IN SHADOWS OF SILVER

BEN GREEN

Loamseed PRESS

In Shadows of Silver (Rimduum Book 2)

Copyright © 2022 by Loamseed Press

Website: www.loamseedpress.com

Cover art © 2022 by www.seventhstarart.com

eBook ISBN: 978-1-7348218-5-7

Paperback ISBN: 978-1-7348218-4-0

To all the worldbuilders.
You know who you are.

ROYAL CRAFTS

GOLDCRAFT

PHYSICAL AUGMENTATION
METAL: GOLD
BODY & FORM

SILVERCRAFT

MENTAL AUGMENTATION
METAL: SILVER & NICKEL
MIND & SPIRIT

SHIELDCRAFT

PROTECTIVE AUGMENTATION
METAL: TUNGSTEN & LEAD
PROTECTION & HEALING

INDUSTRIAL CRAFTS

COPPERCRAFT

ANIMAL DOMINION
METAL: COPPER
ANIMAL CONTROL & COMMUNICATION

TINCRAFT

PLANT DOMINION
METAL: TIN
PLANT CONTROL & COMMUNICATION

IRONCRAFT

ELEMENTAL MANIPULATION
METAL: IRON
FIRE, WATER, AIR, EARTH, SHADOW, LIGHT

BUDGECRAFT

SPATIAL MANIPULATION
METAL: ALUMINIUM
TELEPORTATION

MODERN CRAFTS
(REQUIRES GESTURING)

MECHCRAFT

MECHANICAL MANIPULATION
METAL: TITANIUM & PLATINUM
MACHINE CONTROL & MANIPULATION

BLUECRAFT

ELECTROMAGNETIC MANIPULATION
METAL: COBALT
COMMUNICATION & ENERGY

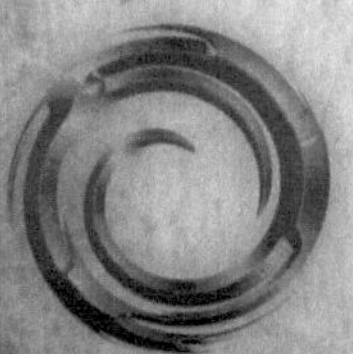

TIMECRAFT

TEMPORAL MANIPULATION
METAL: MERCURY & CHROMIUM
SLOW TIME & SPEED TIME

FORGE A DREAM

ALONE IN MY VAULT, a mile beneath Tungsten City, I set a glowing forgeseed inside a ten-gallon furnace. The size of a flattened baseball, it's the only heat needed to keep the furnace blazing, but I measure a good amount of fuel pellets and bury the light of the forgeseed. The pellets sizzle. An acrid odor rises into the air like the floor of a barn—that's what I get using pellets made from wood and buffalo dung.

Standing back, I rub my stubbly chin with the back of my arm. I need my quick clean—the little ironcraft flask Rugnus gave me when we first met.

Bluelink chimes with a notification. I don't have to check who it's from—Rugnus.

"Clayson, have you seen Icho? You locked me out of your vault again. Know you're probably forging stuff. I... well that kind of thing can be... you should leave forging to the professionals. I just get worried you're doing something—"

I mute the audio. "And... don't care."

This has to work. Forging this object, using it, might leave me paralyzed or blind, but if it works, I'll be able to access my dreams directly, dreams my grandfather planted in my mind. All part of the still unexplainable craft he used on me and my mom.

Even after five months of access in the archives at Whurrimduum —my sister provided me an unlimited royal pass—I'm no closer to answers.

Two months ago—a quarter season to Loamin—we found one reference to a memory garden, a type of silvercraft that allows a person to visit someone's memories. Since then, that's what we've called the canyon from my dreams. But nothing explains my mom's memory loss or why I don't feel the surface effects.

The forge is ready, so I begin the process.

Over the forgeseed and the wood-dung pellets, I add coal flakes and a flagstone of shale rock—these are what coders and smiths call the means. They go inside the furnace, but not in the crucible with the metal. My mind flashes on my brawny grandfather, Yinzar Copperoath, to his secret forge under Lake Onthratia, to the slimy pieces of oak that fueled the creation of the mithrium shield.

When I forged the shield five months ago, I had no terms or definitions. I made the most powerful object under granite—in all Rimduum—and I didn't even know what to call the ingredients that go inside the furnace. Dad taught me about some of the tools, just not in Loamin terms. That was long before Bazalrak attacked our cabin last season, October by the human calendar.

The alarm for the vault goes off, pitched tones accelerating into an understated beat drop then slipping into an icy melody. At least I set it to play some decent music. It will be the soundtrack for my descent into madness the moment I use this object.

I check bluelink. A barrage of new messages since the last one, all from Rugnus. I don't open them. I know what they say. In succession, it's probably a load of questions spiraling rapidly into a series of accusations. Something like: Where did you put Icho? Are you even in your vault? You keep doing this to everyone. You can't shut me out. Then: Let me in! —repeated until five seconds ago when he must've decided to hack into my vault by force.

To be fair, I did steal Icho from him. He was sleeping.

I blow out a breath. That was not my favorite choice today.

Also, I distracted Winta with the chance to drive Dad's flatbed at the cabin. Five months pregnant, but she couldn't resist. Now Rugnus can't get her to do his dirty work. She could've busted down my defenses in under a minute. But Rugnus? It will take him a lot longer. Maybe if he and Andalynn didn't feel the need to check on me every hour of every day...

When the means are blazing, I set the ceramic crucible on the slab of heated shale and begin adding the ends.

The ends are everything coded into the metal inside the crucible. I drop two small silver coins; they clink against the ceramic bowl. That's the key for this recipe, using silver luck-coins retrieved from one of the dead cities, the mithrium fallout zones.

Who knows, Rugnus himself might have brought these objects back from some wasted city through his work as a surveyor. He probably won't care to have a casual conversation about it once he breaks in.

The volume on the alarm increases. Rugnus is getting closer to opening my vault. I cast an eye over to the wall where Icho leans at an angle. Rugnus' budgecraft billy club is his most prized relic. "I'm gonna be in a whole lot of trollbrick."

I glance at the coding for this object projected onto the wall. This is the complicated part.

When the silver is molten, I take two square plastic beads from the shelf and drop them in the metal. If craft wasn't involved, they would melt, but I grab the UV flashlight I've prepared and shine the light into the crucible. The beads remain intact. I use the flashlight like a spoon, stirring counterclockwise. Tiny slivers of pink light move from the metal into the plastic cubes.

I'm drawing the luck from the coins, leaving behind only a curse.

When the metal is devoid of pink slivers, I use tongs to remove the swollen cubes. The mold for the object waits nearby. I grab the crucible with my bare hands. The tungsten bracelet on my left wrist activates immediately. I feel only a little warmth from the blazing crucible.

Last week, I finally replaced Ergal—the tungsten ring I made the mithrium shield out of—with a bracelet I forged out of a few expensive relics. Rugnus might think I'm still an amateur, but I had the bracelet appraised. Its Total Object Rating is nearly unmatched, especially when combined with my peerless shield-craft score.

Carefully, I pour the liquid into a small hole in the sand form.

I grab a mason jar filled with dark Lake Onthratia water. After Rugnus and I moved the Great Smoke that swam its waters, the water itself has become a huge commodity in the markets of both Whurrimduum and Tungsten City. It has a stabilizing effect on nearly any recipe, meaning my improvisation today might not blow up in my face. These are exactly the type of decisions Rugnus frowns upon.

Unscrewing the lid, I take a small scoop and drizzle the water over the mold.

I break away the form and dig the object out from the sand. It's a long silver pick, narrow enough at the tip that it could be a needle.

It's called a dreampick. The object allows the user to access their subconscious directly—to dream but to remember. Loamin don't dream, though a rare few have nightmares after years of life on the surface. The thrill of this object for others is the experience of manipulating the subconscious. For me, that could mean choosing which of Yinzar's memories I enter. I hope.

For the last five months, beyond a season, every time I've slept below the surface, I've had the same vision. A rounded mineshaft. At its base, hundreds of drill-marks the size of manholes. Dark vines snaking down one of the drill holes into darkness.

It has to be the entrance to Mithriumbane, the lost dungeon created when my grandfather destroyed a piece of the mithrium before I was born. The vision always ends before I grab the vines.

With the dreampick, I hope to go deeper, climb down, and prove to everyone—Rugnus in particular—that the dungeon is real. I might only be fourteen, but it's my job as Yinzar's grandson.

With a breath, I bring the point of the pick to rest unsteadily between the nail on my index finger and the nailbed. I wiggle the pick inward, but not far enough to break my skin, though that's what must be done for this to work.

In a flash of light, Rugnus appears on the other side of the room. His dark eyes soak in the reflection of the forge. He's dressed for a party in a brown suit with pink, flaring lapels. Tonight is the opening of StoneYoke, a redesigned area on the outskirts of Tungsten City, a symbol of harmony between the two major populations left under granite. Andalynn and Rugnus are the chief architects, so they'd probably be more upset if I didn't make it to the opening than if this experiment blinds me.

Sular, Dad's relic pin, is attached to Rugnus' lapel like a military award. I don't regret giving it to him, but it's a stiff reminder of Dad's disappointment that I'm not an ironmage like many other Brightstorms.

Rugnus' eyes flick between my face, Icho resting against the wall, and the dreampick. "Fizzblooded idiot. Think before you—"

I jam the dreampick under my fingernail.

My vault dissolves into a blurry sea of static. I still feel the prick underneath my nail, but a pulse of clarity, of revelation, delivers me over to the dream. The moment the dreamscape materializes around me, my hope bursts like a balloon. This won't help me dig deeper into Yinzar's memories.

The diamond-hard scales of a dragon form beneath me, large wings rising to my right and left. We take flight from a wide meadow that has somehow appeared around us. One beat of its wings takes us into the clouds, and we twist toward a white sun. If I were a normal Loamin this would be thrilling; even the mention of long extinct dragonkind is taboo. This is a forbidden experience. None of this matters. The failure of all my research and time rests in my bones like cast iron.

I know what Rugnus will say to me: I was foolish and rash; I should've checked with him; even if an object isn't dangerous, it's a waste of time and ferrum. He doesn't understand what solving this problem would mean to me and others waiting to enter Mithriumbane Dungeon.

Invisible hands grip my biceps, and the fake dream begins to peel back around the corners of the sky. The clouds deflate, the dragon turns to sand, and the dream ends as quickly as it began.

Rugnus shakes his head, holding the dreampick by the thick end with his thumb and forefinger like it's infected. I didn't feel him pull it out, but for a second, a sharp pain pulses under my nail. I let it linger for a minute before I heal the wound with my bracelet.

Rugnus flicks the dreampick to the ground. "Never seen one of these. What's it supposed to do?"

I pluck it from where he threw it. "Doesn't matter. Thought you'd be busy today."

"I am. You should be too." He considers the pick again. "Best guess? This gives you dreams you can control."

Of course, he would guess it. I must look exhausted. I haven't been to the surface in over two days. Which means I've only slept restlessly, plagued by the same reoccurring vision.

"I needed to see more."

Rugnus knows the dream hasn't changed since the day they returned, a couple weeks after I made the mithrium shield. "So, the solution was to look up some crazy recipe on bluelink and—"

"I knew you would react this way. That's why I—"

Rugnus rolls his eyes. "I think I made it clear how dangerous this kind of thing can—"

"Forget it. I don't expect you to understand. Your life is simple."

Rugnus scoffs. He turns his attention to the shelves around us, to the wall full of newsfeeds, to the large furnace and the river of lava that runs the length of one side of the room. The main forge sits at the center of that wall. Our two vaults reveal vastly different life experiences.

I've eliminated the two connected rooms to make more space for forging. For Rugnus, a vault needs a testing room, separate areas for different tasks. I'm not as good at keeping my life compartmentalized.

He lifts a copper bracelet from the shelf. It belonged to one of the ironheads we fought in Silverlamp to get to my parents. It controls insects, arachnids, and rodents—all things creepy-crawly. Its allegiance changed when I won it in the dungeon. That was the day Koglim lost Elbaz, his gemstone pendant. It was also the day Hemdi lost tincraft forever when the three wraiths in Silverlamp Dungeon attacked us.

The bracelet must remind Rugnus of these lost things. He grimaces.

After a second, he moves to the wall and takes Icho, grumbling about my lack of respect for the most important thing in his life. I don't bring up his relationship with my sister. He turns to the sea of videos, text, and icons on the other side of the room. In one video, Lagnar Emberfence tests strengths with a few members of the Keeper's Council, grasping their forearms with a strength he never had during his years on the surface.

My blood thickens.

A month ago, when Lagnar started to resurface on bluelink, Andalynn told all of us the secret reason for his exile. Dad knew of course, he'd even shared it with my mom. Lagnar was the assassin who placed a mithrium bomb in the last city of Hngaal—Malguk. It killed my grandparents, the former king and queen of Rimduum. Everyone still believed it had been a spy of an enemy kingdom, an agent of Zal Kakraja, but it had been Rimduum's own General Emberfence.

For unknown reasons, my father had fabricated other charges and gotten him exiled.

In the video, one of the council members, Moburan Hardkeeper, throws an arm around Lagnar, and they laugh. They're old friends.

"Can you believe this?" Rugnus points to the video. The look he passes me says: *We're not going to agree, but it's better if we both just forget our arguments and focus on what we have in common.* Must be nice. He gets to dismiss all my worries and pretend I can live a normal life around here.

I retrieve the hot forgeseed from inside the furnace and set it on the stone to cool. I brush the ash from my hands, looking from Rugnus to the video. "They're giving Lagnar a free pass."

"The council thinks that pardoning him will build better relations with Tungsten City's businessmen, particularly in bluecraft markets. And they love him. Look how smug he is. Andalynn's been against it from the start. They're trying to say your dad pushed his exile through and overrode the council."

"He did push it through, but it doesn't mean he was wrong."

"Don't have to tell me that." Rugnus glances at the title of another article: RUGNUS AND ANDALYNN: REAL OR ROYAL FLING?

"Sorry." I close it. "I-I didn't read it."

He gives me a dubious look, scanning the wall for other titles.

CITIZEN'S CONTRACT EXTENDED TO WHURRIMDUUM

TWO SIDES OF A COIN: CLAYSON AND YINZAR

WHO IS RENSIRA SILVERLAMP?

WILL STONEYOKE BE SAFE?

He stops on this last one. "Fearmongers."

"There'll be a lot of people there."

"Understatement. The opening festival's likely to empty out half of both cities, or at least bring them to a standstill for the day. But the more people, the safer the event will be. There's no greater power than millions of united Loamin."

I shrug. He's right, of course. If anyone tries something at the opening of the StoneYoke district, millions of people will stand up to stop them. It puts the *dem* in democracy.

"I wish my parents could come. They won't even have a way to watch."

"Stayed behind that shield for a reason. To them, Geum Ide feels safe. And for now, there's nothing we can do. Your grandmother and her conjurer goons won't let us return. At least the festival will give you a distraction, something to do besides think about what you can't have."

"I have something to do. Finding Yinzar's dungeon."

A frown cuts a few lines between Rugnus' thick eyebrows. "You don't have to solve all the world's problems."

"How about my own problems? Figuring out what's wrong with me and—"

"Nothing is wrong with you... or nothing you can fix, anyway. Really want to pull on that string? Find your grandfather's dungeon?"

"Seventy-five."

Rugnus shakes his head. "Seventy-five what?"

"That's the number of initiatives that have been called to Mithriumbane Dungeon. People that can't get an AMP score until it's found."

"Is it? I didn't—"

"I'm the dungeon's expected keeper. I have to figure this out. The only clue I have is that his second forge is somewhere in the mines. That's all I've got. A single dream again and again. But the mines are closed, and the Keeper's Council won't hear my request to open them. And because of the deal Andalynn made, she can't override them. People are counting on me. If it was your summation... or Koglim's..."

"You're right." He hangs his head and sighs loudly. "Ide keep me, you're right. I'm sorry. Look, Andalynn and I have been putting this festival together for months, and I promise: Finding Mithriumbane Dungeon will be my next priority. But... about tonight. Come. Interact with people. Take a quick break from this."

"You think I could get out of it? Andalynn would melt me."

When Rugnus smiles, there's something so genuine about it I almost forgive him for being dismissive of my search for Yinzar's dungeon. He must sense a way around my defenses because he asks, "So, besides your newest creation,"—he purposely avoids looking at the dreampick— "how's forging your own things?"

When it comes to craft, Rugnus will never change. He loves unique objects, whether they're relics or made professionally.

I smile, holding up my new paracord bracelet. "Total Object Rating is nineteen."

"Nineteen TOR? That can't be. Anything over eighteen has to be—"

"Forged from relics?" My natural ability at forging isn't something he can easily sweep under a rug. "Yeah."

"Complicated stuff. How?"

I shrug, trying to look innocent. "I took the instructions for another object and adapted it for the bracelet."

"And the relics? I mean, I know you make good ferrum with the Spangler Eggs, but—"

I pass him a bright yellow and orange bin from the shelf, uncut lead and tungsten keys fill them both about halfway. "Andalynn helped me find an object depot in Forgebreath."

"Keep Ide. When did she find the time?"

This I understand. This we share. Trying to carve an hour from Andalynn's time is like breaking into Keelcrawl prison. I've been debating about sharing something with Rugnus. Maybe today is a good day.

"Let me show you something else. We have a few minutes, right?" He follows me to a corner of the room, where another bracelet rests on my workbench. "This one's yours."

"My what?" he asks.

"Bracelet."

He's suddenly uncomfortable. "Made me a matching bracelet? My shieldcraft is brick."

I'm prepared for this reaction. I smile. This time I pull down a bright pink bin filled with cast iron marbles. I hand it to him. "Not exactly."

"Double orbs? Wraithspit." He looks to the bracelet, eyes wider than the marbles. "No way. You didn't have to... I can't—"

"Oh, no, you'll take this and be grateful. It's a gift. For all your work on the festival."

His grin widens. "If it works, I'll be able to use two types of ironcraft at the same time. Fire and stone. Without splitting my AMP score between two objects. How much ferrum did—"

"No, no, no. You don't get to ask that. Here."

I lift it from the bench and pass it to him. My frustration, my worry about his perceptions of me, that all melts away as he takes the bracelet in complete awe.

He stands back, an eager smile spreading across his face. "Time for a test."

Once the bracelet is on his wrist, he opens bluelink, making a few quick gestures and tapping the bracelet against his new cobalt wallet chain. He smiles. Globes of molten red break from the surface of the lava pool at the side of the room and swirl around us in a symmetrical pattern. Ironcraft usually isolates an object down to a single type of element, but the double orbs do exactly as advertised.

The wall above the lava pool breaks off in tiny dice-sized blocks. The stone dice join the globes of lava swirling around us. He can control earth and fire. And with Sular, he can heat metal as well, though he'd have to switch from the bracelet. Instinctively, I extend a layer of protective white light around me using my own bracelet.

The forge is cast in spinning shadows and red-orange light. It's beautiful.

"Perfectly balanced," Rugnus whispers.

The globes of lava and tiny blocks of stone zoom back toward the wall, coupling together, each turning into brilliant pieces of glass, which Rugnus affixes to the wall. The effect is immediate. As the tiny nodules cool, a glass tiled mosaic emerges in geometric patterns.

Rugnus smiles. "Thought this place could use some texture."

"Nice."

"Life's all about the flourishes." He smooths down his pink lapels.

I step closer to the wall, examining the details, a patchwork of frosted glass squares and porcelain white rectangles. The color reminds me of the glaring white of shieldcraft. It's a way for Rugnus to give me a gift in return.

"Just what this place needed." I wiggle my bracelet at him. "Well, do you think my bracelet can counter the effects of the surface for both of us?"

"Easily. Why?"

I scrunch my mouth, trying not to reveal the other part of my plan, but it comes out anyway. "About that. I may have let Winta—uh, and the others—drive Dad's flatbed up at the cabin."

Rugnus' face becomes stone. "Why would you do that?"

"I wouldn't have had time to make the dreampick. You'd have gotten Winta here, and... I just did, okay? Not a big deal."

"Except that Andalynn will actually melt you. We're supposed to be looking after Winta. She's due within the next week, Clayson! Can't believe you would exploit a reckless pregnant woman for your own gain."

Everyone has been treating Winta like she's a piece of cobalt glass. Loamin pregnancies are only five months long. That shocked me for about three seconds. But Loamin are shorter, we mature faster, we begin work and family sooner, and we only live into our sixties. That wasn't fun news either.

I hold up my hands toward Rugnus. "If it's not driving a truck at high speeds, it'll be something else."

Rugnus raises his voice. "Did you even think about how Hemdi is feeling right now?"

I break our eye contact. So much for fixing our relationship. "Leave him out of this."

"You didn't!" His knuckles tighten around Icho. "We're getting them. Now."

"Fine. That's what I just said I wanted to do."

He tries to hand his bracelet back to me.

My lip curls up in disgust. "No. I'm not taking it back. Keep it."

"You didn't have to make this. Maybe I don't want it."

"You're keeping it." I bring my eyes up, daring him.

He jams it in his pocket. "Sometimes, I think I should just budge you somewhere far away. Maybe through the shield over Geum Ide. Then you can be Therias' problem again."

I work my mouth open, unable to process the mixture of hurt and anger I feel, but he budges us to the surface before I say anything.

The cold immediately creeps in. Last week's snow hugs the edges of every building. We've appeared near the new chicken coop. My family crest hangs over the coop. Instead of Brightstorm, it reads Spangler Eggs.

Three madly barking labs burst from the tree line. Hemdi and Winta's labs. I've been dog sitting, too. Pretty much all things farm and country for me these days. Well, nights really.

After Silverkeeper's funeral last fall, I returned to the surface so I could finally sleep. A few weeks later, I ended up buying two dozen pullets, which Rugnus had said was just a way for me to avoid the world altogether. He wasn't wrong. I needed time. Now I spend my days in Tungsten City or Whurrimduum and my nights here. Taking care of my chickens had been a good excuse to stay away.

When I didn't return to Tungsten City one morning, Rugnus came to the surface with an object that could automate feeding, cleaning, and egg collection; a cobalt and aluminum funnel alongside a set of small aluminum stars that could be tucked into each roost to transport fresh eggs to the food markets.

They're a hot seller. Eggs made on the surface by chickens raised by the prince of Whurrimduum. When the ferrum started rolling in, I kept only twenty percent, giving thirty percent to Rugnus and the other fifty to the refugee fund in Tungsten City.

I pet the closest of Hemdi's labs, Nox. They're named after three of the four Loamin months—Nox, Gem, and Stone.

Rugnus tries but fails to push Stone away. He kneels and gathers all the puppy's loose face flesh in his hands, scratching her underneath her chin. Even this doesn't change his mood. His normally dark, sandy complexion is a fleshy pink. He's upset with me, or maybe its the surface effects—fizzblood. I'd offer to lend him my bracelet, but he'd turn me down for sure. He's usually equipped to handle the effects for at least an hour.

I just hope he doesn't tell Andalynn about the dreampick. Not to save me from getting melted, but because on the day of Stone-Yoke festival, she doesn't need the added stress.

A loud whooping sound that can only be Koglim draws our attention to the gravel road. Dad's twenty-year-old flatbed truck skitters over the loose rock. A flood of spring mud and dirty snow splashes behind it. Winta's gleeful face is clear through the windshield, even at a distance.

Koglim and Hemdi squeeze together on the passenger side. Koglim is closest to the door, leaning out the open window, his new silver tattoo glimmering on his upper arm. Winta whips around the last turn like she's an inch from first place at some truck rally. Hemdi's face has no color left.

I can tell he's pouring everything he can into a bit of shield-craft. Both for the surface effects and just in case anyone goes flying out a window. Right about now, he's probably cursing himself for humoring Winta's wild side.

A swirl of mercury whips from the driver's side and ensnares the truck's wheels with timecraft. The whole car enters slow-motion as Winta slams on the brakes. I release some tension in my shoulders when the truck finally skids to a muddy stop a few yards away, returning to real-time.

Koglim leaps from the truck, patting down his body parts like he's trying to make sure they're still in one piece. "Wraithspit and nulls, Winta. You are crazy."

She pulls herself up to sit on the edge of the door, arms resting on the roof of the truck. She takes a deep breath, smiling that rare, dazzling smile she usually keeps tucked away. "Amazing," she whispers. When she sees me, a glimmer of mischievousness widens her eyes. She knows I used her, but she used me, too. She winks.

Hemdi steals a glance at her pregnant midsection, perhaps using craft to check for a tiny heartbeat. He climbs out of Koglim's door and rushes to the other side of the truck to help Winta down. She shrugs off his protection. I brace for her reaction. His protectiveness of her has been the source of all their very public, though one-sided, arguments.

"I don't need help," Winta says. "Ide keep me, Hemdi, I can take care of myself. You saw me drive this thing, right?"

"Like an expert. And I know you can take care of yourself, I just…"

Something softens behind Winta's mask of grumpiness. "Okay." She offers her hand, and he helps her the rest of the way down.

Rugnus clears his throat. "Get your fix, Winta?"

The ice returns to Winta's eyes. "Look who it is: Andalynn's midwife paladin, coming to make sure I'm wrapped in bubbles with my feet reclining. I'll be—" She closes her eyes, hunching forward. Her normally stained-pine skin is patchy, flushed red along her cheeks and neck. Hemdi places a hand on her back.

Rugnus turns to me. "See what you did?" I must be an easier target.

Winta stands straighter, her hand bracing her lower back. "It's the surface effects, Rugnus. Not this little latcher." She pokes her abdomen.

"The baby has to come out soon," Hemdi reminds her.

"No, it doesn't!"

I come around to the driver's side. "Let me just park the truck."

"I've got it." Rugnus places a hand on the hood of the truck, and it disappears.

"It would've only taken me a couple minutes to drive it back to the garage."

Koglim whistles. "You know how long a minute can seem in a dungeon? That budge patch you put on the truck was worth the ferrum. Along with all the other improvements you've made to the cabin. And those Spangler Eggs... delicious, by the way."

Winta huffs. "I suppose now that you're a professional raider, you can buy all the Spangler Eggs you want."

Koglim smiles with pride. His new status has been one of the positive things to come from Silverlamp Dungeon. Professional raiders make a living trying to get as far as possible into each dungeon, usually in teams of five. When I first met Koglim last year at Kel's Lounge, he and Rugnus had been watching a few rounds over bluelink.

Like many other things about this world, I hadn't understood how the dungeon rankings worked. But now it's clear: the harder it is to advance through a dungeon, the higher the dungeon is ranked. The Keeper's Council is made up of the top ten dungeons, which can change season to season. So not only does the work the raiders do matter, but it can also have a political effect if they find a new weakness in a dungeon.

But Winta's not thinking about that. She's thinking about the cost of eggs. Since Hemdi's loss of craft he's had a harder time making ferrum. Even with the sale of their nursery of beautiful plant life, which left them both hurting in more ways than one.

"I'm working to bring down the price," I say. "Chicks should get to the local markets pretty soon. Just have to convert some ferrum into dollars and get over there. Besides, you guys can take eggs anytime."

A notification chimes, and we all check bluelink. Rugnus opens a live video, grabs it with a gesture, and moves it to where we can all see against the side of the coop.

It's Andalynn, a crowd behind her. "What are you doing? The festival has already started. The opening ceremony is in less than an hour. Wait, where are you? Are you at the cabin? Is Winta there?"

"Relax, queeny," Winta says. "I'm fine. My overseer"—she pats Rugnus' back—"is keeping me safe from harm."

Andalynn shakes her head. "You're on the road. Where's the truck? You didn't—"

"I did. Clayson's idea, though mostly he wanted to keep me from helping Rugnus break into his vault so he could do something secretive and idiotic—that's my bet anyway."

Hemdi glances at me, his mouth transforming into a hard line. "Is that what this was about?"

My stomach feels sick. No one does parental disappointment like Hemdi.

Andalynn begins scolding both of us, her words pointed and fast.

I interrupt her. "Let's talk at the festival. It will be nice to see you in person for once."

Andalynn's shoulders droop, her head bows slightly. "I know. I know we need more time. I—" Someone off-camera drags her attention away. "Sorry. I need to—I'll see you after the ceremony."

The video blinks off.

Rugnus scowls. "Shouldn't make her feel guilty like that."

"She doesn't need to get on my case about Winta."

Rugnus points a rigid finger at me. "Shouldn't have involved Winta in your stupid idea in the first place."

I step toward him, but Hemdi nudges between us. "You are both correct. Stop arguing."

"Let them," Winta shifts her weight from one foot to the

other. "Sooner or later, you won't be here to stop them from killing each other, dear."

Koglim scratches his head. "That would be worth going live again, Rugnus. I could bring some roasted Cheya nuts."

Winta adds, "I'll make popcorn."

Koglim nods vigorously. "You do make good human snacks. We could—"

Hemdi cuts them off. "No one is fighting today." He looks around.

Everyone's on edge. Rugnus brushes the pink lapels of his jacket, unable to even look at me. Winta cracks her neck. Koglim's oblivious, but that's more of a symptom of his life in the dungeons. You can't care too much about the little things when you're risking life and limb every weekend.

Hemdi continues. "The festival is supposed to bring everyone together. Heal two cities that have been divided for the last fifty years. Maybe we should act like it is important. People have already lost so much."

None of us can hear the word "lost" from Hemdi without thinking about what happened five months ago in Silverlamp.

Koglim grimaces, placing a hand over his silver tattoo.

"What is it?" I ask. Koglim's new tattoo isn't as powerful as Elbaz. It gives him flashes of the future in still images but no warning about what's to come. One time he got an image of me eating breakfast. Not everything's prophetic.

Koglim's eyes flicker. "Smoke and machines. That's all I got."

Rugnus frowns. "It's probably tonight's performance. Andalynn thinks there might be close to five million people."

I shuffle back a step, staring at Rugnus. "Will it really be that many?"

Winta slaps me on the arm. "Can't avoid people tonight, large boy."

"Fizzblood, Winta. It's big boy. And I haven't been"—she squints at me— "Okay, so I don't like everyone watching me. But to be fair, I've been occupied with other things. I know the festival is important. That's why I'm going."

"Maybe turn your camera on a few times," Koglim advises.

"I'll think about it. Can we go?"

Rugnus nods, removes Icho, and we budge.

The moment we appear on the budgeport, my senses are overwhelmed. We're still far above it, but the festival seems to fill the entire world.

Koglim blinks rapidly. "Incredible."

We stand at the edge of Tungsten City, the exterior wall of the citybarrel to our backs. At the center of a massive valley, a mountain of connected structures towers into the sky, alive with color and craft, made from dozens of terraced fields the size of football stadiums, built one upon another like stairs. The top of the mountain of construction is like the crater of a volcano, and inside, an amphitheater packed with people crowns the whole district. The crowd awaits the start of the opening ceremony. Timpani sound from one of the lower stadiums, followed by a wave of ethereal music, melodic but heavy with bass.

A dozen giant, crystal stalactites hang above the district like reverse skyscrapers, alive with dangling plant life and the steady moving pulse of festivalgoers. Banners of every conceivable color combination jut out at all angles. Far in the distance, Tungsten City's brightstorm dazzles the sky, sending out white rays that bounce off a million geometric surfaces of the upside-down crystal skyscrapers.

Three days. It took mechsmiths and ironsmiths three days to repurpose and redesign this whole area of Tungsten City. It doesn't seem conceivable. A new district where the markets and cultures of the two cities meld together.

I wonder for a moment if the human Olympics could bring five million people piling into a celebration in a half-mile circle. I bet we're far beyond the limits of safe occupancy for humans. But every Loamin has emergency budges and shieldcraft, if—Ide keep us— something was to happen.

Rugnus smiles, gestures in the air, changing some settings in bluelink. "Open the overlay."

Though I'm not sure my senses can handle more input, curiosity forces me to open the festival settings in bluelink. When I make the gesture to open the overlay, I stumble backward.

A second reality joins the tangible world.

Two pale worm-like dragons weave through the crystal buildings, dancing around each other above the amphitheater. Their bodies and tails stretch in coils around the circumference of the whole StoneYoke district. They remind me of the Great Smoke, the giant eel under the dark waters of Onthratia, but more than that, of the dragon from my failure with the dreampick. Dragons and information about them are hard to come by, forbidden by law in Whurrimduum, and taboo in Tungsten City.

Rugnus grins. "My idea. Figured StoneYoke festival should have something historical that could represent the two cities. I know dragons are a bit—"

"Sadistic?" Winta offers.

"Illegal?" Hemdi adds.

Rugnus shrugs. "Not standard. We wanted to break some traditions with this celebration. It will show the people that we need to accept what is different and strange about each other."

I can't look away from the festival. "It's… amazing."

Rugnus watches us. This is his moment. The pride in his eyes is unmistakable. I wonder for a brief second how much besides the dragons was his design. Did his mother help to plan this event? He smiles, leading us down to the next row of budgeports. "Wait until you see it up close."

CONSULT WITH KEEPERS

Our luxury box sits on the rim of the festival, the amphitheater below us on one side and the terraced stadiums on the other, packed with joyful sights and sounds—games, food vendors, and performances. Host to a million new experiences, and that's not an exaggeration.

So many people. I wonder if the crowds would see through a goldcraft concealer? I don't have anything close to my mom's craft—the one she used to hide me from Bazalrak last fall. I'm not even sure where to get concealer.

"StoneYoke," Hemdi says. "It's a beautiful name for the reuniting of two places." He takes a deep breath through his nose and lets it out slowly.

On the stage of the amphitheater, the Knights of Shale stand row upon row in their homespun uniforms, glittering with bits of crafted objects, prepared for any eventuality—in this case, spectacle. At another corner of the stage, dressed in bright neon clothing, an equal number of citizens from Tungsten City gather into clumsy lines.

The two groups appear as equal partners, but Whurrimduum's population barely holds steady at two million. With all its refugees and the generations that followed, Tungsten City has a bustling six million Loamin packed inside the citybarrel, a space about fourteen cubic miles, at least in human measurements. I could make the conversion to blocks and tens, but my brain still doesn't work that way.

Koglim taps my arm. "Clayson, look." He draws my attention back into the luxury box, where maybe a hundred people mill about, drinking, and eating hors d'oeuvres. It reminds me of last year's Keeper's Social when I was naive enough to believe I could get Silverkeeper's key.

"Is that Cessar Bluekeeper?" Koglim points his head toward a man with a clear glass face-covering in a citrus yellow suit. "And wait," he points another direction, "th-that's Moburan Hardkeeper? No one told me we'd been invited to the keeper's box. Wraithspit, this just keeps getting better. Do you think they'll give me any tips?"

Winta rolls her eyes. "Get melted. You're a raider now, Koglim. Be lucky if they tell you to eat brick."

I finally connect the dots. "This was Andalynn's idea. The luxury box."

Rugnus nods, but the look in his eye says I should have known.

Andalynn is notoriously thoughtful. It's a common topic for the pundits on bluelink. They say she must have an army of assistants, that her inspired gift-giving and impeccable timing must be the work of craft, but they don't know Andalynn like I do.

It's not craft. She remembers what people ask for, and sometimes even what they only hope for, then out of nowhere, she delivers. I've been trying to get an audience with the keepers all season. And she's wrapped them in a bow for me, in a place where there are only a few prying eyes. No wonder she tried to get me here earlier.

"Koglim"—a grin appears on my face—"find me the highest-ranking keeper."

"Yes, boss." Koglim adopts a look of focus and determination, like he's about to enter a dungeon. He's the oldest in our group by a whole year, but when it comes to dungeons, he's a kid with a new bike.

"Bleh," Winta groans. "This is what we're doing? No thanks."

Hemdi intercedes. "Let's go find something exciting to do."

Winta's eyes widen. "Seriously?"

"Well," he says, showing the palms of his hands. "Not dangerous, just exciting."

Winta's shoulders fall, but she keeps her smile. "Or something delicious."

They disappear, leaving Rugnus looking out over the amphitheater.

"Just go," I say. "You're more help to Andalynn than you are to me."

Rugnus looks between the two of us. "Don't cause too much trouble."

Koglim's eyes shine. "No promises."

After Rugnus budges, I turn to Koglim. "Okay, let's cause some trouble."

His hearty laugh warms something deep inside of me as he leads me out into the crowd.

People are gathered around a large circular tank, like a fishbowl. The tank extends below the floor but rises waist-high, so we can watch the performers. The surface is still settling from their last trick, but with a splash, a pair of Loamin erupt from the water in perfect synchronization, flipping and tumbling over suspended hoops and bars. I catch a glimpse of scales along their arms and legs and a flash of dull copper, though it might be an alloy of copper and iron.

A third figure resides in a globe of water above the tank. It's the same Dura performer I saw in the park with Sira last season. Gracefully, he flips and turns, stretching his body into an arch and pinwheeling downward with mesmerizing precision.

Koglim, scanning the crowd for council members, gulps as the two Loamin performers disappear under the water. Like any other sane Loamin, he's afraid of water. No one has offered me an explanation for this, but I suppose many humans have a fear of heights. It had to be something.

"How do they do it, Clayson?" Koglim says. "How do they do it?" He stops walking and points his head at Hardkeeper.

This is my cue. I circle around Koglim and stand next to the keeper.

I clear my throat and try to start a conversation. "Have you seen this use of coppercraft or—"

His head swivels in my direction. His face matches his name: thin lips, cold, narrow eyes, and a nose you could chop wood with. One of his ears is pierced, studded with rubies. "Leave my presence, Clayson Brightstorm. I did not summon you, and you do not belong here among the friends of the council."

I've been dismissed by the council for a season now; maybe that's why something inside me transforms into a rough stone. "I'm pretty sure I'm invited. I'm willing to bet my sister talked to enough of the council to allow me to be here."

"Insolent. Why are you troubling me?"

Koglim steps to my side. "Keeper, if I may. I'm Koglim Felsight." He extends an arm to test strengths, but Hardkeeper doesn't even look down. Koglim slowly drops his arm. "Uh, the trouble is, my friend Clayson has been asking for an audience with the council for a half-season."

Hardkeeper returns his attention to the performance. "For what reason?"

His ignorance hits me like a barrel of rocks. "How could you not know? I've made so many—"

"Our assistants and servants screen our requests. This is the first I've heard of it."

"But Andalynn—"

"The *Queen* has not sat in council with us in the last five sessions. Busy with StoneYoke."

A lump catches in my throat. She didn't tell the council I wanted access to the mines. All of my requests of her take on a new color. Phrases she used like *try my best* or *see what I can do.* Why didn't she tell me she didn't ask them directly?

I swallow the lump in my throat. "The mines. I need the council to open the mines."

If possible, his eyes narrow further. "The mines?"

"I believe if I—"

"Clayson Brightstorm." The twang of Lagnar Emberfence's accent seems to reverberate off the glass. He steps from around Hardkeeper. "Ide keep us. Did you come here to harass every member of the council?"

I try to pick a single reason to hate this man but fail. He called the knights on us when Rugnus and I tried to get a fake AMP from him. He was there with Chainkeeper when we broke into Keelcrawl prison. He came up with the deal that placed my sister on the throne in exchange for a percentage of her power to cast decisions. He killed my grandparents. He used the mithrium to murder over three million people.

There. That's the reason. "Get melted, Lagnar."

Hardkeeper's back tenses, and I realize I've stepped in social trollbrick. Hardkeeper and Emberfence are friends. I knew this. I should have been prepared.

Hardkeeper fully turns my direction, his chest swelling, nostrils flaring. "How dare you speak to my guest this way. He is a former general of the Knights of Shale. He fought in the Last War. He is the seer of Bluebottle Dungeon. Your informality will not be tolerated."

Lagnar flaps a hand in the air. "Oh, don't hold it against the little whelp. He don't know any better, and he don't play his cards very close to his chest."

Leave it to Lagnar to use a human phrase to insult me. A reminder of how long he lived on the surface. Somehow every word out of his mouth seems like a calculation disguised as lack of concern.

"You will leave my presence at once," Hardkeeper orders. He points to Koglim. "And take this raider with you."

"I didn't mean to... I need access to the mine, it's—"

"Begone." Hardkeeper's voice echoes across the room. A dozen people turn and stare. Even one of the Loamin performers misses a jump, trying to crane her neck toward us.

Koglim pulls me back from the crowd. "That didn't go well. You really have something against Lagnar Emberfence, don't you?"

"What? Of course. He's responsible for the death of Dad's parents. Maybe even planned their assassination."

Koglim glances around nervously. "Don't get brittle boned on me. I'm just... there's not much evidence that—"

A bubble of anger rises to the surface. "If my father said Lagnar did it, then he did it."

Koglim looks like a scolded puppy. "Okay. Well, maybe we should try talking to another council member. I think we picked the worst one." He pushes me back into the crowd, this time the other direction away from the fishbowl, toward the bar. "There. Cessar Bluekeeper."

I've seen him on the news. Bluekeeper isn't as closely tied with Whurrimduum, maybe because the champion he represents —Glyshur Bluebottle—discovered bluecraft, which led to the creation of bluelink—the people's avenue for freedom of information, which is one of the council's least favorite things.

Before we reach him, Vor materializes behind the keeper. The familiar face is welcome. This is the Dura man who has served the council and the royal family for as long as there have been Brightstorms on the throne.

As we approach, Vor sees me. Like other Dura, he doesn't make eye contact. It's why his whole race has been branded as vacants. Even the thought of the dismissive word puts a spark of anger in my fists.

His feet angle my direction, and he nods. His clothing is simple and gray, hanging on him limply. A shock of jet-black hair crowns his head in hundreds of sharp directions. He smiles and whispers to Bluekeeper.

Bluekeeper looks over to me and tugs on the hem of his lemon suit. "Young Brightstorm, hello." He may be speaking with me, but his attention is on the inside of the glass face shield. He's reading something. With bluelink, anyone can have a private or public feed running as augmented reality right in front of their faces twenty-four seven. So, the craft behind his face shield seems older, or maybe just something I don't know about yet.

"Bluekeeper. It's an honor." I extend my hand to test strengths.

Koglim whispers, "Much smoother."

"Glad you could join us." He glances in Hardkeeper's direction. "You'll find we're a little more friendly to the crown over here. Andalynn has done marvelous things to open the kingdom to all kinds of new trading opportunities. The Targlass Music Library alone—I digress. I hope Moburan didn't rattle you too much."

"Uh, no. It-it's fine."

"My cousin, however... well, Lagnar can hold a grudge for a long time."

Koglim slaps his forehead. "That's right! He's your cousin."

"Shame, really. Closest living relative I have. He would've been Keeper of Bluebottle... but banishment is banishment. Anywho, how can I help you today?"

I catch it now, the hint of Bluekeeper's western accent. Not as pronounced as Lagnar's, but it's still there. I always thought Lagnar adopted the accent on the surface, but maybe he exaggerates it on purpose.

"I was hoping to bring your attention to something," I say. "I've been requesting—"

He holds up a finger. Andalynn's face appears inside his shield. The audio is open. "Attention all members of the Keeper's Council: Your presence is required on stage for the opening ceremonies."

"Ah. Sure enough. Sorry young man. I'll have to hear your request later." Without another word, he budges.

Koglim whistles. "No wonder Lagnar has it out for y'all all. I'd feel the same if I were denied keepership."

"It's y'all. And don't defend him."

Vor gets our attention with his sing-song voice. "Maybe I can help you?"

I look him over. He's not like Ara. His only purpose is to serve the council and the monarchy. Andalynn told me he served my parents for a time when they were first married. Vor brought Silverkeeper's leaf—undoubtedly filled with useful information—to Dad during the funeral last year, but he refused to open it.

"Could you help?" I ask him. "It's been hard getting an audience with them."

An innocent smile comes to his face, but he keeps his head inclined toward the ground. "I'm glad to assist you."

Then Vor budges. Simple budges, simple ironcraft tricks, and simple shields. This is the extent of a Dura's power. Though with Ara, it's different. She can absorb Dad's craft. She helped to heal the damaged brightstorm for the conjurers in Geum Ide.

Koglim shrugs and laughs. "I guess he meant he'll go right now. Come on, let's get something to drink."

A few people stand between us and the bar, but a girl with harvest moon skin rises from a stool, stares at me for a moment too long with electric eyes, and walks away. I lose the magenta highlights of her hair and her shimmering black top in the crowd as Koglim places a hand on my shoulder, pushing me toward a stool.

"Did you see that girl?" I ask.

Koglim scans the room. "There's a lot of girls. Which one?"

"Never mind."

As Koglim orders us drinks, I open bluelink and scan the VIP guestlist until I find her. She has only one name, meaning she was born in Tungsten City like Rugnus. But from her appearance, my guess is that her family were refugees from Hngaal, the former kingdom under the Alaskan Rockies.

Jeiahlir. I open the link for her name, which brings me to a living picture of her. A lot of people wave or smile for their identification picture, but not her. She scrutinizes the recording, almost like her cobalt eyes can see me through bluelink.

Behind the bar, there must be a shift change because a woman disappears, replaced by a man who wipes his hands down a golden vest, grows two more arms, and says, "What can I... you're Clayson Brightstorm. What an honor." He looks to the side of me where Jeiahlir's picture hangs. He leans across the bar. "Your, uh, search... did you want it public?"

The blood drains from my face. I change the settings, but people are watching. I keep making this mistake. Every time I budge back to Tungsten City, my search defaults to public. "Brick," I swear.

Koglim cringes. "Yikes, Clayson. You got to remember that." His smile turns mischievous. "Worse yet, this girl's a paladin for Bluebottle Dungeon, works for Cessar Bluekeeper. She can spot you ten tenblocks away on bluelink. How do you think you pronounce her name? With a gee sound or a jay sound?"

"Keep Ide, Koglim! I don't wanna talk about it."

"There you go getting a tilted beard again. Relax, stalking people in Tungsten City is a favorite pastime. And she's quite the slayer."

"You're not helping."

"Maybe this will." He slides me a silver mug brimming with purple-amber liquid.

The mead is designed to put me in a good mood—silvercraft. Koglim guzzles down half of his mug and taps his fingers on the counter, whistling softly.

The barkeep fills more orders as we sit there, passing out mugs and glasses filled with strange, heady liquids, bursting with color and flourishing garnishes. At the same time, he washes things out with his other two hands. A younger kid comes and sits at the end of the counter, but after asking for his AMP score, the barkeep shoos him away.

Koglim mutters something like, "This is supposed to be *the* party." He slaps the counter. "How about we approve your guest list? Rugnus said—that Andalynn said—that we could invite some people. Give them budge permissions into the lounge. So..."

A sigh escapes me. "Okay, sure."

He tosses something invisible to me with a gesture.

A new icon appears floating near me. I open the list and click on the first entry. It's immediately apparent that Koglim stocked the list with beautiful models and dead-eyed professional raiders who look as if they've just got out of a stint in Keelcrawl prison. I can't help but smile, but I shake my head and flick the list back to him. "No."

"What? These are important people. I—okay, I had to try. How about this one?" He clears his throat and flicks me another list. This one is more diverse. I scroll through it and find a few pro raiders from Koglim's new team, two or three keepers—not from the council—and a host of others. I stop when I reach two teenage sisters.

I shake my head. "Not the ClaySlay girls."

"Oh, come on." I don't look his direction, but I can hear him pout.

"This is why we have trust issues, Koglim. Not these two. They run a channel that—"

"Everyone loves them, though."

"They're obsessed with me. They make fake videos of me doing extremely Loamin things like chopping wood with a double-sided ax, or—"

"That one where you break through an obsidian wall with only the power of your pecs. That one is so..."

I frown at him.

"...uh, inappropriate. They can go, I guess. I'll add a few more raiders from another group I know."

Once he deletes the sisters, I accept the list. "Now, if I could only change the music."

"Change of music?" the barkeep asks.

"You can do that?"

"For Clayson Brightstorm? Get melted. Sure. What do you like?"

"Anything. Just no Duumian bass-chants."

"You got it." The barkeep spins something on bluelink like he's scratching records.

The background music instantly changes to something closer to human trap music. Koglim pops his shoulders to the beat and pushes the mug closer to my hand. I grab it and spin around on the stool. I suck in a breath, holding it in anticipation.

"Half of the world is standing on your doorstep waiting to talk to you, Clayson."

"That's what I'm afraid of. Open the gate."

A few people budge in on the other side of the suite. They spot me, and I read the excitement on their faces. Before I can acknowledge them, twenty more people blink into existence around the lounge, then fifty more. We've tripled the size of the party. I take another deep breath, only to realize the whole room is unearthly quiet. Waiting on me. They're my guests.

Koglim speaks out of the side of his mouth. "Don't just stare at them."

I awkwardly raise my mug, but no words leave my mouth.

After another few seconds, Koglim yells. "Let's party!"

The guests shout back a cheer.

The barkeep gives me a loose salute and sends out aluminum trays of steaming food right on cue. The area around us erupts with dancing. At the same moment, dozens of excited conversations join the murmur of music.

"Now," Koglim says, "I welcome you to the party, within the party." A ripple of orange light pulses through the curving transparent aluminum ceiling over our heads. Koglim spots one of his fellow raiders a rail thin boy named Brude, with a complicated set of glasses. He leaves me sitting by myself with two drinks. No one immediately accosts me, so I turn toward the bar.

In the reflection of the mirror behind the bartender, blue eyes watch me—Jeiahlir. But when I turn around, she's gone.

A howl erupts next to me, and I twist to my left where a man stands flanked by two large dogs, a mastiff and a husky. Another dog—a golden retriever puppy—rests in the nook of his right arm. Coppermages always have animals around, but the mastiff is particularly intimidating. Before I can ask his name, the man tilts his head back and belts out another howl, the graying beard on his face shaking with reverberations.

His dogs join him for the last few seconds, but then all three stop, and the man extends his empty arm to test strengths with me. I grasp his forearm. His sinuous muscles are thick through the rough canvas of an old knights jacket he wears. Two distinguished master's pins and one peerless honor pin show his military record. I scan his face, hoping for some recollection to dawn on me, and there is something familiar about the shape of his eyes and the coarseness of his hair, but I can't place it.

"Tarden Wolfkeeper." His voice is a steady breath, almost like a long gravelly sigh.

I blink and scan his face again. "Then Torlina is—"

"Please. Wolfstaff is the proper way to refer to her."

"Right, sorry. Wolfstaff. She must be—"

"I am her direct descendant. Keeper of Wolfstaff Dungeon."

"Oh." I cycle through my mental list of the Council of Ten Keepers, but I know Tarden isn't one of them. Wolfstaff Dungeon lies somewhere in the middle of the rankings. It had been higher, but my summation crossed into some places that had yet to be seen—the mirror room, staring Landred Wolfstaff at his mother's funeral brunch.

"I've come bearing good news. We finished our review of your summation in Wolfstaff Dungeon last Gem, and it's conclusive."

A few tables behind him, Jeiahlir weaves between the crowd. Something glitters in her hand—blue glass. She steps behind a man with a giant fox head—must be coppercraft and goldcraft combination—and disappears again. Something's off with this girl. I need to find Koglim and—

"Young Brightstorm?"

Wolfkeeper's eyes draw me back to him.

"Oh, sorry. You were saying."

"I've been trying to contact you for weeks."

"I've turned off a lot of my notifications. I couldn't process it all."

He looks around at the party. "Silencing the host of people is wise. Wolfstaff would certainly approve. I'm glad you accepted my request to enter here tonight."

"You said you reviewed my summation? I didn't know it was under review."

The Mastiff growls, and Tarden pats the dog's head. "Yes, it was conclusive. Your summation alone reached the greatest depth in the dungeon anyone has ever achieved."

"That can't be right."

"They say you spoke to her son—the only known wraith in Wolfstaff Dungeon—and lived to talk about it. The review has granted you seership of the dungeon."

The mug in my hand almost slips. "Seership?"

"Yes. And many tasks await you. The worshiper pool is at an all-time high, so your first task will be to complete a devotion analysis. After that, there are several other—"

This is a job offer of sorts. What would Andalynn and Rugnus say about this? Finding Mithriumbane Dungeon already takes up most of my time. "I'm sorry. I don't think I can do that right now."

Wolfkeeper leans back, blinking. His eyes search my face. A low growl enters his throat, more of confusion than anger, but the Mastiff picks it up, and the hair on its back prickles.

"Perhaps I wasn't clear, or perhaps you are unaware of what this means, living above granite as you do. Being granted this status is no small thing. One does not simply pass on the offer of seership."

I swallow, looking down at his dogs. What am I supposed to say? I can't accept such a high position. The only seer I know is my mom. That's why she was dragged into Silverlamp Dungeon last year. I'm almost positive I will do a horrible job trying to fulfill the responsibility that comes with the status. It's too much. Though I can think of one possible excuse.

"I would be in direct conflict. My grandfather's dungeon—"

"Mithriumbane?"

"Yes. I'm trying to find it."

Very slowly, he inclines his head, stroking the golden retriever puppy in his arms. "I can see this is meaningful to you. But in all these years, no one has located it. Most are convinced that it was fake to begin with."

"It's not."

"How can you know this?"

"Tarden—uh, Wolfkeeper. I'm trying my best. I'm still learning about this world. Mithriumbane Dungeon is my priority. It's been hard to get the council to take my request, and now Lagnar Emberfence just made that even more—"

"Curious." A rich, playful voice speaks from out of the crowd. "Excuse me, but if I'm not mistaken, Clayson Brightstorm, there is some evidence that you are working with Emberfence."

It's Jeiahlir. From her position sitting at the long-legged table, she meets my stare, investigating every angle of my face, testing my reaction to her words. From the cobalt of her eyes, I know how to pronounce her name: the sound of a jay as in blue jay.

Wolfkeeper growls again, and for a second, the ground vibrates under me. "Do not speak that name."

Jeiahlir's electric gaze doesn't flinch from me. The high-hat drops on the music, and her bronze eyelids fold and unfold, bright and alluring. I take in, only briefly, the clothes she's wearing, a nebulous black top and gray cargo pants. I thought paladins were basically security guards. I guess I expected a uniform like the knights.

She leans forward in her chair. "Sorry, Wolfkeeper. I know

many keepers are wary of Emberfence, seeing how adamant he is that he should replace Bluekeeper on the council."

"Yes?" Wolfkeeper draws out the word into a question.

"Did you know"—the girl smiles at me, and my stomach flutters— "Clayson Brightstorm purchased a fake AMP from him last year to pose as a refugee?"

The flutter inside me settles into something cold, the same sensation I get when my hand comes free of a groove, and I'm not sure I'll stay on a cliff. My hand reflexively encircles the bracelet on my wrist, and I let white defensive power light my body up from my bones outward. If she's recording, I've blocked her out. I hope.

"How did you know that?" I ask.

Wolfkeeper takes a step uncomfortably close to me. "It's true then?"

I back up, but his dogs are so close. One sniffs my hand. "How was I supposed to know who he was at the time? I had lived under a rock for fourteen years."

He leans in closer for a second but finally backs off, grabbing the lapels of his knights jacket, his face wrinkled in confusion. "Lived under what rock?"

"Sorry. It's a human phrase that means I didn't interact with the world much."

"Ah," Wolfkeeper says, still wearing a perplexed look. "Why a rock?"

"I—"

"The problem," Jeiahlir adds, "is not that he lived under a rock, it's that he *didn't*. I don't think he understands how complicated things are in our world. Like his relationship with Emberfence, a known criminal."

"Jeiahlir, right?" I pronounce it with the jay sound.

"Jeiah, please."

I roll my shoulders back. "Well, Jeiah, I've got nothing to do with Emberfence."

"Why does he keep showing up in your location data?"

Now I'm confused. "What?"

Wolfkeeper growls. "We've been interrupted, Brightstorm. Consider my offer. I can honor your hope of finding Yinzar's dungeon, but your time would be better spent as the seer of Wolfstaff. I give you two days to change your mind."

He budges, leaving only Jeiah and me. She removes the same glass rod I saw in the crowd and sets it on her lap.

I point to it. "I'm a bit paranoid about what people see on bluelink. Are you recording?"

"No."

"Okay, so you've been, what, spying on me?" I wince slightly, knowing that I was just looking into her.

"I'm a paladin, Clayson. I don't spy. I figure things out and reveal them to the public. So, are you working with Emberfence to help him steal Bluekeeper's spot on the council?"

"Am I... are you nuts? Ide keep me, of course not!"

The blue glass rod comes up. She waves it slowly over me like a magnifying glass. "And that's the truth?"

"Yes. Would you put that thing away? What is it anyway?"

"You don't know what a beholder is? Boy, you did live under a rock. It helps me see things. For example, that bracelet. It's unregistered. And another thing: You used something called a dreampick in the last twenty-four hours. You've been to the surface recently. No surprises there. You've been looking into the effects of the surface and... dreams. Which is strange."

"Figures none of that's private."

"What you see as privacy violates the principles of community."

"So, a good community knows each other's search history?"

"I wouldn't let your friend Rugnus hear the doubt in your voice. Makes you sound like the true prince of Whurrimduum."

"Not likely. The council barely knows I exist."

"That's an overstatement. Next question: Why does Emberfence show up on your location data?"

"What do you mean?"

"He's been close to your location multiple times in the last week."

"News to me."

Jeiah stands up from her table and looks me over, weighing something. It's the investigator in her working something out. I wonder for a moment what her work for Bluekeeper includes. Obviously, the keeper is concerned about Lagnar's growing interest in retaking the council seat.

I'm about to turn the question to her when she says, "Hmm, then you weren't involved? You didn't even know." Her empty hand stays face open toward the transparent ceiling, and she spins it around the glass rod clockwise. This investigation is unnerving.

The cobalt ring on my finger shines, and a notification icon enters my field of vision: Its Andalynn. "It's my sister. Been waiting for this call."

Jeiah keeps her eyes on me as she sits back at the table. She accepts a small plate of food from one of the floating aluminum serving trays.

As I turn to find a quiet corner of the room, Jeiah says, "Ask her about Emberfence."

Turned away from her, my breathing catches up with me again. What's my problem? All her questions and her piercing eyes, her strange bluecraft object. She sucked all the air out of the room. I either feel attacked, or I'm infatuated with her. Probably both. I clear my thoughts as I search for a good place to talk to Andalynn.

There's no such thing as a quiet corner, so I find a wall and open the icon.

"There you are." Andalynn's smile, as always, is infectious. She looks down at my mug and then behind me. "Good. You're letting people in. How's the festival from where you're at?"

I shrug.

"I see. You drinking that, or just holding it?" she asks about my mug.

I almost feel my eyebrows knit together in frustration. "Holding it. Why?"

"Twenty minutes until we start. I think it would be good if you..."

"What?"

"Maybe go out to the festival."

"With people? I'm blocking recordings for a reason. I'd really rather—"

"You think you can block that much craft without Ergal? If the first hundred onlookers can't get through your privacy defenses, the next hundred will."

First, this paladin girl sorting through my bluelink search history like it's her personal laundry. Now my sister—the leader of the most historically undemocratic kingdom in the world—thinks I need to be more open. Something in me finally crawls into a corner and dies. I think it's hope.

A woman greets my sister at the edge of the recording. Andalynn smiles and waves.

"You know everyone yet?" I ask. It's a common question from me. She must know the names of a million people.

"Almost," Andalynn says. "Look. This is just the new reality of the world."

"You sound like Rugnus."

"Don't you dare," A smile betrays her real thoughts about Rugnus. "I'm trying to bring people together. Help me out, will you? If it makes it easier, find a place that looks fun and budge there. You could try the forge celebrations."

I sigh. "Why not."

"Good. You need this. I've got to go. Wish me luck." She uses the human phrase.

"With Ide." I like the phrase. It means the ancient earth will provide everything.

After we're disconnected. I find myself staring into the purplish liquid in the mug. "One way to be cheerful about all this." I let my defenses down and take a long drink. The taste is sweet and rich, with an after taste like apples in the fall. Loamin don't work in sugar, so it must be sweetened with something else. Honey? My imagination conjures up the image of some Loamin happily covered in a buzzing swarm of bees.

There's always something that surprises me about the way Loamin use craft. More industrial than magical. Maybe getting a look at the festival up close will be exciting. Where's the kid who wanted to see the world and watched travel documentaries religiously? Okay, that could be the magic liquid talking.

I open myself up to the idea of exploring: I can do this. The block on my camera through bluelink is easy to find, a silver and blue lock and chain across a holographic door. The lock expands as I extend my arm outward. The silver and blue icon greedily accepts the code from my bracelet, and I rotate my fist until it shatters both the lock and chain.

I scan the crowd in the suite, but Jeiah is gone, along with all of her accusations.

"Alright," I say to pretty much everyone. "Show me what this festival has to offer."

EXPLORE THE FESTIVAL

I ENTER the world of the StoneYoke festival virtually, searching for a good budgeport, a place to start, to spend some time and ferrum.

Every corner of the festival is lit by the brightstorm.

Today is the first day of Stone—zero one—and over the last few days, Loamin ingenuity and craft have carved out a home for thousands of groups, worshiper pools, craft interests, and political enclaves—a permanent place to link the last two cities under granite. For a boy who grew up in isolation in the Blue Ridge Mountains, it's a feast for the senses.

One section of the new district is made of glittering pink and green ice, carved into towering castles and frozen markets by ironcraft masters. Another section is so thick with trees there's no room to stand on the ground, so people scramble around in the canopy launching themselves from bough to bough with thrilling screams. All these microcosms of culture and craft can be seen at a distance from the ridge of the central amphitheater looking outward.

Inward, inside the crater of the super-volcano shape, the amphitheater crawls with people finding seats for the opening ceremony. It will begin shortly after the brightstorm shifts to night. As a virtual presence, I can speed through the air. I zip over the crater and pass to the other side of StoneYoke, where I find even more biomes designed for adherents of the many crafts.

A strange lizard rodeo for the coppermages looks interesting. Speed dating tables boosted with silvercraft—that's a pass from me. These larger sections are nestled within a maze of shops and smaller testing areas. It all reminds me of the Keeper's Social, the night Bazalrak exposed my presence in Tungsten City to the world.

For me, the most curious part of the festival is where the crafts begin to blend. Goldcraft base jumpers shoot into the air, only to come plummeting to earth, drilling deep into the stone, protected by shieldcraft. The stone repairs itself with ironcraft. Cart owners throng the pathways hocking food and craftsmanship. A group of hairy giants, using goldcraft to change their strength and appearance, stomp past an area where a handful of unruly kids try to turn themselves into molecules and pass through a brick wall. I'm impressed when one actually does it.

I'm floating five feet above the crowd, but the virtual avatars of hundreds of others are there with me. There is some customization, but—the best I can guess—most people don't divert far from their true physical appearance. Maybe that's because there's a mountain of surveillance that makes it easy to know who you are anyway. Plus there are objects made of gold which let you walk around with instant plastic surgery, though those can only conceal you if no one's actively scanning for your location.

A parade of mechanical dragons race by beneath me, titanium claws clicking against the stone. A large maroon dragon swallows a smaller yellow one, and I see a hint of the person inside controlling it. As the smaller one is consumed, the two transform into a single orange centipede.

At this moment, when the beauty of the festival is on full glittering display, the brightstorm shifts from day to night.

There's a second where it's like someone switches off the

light, but only a second. Then, neon flares and spotlights blossom all around, red and orange and pale blue. Even the people seem to glow all the brighter, their faces flecked with gilded blush. Studded jewelry and streamers of light add even more radiance. The colors of every craft appear vivid against the darkness.

I find myself ensnared in the beauty of this strange world once again. My body is still inside the VIP lounge high on the ridge. Instead of returning, I join the festival firsthand at the closest budgeport. It's strange moving from being what amounts to a shadow on a bluelink server to flesh and blood in an instant.

More sensations hit me. The smell of fatted meat cooking and the sound of it sizzling in a nearby food stall. The electronic music is not only crisper and more authentic, but the music physically shakes the ground.

If I lived a thousand years, I'd never be in another place so crowded with people. Everything I fear about existing in Tungsten City—in the world of my people—was wrong. I thought there would be a hundred thousand requests for interviews, a million messages over bluelink, that I would be overwhelmed—like when the honeysuckle comes in early summer and chokes out all the native species on the border of the northern meadow—it takes weeks to fight it, and it's always a losing battle.

But that doesn't happen. The crowd allows me space to breathe. Knowing eyes acknowledge my presence with a sense of respect and agreement. There are smiles and cheers wherever I wander, even groups of gawking fans, but they don't throng me like paparazzi. Until now, I had been unwilling to believe that the people of Tungsten City could respect my need for space. I can't count on my fingers the number of times Rugnus has tried to tell me this.

"It's not in their blood," Rugnus had said.

Sure, they tried to throw us out of the city last year, and sure if I wanted to, I could pull up an unwatchable amount of commentary about myself, but Rugnus also said, "We understand your need for space."

Maybe he was right. With all the invasion of privacy—bluelink tracking my movements, listening to my conversations, a hundred thousand VR cameras recording me every time I scratch my nose—the people themselves like freedom too much to form a mob against me. They may enjoy an unhealthy level of spectacle, but at least they won't talk to you about it. And I could always put my blocker back on, though I doubt my bracelet could scrub me out of every nearby recording. There are just too many. Maybe Ergal could have, but not my bracelet.

I spot a curious market stall where bronze and copper cookware dangles from sturdy racks. I chart a course toward it, but a food cart cuts off my path. "Harmony links!"

"What?"

"Sausage." A man, with an impossibly clean apron, holds up a ring of meat suspended by two connected silver skewers. "If you've never tried harmony links, it's worth the price."

I ask myself what Rugnus or Koglim would do, then take the ring of meat from the man. The icon for ferrum spins at the corner of my vision, and I know I've paid for it.

"Wonderful!" the seller says. Leaning in, he adds, "Spangler eggs are a hit. But a word of advice. Use some silver before they go out. Give us—I don't know—the feeling of living in the beautiful woods by your cabin."

"How do you—"

"Oh, well..." a pink color fills in his giant ears. "Don't mean to pry. Just something to consider. Here, how about this one's on the house."

The ferrum icon spins in reverse as he gives my money back. Before I can persuade him to let me pay, his cart rumbles away over the stone.

I take another look around at the crowd. It's like Rugnus told the whole world to treat me with kid gloves. He knows I don't follow his feed that carefully. Could he have advertised to all of Rimduum to give me some space? I'm just being paranoid.

One bite of the sausage and everything but the music fades into nothingness.

The sensation of each note stretches across my mind. A trill, composed of a hundred overlapping notes, breaks down into distinct components, every pitch taking on meaning, telling a story that, when weaved together, reaches into my body, and pulls at my sinews. Tears come to my eyes.

It's the skewer, tainting my mind with silvercraft. Beautiful, alluring craft. I budge one section over, and the music changes slightly. There is less bass and a man's voice instead of a woman's. I notice bagpipes somewhere in the distance. Am I hearing music from the next section over?

When I budge there, I barely notice the swirls of mercury. People move in either slow-motion or a rapidity not possible for humans. I ignore the hoard of people using timecraft. For me, the music is alive. Bagpipes added to the same song from before, but now hammering has replaced the bass notes.

The effect almost fades, but I take another bite of the sausage.

And I continue in order around the side of the massive amphitheater, stadium by stadium. Each time I budge, the music changes slightly. I move quickly around the outside of the amphitheater, trying to confirm my suspicion about the music. Whoever spent the time orchestrating the festival understood how each type of music related to the next and made it ebb and flow in waves that all fit together naturally.

The effect fades, and I discard the skewer into the closest craft recycler.

A girl brushes past me, dragging a familiar summer scent across my face in a cloud. I catch a swirl of blonde hair, and my blood cools. It reminds me so much of Sira I take a second look, following the swish of the girl's silver-white shirt. It can't be her. She's locked in maximum security in Keelcrawl prison. I stumble forward, shaking my head.

A crowd of people wearing wooden masks passes between us,

and I lose her for a couple of seconds, but the girl—light on her feet, playful—stops and swings toward me.

Unmistakably, it's Rensira Silverlamp, standing next to a small knot of Loamin playing maltobi. She smiles. The crowd between us is gone, but my feet refuse to move.

It can't be her.

Her face is pale and gaunt, eyes haunted, but her smile widens as she begins to interfere with the players. There are bags under her eyes as if she's taken a bad budge, or in Sira's case as a near null, any budge at all.

She's focusing on the game of maltobi. I've seen versions of this game before, but much smaller. Koglim made me spend a day playing it because, in his words, I needed to "have a real child-hood." A massive twelve-sided hologram, like a game die, hovers between the six players. They take turns marking sides, trying to connect all their lines inside the shape. The trick is, they can't see the lines, only the points where the lines begin and end.

The girl—it can't be Sira—removes something silver from under her shirt and steps toward the woman whose turn is next. It's Onrix, Sira's silver knife. I would know it anywhere. How? It's locked away in the royal castlestack in Whurrimduum. Did that drink do something to me? Did the sausage?

She nudges the woman's hand, forcing her to choose a spot on the shape that will connect it with the most lines possible. The crowd oohs at the woman's choice. As the line snaps together, the hologram shimmers white. The girl's smile drops a bit, and she shakes her head, vanishing, budging somewhere.

Budging.

It can't be Sira. Her AMP score in budgecraft is a one. She hates budging. It makes her nauseous. But didn't she look sick? As if she had been budging everywhere? My senses return to me. I need to track the girl's movements. I gesture open bluelink and try to connect with Rugnus. His face appears.

"Rugnus. Rugnus! Something's happening. It's her. She—"

It's a recorded message.

"Connect with me—now!" I disconnect.

Next, I try Andalynn. No response. The performance is minutes away. Of course, she can't answer.

The moment I call Koglim, it connects, though he doesn't pause his dancing to talk. He's a head taller than everyone else, a gleam of sweat across his forehead. The music is so loud he only squints at me, mouthing something I can't understand.

I try to tell him, but he shakes his head. "Come back to the party!" he yells.

"Sira!" I yell at him.

"Syrup?!" He barely glances at me, neon light coating the surface of his dark skin.

I hang up.

Maybe I could try Winta and Hemdi. But before I find them in my contacts, another idea pops into my head. The paladin girl from the suite, the investigator, Jeiahlir. She immediately answers when I call but doesn't say a thing. Her face reads like an expectation.

"I have a problem," I tell her.

She searches my face, squints. "Okay."

I send her a budge match. Within seconds, she appears in front of me with raised eyebrows.

I shake my head. "You're gonna think I'm nuts."

Her eyebrows inch further upward. "That word again. Nuts. That's a human saying?"

"Crazy. You're gonna think I've lost my mind."

She scans the crowd. "Wait, where did you see him?"

I shake my head. "Him? You mean her?"

"Her? No, Lagnar Emberfence. He's—"

She whirls back to me, fear in her eyes. "Is this some type of trap by Emberfence? What do you want from me?"

"I—no—what? I called you because I saw Sira." I point to the game where she had stood. "Playing that game."

She straightens. "Rensira Silverkeeper? But she's in Keelcrawl prison. You saw her? And she was playing maltobi?" The doubt in Jeiah's voice doesn't inspire confidence.

"That's what I'm telling you. It doesn't make any sense. She's locked—"

"Give me access to your history."

That's when it hits me. "Wait, why are you worried about Lagnar?"

"Come on, quick. Give me access. This is what I've been investigating, why I even came tonight. Well, that and you."

"What is?"

She stands waiting, so I open my history and add her to approved reviewers.

The blue of her eyes deepens for a moment as she relives my last few minutes. "She's not in your history."

I scoff. "That can't be right." I access it myself and scan back to the point I saw her. Nothing. "There's nothing there. How—"

"Almost nothing. Look closer. See the shadow. The light against the stone there... and there. Something is blocking it out. And look. Did she touch that player?"

I nod when the player makes her choice.

"Okay, so did I see her or not? I'm not following you." My heartbeat is thudding against my eardrums. Something terrible is happening.

"Think about it. Your shieldcraft rating is peerless, meaning if you wanted to screen individuals from capturing you on video, it could work. But if a hundred people were recording you? A thousand? There's always a point when one person's craft can be overpowered by the people."

"So, she just blocked us?"

"Are you trying to—why aren't you getting this? Look around. Thousands of people, all recording. bluelink history takes in all that data. There are so many recordings of this that it would overwhelm even the strongest privacy craft. Rensira Silverlamp's shieldcraft is terrible. Even if it wasn't, it's not possible for her to erase or block that much information."

"You're right. So, what does that mean?"

"That's the problem. That's what Bluekeeper wanted me to investigate. For the last few days, these glitches keep coming up around the city with one common connection. They're breaking all the rules about bluelink."

"A connection? Like what?"

"You. All of the anomalies are happening around you."

My head spins. "How come no one told me?"

"Why would I tell you? It's you I'm investigating. I thought you were involved." She looks at me carefully. "Maybe I still do."

A sinking feeling turns my feet to lead. This can't be happening. How would Sira get out of Keelcrawl? But I know exactly how.

"You think Lagnar is involved?" I ask.

"I went to investigate one of the anomalies that came up early in the day, near the amphitheater at the forges. He was there. I figured he was enough of a connection to you that it couldn't have been a coincidence."

"Is he still at the festival?" The weight of responsibility settles in my gut. "I'll confront him."

Jeiah almost smiles. "You'll what?"

I pull up the festival map and, in the snap of a finger, I find him. A little orange dot among blue dots, in a section dedicated to forge worship which sits on a part of the ring of the volcano. "There, see. Found him."

"And you're going to walk over to him and... what?"

"I-I don't know. I can't just stand by and do nothing."

"That's interesting coming from you."

"What is that supposed to mean?"

"You practically live on the surface, disconnected from everyone."

Hearing this from a stranger is like a battering ram. I've spent the past few months hiding, looking into dreams, searching records about my grandfather. I've made myself as unavailable as possible. A hundred thousand expectations catch up to me all at once, not the least of which is finding my grand-father's dungeon.

I could've helped with the festival. Maybe I should accept the invitation to be the seer of Wolfstaff. Or at least become a mentor for other shieldmages. Maybe I should've even done an interview with the ClaySlay girls. But none of that matters now. Sira and Lagnar are up to something, and it involves me.

"If Lagnar is here... what I'm saying—" I blow out a breath. "I'm not defenseless."

Jeiah's face remains impassive, if not somewhat amused.

"Follow me if you want," I add.

I budge to the forging area, careful to put some distance between me and Lagnar's location—about fifty yards. Jeiah appears next to me. "What's the rating on your unregistered bracelet?"

A cloud of heat swells the air around us from a hundred forges. The whole area glows a molten red. Next to us, someone pulls a huge, rusted lever, dumping a tank of graywater over a furnace. It hisses, and yellow steam plumes into the air. To a human, it might look like work, but this is a festival—its perfor-mance. They're worshiping the forge.

"Nineteen."

"That's—and you made it? I could get you a job at Bluekeep-er's forge."

"Get in line." I walk through the newly created yellow fog. The woman working the forge nearly drops the hot metal from a pair of tongs when she sees me.

Jeiah looks from me to the woman, then steps closer to my right between us like a bodyguard. The woman turns back to her forge sheepishly.

"Hmm." I glance at her. "Maybe I could hire you for personal security."

"You don't need it. Though, not sure you could pay me enough ferrum to follow you around and make sure no one looks at you." Her face is mostly serious.

"You're making fun of me?"

"You make it pretty easy. Can we focus on finding Lagnar?"

We pass through the steam, but Lagnar is nowhere to be seen. I check the map one more time, but his orange dot is gone. Even with a wider search of the festival I can't find him.

"He's gone." Jeiah spins slowly, double-checking with the beholder.

How is she still calm?

"The closest bluelink hub isn't far." A fringe of urgency sharpens her voice. "I'm going to trace his budge. Stay here. Find out where he went."

"How am I—"

"If you're not involved with any of this, which I still doubt, then help me. Ask people. Looks like he was working over in that forge. Check around."

She disappears.

Curiosity tries to break through my urgency as I make my way through. I take in the contrasting energies. The fires in the forges —pulses of lava, or coals, or burning wood, and some forgeseeds —meet with a variety of cooling agents, elemental magic, snow, ice, water, and in some cases, a white semi-solid gel which, as it contacts newly formed metal, sizzles and releases a medicinal eucalyptus scent that cools the inside of my nose and throat. My eyes sting for a second, but it's fleeting.

Five people work the forge where Lagnar had been.

"Excuse me. Was Lagnar Emberfence just here at this forge?"

A younger man at the edge of the group wears a large clear bottle, settled like a hiking bag on his back. The bottle is half full of clear liquid. He wears two circular disks over his hands, reaching up in the air to grab steam. It's a technique I've only heard about, but something about capturing the water vapor from the forge to use in future recipes.

I catch him glancing my way, but he ignores me, slipping off the metal steam collectors and moving in closer to an older man.

The older man whistles loudly, and the remaining three

workers pack up their gear. Before I can ask any other questions, everyone but the old man is gone. He makes a gesture closing something, and the portable forge closes in on itself and vanishes.

Something is not right about all of this. "Who are you?" I ask.

"Lagnar's sorry he couldn't be here," he says, then budges.

That was weird.

The countdown to the ceremony pops into view. It's only a minute away. Is that why everyone is leaving? Maybe budging to their seats in the amphitheater?

I jog up a cascade of stairs to the height of the rim to look down into the amphitheater. With night settled on the festival, the columns of seats are lit only with occasional flares of craft. The crowd is awaiting the opening ceremony. High above me, hundreds of small surfaces on the crystal stalactite buildings shift like scales, turning spotlights to the stage; otherwise, every light around us turns off in preparation for the performance. Between the reverse skyscrapers above, adhering to the surface of the cavern ceiling, I spot a flicker of black metal. The construction drones that built the district hang like bats.

At center stage, a green light falls on my sister, sitting on a throne as tall as a pine tree woven from plants and jungle flowers, neon green, purple, and white. Even from this distance, her crown glitters almost like mithrium.

Her voice is amplified across the StoneYoke festival. "Welcome to all. Tonight, we once again witness our commitment to one another, to our species, to our culture, and to our mutual survival. We are stoneyoked, one pulse, one body, glimmering in metal, and basking in the light from every brightstorm. We keep the dungeons of our ancestors..."

New orange spotlights find dozens of keepers, nearing a hundred, moving in a half-circle surrounding my sister's throne. "We are citizen-leaders with influence and power..." Another spotlight, this time on an equal number of Loamin rising like a tide at the far end of the stage. I recognize a few of them as powerful leaders from Tungsten City.

"...and we come from families as old as metal and stone itself." A final yellow light settles over a group of men, women, and children, representing important families from Whurrimduum.

Each group moves forward. The amphitheater rumbles with craft. The men and women on the stage raise their hands into the air, dragging metal coils from unseen places. The long strands of metal come together, forming a huge basin. It can only be a representation of the quest agent, the summator, a nest-like object symbolizing the connection of all things. Andalynn's throne lowers to the stage, and she joins the group of people. The giant summator remains propped up by a forest of metal limbs, some spouting fire, some light, others blossoming with vines.

A buzz of belief fills the air. I feel the craft in my bones. All the crafts combined to form one great whole, and for a moment, I'm filled with guilt. Why haven't I embraced life down here? It's a life rich with beauty and magic.

Far above us, the two circling dragons merge into a single globe of energy, a mock brightstorm. It's a symbol: something forbidden becoming something life-sustaining.

There's a sudden alarm over bluelink, an emergency broadcast.

Words appear in the air. Everyone around me is getting the same message.

KEELCRAWL PRISON'S DEFENSES OVERWHELMED. INMATES ESCAPED.

The joints in my knees nearly buckle. I mutter a curse—something human. It *was* Sira I saw. Who else has escaped from Keelcrawl?

The circling dragons above the festival swell with blue light. When the light fills the whole sky, there's a loud pop, forcing gasps from people all around me. The dragons are gone. The group on the stage tilts their heads back, looking to the sky in confusion. None of this is part of the ceremony.

Koglim had seen smoke and machines.

My mind whirls. Dark shapes on the cavern ceiling, the construction drones, swarm around the base of each of the crystal stalactite buildings, which loom like glistening daggers.

I blink. One of the hanging buildings detaches, plummeting toward the festival. As it falls, the world slows to a crawl, not by craft. Silence. Watching eyes filled with horror. An ear-shattering sound, like someone compressing a billion glass bottles through metal teeth, rattles into my skin. It's a nightmare of sound. A cloud of glass plumes toward the sky.

My muscles contract, jaw tightens. I feel the grinding of enamel. Andalynn was in the Amphitheater. A man next to me screams. A sharp voice yells, "I can't budge."

This declaration echoes around me.

I gesture open bluelink, but it fails. I try to budge back to the VIP lounge, that also fails. I follow a woman's long, trailing finger back up to the sky as two more glass buildings are severed from the distant cavern ceiling, falling into the city below, sending up waves of smoke and glass. Those buildings were filled with people. Were they blocked from budging also?

That's when the millions of people on the ground—who can't budge, who can't escape—run for their lives. StoneYoke is under attack.

SHATTER ON STONE

Darkness and broken neon light. Muted fires and muted voices.

My bracelet. I extend the protective glow of white around my body, and though the light doesn't pierce the dark cloud of debris, I can see my skin, lacerated and covered in sand, or gravel, or bits of glass and stone. Nothing's clear.

"Help." The word is so soft that, for a second, I think it's coming from me.

No, someone is out there within the cloud.

"Help!" It's louder this time, and my legs come unglued. I stumble through the fog and confusion toward the sound. My legs smash into a knee-high wall. I pinwheel and barely catch myself on its cratered surface.

Another step forward, and I run into a woman. A man stands next to her holding a bundled infant. I grab the woman's arm and extend the power of my bracelet. A bubble of shieldcraft forms over us.

My ears ring, and for a second, I can't remember if that's normal. Did the buildings really fall? How? Dust coats my tongue, but my mouth is too dry to spit it out. This can't be happening. Whatever *this* is.

The father, with the infant in his arms, touches an iron ear-covering. Swirls of debris inside the protective bubble coalesce into a ball of mud and crash at our feet. The air inside my protective bubble is clear, but the debris cloud pools over us like we're under a glass bowl.

The mother's eyes squeeze and un-squeeze as if she is trying to wake from a dream. All she finds is me. Confusion shows on her face, then fear, then confusion again. She tries to speak, drawing her mouth open, but no sound comes out, and the frozen expression makes her look as if she's screaming.

"Are you okay?" It's such a stupid question. Of course, she's not okay.

The father hands the baby to his wife. "You're a Brightstorm. Did you"—he looks at the surrounding cloud of darkness— "are you doing this?"

He thinks it's me. He wants to know if I did this. But I don't even know what *this* is. His wife shakes her head, finally speaking. "No. I-I saw the building falling from the sky. But wh-what's happening?"

"I don't know. It's an attack, I think." Every word from my mouth is dry, meaningless.

"I can't budge. Can you?" the mother asks.

The father puts his arm around her. "No, something stopped me. Stopped everyone. And took down bluelink. What could do that? How could someone prevent bluelink connections? Ide keep us."

In the depths of the cloud, someone cries out. The anguished plea sets off a wave of other shouts and screams. The father tucks the baby's blanket gently around their head. I deepen the protection of the globe around us. The light increases. The sounds fade into dull murmurs.

The father says something. His lips barely move. It might be, "Thank you."

We stay like this for a while, huddled in the darkness until deep, red firelight bleeds through the cloud. I become aware of small pieces of floating ash in the debris cloud. A flash of pale orange light and muddy rain patters against the protective shell, slipping to the ground.

The mother's body tenses. "Something's happening."

My mind can only register the rain as another attack.

The father looks out into the debris cloud. "Ironmages are trying to clear away the cloud." he pauses thoughtfully. "That could work."

"Oh." My mind flashes to Rugnus. He could burn the atoms of this debris cloud into nothing. Others must be thinking the same thing. There are millions of people here at the festival. I don't know how widespread the attack was, but even one building... without budges, how many people would be dead?

The construction mechs parked on the ceiling, how many were there? They cut down the buildings. That's what I saw. Rugnus said each construction mech was run by twenty mech-mages. The dots are beginning to form into a coherent picture, but how many people would it have taken to cut loose whole buildings? Was it an accident? But the timing of that emergency warning about Keelcrawl. And I saw Sira. I saw her.

The father caresses his child's soft, tangled hair. "I can help out there. Can I step through the shield?"

I nod, and immediately he walks through the shield. His figure is like a shadow in the cloud. He grows larger. Or maybe the dim light is playing a trick of perspective. The cloud thins even more, and I catch a glimpse of his head and torso, covered with a thick layer of dirt and glass particles, clinging to his skin as if he crawled out of the center of the earth. After only a minute, he's doubled in size, a whirlwind of debris around him.

He forces himself out of the giant monster he's made, leaving behind a shell like a cicada fleeing its exoskeleton. His body is covered with scrapes and abrasions. He sprints back, and I let him inside the shield. I wanna reach out and heal him, but I'm afraid to drop the shield.

He stumbles toward his wife and child. "There were bodies

out there. They weren't breathing. I—"

"Bodies?" My thoughts are washed-out, far away. This killed people. No one could budge. No one can communicate.

"We should... we need shelter," the mother says through gritted teeth.

The father shakes his head. "I should keep going."

His wife grabs his arm. "Shelter first. Please."

He hesitates, then nods.

I try bluelink again. The icons are all out of focus, tilted. None of them respond to gesturing. What kind of craft could block millions of people? As we walk back toward the forges, I'm able to call up a map of the festival, but no location data.

It shows a circular building not far from where I think we might be.

"This way." The protective bubble moves with us, pushing aside the cloud. A pulse of fire in front of us reveals two girls, barely my age, gathering dirt into a fiery orb of molten glass. When it's as long as I am tall, they set it down to cool and begin another orb. Behind them, the circular building comes into focus. Ironmages, all around us, are clearing the debris. Nothing landed on the building. It should be safe.

"There."

Once the family is safe inside, I rush back into the cloud.

How long has it been? If every ironmage is trying to pull debris from the air, how long will it take? The father saw bodies. How many died at the moment of impact? Questions churn my mind into a worried frenzy.

For a moment, I find myself staring at an amber-yellow light out in the cloud, unfocused, frozen. I feel my pulse, hear my breathing. I'm aware of everything and nothing. The ringing in my ears could be real, but it could be something I'm imagining. Minutes seem like hours.

I respond to another call for help, healing a man whose shirt is soaked in mud or sweat. As I stumble away from him, I realize it was blood.

Tungsten City has protections against this type of attack. People have emergency budges, shieldcraft. The power of a few destructive people is easily overcome by the millions. Crowdsourced protection. It's the reason they believe they need no police, no government. The people can prevent this sort of thing. That's what Rugnus believes.

But this is something new, something terrifying. I'm seeing the city overwhelmed for the first time in its history. It escaped the mithrium attacks during the devastation of the Last War.

It hits me.

Is this mithrium? Did someone find one of the other two pieces? The thought sends electricity along my spine. But that can't be true.

One piece lies in Mithriumbane. My mind returns to the single dream I've been having, the slow descent into the darkness of an abandoned mineshaft. *Don't let him have it*, Yinzar's voice called to me.

Don't let *who* have *what*?

I hear my name in the cloud, growing closer. The sensory input draws me back to the here and now. How long have I been standing in the same spot?

The voice is familiar and strange all at once. I can't place it until Jeiah steps into my path and literally shouts at me. I extend the shield over her. The look on her face is grave, angry even. A large gash at her neck leaks blood. Without thinking, I drop the shield, heal her quickly, and throw the shield back up, trapping a light haze inside the bubble with us.

"You okay?" I ask.

"No. No, I'm going to find who did this and drop a mountain on them." Her eyes cut into me. "Were you involved in this?"

"Me? No. I... how could you even... it was Sira."

She shakes her head sharply. "Sira? No. Emberfence."

"Both of them."

"If you're truly not involved, then I don't know. You might be right. It's a working theory. Both of them." She pauses. "Here. I'll patch up your bluelink connection."

"Bluelink is working for you?"

"We'll be able to find your friends now."

"Perfect. That will help, but…" A thought strikes me. What would they be doing right now? The same thing I'm doing—helping anyone they can. The closest people around them. "But there are so many people hurt."

"Understood. Okay, I'll help. You get people patched up. I'll get them patched in. Then maybe they can budge."

My bluelink icons are no longer blurred or tilted. When I open the map for the festival, location data comes up, but not with the usual information. The dots are heat signatures, not bluelink connections. The closest survivors are huddled in a small group only a fifth block away.

"Follow me." I scramble over the broken stone toward the group. Two of the group draw rain out of the air, turn the gray smoke into charcoal mud, and cast it into a pit.

"Anyone need immediate assistance?" Jeiah asks.

The two ironmages ignore us, but one man blinks, clears his throat, and says, "Nothing serious. Though… a woman, uh, back that direction. I couldn't do anything for her. Seemed bad. Maybe…"

Jeiah moves from my side to take the lead. "We're on it."

I spin the map and zoom in on the area where the man had pointed. A single dot hovers ahead of us. The air is growing lighter, the smoke and ash relenting to time and the work of all the ironmages. When I recheck my map, the dot is gone. "Jeiah? The woman."

We both see the body lying in the rubble ahead. A body but no biometrics on bluelink. No. My feet stop. I don't wanna get closer. But Jeiah takes a few more steps. She scans the woman with the blue glass rod she had called a beholder. She looks back at me, shakes her head.

A new dot appears alongside us, still out of visual range. I freeze. This person is connected to bluelink, and the name stops me in my tracks: BAZALRAK STONEDOOM.

"No." First Sira, now Bazalrak. One impossible person after another.

"What?" Jeiah asks. When I don't answer, she rests a hand on my arm, "I'm sorry you had to see that, but it will be okay. Everything will—"

Jeiah's words reach my ears, but I barely hear them. "It's not that."

I squint into the gloom. There it is, exactly what I expect. An unnatural shadow curling around the edges of the haze like someone's mixed two colors of smoke.

"Bazalrak."

He steps into view. The same ring-studded face and cruel smile, but something else too. Satisfaction. Like a man possessed with the knowledge that he has nothing to lose. His torturous nature doesn't have to hide behind a mask of invested authority. Free from Keelcrawl prison, it's clear what he wants—revenge.

Everything clicks. It's Emberfence. He broke Sira and Bazalrak out of Keelcrawl prison to help him rain terror down on Stone-Yoke. They're not here to fight for Whurrimduum or for some sense of justice. They wanna inflict the greatest amount of public damage they can, to bring this world to a grinding halt.

Bazalrak smiles, lip ring twitching. "Gonna enjoy this." Deep shadows leach out where his hands grip his shadow ax.

With Ergal, I had kept his attacks at bay, but with this bracelet, I'm not sure I can defend myself, let alone another person.

I push Jeiah behind me. "Run." The word barely comes out.

"I'm not going anywhere."

The shadow hits my circle of defensive magic. Bazalrak leaps toward us and smashes the ax into the ground. A legion of inky fissures rip over the stone. And that's all it takes.

Shadows pierce through my shieldcraft, and I dodge to the side, avoiding a tendril of the poisonous gray fingers. Jeiah cries out. A shadow grips her leg just above the knee, working toward a second loop around her thigh. Her eyes are wide in fear and pain. She grits her teeth and reaches down to try to peel it away.

"Don't touch it," I yell.

"Oh please, please do," Bazalrak says, circling us.

Jeiah falls to the side and gasps for air with a strangled, grief-stricken moan.

I scream. "Stop it!"

I draw closer to her, shrinking the size of the protective barrier around us and pouring every ounce of my mental power into the shield. The length of tangible shadow attached to Jeiah's leg is severed where it meets the energy bubble around us, and then it fades from her leg. Even the fabric of her clothes is discolored from the acid. She touches the dark wound with her fingers, wincing.

Maybe I could heal her, but I would have to take the shield down.

From my left, someone shouts, "Hey, bricksack. Eat this!" A stone comes hurtling toward Bazalrak. He snarls and sidesteps the attack. But the stone stalls in the air next to his face.

Jeiah nods at the figure emerging from the haze. "One of your friends."

"Koglim, he's not iron mage. Who's controlling the—"

The large stone bullets toward the ground, shattering the area around Bazalrak's feet. The former general draws the tendrils of shadow back toward himself, striking out at the shards of swirling rubble, but it doesn't work. The shards become super-heated and begin fusing together. Jaws of molten stone clamp down over him and drag him beneath, like the earth has become a Venus flytrap. Fiery chords of stone roll together like the muscles of some giant beast until the whole mass disappears, leaving a smoking crater in its wake.

Koglim whistles softly. "Well, that's some thick spit."

Rugnus steps into the light on the opposite side of the crater. Even with a film of dirt over his clothes, the pink lapels of his suit coat stick out, the canary yellow of his button-down shirt. The stubbled hair on his head and his olive face coated with ash. He forces the last of the debris cloud down to our feet with a wave of his hand, my iron bracelet glinting on his wrist.

My forgework glimmering as something bright in the dark.

I retract my shield and attend to Jeiah's leg. It closes halfway. Maybe Rugnus and I could manage the task together; light healing takes mastery in iron and tungsten, but I don't know enough about it. It will take extra time and a lighthealer to counteract the shadows. Napcraft works too, but I don't have access to Rugnus' vault.

I suddenly realize that my hand has overstayed its welcome on Jeiah's leg, and my face grows hot. Wraithspit. This girl is not what I should be thinking about right now. I help her up, and we both stare back at the crater where Rugnus buried Bazalrak under the rock. How long will it take him to dig out?

"We gotta go." Rugnus urges us over to him, even as he walks around the crater. "That won't hold him long." He draws out Icho.

"Is Icho working?" I ask. "No one else can budge."

He nods and smiles. "Whatever blocked everyone from budging, still can't touch Icho."

Jeiah snaps her face toward him. "How is that possible?" She winces at the wound on her leg.

Rugnus taps Icho against the side of his leg. "Just how this thing works. Family relic."

Koglim plods over to Rugnus' side. "Knew it was strong, but good garlic, brother. Your mom knows how to give a gift. I would *not* have passed that down to my kid."

Rugnus looks at me. "Ready?"

I nod. "People need our help."

"We'll check in at the amphitheater. Get marching orders from Andalynn."

My eye squeeze shut. Tears rise, but my mouth eventually works open. "She's okay?"

Rugnus gives me half a grin. "She's coordinating everything already. I'm having trouble adding people on Icho. Just put a hand on it."

I place a hand on Icho. As Koglim reaches over, Jeiah slips her hand next to mine.

"I'm going with you," she says.

Rugnus opens his mouth to say something, eyebrows knit together, but I cut him off. "She's with me." Even in all the madness of the attack, my heart rate reminds me that our hands are side by side on Icho. Stupid thought. Focus on what's in front of you.

Koglim smiles, placing a hand on Icho. "Good enough for me."

Rugnus budges us to the foot of a tangle of vines made from metal, stone, and plants. We're on the stage now. The nest from the performance has been flipped over, but nearly buried in ruble. Beyond the stage, the amphitheater lays in ruin under mountains of glass and stone rubble.

But with the debris cloud nearly settled, dozens—no hundreds—of bodies are visible all around us, shapes as lifeless as concrete. As if these festivalgoers merely laid down and slept. Many more must be entombed inside the rubble. My dread turns from sickness to calm to rage in a matter of a second. The fire in Jeiah's eyes looks about like how I feel right now.

How many bodies are out there?

I pull up the map in bluelink. There are still a lot of heat signatures in the stands, but not as many as there are bodies in front of me. I swallow the feeling of sickness that threatens to close off my throat. My heart drops deep into my stomach.

Rugnus leads us into the tangle of vines, weaving over and under them, until we come into a small clearing, where Andalynn stands, flanked by Hemdi and Winta, her glimmering dress dimmed with dust. Behind her, a few members of the council stand huddled in conversation, Vor healing a bruise on Chainkeeper's arm. Behind them, a rough line of bodies, perhaps a half dozen, face down on the stage floor.

The second Andalynn sees me, her hands fly to her mouth. I rush forward and wrap her in my arms. A sob breaks through when she tries to speak. "I-I couldn't find you. I thought..."

"It's okay."

"This should be... I'm sorry. You could have died out there. I haven't meant to ignore you. I—"

I wipe a tear from her cheek. "Please, don't do that. You haven't ignored me. We're both okay. We're both okay."

"Clayson, Rugnus and I... we didn't send your request to the council."

It's such a strange comment, so out of nowhere, that I'm unable to respond. Why is she telling me this now?

Rugnus stares at her. "Is this really the time—"

"You could have died," she says. "He could have died, and we were keeping secrets from him. I'm no better than our parents."

Rugnus looks between us. "Don't blame her. I convinced her to wait until after StoneYoke to ask the council about the mines. Didn't have enough influence among the keepers to do both."

Andalynn keeps my hand in hers. "I thought I lost you today."

My eyes push shut. I shake my head. "I... we're alive. You're safe. I'm just glad you're safe. But... what happened when the building fell?" I glance at the line of bodies.

"Buildings," Rugnus corrects.

Andalynn looks down.

A chill hardens in my bones. "How many?"

Rugnus says, "From what we can tell, all of them. They dropped down everywhere."

"And if no one could budge out..." Jeiah didn't finish the sentence.

There could only be one result. I can't process a death toll for this act of terror.

"Clearing the debris and finding survivors is our first priority," Andalynn says, letting my hand fall away, her voice masked with official authority now.

"And after that?" I ask.

"Not after. At the same time. I'm putting Winta in charge of restoring bluelink and discovering who was behind this."

Winta's studying Jeiah through narrowed eyes. That's when I realize: Everyone I know is safe. My mind flashes back to the woman Jeiah and I were too late to save, to the bodies on the stage just outside this nest of vines.

I don't look at the line of dead that lay the closest to us.

Jeiah raises her beholder. "I can help. I'm Bluekeeper's paladin. I've already restored one hub."

Rugnus and Andalynn share a quick glance. Andalynn's head turns slowly toward the knot of council members. She clears her throat. "Cessar Bluekeeper is dead. I'm sorry."

Jeiah stumbles back like someone physically strikes her. "He... I was just... he was in the lounge. I... Ide keep me, no. That can't be right. Where—"

But Jeiah follows my sister's eyes back to the line of bodies near Vor and the other council members. Bluekeeper's citrus-colored suit is there, the glass screen over his face shattered. He's gone.

Jeiah rushes forward. Ogrekeeper—the most muscular Loamin I've ever seen—blocks Jeiah's forward motion. "You don't need to see that, paladin. He's with Ide."

Chainkeeper calls for the council's servant.

Vor approaches him. "Yes, keeper?"

"Does this block affect your vacant craft? Can you still budge?"

"I believe I can."

"Good. Start moving the bodies of any of the keepers and their families to Edium Fiarie, to the preparation house where they can await their return to Ide."

Vor nods, hunches over Bluekeeper, and vanishes.

"Queen," Chainkeeper continues, "I'll convene the council and see what information we can gather."

Jeiah regains some composure. "The evidence points to Lagnar Emberfence."

"Why would Emberfence be involved?" Chainkeeper says.

"It's what he wanted. He and Hardkeeper. He's next in line for Keeper of Bluebottle Dungeon."

"That may be," says Chainkeeper, "but why this? No, this is greater than one man's greed for power. Something else... this will take a longer investigation, paladin."

She shakes her head. "There's at least a connection. There have been disruptions to bluelink data at his location over the past few days. The disruptions are similar to what's happening right now. And there's more. Clayson Brightstorm's location data matches some of the disturbances as well."

"What?" Andalynn steps next to the group of keepers. "I hope you have clear evidence to back up your claim."

"Always," Jeiah says.

Chainkeeper asks, "What is your name, paladin?"

"Jeiahlir."

"And you are the paladin for Bluebottle Dungeon?"

She nods.

"Good. As the head of the Council of Keepers, I charge you with responsibility over this investigation and grant you access to all the resources I have under my authority. Report everything you have found and will find to the council and to the people of Tungsten City. Including anything about the involvement of Lagnar Emberfence and Clayson Brightstorm."

Andalynn shakes her head. "Keeper, I—"

"The paladin can be objective where we cannot. That is her training. I trust you and the other official paladins will find evidence of who did this. And one other thing..." He glances at Andalynn. There's a long pause as we wait for him to speak. "I reported the break-in at Keelcrawl prison, but there's more to that. I-I'm missing eight minutes."

Rugnus shakes his head. "What does that mean?"

It hits me like a bad budge. Chainkeeper is in charge of the prison. He's a stronger timemage than Winta. If he lost eight minutes... "Do you think someone made you free Bazalrak?"

Slowly, his mouth works open. "Queen Everbloom, when you called for the keepers to gather, I budged there, but time had jumped forward eight minutes. I have no explanation. Your brother's theory is not unfounded. I am the only one that could have unlocked the prison for Bazalrak to escape."

Jeiah scrutinizes him. "I will look into it, meanwhile... here." She takes her blue glass rod and taps it to a ring on Chainkeeper's finger. Then to other objects for Ogrekeeper and the other councilmember. "I've repaired your bluelink and budge capabilities."

Chainkeeper nods. "Find out who did this."

The group of keepers budge from the amphitheater.

Andalynn looks at Jeiah. "Paladin, I'm going to need another explanation. What information do you have on Emberfence? How is it connected to Clayson?"

Jeiah doesn't bat an eye. "He's been erasing data on bluelink for days, scrubbing his presence from every camera. I think he may have been testing something. Clayson has been within the radius of the effect nearly half the time."

"That's a coincidence," I say. "I had nothing to do with this. But Sira's involved. I saw her just before the attack."

Koglim's head snaps up. "Wait. You saw Sira?"

Jeiah answers. "She was using the same object or craft to scrub her data. She should have been in Clayson's video, but it's like there's only a shadow there."

Rugnus clears his throat. "Must have gotten out with Bazalrak."

"You think Emberfence manipulated Chainkeeper? Broke them out?" Winta says.

"It's a good guess. And—"

Winta cuts me off. "And Lagnar caused all this? He's good with mech, but come on, I'm better. And I couldn't cause this kind of malfunction with years of planning, let alone block every budge out of the district. You'd need thousands of mages each with mastery in at least one craft. And pulling down bluelink? Not a chance."

I shrug. "Maybe he—"

A crack-thump shatters my words, and the vines all around us reverberate as if the flipped-over nest was struck by a mallet.

Hemdi looks up, wary. "What now?"

When the massive arm of one of the construction mechs tears through the metallic ceiling, I don't register the danger. I'm in shock. It must be shock.

Rugnus shouts, "Shield!"

But I cast my shield outward too late as one of the mech arms rips down the ceiling.

Chunks of metal drop all around. Rugnus stalls a large piece of shredded metal in midair and sends it flying toward the mech. Andalynn reinforces the ceiling with thick vines, but doesn't see the piece of debris speeding toward her.

I throw an arc of protective magic over her, and the metal ricochets toward the floor.

"Clayson," Hemdi yells.

A gust drives me toward the ground, but something heavy clips my head right above my ear. I stumble forward. Everything is oddly quiet, and the pain in my head blocks out any other sensation. I close my hands into fists... or maybe I don't. I can't tell what are physical sensations and what are thoughts? Maybe I only imagine I close my hands. Then, I can't feel my hands and feet altogether. My heartbeat is slowing. I can feel that, at least. I'm facing the ground, but someone turns me over.

Jeiah's eyes widen. What is she saying?

"...awake. Clayson..."

My eyelids don't open back up. Everything is black. As I slip into the darkness, my fear isn't that I will die, but that I will lose consciousness under the surface, that I will dream again. And I'm not wrong.

I pass from the scattered light of reality into the canyon of Yinzar's memories.

DISCERN THE COST

A STROKE of blue-sky gleams between the canyon walls of my grandfather's memory garden. It's never been daytime before. Something has changed. Neon butterflies, representing moments from Yinzar's life, swarm around me. For months, the only one I've been able to catch has been marked with orange and white lines, and it leads to the mineshaft. This time, in the light of day, they appear more visceral, less like bulbs of light, and more like real butterflies.

After so many attempts to catch a different memory, it's a bit annoying that it happens because I've been knocked unconscious —I think.

Did I get smacked with a giant boulder? My recollection of real life is fuzzy. Maybe I'm dead. I don't feel dead, but I bet that's what most dead people say. "Okay, Yinzar. Show me something I haven't seen."

A pink and turquoise butterfly unfolds its wings and alights from the wall. Words come out of it like a speaker. "Yes, yes. It's ancient. Good, ancient. Ide corrects itself, yes."

I know the repetitious voice: trollslayer, an azdeth. The azdeth were living mountains that swam through the earth and communicated with Ide itself. They ate lithic trolls and fed off energy from the molten core of Ide. Andalynn helped me track down that much information in Whurrimduum's records, but no one has seen an azdeth in a couple thousand years, long before the death of the last dragons.

Except for Yinzar, if my visions of last year are to be believed.

The light from the butterfly expands, transporting me into his memories. I'm standing with Yinzar, facing the azdeth across a wide chasm. The ancient beast appears as acres and acres of stone. One more unfathomable thing in an unfathomable world.

My grandfather's already forge-baked face reddens in blotchy patches. His shock of faded orange hair pulled back into a bun. I've seen a part of this memory last year. He wants information from the azdeth about the mithrium—how to use it or destroy it.

"Then it can be changed?" Yinzar asks.

"Yes, yes, good, a sacrifice, though. Change requires this."

"But Daglusk—"

The mountainside groans, shifting in the single light from the vines at Yinzar's hand. "Evil. No. No, no. The worms are not light. They are dark. Not better than trolls, worse. Evil. Evil, no."

I issue a silent thanks to the unknown for showing me more of this encounter.

His grip slips on the tangle of glowing vines at his right hand and the vine lengthens out, dragging him toward the edge of the cliff. "Okay, I won't mention the dragon. Just"—he digs his heels into the ground and the stone chips— "relax. Worms, no. Evil. Got it."

The pressure from the vines eases, and Yinzar stands upright again. "Then I can change the mithrium into something good?"

The mountainside shifts again, enlarging the chasm. For a long time, there's no response. Yinzar waits in the darkness.

"Yes."

A visible weight lifts from Yinzar's shoulders. "It will work. All the elements together. Like in a summator? Wait, that's it! The Cradle!"

Trollslayer continues, "Yes. Good, good, good. A fire in the sky, but deep, deep, yes, deep. Good into the heart of Ide. Yes."

"The energy in the Cradle is only potential energy. Is that the key?"

Silence from the trollslayer.

Minutes go by, an hour maybe. The light around my grandfather's arm fades, and we are left in the dark. Something touches my shoulder. A haze of light surrounds me, but it's not the sandstone canyon of the memory garden. Another dream? Voices calling out something. My name.

Clayson.

"Clayson. Clayson, can you hear me?"

I open my eyes, and Andalynn's rounded face awaits me. Still delirious, I try to scan her eyes for fear or worry but find only her compassion. "He's coming out of it."

I try to sit, but my head throbs. A wave of nausea hits me, and I squint at the faraway brightstorm. It's day again?

On my right, Hemdi winds lengths of a spool of lead around his fingers like a religious charm. It's a type of shieldcraft I've not seen him use. He places this hand on my forearm, and the pressure in my head eases back.

"The attack. And..." I try to add more about the dream, about Yinzar and the azdeth, about this place he called the Cradle, but my stomach reels as I look around me.

A sea of healers scramble to triage a host of injured Loamin. Groans fill my ears. Hundreds of makeshift beds line the walls. To my left is the bar of the VIP lounge. The fishbowl—where only hours earlier acrobats entranced the members of the Keeper's Council and their families—lays in a ruin of glass.

Glass.

I tip my head toward the ceiling, my mind reeling both from pain and from a horrifying realization: far above me, there are no glass skyscrapers. "They all came down."

Andalynn helps me sit up.

"It's over," Hemdi glances at Andalynn. "We think."

"The mech," I say to Andalynn. "It was gonna crush you."

"It didn't. You made sure of that. Though you took a beating for it." She nods at my head.

An announcement blares out, *"Please update your status and location over bluelink. If you or a loved one are injured, proceed to a designated healing station."* The message repeats two more times.

"How many people... the attack, did it—"

"Too soon to tell," Andalynn says. "But it's bad. The House of Ide, at Edium Fiarie, can't take all the dead. We'll have to..." Her voice goes dry. Her eyes brim with tears, but nothing comes out. She blinks them away. "I messaged Rugnus and the others. He'll be here in a second." She looks up to read something in the air. "See if you can heal yourself a little better. I'll be right back."

She disappears, her hand leaving a warm imprint on my shoulder.

Hemdi stands back in anticipation as I adjust my bracelet and focus on healing my head wound. I take a deep breath as the throbbing pain releases its grip. Clarity of thought comes more naturally now, though the pain spreads if I move too fast.

"Better?" Hemdi asks.

"Yeah. Thanks. I could've died if you hadn't been there."

He sighs. "I'm glad I can help." But his words carry a strange tone of defeat. We've all adjusted to his lack of tincraft, but he doesn't often come to dungeons or do surveying work with Rugnus anymore. In an emergency like this, I'm sure he must be feeling its loss more deeply.

"Really, thanks."

Hemdi's true strength in our group was never tincraft. Or any craft. He has a way of seeing things from everyone's perspective, helps the group compromise. Not to mention the handful of times he's talked Rugnus and I down from an argument.

The announcement sounds again, and it gives me an idea.

"I should start helping around here."

Hemdi steadies me as I stand. "Maybe you should take it easy. I—"

"No, here..." I stagger to the next cot, where a young man grips his injured leg. The second I extend the power of my bracelet over him, every ounce of strength I had just restored drains from out of me.

The young man sighs in relief, even swings his legs out over the cot and stands. He smiles, eyes widening. "Thank you."

"Sure, I..." My words slur. The throbbing in my head grows, and I drop back down to my cot. "Th-that was... hard. I think—"

"Focus your craft on yourself for now," Hemdi orders. "You were unconscious for a long time. It-it was a bad injury."

Unconscious. Of course. "Hemdi. I—" Why can't I catch my breath? "When I was unconscious, I saw Yinzar's memories again."

He nods, but he focuses on adding his healing craft to my own, helping to steady my breathing. It takes a few moments, but the dizziness abates.

"It was different this time. I saw the azdeth again, but Yinzar mentioned something about potential energy and the Cradle."

Hemdi sits back. "Interesting. You've thought the memories might be leading you to the mines. That's where the Cradle is. It is where Erikzin Brightstorm forged all the brightstorms. Though the exact location of the Cradle has been lost for centuries."

"That has to be the location of Mithriumbane Dungeon, but..."

Hemdi glances at me from over his leadcraft. "But what?"

"It's more than that. Everything seems connected. This attack, the mithrium, my dreams." Where do I start with this? "I want answers, but I can't escape the feeling that I don't have a choice in where this all leads. I don't wanna follow Yinzar down another rabbit hole, but what choice do I have?"

"Oh, I've heard that expression before. Winta uses it. A rabbit hole—like a wraith's cradle. A problem that is difficult to solve because it is impossible."

"Kind of. More like falling into something that messes with your mind—that seems to be one thing, but really it's another."

My head throbs again, and I reach up to massage my temples, but Hemdi nudges my hand away.

He uncoils the lead from his fingers but laces it around the other hand. When he sets the hand against my temple, the pain dulls into a soft buzz. "I may have asked this before, but do you have any choice over the memories he shows you?"

"Last year, it seemed like I could choose the memory. But I... maybe I've just assumed that Yinzar is only showing me what he wants me to see."

Hemdi shifts to face me directly. "From what I know, Yinzar was a man who believed in the impossible. He valued freedom and choice. Made all his own craft when he could. Whatever craft he used on you and your mother, perhaps it expanded your choices, not limited them. He sought a path forward with the mithrium. You made that a reality in Geum Ide."

"But it almost led to something much worse. If Sira—what if the memories lead me to Mithriumbane Dungeon and... we're wrong. And he didn't destroy it. It could be Silverlamp Dungeon all over again. What if this time something terrible happens?"

Hemdi gives a short laugh. "That's a lot of what-ifs."

He stands. After a breath, he shakes his head, glancing at the destruction and ruin of the VIP suite, at the bustling healers. I follow his gaze around the room. The healers look exhausted. They move like hummingbirds, the glow of white shieldcraft pulsing wherever they land. There's even a Dura woman—making that only six Dura I've ever seen from either city—making her way through the injured using the simplest Dura craft to heal minor wounds.

Would any of this have happened if I had stayed on the surface?

"I know what you're thinking," Hemdi says. "But whoever did this... it's not your fault."

I shake my head. "It's weird you can read my mind without silvercraft."

His broad smile appears for a split second. "It's written on your face."

"Sira made sure I saw her right before it happened. And Emberfence, he hates Andalynn and me."

"But two people alone couldn't do this. It's not possible. Craft balances craft. If someone wants to harm you, they must have enough craft to overcome your latent defense. And shieldcraft is typically a degree stronger than other craft. Which you know. Almost as if Ide itself has balanced some grand equation. This type of thing is not supposed to happen. It can't happen."

"A wraith's cradle?" Maybe for the first time, I understand the use of the term. Difficult to understand because it's actually impossible.

"Yes, you understand now. Two people alone could *not* do this."

"They could've had mithrium."

"But mithrium has never been used like this. The attackers prevented five million people from budging, and at the same time severed any connection to bluelink. Not to mention controling the mechs in order to cut down the buildings. That's too delicate for mithrium."

"Right." I grasp at an understanding. "Mithrium has only been combined with one element or alloy at a time. A single object."

"Yes, and the power of destruction was magnitudes greater. No one survived."

"Then what was *this*?" I ask.

He shrugs. "Andalynn thought maybe it was the people."

"What does that mean?"

"That there are people on both sides of this that wanted the festival to fail. They protested the creation of StoneYoke district entirely. Emberfence, Sira, Bazalrak—they might be involved, but they would need hundreds, thousands of citizens to combine craft to make an attack like this. Whatever this is, it is much closer to a military attack, where a hundred thousand soldiers used targeted craft, like during the Mithrium War."

"We would have noticed, right? A few hundred thousand people?"

"It's not the people." Rugnus' voice startles me, and I spin around to find him cutting past the sick beds. His usually well-kept clothing shredded in places and coated in grime. His face is a stone of rage. "Andalynn is wrong."

I search Rugnus' face for a sign that he will be willing to talk this out. My mind's still cloudy from the head injury, but I can tell some of his annoyance and anger are pointed right at me.

"Sira must have been after you," he says. "And Bazalrak and Emberfence. This is some vendetta they have against the royal family. And they took it out on millions of people instead."

Hemdi drifts between us. "They couldn't have done this alone. And this is not Clayson's fault or Andalynn's."

"Well, the royal family then. They have a thousand years of enemies to account for."

"The people aren't that innocent themselves," I mutter.

Rugnus swallows hard like he is trying to eat a vegetable he hates. "What?"

Hemdi shakes his head. "Rugnus, please. Please. Whoever did this, made their choice. They made sure they couldn't be stopped."

Rugnus looks to the ground, grinding his teeth. "The council is planning an emergency meeting."

"I could help," I say. "What if there's a connection with the mithrium? What if Yinzar—"

"Just stop. There's not a connection. Ever since... well, the day I met you... just better if you stay out of this." He rushes through these final words.

This attack is the tipping point for him, but it's clear that some version of this has been rattling around in his mind since Silverlamp, maybe even since I got Ergal out of Wolfstaff. I understand why—he's afraid. Stark, plain fear. And this attack has heightened the sensation. Everything he values is under attack, and I'm the common denominator.

The announcement for the injured and lost sounds again, repeating three more times.

I come to my feet and, with a few steps, draw closer to Rugnus until we're face to face. "This is my problem, the same as yours. Shutting me out of this—"

He stiffens his arm and nudges me back. "Get out of my face."

"Rugnus. I'm not trying to screw things up. I'm trying to find answers." A burst of pain lances through my mind. I grip my forehead and squeeze my eyes shut.

Hemdi comes between us. "We all need patience right now."

Rugnus grimaces. "Fine. Just... this festival... things were supposed to get better."

The pain in my head ebbs. I scrape my foot back and forth in the layer of dust on the floor. I think about the family I helped. "Do they need help finding survivors?"

Rugnus shakes his head. "It's been five hours. Our ironmages have moved all the debris. We may have found everyone that can be found."

"Already?" I ask.

"Yeah."

"First things first, we track down Bazalrak and Sira. They must know something."

Rugnus finally meets my stare directly. "That we can agree on."

Winta and Koglim suddenly appear behind Rugnus. The new heartbeat in my head skips a measure. I take a deep breath.

Koglim must notice our stance. "I swear if I have to listen to either of you arguing, I will melt you both. You two need to knock it off. I'm done playing sneak the relic with everyone."

"Sneak the relic?" I ask.

Koglim's eyes widen. "Add that to the games I have to teach you. I mean, I knew you didn't have a childhood, but seriously... and they are looking at you as a potential seer for two dungeons?"

"Two? I know Wolfstaff, but—"

"Silverlamp. The dreamwell? Hello." He moves over and taps my forehead. It sends a ripple of pain over my scalp. He winces. "Ooh, sorry, head wound."

I glance at Rugnus. I just got another clue from Yinzar's memories, but with Rugnus this way, I can't work on that right now. Besides, there are more important things to do. "I'm not going to deal with the Council of Keepers right now. It's more important to track down who did this."

"Definitely," Winta adds. "There's time for a council meeting any day."

Rugnus clears his throat. "The council is considering turning on the foilgrips around Whurrimduum."

"What?" Koglim shouts, drawing looks from the healers. "There are raiders I work with behind that foilgrip!"

"That's not all," Rugnus continues. "They want to close the dungeons as a precaution."

"The tilted beards these days. I need the dungeons open," Koglim says. "Brude and I... well, my pro-team has already been talking about doing some sort of tribute to all of this—a memorial raid of Runearmor, to raise ferrum for families and stuff. So, I vote that Clayson tries to appear before the council. They'll listen to him."

"Can't be that simple," I say.

Rugnus agrees. "It's not."

Hemdi holds up both hands. "Maybe working with the council is a good idea eventually—a goal for another time—but, as Clayson said, there are more pressing matters."

The sound of a construction mech blurs above our heads, and we all flinch. The mechs carry large pieces of debris. They're back under the control of the mechmages and ironmages, but I can't shake the worry that they're aiming at me. A pulse of blood in my temples answers this thought. I take a deep breath. There's something everyone's forgetting. Sira is connected to all this. She knows what happened.

"So, we start with Sira."

"And... track her down?" Koglim says. "How?"

"Jeiahlir," Winta adds, "I mean, she's amazing. Even I haven't been able to trace these bluelink disruptions, shadows, whatever you want to call them."

"The shadow wound on her leg?"

Koglim waves a hand. "Lighthealers made short work of that. And they cleared all the shadows from the area where we buried Bazalrak. But he was long gone."

"You think she'll be able to help? She pretty much accused me of being involved. And now she's working for the council." All of this should trigger a warning for me, but a flutter of curiosity expands my breathing.

Winta scoffs. "She took out the mechs."

I blink. "Wait, what happened with the mechs?"

Rugnus opens his mouth to speak, but Winta talks over him. "After you got your skull crushed by a giant piece of building, everyone else pretty much lost their minds. Everyone except Jeiah and me. We tapped into their instructions through bluelink and changed them."

Koglim giggles. "They made them fight each other. It was—"

"Should have just shut them down," Rugnus said.

A smug grin dawns on Winta's face. "Killjoy. Come on, we needed them to be active so we could start digging through their craft. I mean, they came straight for us."

"Well," Koglim says, "after they pulled down a hundred buildings on top of the festival." Everyone seems to look at the ground at this moment. "Sorry, I shouldn't... I didn't mean to—"

I clear my throat. "That's why we have to find out who did this. The council can wait."

Rugnus takes out Icho. "Okay, so where to?"

"Bluelink building," Winta says. "That's where Jeiah keeps her office."

Koglim smiles. "Someone's in love."

For a brief, foolish second, I think he's talking about me, and I start to protest. Winta glances at me. "She *is* awesome, but I'm taken." As an accent to what she says, Winta sidles up to Hemdi. He rubs her back gently, and she settles both of her hands on her midsection. "Koglim, when was the last time you even spoke to a girl—"

"Hey, I—"

"About something other than a dungeon?"

Koglim's mouth closes.

Winta winks at him. "I'd say you should go for it, Koglim, but I think Clayson likes her."

I swallow hard. "No, wait... what?" My mind must still be fuzzy from the head wound.

Winta smiles, but Rugnus is the first to comment, though the tone of his voice lacks any humor. "No surprises, Clayson likes every girl he sees."

"Hey, that's not—"

"True," Koglim says, chuckling.

"Well, you liked me," Winta says, as my cheeks flush. "And I'm married."

Hemdi smiles at this, and for a second, I could almost let this conversation go because Hemdi doesn't smile that often anymore, but they keep going.

"What about the Dura girl?" Koglim adds, wide eyed.

Rugnus nods. He's taking a grim pleasure at making fun of me. "Ara. Yeah, that one's weird. She's like a foot taller at least."

"Oh, don't forget Sira." Koglim's voice reaches a higher pitch.

"I didn't like Sira," I say in an attempt to end the conversation. It doesn't.

"Of course, you did," Winta dismisses, "but don't feel bad. So did Koglim."

Koglim smiles for a second longer until he realizes what Winta said. His face hardens. In a deeper voice, he says. "Whatever. Everyone liked her. No one could help that."

My smile melts as quickly as it came. Why did Sira come to me? Just to gloat? Was she in on the attack? She wanted to control everyone, force them to feel safe and happy. A terrible plan, but well-meaning, in a twisted way. I look around at the dusty floors. We're far away from the epicenter of the attack, but there's still a haze in the air. Something wars inside me. I want there to be a simple answer, but this wasn't her.

"Let's get over to the Bluelink building," I say. "Find Jeiah, and work toward some answers."

Everyone moves in closer to Rugnus, and we budge.

We arrive in the park outside of the Bluelink building, where the dangling vines of a hundred willows shine like strings of emeralds. The Bluelink building's characteristic mercury-veined, blue-glass walls inviting us closer.

The brightstorm hangs above us in the cavernous sky, fulsome and glittering. Not quite a summer night sky above granite, but still alluring and beautiful. The idea of the peaceful moment drops like a fifty pound bag of feed when I realize there's nearly no one in the courtyard. The time of day is right for a crowd, but the place is empty.

"This is weird," Winta says.

Koglim scans the courtyard. "Isn't there usually a potato bar vendor here?" He gestures open bluelink. "Yeah, Kaxdin Taters."

Winta twists something invisible on bluelink. "Koglim... Kaxdin is on the list."

"What? No. No."

"What list?" I ask.

Rugnus says. "Confirmed dead."

Koglim's eyes grow glassy. "Kaxdin was an awesome person. I stopped here for lunch just, what, a week ago. She gave me a tip for raiding Bearcloak. Ide keep me, this... this is not right." I haven't seen Koglim get emotional like this. It's hard to watch.

Bluelink chimes with a public message. Rugnus casts his screen between two pillars. No one moves. No one speaks. I doubt any of us even blink.

BREAKING NEWS

Connected to the headline, the icon for a virtual walkthrough spins. As Rugnus reaches for it, I put a hand up. I don't wanna see where it will take us, but he ignores my movement. He extends the festival scene into the space of the courtyard. All around us now—whether it's a live video or not, it doesn't matter —lays the wreckage of the festival. The dust has fully cleared, leaving behind strange shapes created by the ironmages as they cleared the amphitheater. Monstrous cylindrical shapes—charred stone bubbled with glass—rise like new ungodly buildings around the festival.

Body bags spread out as wide and deep as an ocean. There's nothing for any of us to do but to stand here. My pulse throbs against the inside of my skull. A wave of dizziness sweeps over me. My eyelids flicker closed. I hear Yinzar's voice again, more memory than craft.

I stand at the cusp of the same vine-choked hole I've been seeing all winter. All around me, the wall shimmers in metallic hues. Two beady lights—eyes—meet mine from out of the pit. I hear Yinzar's muttering voice as an echo rising out of the hole. "Can't let him get it. Can't."

"Clayson," Rugnus says. "Clayson!" He shakes me.

When I open my eyes, I'm staring at the death toll.

459,341 CONFIRMED FATALITIES AT STONEYOKE FESTIVAL

Shock numbs my body, and my knees tremble, but I stay upright. A flock of birds erupts into the air, and the sound yanks my heart into my throat. "That can't be right."

"Ide keep us all," Hemdi murmurs. "Half a million."

Everyone echoes this shock, everyone but Rugnus, who looks ready to melt this whole courtyard down in rage. If he finds out who did this, he'll turn them to ash.

But all I can hear is Yinzar's muttering. "Can't let him get it. Can't."

EXAMINE THE FACTS

T H E   A Z D E T H and the curling brown vines of Yinzar's plant arm rise before my eyes, but Rugnus' voice is somewhere behind me, muted and warped. Is Rugnus in this dream? What is my mind doing to me?

The bright snap of fingers finds me in the void.

"...still in shock," Winta says from somewhere to my left.

Rugnus, hovering in front of me, is pushed aside. Intense blue eyes scan me.

"Jeiahlir?" I half mutter, half gasp her name. It's like I can't get enough air.

"It's Jeiah." Her blue eyes dazzle me. "And what are you doing walking around? You had a massive indentation in your skull. Keep Ide. I thought you were dense but—"

"I... we needed your help," I groan.

"What am I supposed to do? I'm a bluemage. You're the healer."

"We didn't come about his injury," Winta adds.

Koglim adds something, but my head is still rattled, and I can't understand him.

I shut my eyes against the pain. Rugnus guides me to a bench against one of the courtyard pillars and forces me back down. "How many fingers am I holding up?"

He's holding up three fingers. I make a few attempts to tell him but end up scrunching the skin between my eyebrows, taking a deep breath, and settling my head against the pillar.

"He *was* walking around," Koglim squeaks, "so maybe... not brain damage. I've gotten hit pretty hard on the head a few times and—"

"That's obvious," Winta says.

"Clayson." Rugnus snaps his fingers. "You know where we are?"

I know where we are; we're in the garden courtyard outside of the Bluelink building. But when I try to tell him, I end up just nodding slightly. My breathing is finally slowing down.

"See, he remembers fine." Koglim laughs nervously.

"Well, he remembered one thing," Winta says. "Jeiah's name."

I move my eyes sideways to look at Jeiah, and I swear she blushes. Winta looks between us, a self-satisfied smile on her face, and winks at me.

I look away, which Rugnus mistakes for me going back into a coma. I nudge him away and take an intentionally slow breath. It takes longer than I want, but eventually, I can speak again. "You held up three fingers. We're in the garden courtyard outside the Bluelink building. And..." My mind settles on an image. A sea of body bags. "I'm fine."

"No, you're not," Rugnus said. "You were muttering your grandfather's name."

"I saw him again."

"Okay," Koglim says. "Maybe that head injury was worse than we thought."

Rugnus nods. "We shouldn't be rushing this. You need more time to heal. If you had Ergal—"

"If I had Ergal," I snap, "no one would have died in the first place." The moment I say this out loud, I sense the whole group freeze.

Everyone but Winta that is. Her sigh drops the temperature of my blood. "Trollbrick. Clayson, you're not the only one responsible for everything. For Ide's sake, you barely know how to count ferrum, or the days of the week."

The volume of her voice taps against my head like a drum. I hold up my hands. They're only shaking a little. "I know the days of the—"

"Oh, don't get me started. We can handle whatever this is. Go find a cozy little room overlooking a grove of trees, or better yet just go back up to the surface and tend to your chickens."

"Winta, go easy on him," Koglim says.

She rolls her eyes and steps away.

I stand from the bench, ignoring the pressure on the inside of my skull. "Really, I'm... okay." I glance at Winta. "It was *me* who saw Sira at the festival. And Bazalrak came after *me*. Not anyone else. He was after me. I wanna find him as much as any of you."

"Then we move forward," Rugnus says. "But I'm gonna grab my armband."

"The gold one?" I ask.

He nods. "It should help. Not sure what's happening when you pass out, but if you're dreaming like last time, sleep may not have the healing effect it should." Rugnus glances at Jeiahlir and budges.

"Dreaming?" Jeiah surveys my face. "Like surface nightmares?"

"No. I don't dream up there. Only down here. Though... that's not common knowledge."

Winta searches Jeiah's eyes. "Keep your recording private, paladin."

"Don't worry"—she touches my arm— "I know how Clayson feels about his privacy. No one will hear that from me."

"Good," Winta says.

"Though my little brother would kill for that information."

I blink at her. "Your brother?"

"He's kind of obsessed with you. Though... I haven't heard from him yet. Since the attack."

"Wait. Is he okay?" I ask.

"Bluelink's all scrambled. He's alive. I just can't get a read on him. It's happening to a bunch of people right now." A weight drags her shoulders down. Something else is wrong.

"Did you... lose anyone close?" I ask. Winta slaps my arm. "Sorry, I shouldn't—"

"No," Jeiah says. "It's an innocent question. My aunt and uncle were in the amphitheater. They're gone. They've been the ones to check in on my brother and me since my father passed last year." Jeiah states these facts like something in a report, but I can see the depths of her feelings rising to her eyes. "Okay, you guys came here for something, right?"

"Full amp." Koglim gives a human thumbs up. "Figured you and Winta combined could make short work of tracking down those glitches over bluelink."

Jeiah looks at Winta and smiles. "We did make short work of those mechs."

"I was just warming up," Winta says.

"I'll show you where I'm at with my search. Come on." She looks me over. Even without her beholder object, her stare seems to judge everything about me. The depth of color in her pupils, the flecks of dark blue against the light, hold me in place. Finally, I blink. This is stupid. I need to focus on what we're doing. And I don't know for sure if I can trust her. "What about your investigation of me?"

"Ongoing." Her voice is deceivingly mild and polite.

"But you'll help us?" I ask.

A soft smile plays over her lips. "More like you'll help me. I'm leading this investigation."

She walks us into the building, where everything takes on a reflected shade of purple-blue. We take a tower of glass stairs along the sidewall. As we make our way up, Winta runs her hand against the wall. With each pass of her hand, the pulsing mercury veins inside the walls seek out new paths around her presence. She smiles, standing a bit taller.

On the third floor, we exit into a hallway of concrete. Neon purple lights bend like waves along the wall. On our right, the wall is replaced by glass frosted with ice on the inside, like someone left a freezer open. We turn into a large room with two walls made of the same glass. The air temperature drops. In the center of the room, five blue glass panels, as thick as Koglim's neck, are suspended from heavy-duty wires. They form a pentagon, but with enough space for our party to slip through the panels.

Once inside the pentagon, Jeiah places a hand on each panel, one at a time, nudging them to different parts of the room. They come to life with strings of light and floating icons. I take in a sweeping view of each section. It's a collection of evidence, like something you would see in a crime scene investigation show, but instead of corkboard and pushpins, there are three-dimensional headshots, maps, and dungeon relics on display, all with shimmering lines of connection and Jeiah's digital handwritten notes.

For a brief second, music with bright vocals and a harp reverberates in the room. Jeiah gestures and the music is gone, but I take quiet note of her tastes.

My head goes dizzy again, and for a second, I feel like I could faint. My muscles tighten. I clench and unclench my hands, trying to ground my mind.

Rugnus slips in behind us as Jeiah begins her explanation. He hands me the armband, but when I slip it on, it has little effect. It takes a herculean effort to focus on what she's saying. The dull thump tap at the crown of my head shifts behind my eyes, and I try to blink away the pain.

"What's on the closed one?" Winta asks.

I squint at the one rectangle of glass that didn't open.

Jeiah shrugs. "My eyes only."

"Forget about that," Rugnus says. "Jeiah, walk us through it."

Jeiah steps over to another panel where a map of Tungsten City rotates in orange. It's always strange seeing the structure of the city disconnected from the citybarrel where it lies. The agricultural area—a stretch of fields, woodlands, and a scattering of squat buildings—sets at the center, directly beneath the brightstorm. Tungsten's characteristic skyline rises in an oblong ring around the field.

But the thing that makes it most odd is the map's depth and breadth, the places that go mostly unseen. Large areas carved into the city's foundation and at its edges where the city's people sleep and work, a million tiny grottos, taverns, workshops, kilns, and research facilities. A cluster of millions of large rectangular boxes—the vaults—form the lowest level.

How many of them won't be visited by their owners again?

On one side, where the cavern's heights become less of a sky and more of a ceiling, the concentric circles representing the StoneYoke District lay darkened in red. Jeiah begins pointing out the many bluelink disruptions over the last three weeks. A relic shop on the southern side of the city, the practice blocks, Kel's Lounge, and a dozen more. A little less than half of them were places I had been, at times when I had been there. Next, she shows us the bluelink disruption where Sira appeared at the festival. And then one last massive disruption occurred, this time sweeping over the whole festival.

That's when everyone begins to argue. Koglim brings up Andalynn's theory about how a mass amount of people could've overwhelmed the latent security of the other festivalgoers. Rugnus swears Emberfence and Bazalrak must be in charge. Winta thinks Sira is using her knife to control everyone again. The argument continues to grow louder until the roar of their words blends into the pain of my injury.

Suddenly, Jeiah whistles. When everyone is quiet, she says, "Those are all very nice theories, but your speculations aren't going to help us learn the truth about what happened at the festival. We need more information."

"Jeiah?" A boy's voice comes from the door, and we all look over.

I recognize him at once. "Brig?"

His mouth opens and shuts. "Ho, Jeiah, you've been holding out on me." He steps into the room, jabbing a finger in my direction. "Shield boy—I've been trying to get a hold of you forever."

It's been nearly a season, but I can't forget the day Sira brought me to Handler when I worked in the testing forge with Brig making animal tags from copper. He's a season older, but he's wearing a bolo tie and a dress shirt again, though it's smudged and torn in a few places.

"It's good to see you, Brig," I look from Brig to Jeiah, then back to Brig. They both have skin the color of a brownish harvest moon. Both have dark hair dyed half neon, hers magenta, his bright pink. It hits me. "Brig's your—"

"Little brother." She sighs. "Took you long enough to check-in."

"You're not Dad," Brig tells her.

She adjusts the map on the screen. "Give me a minute." Glaring at Brig, she pulls him from the room, though not without protest.

It doesn't take long for the conversation between everyone else to circle back to arguments. I ignore them, moving over to the map of Tungsten City. All the disruptions are the same size and shape except Sira's. A creeping sensation worms its way into my thoughts. Sira's forlorn face, so uncharacteristic, refuses to fade into memory. It's still crisp and telling. Why would she find me at the festival?

I spin the map, but as I do, a notification pops up: INCOMING DISRUPTION DATA.

I hesitate only for a second, glancing to see if anyone else is watching me, then I open the notification. Six more disruptions since the festival, but each is smaller than the earlier disruptions. They're identical to Sira's disruption.

Jeiah returns to the room with Brig in tow, but immediately she sees the new data. "What's going on?"

She looks between me and the map. Her discerning eyes no longer hold any ill judgment of me. She's genuinely curious about the new information.

"Six more disruptions," I say. "I think it's Sira."

All six original points are connected to me from last week, but these six new points seem more random.

Everyone gathers around the map.

"So," Koglim says, "should we budge to those places and see if Sira is there?"

It doesn't add up. "Sira's a near null. Why is she budging everywhere? It must be awful for her. And these disruptions don't do anything. They're just like the one I saw when she..."

Maybe it's a trick of my imagination, but something occurs to me.

The game. Why did she interfere with the people playing maltobi? "The day I met her, we saw someone playing maltobi in the park. She told me she'd have to teach me one day, said she used to play the game with her father."

That's when I see it. I reach out and trace a finger from the first disruption connected to me, the ones from last week, to Sira's first new disruption, creating a long string across the map of Tungsten City. The second disruption connects as well. I keep connecting them until I have six lines all connected on a single point.

I stand back and look at the map. "Maltobi."

"No way." Rugnus' voice startles me.

I hadn't noticed everyone grow silent.

Brig comes to my side eagerly. "Ho, perfect game."

"What did you do?" Jeiah asks, spinning the map.

"Sira was standing by the maltobi game. I connected the dots."

"Hey, you remembered how to play." Koglim nods his approval. "Wait, are they all connected? That's not likely."

Winta scoffs. "Likely? No. Even playing the game, you might be lucky to intercept a single line, let alone get them all to cross at a single point. You don't get to see the inside of the shape until the game is over. Whoever did this knew what they were doing."

Rugnus clears his throat. "I know where this is." He points to where all the lines intersect, deep beneath the surface of the city. There's a breath as we all wait for him to speak again. "Emberfence. He practically ran that whole ten-block during the Mithrium War. The Mirror Market. Unregistered relics, severedferrum, copper-staves, silver-tongues, pry-vaults, you name it. Strange that it points right to him. Seems like a trap."

"I don't like it," Jeiah adds. "It's like... Sira wants you to go there."

"She was in Keelcrawl during the first set of disruptions."

Rugnus shrugs. "Taking any six points, you could connect them to a single location. Maybe Emberfence made the first set, following you around the city Clayson. Then Sira completes it, knowing that you will want to go find her."

"Yeah," I say. "So that's where we're going."

"Ho! That sounds fun." Brig shows a huge smile.

Winta's not so pleased. "Hold on. Hold on. This is Sira we're talking about. She's peerless in silvercraft. She could be controlling this whole thing again."

"I don't know," I add. "It was more than that last time."

"More than what?" Rugnus asks. "An unhinged sociopath and her murderous friends trying to take over the minds of every living Loamin?"

"Look, I'm not defending—"

Winta scoffs. "Yes, you are. I mean, were you even there?"

"Yes. In fact, I was there. I was the only one listening to her."

Rugnus shakes his head. "We had her cornered. She didn't have a choice."

"No. That's not true. Her father died... she changed. She doesn't have control over—"

Winta whistles. "Maybe Clayson's *still* under her control."

My head throbs again, forcing me to close my eyes for a few seconds. When I open them, I find Jeiah holding out the beholder, searching my face. Her pupils have turned to molten silver. "No. He's not being controlled right now."

"Beholdercraft?" Koglim says in wonder. "That's pretty awesome. What else can you do?"

Jeiah raises an eyebrow as if in warning, and Koglim holds up his hands.

"I know he's not being controlled," Winta snaps. "Not by craft. But his feelings for her are going to get him—or us —killed."

"I don't have feelings for her. No one was there. She was doing what she thought was right."

"But she was wrong," Rugnus says, his voice flat.

"Yes. I know that. I know that. But her life... ever since Silver-keeper's accident, everything she did... it was like a defense mechanism. She willed her father to stay alive during the accident. She was five. What if you had the power to control everyone around you when you were five? What would you have become?"

Winta's shoulders tighten. She shakes her head. "Not her. Not that."

The room is quiet for almost a minute as people scan the panels, until Jeiah consolidates them down to one, where a zoomed-in image of the intersecting point hovers in the air. She looks only at me. "Okay, Clayson, how would you go about this?" Her stare is so intense, so discerning I can only bear it for a moment before I turn to the panel, trying to find a solution.

At a loss for words, Rugnus saves me. "Obviously a trap. But that doesn't mean we can't turn that on its head."

Koglim begins nodding. "Hmm. Interesting. Kinda like the third grotto in Greatfish Dungeon. You know it's a trap. You just work around it. I'm liking this more and more."

"Agreed," Brig says. Jeiah burns a hole through his face with a glare. "I mean... I'm just happy to be here. Please continue."

"Good," Koglim says. "The latchmage is in agreement."

"Latchmage? Already had my survey,"

Koglim tisks. "And your summation? It's complete?"

Brig looks at me. "It's more complicated than that. I—"

Rugnus rolls his eyes with a loud sigh. "We don't have time for this."

"Time for what?" Andalynn walks through the door with three royal guards, all dressed in lead-lined body armor, like they're about to pass through a giant X-Ray machine. Metal objects, some relics probably, dangle from holsters at their side, each wearing grim, determined faces. She walks over and hugs me. Looking into my eyes like a doctor checking to see if I'm healthy.

"Nothing," Rugnus says.

A ripple of pain flows across my scalp. An image of butterflies rattles around my skull. The voices in the room become cloudy and muffled until my sister gently shakes my shoulder, "Clayson."

I try to respond to her, but the words don't come out.

She leads me out of the room and into the hall. I squeeze my bracelet, trying to will more healing power into my body, but I think I've reached the extent of what the bracelet can heal. She helps me down against the wall and sits next to me.

After a minute, she says, "Rest." Then she stands and walks into the room.

I close my eyes, but I don't think I should let myself sleep, even if it means more information from Yinzar's memories and time to heal.

Brig's voice forces me to open my eyes again. "You doing alright?" He takes a seat across from me against the opposite wall. I can feel excited, nervous energy rolling off him. He glances back at the door and leans forward. "So, I've wanted to ask you something. Well, tell you something, really."

"Okay."

"I'm putting together a sort of... well, a history of-of your life, I guess. People are interested in what you do, where you were all that time, what happened with the mithrium. I..."

"Brig I—"

"Before you say no—and I know you don't like publicity—there's more to it than trying to get a following over bluelink."

"Like what?"

"You must know something about your grandfather, Yinzar Copperoath. You're the keeper of that dungeon."

I'm not sure I like where this is going. "Some keeper. I can't even find the place."

"Ho, that's the thing. Most people agree th-that he wasn't at the level of a champion when he died."

"I know that."

"So how did his death create a dungeon? One that can't be found."

I shrug, eying him.

Brig scoots closer. "You think you know where it is? Don't you? Mithriumbane."

"I've wanted to find it. I had to ask the council for access to the mines, but..." My mind wanders to my sister and Rugnus. My request never made it to the council.

His eyes widen. "The mines? Is that where—"

"Rugnus thinks I need to take it easy about dungeons. I already found one piece of mithrium in Silverlamp. What's to stop me from finding the second or the third? And if I did, what would people do with them? Not to mention that we have a more pressing issue—learning who attacked the festival. Maybe, Rugnus is right. Maybe Mithriumbane should stay hidden."

"Are you serious? People are waiting to complete their summation."

The moment he says this, I know why he cares so much. Something he said a few minutes earlier when Koglim called him a latchmage. "Your survey. You were called to Mithriumbane."

He nods. "Couldn't you find it? You're the keeper, and it's like

—like you don't even care that we can't move on with our lives. You have a responsibility to help us."

His words cut through some of the defenses I've built up around myself. My own summation happened after Rugnus tested me with the summator in his vault. It was simple. I chose rocks representing things like fear and freedom, and power. Then I was called to Wolfstaff to receive my AMP score.

Going through summation is Brig's whole world, and I'm denying him access. Not on purpose, but still. He won't ever have an AMP score if I can't find Mithriumbane.

"I'm sorry. I know it's important to people. And before the attack, I was searching. I just—" Brig's eyes turn red, and when he blinks, he has to turn his face from me. He's right. I'm standing in his way. My feelings swing back the opposite way, though I'll have to get Rugnus and Andalynn on my side. "Okay. As soon as we figure out all this stuff with the attack, I *will* find that dungeon."

That excited energy returns to his eyes. He stands up, stare glued on me. "Ho, I knew it. This will be awesome. Hey... could I send a message out to the other Mithriumbane initiates? They'd love to hear that you're with us."

I take a deep breath. This is the right thing to do. "Yeah. In fact, can you record a message for me?"

Brig gestures. "Go ahead."

"This is Clayson Brightstorm. I know many of you are grieving right now. This is a difficult time. I just wanted to let the initiates of Mithriumbane know something. I've been trying for a long time now, a-and well, I'll make finding the dungeon a top priority as soon as things settle down. We're all hurting from the recent attack. Hopefully, you receive this news as something positive. Thanks."

Brig gestures the camera off. "Awesome."

There are voices in the room—loud ones. Rugnus steps into the hall. "Need to see this."

When I enter the room, everyone is huddled around the map

of the intersecting points. A few dozen dots are meandering around the space, representing people. One dot highlighted in bright white has a name under it. Rensira Silverlamp.

"She's there?" I ask. "Right now?"

"Yep. The heart of the Mirror Market," Rugnus says.

Winta cracks her knuckles. "What are we waiting for?"

Rugnus clears his throat. "Finding her was the easy part."

TRADE OUR FRIENDS

Two hours later, Sira is still in the Mirror Market, but our plans begin to come together. Everyone but Andalynn budges to the Stacks to go over the craft as we wait for her to return from Whurrimduum with backup.

The Stacks are made of sixty-four concrete buildings, each ten stories high, half-buried in the ground, half rising from it. The place looks like a giant 3D checkerboard.

We came here last season to prepare for the Keeper's Social. Sira invited us. Somehow, she knew about Rugnus' connection with Dad. She knew I would go with them to the social. She predicted a lot of the events to follow. What she didn't foresee was the death of her father and the creation of the mithrium shield.

Even so, Sira is a master manipulator. The Mirror Market is a trap, but at least this time, we see it for what it is, though none of us can predict the outcome.

Koglim, flicks his tattoo, hoping for a warning. Nothing. He frowns and looks at me. "Remember the warning I got from Elbaz when you used your ring before the social?"

"How can I forget?" I had used Ergal to block Winta's time-craft during practice. The moment I did, Koglim's necklace had lit up like a hot coal. Maybe the object knew Bazalrak would show up to the social and expose me to Tungsten City as the son of Therias Brightstorm. "Too bad you never found your necklace."

"Worth the sacrifice. Old Challozil Silverlamp must've liked it, so she kept it. Dungeons have a mind of their own. Besides, one excursion into Silverlamp was enough to get me an interview with the recruiter." A broad, dangerous grin comes to his face. "And my new tat"—he slaps the silver diamond on his upper arm — "gives me pictures straight from my future memories. I say, bring on the danger."

Winta slaps his tattoo. "A lot of help that got us. All you saw for the festival was smoke and machines."

Koglim shrugs. "I thought it would be part of the show."

Across the large, echoing room, Andalynn appears with six Behemoth class mechs. Their blue eyes are dim with fire, scanning the area for potential threats. The last time I dealt with one of these, it was chasing me through an RV park.

"Curse us this early, huh?" Winta says to Koglim. She's in an even grumpier mood than usual. Which is fair, seeing how close she is to having this baby.

Hemdi and Andalynn didn't want her putting herself at risk like this. She's due any day now. In fact, when she insisted on coming, Hemdi had mumbled something about the stubbornness of Dashen women and returned to help with the festival clean-up.

"What do you mean, curse us?" Jeiah asks.

Andalynn waves us over. Rugnus blows out a breath, ignoring us, and crosses the distance to her. His hand goes to her elbow as they speak quietly, then he slips his arm around her. I tense slightly. It's weird feeling protective of a sister I didn't grow up with, but that instinct is there regardless. They are so different. Sometimes I wonder how they make it work.

I blink, then turn toward Jeiah, backtracking to her question. "Last time we trained here, the results... weren't so great. It was for the Keeper's Social last fall—uh, Gem. Sorry, I do that sometimes."

Jeiah scans my face again. I know her eyes are a natural bright blue, but sometimes they seem to bring the same scrutiny as a camera. It's pleasantly unnerving.

She ignores my mistake. "I remember seeing that footage. It was the first time people saw you. I was working on a different investigation at the time, or I would have responded when the other paladins were called. Brig came home so excited he didn't sleep for two days."

"Brig sleeps?" I ask, and Jeiah doesn't miss my joke.

The genuine smile on her face draws small dimples on her cheeks, highlighting wisps of golden blush in her brown cheeks. I find I can't look away. She notices, only increasing her smile. "Well, not on days that end with y. You do know your days of the week, don't you?"

"Oh yeah. Dad had a whole song for that."

She sighs and shakes her head. "And by your dad, you mean—"

"The former monarch of Rimduum."

"Just checking."

Winta and Koglim have already made their way across the room to the mechs, leaving me and Jeiah alone. I clear my throat. "Where'd Brig go anyway?"

"Sent him home."

I open my mouth in mock surprise. "You didn't?"

"Actually, he took it well. Seems like someone made a promise to him. He was euphoric. Thanks for that. Your video is going viral."

"So, you saw it?"

"It's quite a promise. Did you mean it?"

"What? Of course, I mean it. I—"

Her shoulders slump. "Is it the right thing to do? What if you find the dungeon and your grandfather didn't actually destroy the mithrium? Seems dangerous."

"If Yinzar went to destroy it, it's destroyed." The words come from my mouth, but I'm not sure I believe them. I suddenly can't avoid the memory of his voice echoing in that hole deep in the mines. Jeiah—being discerning as she is—reads the doubt on my face, but she leaves me alone with the thought. "Is this part of your investigation of me? To see what I'm willing to risk?"

She's thoughtful for a moment. "Maybe."

Rugnus calls out to us. "Going to join us over here, you two?"

We cross the distance to the group. Now, as Jeiah gets a good look at the mechs, she whistles low. "Winta, you need any help with these?"

Winta taps the air, presses a palm to something unseen, and simultaneously twists an invisible control knob with the other hand. The head of the closest mech peels backward. The shards of titanium form into two rail guns, and a gunner's seat pops up from the torso. With a wide smile, Winta climbs up. "Not sure you can handle this much mech."

Jeiah narrows her eyes. She passes a hand over one of the hinges on the polished titanium chicken legs. "In my sleep."

"Maybe, but don't think you can take my spot because of this little latcher." Winta jabs her abdomen with two fingers.

"I wouldn't dare."

"Time for the plan," Rugnus says, calling everyone into a loose huddle. Winta moves the mech, nearly stepping on Koglim.

He stumbles sideways. "Watch it!"

"Oh," Winta says. "Didn't see you down there."

Rugnus speaks over them. "Probably start with the basics. Everyone know about the Mirror Market?"

The whole group looks at me, even Jeiah. My cheeks grow hot. Luckily, I've been combing through information about the Mirror Market for the last hour. I'm prepared.

"It's a black market," I say, as conversationally as I can. "Made entirely of obsidian. You get an invitation to participate from a seller, and they provide a guide for your group—a guide that lives on the surface of the obsidian walls as a reflection. If you or your group gets lost or can't follow the guide, you could become a reflection yourself, joining the other guides in the obsidian. You become part of the market until you're released by a seller."

"Good," Rugnus says. "Apparently, all that time on bluelink is paying off."

Koglim snickers.

Rugnus moves us along. "The Mirror Market spans three blocks in every direction. Sits on the bottom side of Tungsten City. Six access points, each of which Winta will be guarding using the foilgrips on the Behemoths. All from the comfort of mech number one."

Winta punctuates the announcements by shooting off the mech's guns into the distant ceiling, breaking free a chunk of concrete that is immediately regrown.

"Winta!" Andalynn says.

"Keep Ide!" Koglim shouts. "Hold your fire."

Winta winces. "Sorry. Just getting excited."

"Anyway," Andalynn says, taking over for Rugnus whose eyes look like they could roll out of their sockets. "We block the entrances, do facial recognition on anyone leaving, and throw up the foilgrip from the mechs. That way, we can block Sira from budging if she tries to leave the market. Meanwhile, Koglim will lose himself on purpose in the maze and become a guide."

I whirl around to Koglim, who's grinning. "This is going to be awesome."

"Wait. We're letting him get turned into a guide on purpose? He'll be... like a two-dimensional reflection?"

"His idea," Andalynn says.

"It'll work," Rugnus says. "I'll bring an object for sale to the entrance walls. Koglim will pledge his work to the market and become a reflection, a guide. Then I go in as a seller, which should afford me a chance to look around a bit and chose a location for the sale. When we're set, Koglim will return to the entrance and guide you inside."

"And," Andalynn adds, "once our transaction is complete, we will have an hour or so of freedom inside the market. Koglim's short time as a guide should help us find Sira and get out quickly."

"Before what?" I ask. "There're always consequences. I know how these things work."

Winta pivots the mech's head toward me. "Don't worry. It's no more reckless than usual. If we don't hurry, we'll be trapped as guides until someone uses us for a transaction."

"Great," I say.

Rugnus removes Icho from behind his back. "Any more questions?" No one has any. "Let's budge."

I blink, and we've moved from the lighted training area in the Stacks to one of the entrances of the Mirror Market. It's cold. We're in a wide alleyway deep inside the bowels of Tungsten City. If light from the brightstorm can reach us down here, it would have to bend around a half-mile of rock. At our backs, an industrial plant of some kind pumps steam into the air.

Across the wide distance of the alley, or street, or whatever you call the spaces in between things down here, the surface of the Mirror Market glimmers with light, made, not of lamps or neon signs, but of the men and women trapped on the surface of the rock. Ghostly, glowing two-dimensional shapes. Synthetic music pulses from the rock in greeting.

It's an alluring place.

"Wow," Jeiah says. "Did Rugnus just budge all of us and the mechs to different locations at the same time, without physical contact?"

I nod absently. Sometimes I forget how powerful Icho is.

"Does it all the time," Andalynn says. "Icho is unmatched."

Rugnus chimes in over bluelink. "Koglim and I are at the opposite entrance from Andalynn, Jeiah, and Clayson. You guys have one of the mechs with you. Winta's lead mech is at a topside entrance waiting. The other mechs are in place. Koglim's pledging himself now."

And we wait. We sit on a low wall connected to the industrial building. The glowing forms of the guides fill the alleyway in all directions.

After less than a minute, someone emerges from the entrance. The man takes one look at the mech and tries to budge. When he can't, he sprints along the outside of the Mirror Market until he gets out of range and budges.

This happens a few more times, people exiting the market and scattering at the first sign of us. Jeiah uses bluelink to look up information on each of the market's patrons as they emerge.

I think she might be taking notes for future investigations.

As she does, I move closer to Andalynn.

"How are things with the council?" I ask. It's not exactly what I wanna ask. I want to ask why she didn't make my request for access to the mines. But I've already landed on my own conclusion. She didn't have the political capital to bring it up directly. That's why she put me in front of them in the lounge. It was the best she could do.

Andalynn sighs. "Difficult. Two others besides Bluekeeper were killed in the attack."

"Are they filling the positions? What can I do to help?"

She smiles, and the edges around her eyes soften. "Can I just show you?" I can tell she's testing the waters, trying to see if I'm just being nice or truly wanna talk about it.

I nod, scooting closer to her. We lean our heads together, the silver strands woven in her hair rest on her shoulder. As busy as she has been, we haven't had many conversations, let alone shared memories. I open myself to her world. The first image that enters my mind is of Lagnar Emberfence arguing with two members of the council, Ogrekeeper and Chainkeeper.

"Bluebottle's line is dead. I'm the closest living relative and, I oughta remind you, I'm already seer, so there's precedence."

Ogrekeeper coughs a yellow cloud of smoke. "Perhaps."

The next vision is of Chainkeeper alone. "Then Clayson should produce himself to this council and give us a more factual account of what happened in Silverlamp."

I blink and the scene changes. I'm pacing the pebbled paths of Everbloom Garden late at night. A heavy sense of fear and worry floods my senses. Lagnar's words echo in my mind: The Monarchy must come to an end.

The visions pass, but I stay leaned against Andalynn.

"When this is done. I'll take the Wolfstaff seership or Silver-lamp. Help you the best I can. Though I need to find Mithrium-bane as well. I—"

She squeezes my hand. "It's okay. And I'm sorry I couldn't help with the mines, and that I haven't been available. I know, I know it's not easy for you down here. I keep imagining what it would be like if our positions were switched if I had to live on the surface with the fate of the world balanced on my back. I... any help you could give would go a long way, but don't feel like it's something you have to do."

We look out over the entrance of Mirror Market. "I didn't get this authorized," she says, "Coming here. I figured if Lagnar was involved, we would lose the advantage."

"I don't like this place."

Jeiah steps over to us, dips her chin toward the ground in respect, and sits.

Andalynn graciously nods back. "Places like this..." she pauses for a moment. "Before we broke down the foilgrips in Whurrim-duum, there was a black market for...well, even basic things. Food, clothing, budges. I used to go there with donations to help. But this—this is something different. In Tungsten all the necessities are cheap and abundant. Even things that are terrible for you are legal. Whatever sellers are offering in there... no one needs those things."

Jeiah agrees. "That's why Tungsten drafted the principles."

"The principles only go so far," Andalynn counters.

"Very true. Which is why I work as a paladin. Those who try to work in darkness find themselves exposed in the light. And every citizen can act as a paladin to some extent."

Two women appear at the wall of the Mirror Market, accept a

guide, and enter the cavernous opening as quickly as they can, casting looks in our direction.

Andalynn nods to Jeiah. "There are not enough professional paladins, with your wisdom and insight."

A bluelink connection buzzes. Rugnus says, "Koglim's in. I'm generating the seller's request for a guide."

Andalynn stands. "I'm going to check on Winta and help Rugnus with the seller's request." Before she disappears, she inclines her head to Jeiah. "Jeiah, I know the council wants you to investigate Clayson. But I'm asking something different... take care of him, please. He tends to get into trouble easily."

I open my mouth to protest, but she vanishes.

A metallic groan, like a distorted gong, issues somewhere deep inside the wall behind us, and we both turn. The steam, hissing from horizontal smokestacks, trickles to a halt. What do they make down here? It's gotta be a forge of some kind.

Jeiah sighs. "Andalynn is... well, as inspiring as I imagined."

"That's very true."

"Stories of her compassion and service are almost mythical. In Tungsten City, she was the only ray of light coming from Whur-rimduum. You know, if we were to have a monarchy again—which we never should, but if—I would want her to run it indefinitely."

I rub the scruff at my chin line. "As long as it's not me."

"Why's that?"

"You tell me."

"That's a tough one. I'd say evidence points to the fact that you don't like responsibility... but that's not quite it. More like... you're being overly cautious." She laughs at this. "Sometimes."

This idea enters the top of my head, travels down to my toes and back, lodging itself at the base of my neck. Or maybe I'm still healing from the skull wound. "Why do you say that?"

The hard blue of her eyes seems to deepen. On her, it only softens her face, though. Maybe she only shifts into a different light. "You're peerless in protective magic. That's a clue. Some say our craft and our personalities blend over time. Others say it's more direct—our very being gravitates toward types of craft because of who we are innately."

I gesture to her to keep going. She's uncovering ideas about myself I've been struggling to understand.

"Then there are the dungeons," she continues. "In both Wolf-staff and Silverlamp, you broke all the rules and gained powerful objects."

"In Shadowwright last month, I uncovered a relic within five minutes," I admit. "I left as soon as I could. Rugnus is right about me staying out of dungeons."

"See. You're powerful. And—rightly so—you fear that power. You fear the answers to your questions. That you're different from the rest of us. That you don't belong here. You think you will disturb some type of balance this world has."

"I-I... yeah, you're right. Huh."

She blinks at me. "And you didn't know this? You needed someone to tell you?"

"No, I-I guess I knew this about myself. I just don't know what to do about it."

"Ah, that I can't help with." Her shoulders lift slightly, and we sit silently for a moment. Finally, she offers one more idea. "When I find I can't make decisions easily—that I can't draw the right conclusions—I find it helpful to seek out more information."

"I guess we have that in common."

My personal need for answers is another reason I must find Mithriumbane. And it's why we're searching for Sira. I can't move forward without more information.

"It worked with understanding you." Her voice is swallowed up by another metallic groan from the building behind us. "I just had to meet you to get the last few details in order."

Everything about this conversation sends both a warning and a thrill through my body. "You have a lot of details about me?"

"It's my job."

"You knew about my fake AMP score. How long have you—"

"You seemed dangerous. I was trying to decide what to think about you."

"Did you make a decision?"

When she looks up, there's something more in the twitch of her mouth, something mischievous.

"Pretty sure." Her words send tingles into the nerve endings along my scalp and through my shoulders. Have we been sitting this close to each other this whole time? Did I move closer? Did she?

The metallic groan sounds again, this time high pitched. Steam billows out into the street, rolling between us and the Mirror Market. When it clears, Andalynn stands, looking at us. "Rugnus is in place. Time to find Koglim and—" she looks us over.

Standing, I clear my throat. "Everything good with Koglim?"

Andalynn fights off a smile. "We'll see."

We follow her down to the wall of the market, the synthetic music grows loud and driving. Blue-white and mint-colored Loamin reflections float over the surface of the black stone, guides trapped until they fulfill a request. To my horror, some of the guides wear styles of clothing I recognize from centuries ago. Have they been trapped that long? They all begin speaking to us as we draw near.

"Deathfingers," a man says. "For your enemies."

A woman winks at me. "I'll guide you in. I know what you want. A strong boy like you."

I shudder. "Have I said I don't like this place?"

Another guide, tall and bright-faced, with a scar across his right eye, floats into view. "You can get all of that and more with severed-ferrum. Trust me. My seller always has open requests."

"Alright, alright," Koglim's high, clear voice cuts through the din of catcalls and sales pitches. "Get lost, freaks." When we spot him, he opens his transparent arms. "Can you believe how cool this is! I'm just a reflection. Good idea, right?"

"Risky," Jeiah says.

"Raiders don't worry about small things like risk. Besides, even if this goes to brick, I've got you guys to bail me out."

I point to a reflection dressed as if she's from the early Age of Discovery, a woven shawl, baggy skirt, and a metal cap. "What about her? She seems to have been forgotten."

Koglim looks her over. "Good point. Let's make sure we find Rugnus and buy the object he's selling. Speaking of which…" He holds a palm to the rock face, and Andalynn presses her hand against it. A light flashes. Jeiah and I take our turn, and the deal is done.

Jeiah says, "Your fellow raiders—Brude Levenrust in particular —might be upset about the risk you're taking."

Koglim smiles. "Brude can—wait, you follow my team?"

"Came up in my investigation into Clayson."

He smiles. "Just got into the pros last season. If I live through this, they'll be jealous. But hey, let's hurry in." He gestures to the open doorway.

The first room is an impossibly long narrow corridor flanked with the stalls of sellers. Thousands of objects lay in heaps or strung on ropes. Chains, and jewelry, household objects, jarred items, watery tanks bright with things both moving and stationary. In between and above us, even on the floor, hundreds of reflections beg to be used as a guide. Every seller joins the chorus to entice us.

I catch Koglim's voice from a sidewall. "Don't follow any other guides, and if you see a seller, don't speak with them. The second you interact, you won't be able to deal with Rugnus. Could even get trapped as a guide if a deal goes bad. There!" He points to a path between two large vendors.

The hallway past the first room is wider, and more of the guides press toward us, trying to get our attention, but only a few sellers try to interact with us. In the next, much larger, emptier room, we weave around a statue—a man with wide eyes holding a stack of treasure. I don't think he's always been stone.

"Take that as another warning," Andalynn whispers to me.

Koglim's reflection slides to a halt before the next door. "That's weird."

Andalynn shakes her head. "What's going on?"

"The beacon thing I'm following for Rugnus... it stopped."

"What does that mean?" Jeiah asks.

Koglim shrugs. "You guys just hold right here. Give me a second."

Over Andalynn's protest, Koglim glides away through another hall.

"What now?" I ask.

"Guess we just have to wait for him to come back."

We stay close to the statue at the center of the room, trying to avoid the calls of the reflections. After a few minutes, many of them give up and move to other rooms. The darkness encloses us a little more each time, to the point where I would gladly welcome the reflections back.

An apparition of a small girl, no more than ten, creeps along the back wall—a reflection. She gestures for me to approach. I ignore it for a few minutes but freeze when she mouths a name: *Sira*. I move in her direction, but Jeiah and Andalynn notice immediately.

"Clayson, ignore it," Andalynn says.

Jeiah grabs my arm.

But this may be our only shot. "Do you see what she's saying? The name?"

Andalynn peers around me. "We expected a trap. This must be it."

Jeiah must sense the urgency I feel. "Chances are she's right, Clayson."

The girl points to me and adds "and Sira," moving only her mouth again.

"I think she's mute. Or was mute in life. All the other guides have spoken to us. If we follow her to Sira, the girl will be free."

Andalynn tenses even more. "This is wrong Clayson. Sira must be playing on your kindness. You can't trust this place."

Jeiah is silent, but I think she is waiting for me to decide.

"I know that. I know, but it could be the only way to get to her. And I don't think Sira would hurt me. And the guide isn't a trick. I think she's really stuck in the Mirror Market."

"This is not the plan." Andalynn steps between me and the girl.

I lean around her. "You're gonna have to trust me."

The little girl blushes and shyly mouths Sira's name, makes a heart with her fingers over her chest, and points to me.

"Sira... loves you?" Jeiah says, confusion in her voice.

Andalynn hangs her head. "It's her. You definitely can't go."

I let out a breath, then move around Andalynn and place my palm against the girl's reflection of a palm. "Guide me to her."

"No!" Andalynn yells.

I try to calm her. "We can do both things. You two wait here for Koglim. I'm going straight for her. If I get to her, find Rugnus, buy his object, and free Koglim. I'll meet you on the outside."

"This is foolish." Andalynn's eyes beg me to rethink what I'm doing.

Jeiah rests a hand on my sister's shoulder. "I'll go with him."

I start to protest, but they both glare at me. "Okay. Jeiah and I will go find Sira." There's nothing left to say, so I hug Andalynn and turn around. Jeiah presses her hand against the stone, and we follow the little girl's reflection through a series of rooms and hallways. Fewer and fewer guides appear on the walls, and more and more sellers pop up in dark corners in even darker market stalls.

In a room filled with large glowing stones, we find five people standing perfectly still. They hold defensive positions, crafted objects in their hands, ready for use. Their eyes are glazed over. As we pass, one of them says, "Sira will see you."

Jeiah surveys one man more carefully. "He's under some type of control."

"Sira is a peerless silvermage."

"But from this far away?"

"Whatever these people were doing at the market, she's turned them to her purposes. She's must have Onrix, her silver knife."

"Let's wait for your friends."

I gesture to the nearest person under Sira's control. "We must be in range. If she wanted to control us, she'd be doing it already. You don't have to come with me."

"But I do."

We move down a final corridor that opens into the darkness. A silver light glints in the corner of the room. Sira steps forward, her knife in hand. She wears a bright-colored flowery sundress, but her skin is grayish pale like she's been sick. Her eyes are rimmed red. Budging all over the place has left her drained.

Our guide smiles, and her tiny frame fades into the stone, mouthing her thanks.

Sira rushes me like a feral animal, a cruel smile on her face. I flinch, activating my defensive bracelet, but the closer she gets, the more I change my mind—or is it her knife? A feeling, like a sudden understanding of a math problem, shoots through my skull. I shouldn't treat her this way. I expect her blade to fall into my back. Instead, she wraps me up in an awkward hug and kisses my cheek.

"Clayson," she says, pulling away and slapping my arm playfully. "I knew you would come."

RAID A DUNGEON

D ESPITE MY PEERLESS rating and my bracelet, I'm no match for the knife. The flow of silvercraft pushes its way past my defenses. My whole body freezes.

"Sira, stop!" My teeth clench.

She squishes my chin and bats her eyelashes at me. "Oh, Clayson. I hate controlling you. If I put this away, can we just have a nice conversation? Like the first day I met you... we had that beautiful moment at breakfast."

My teeth grind together. "I couldn't attack you if I wanted to."

"Good. And this one?" She brushes Jeiah's arm sweetly. My stomach turns. Jeiah's face is frozen, eyes wide with fear. No, more than that. Anger.

"Let. Her. Go."

Sira takes a step closer to Jeiah, the hand with the knife hanging at her side. I wanna reach out, twist the knife away, and turn it against her, but my mind is sending other messages to my body. A general sense of revelation and enlightenment permeates the whole room. I hate that silvercraft feels this way. I should be angry, but I can't hold any negative feelings in my mind.

Sira blinks confused. "It couldn't be... I remember this girl."

Retreating halfway back to the corner, she hides the knife

away in a pocket of her sundress, releasing both of us from the silvercraft. In an instant, Jeiah produces her small glass rod, pointing it coolly at Sira. "Tell me how you attacked StoneYoke. Who else is involved?"

Sira returns Jeiah to a frozen state with a quick reach into her pocket. "Clayson, will you take that from her, please?" There's still an edge behind her voice, like a parent that's about to lose patience with a child.

My mind pushes against the silvercraft.

"So strong, Clayson. But still, I'm in charge here." I reach out and take the rod from Jeiah. "There you go. Throw it this way." I obey. She catches it, looks it over, and tucks it into the front pocket of her sundress. "Jeiahlir, right? I'll release you if you promise to be nice."

Jeiah's body tenses when she's released. Her stance widens. Her voice is fierce. "You think you know me from somewhere. How's that?"

"Last year"—her voice drips with false innocence—"when I worked with Brig. You started following me around, looking into my records. I couldn't have that. I took all your memories of me. Nothing against you, though."

"The scar on my shoulder..."

Sira curtseys.

This new connection, this revelation—another thing that Sira did to control someone—causes wrath to bubble to the surface of my skin. I extend the protection of my bracelet around us, though I know it can't stop Sira from invading our minds. She notices the shieldcraft I've put between us, and she pouts.

"Clayson, is there ever going to be a chance for us? There's already another girl. She's not even as pretty as I am."

Now I'm thinking about the mist of freckles across the bridge of Sira's nose. The way she walks. What she looks like under soft silver light. About the smell of her hair. I try to shake the thoughts from my mind. I know Sira's influencing me.

Jeiah's voice cuts through. "Give me my memories back."

"I might be able to. But why would I do that?"

"Give her the memories back," I say, "and we can talk."

"That sounds nice," Sira steps back over to Jeiah, putting us both under her control. With a quick movement of her hands, she jabs the knife into Jeiah's shoulder. Blood spreads down her shirt. I try to scream at Sira to stop, but nothing comes out.

Sira backs away. "She'll be fine. Just heal her."

The second I'm free to move, I use my bracelet to heal the cut. Jeiah winces, then breathes a sigh of thanks. She blinks. "No. I... no way. I did follow her. Her AMP... it was a high-quality fake. Made by... is that possible?" Jeiah looks at me with renewed suspicion.

"Lagnar Emberfence," I guess because Jeiah's reaction says I'm connected somehow.

"You're very good at that," Sira tells her. "All the little dots connecting."

"What do you want from me?" I ask. "You called me here, right?"

"To business then? If we must." Sira shrugs off some of her cuteness effortlessly. "I need a favor. And just so you're aware my, uh, associates don't know I'm here. And they don't know I led you here."

Jeiah's map of Tungsten City flashes in my mind, the many shapes and sizes of the bluelink distortions. Without the context of the maltobi game Sira showed me, no one would have guessed she wanted to meet me here. She'd been trying to lead us without someone else knowing.

Jeiah shoots daggers at Sira. "Who caused the other disruptions before the attack?"

Sira shrugs. "They were testing things."

"Who was?" I ask. "Who broke you out of Keelcrawl?"

"Oh, sweetie. I made a promise not to say, but that's a good lead-in for my request." She holds up Onrix again. "Hide this for me, will you?"

Jeiah and I exchange glances. If anything's a trap, it will be this.

"You want him to take it from you?" Jeiah says.

"Hide it." The urgency behind her voice is raw. "Don't even tell me where you put it."

A prickle of suspicion runs up my spine. "Why?"

Sira glares at Jeiah. "Why did you have to bring an audience, Clayson." She stands in front of Jeiah and extends an arm. "Swear that you won't say a word about my knife to anyone."

Jeiah's arm trembles as she fights against the silvercraft, but she reaches out and tests strengths with Sira. "I swear it."

"Good." Sira smiles brightly, revealing her voracious canines. She gives Jeiah back her glass rod. "Now your turn, Clayson. But I won't force you."

Someone—one of Sira's guards maybe—shouts. The sound echoes off the wall. There's a flare of firelight from the same direction. It must be Rugnus and the others.

Sira rushes me, shoving the knife, hilt first, toward my hands. "Hide it. Swear you won't tell anyone. Please, Clayson."

I swallow, and for a brief second, my breath catches. I grab the hilt, but she doesn't let go. Her other hand settles over mine. "Hide it. And run away. Anywhere. The surface, but not the cabin. Just stay hidden."

Fear. I see it in her eyes. Fear of something else, someone else.

"I swear."

She lets go. The knife's heavier than it looks, and I tuck it into my bag. A tingle of energy charges from my palm, up through my arm and shoulder into the back of my head. That 'aha' you get when you learn something new. I've made a promise I can't break without consequences. There's silvercraft to it I can't take lightly.

Koglim bounds through the door, no longer a reflection on the wall. "Got her." His arms burst into brown flames, and he launches forward, capturing Sira.

Sira wipes the fear from her face, adopting impatience and

boredom. "Koglim, I've been budging all morning. I'm exhausted. I'm not going anywhere, sweetie."

Rugnus and Andalynn enter the room surrounding Sira like two bookends. Rugnus rumbles the floor using his bracelet to control the obsidian. It's a warning to Sira. If she still had the knife, my friends would be under her control. Why did she give it to me?

Rugnus scans me up and down, but his shoulders relax. "Does she have the knife?" He asks.

Jeiah watches my face so intently, I almost reveal the knife right then and there. "No." When Jeiah nods, it is so imperceptible it's hard to notice.

Andalynn pats Koglim on the back. "I need to check her for objects."

Koglim flinches. He seems to only now notice the others in the room. His arms peel away from around Sira, but his fingers remain wrapped around her arms.

Rugnus juts his chin out toward Sira. "Did you bring us here?"

"I only needed Clayson. I set a guide out. I think she's free now. I hope she is, poor thing. Been here such a long time."

"Why did you want Clayson?" Rugnus asks. "Was it some kind of trap?"

"Of course not, silly. I wanted to see him, that's all. Have you seen the cute video of him rescuing a whole little family during the attack? He took such good care of them. It's precious. The ClaySlay girls posted it."

The family I helped. Someone must have recorded it. Maybe even the mother or father. I told them I would check on them. Another responsibility pushed to the sidelines.

"Got something." Andalynn pulls another object from one of the pockets of her sundress. A blue glow fills the room as soon as Andalynn holds up a tiny vial. At first, I think it's Jeiah's beholder, but Sira had given that back. Jeiah takes a step forward, emitting a soft gasp.

"Great brick!" Koglim says. "Is that—can't be?"

"What is it?" Rugnus asks.

Koglim's hands loosen on Sira's arms, but he thinks better of it, and the flames brighten. "Is that... is it the heart of Bluebottle?"

"No." Jeiah shakes her head. "But it explains a few things. It's a craft battery. A relic that can only be found in Bluebottle."

Andalynn holds it up to Sira's face. "What does it do?"

Sira shrugs. "Makes it so no one can see me."

"The disruptions in bluelink?" I ask.

Jeiah steps closer to Andalynn. "May I?" Andalynn passes her the vial. "It does more than that. It's a receptacle. You can store tremendous amounts of craft inside of it. Anyone can use it, even nulls."

"Like mechcraft or antibudge?" Rugnus asks.

Jeiah squints at the craft battery. "Maybe. But I don't think it can hold that much power."

"You think this caused the attack?" I ask.

Andalynn and Rugnus trade looks. "Could it have?" Andalynn asks Jeiah.

"Not alone. You would need a few hundred to cause the type of damage we saw at the festival. And they're very, very rare. One of the two I know of... Emberfence won it in Bluebottle. But the craft doesn't add up."

Rugnus persists. "But it's possible?" He refocuses on Sira. "Is this how you caused the attack?"

Sira blinks. "Me? I didn't cause the attack. I warned Clayson." She looks at me for help.

Koglim adjusts his grip again. "You expect us to believe you? After everything you did to us?"

Sira's expression transforms into a pout. "You guys are being so mean. I—"

"Then tell us exactly what happened," Rugnus says.

"Well, I obviously can't. I swore to keep it a secret."

"Emberfence." Andalynn and Rugnus say at the same time.

Sira's coy shrug almost confirms it.

Jeiah shakes her head. "That doesn't add up. Without additional batteries, he couldn't—"

Rugnus interrupts her. "Lagnar is now the keeper of Bluebottle."

Jeiah blinks. "That's official?"

Andalynn answers. "Yes. They'll be announcing it soon, along with filling the two other vacancies on the council."

Jeiah looks down at the blue shine of her beholder. Something's wrong.

"What is it?" I ask.

"As Bluekeeper, Lagnar Emberfence will appoint a new paladin. I think I just lost my job."

"Maybe that's what he wants," Rugnus adds, looking at the battery. "As paladin, you could check inside the dungeon, see if he removed any more batteries."

"Is there a way to check?" I ask.

Jeiah leans her head from side to side. "It would be pretty challenging dungeon work even with a paladin's key."

"But it's possible?" I ask.

"Maybe with your help," Jeiah says to me, a hint of a smile. "From what I've heard, you're pretty good in a dungeon."

Sira clucks her tongue. "That would be a waste of time."

"Why are you still talking?" Rugnus snaps. "You're on your way back to Keelcrawl soon enough."

"Rugnus," Andalynn says. "Why don't you go with Clayson and Jeiah? Check out Bluebottle."

Rugnus is already taking Icho out. "Yeah, that works. What about you Koglim?"

"As much as I'd love to, professional raiders aren't allowed into the dungeons accompanied by an official paladin, especially when she has a dungeon key."

"Right. Forgot. Okay so, Sira goes before the council, and we head to Bluebottle to see who's been farming batteries."

Andalynn squeezes Rugnus' hand and finds a position next to

Koglim, producing an aluminum slap bracelet. She locks it around Sira's wrist. My sister wears a familiar gravity on her face. Her sincerity and openness, people say, makes her a great queen. When her attention shifts toward Sira, I sense something grimmer and more determined.

I feel the silver knife through the cloth of my bag. What am I going to do about this? Why did I take it from her? It was fear. Not mine, but Sira's.

"Be good, Clayson," Sira says. "I'll see you later."

They budge, and I can picture them arriving at the shale doorway to the Keeper Council in Whurrimduum, Sira vomiting from the shock. It's almost like torture.

Rugnus is trying to read my mind through my expression. "You think she's telling the truth."

"It's a possibility. Maybe, sending her to the council is for the best. If she swore by silver that she wouldn't reveal who made the attack, then maybe they have a way to remedy it. Find out the truth."

"An oath by silver can't be broken," Jeiah says matter-of-factly. But when our eyes meet, there is something else to be said between us. And I know what it is. She's curious about why I made the promise to Sira without being forced to do it. "Rugnus. I assume, being a surveyor, you have a few good relics lying around."

He smiles. "Have a few. But will we need them? Won't your paladin status get us through fairly quickly?"

"It will still be difficult. We should be prepared for the unexpected."

He shrugs, and we budge to his vault. It's warmer here. His aquarium must hold in some heat. Or it's just the time he spends here playing with fire.

Jeiah looks from Rugnus to me, her eyes wide. "Did you just budge us to your vault without making contact with either of us?"

"It's Icho," I remind her.

Jeiah turns her attention to the object-filled, built-in shelves that form the closest wall. "Wow." She glances at my bag and looks around the room with an encouraging eye. She straightens something on a nearby table. "Rugnus, this place is hyper-organized. What's your system?"

Rugnus, who's already searching through objects on the shelf, starts to explain how he catalogs things, which is a good distraction because he has a lot of objects from surveying the ruined cities, and he loves to show them off.

She's distracting him. This would be a good place to hide something. But why would she help me hide the knife from everyone? Sira forced her to promise not to tell anyone, but that doesn't mean she has to help me.

"Ooh, what's this shelf?" She bounds forward to a shelf I know has the most relics. I glimpse the flashlight that took me to Thiffimdal, and for a moment, a cold chill ripples down my spine, reminding me of the frozen city.

Rugnus takes three hasty steps forward, his hands out defensively. "Don't! Don't touch anything."

His attention turns to managing her curiosity, and I slip Sira's knife from my bag, hiding it in an opaque green glass vase on Rugnus' silver shelf. Rugnus whirls on me.

"And you. Don't touch anything either. Last time—"

"Last time, I was a total latchmage." I try not to look at the vase where I just hid the knife.

"Still are," Rugnus says, smiling. "Okay, what kind of relics will we need? Jeiahlir probably has us covered on bluecraft. I wonder..." he picks through his shelves filled with gold. "This?"

Jeiah takes what looks like an ace bandage woven from gold. She inspects it. "Hmm. Looks like it's from Shadowwright. Which is good." She looks at me as if I need the explanation. "Relics from dungeons created during the Age of Discovery tend to play nice with each other. What does it—"

"Out of body experience. Blocks pain receptors."

I sigh. Dungeons are really the worst. "And we'll need that because..."

Rugnus smiles. "Well, for some reason, you seem to attract all the wrong kinds of attention in the dungeons so..."

I guess I didn't have to ask.

Jeiah considers this with a shrug. "Glyshur Bluebottle wasn't particularly malicious in life if that's what you mean, but the dungeon has a strong pattern of forcing raiders to use every form of craft possible." She looks at the wrap again. "Let's take it. And these reds." She picks up a pair of orange-red tinted sunglasses from the silver shelf. "And grab those cloud marbles from the tin shelf."

"Nice choice," Rugnus approves.

"That should cover us. Bluebottle usually presents objects that can be used for each challenge, but it's nice to be prepared. Can you budge us to Bluebottle entrance?"

"Haven't been there in a long time. I'll look up the budgeport."

Rugnus opens bluelink by separating his hands like a reverse prayer. Each gesture using bluecraft is unique. He navigates to the budge settings by snapping his hands down as if he's slamming a box on a table, though that's a shortcut. You can just scroll through all the features in the wheel of 3D icons. After a second of scrolling and a few taps, he finds the budge icon for the Bluebottle lobby and looks at us in anticipation.

"No shoes," Jeiah says. "Budge them to the exit lobby, though."

Rugnus grins. "That's right, forgot about that."

They both begin to take their shoes off, and I follow them. My days of asking for clarification about every new piece of information are over. I can just look it up on bluelink later if I'm curious —which I am.

When we're all barefoot, we budge into the lobby of Bluebottle, and for a second, I'm disoriented. Not because of the budge, but because of the strangeness of the location. It's like no other place I've been in the Loamin world. We're in a grove of gnarled oak trees, heavy with strange, silver-vined bark. Some of them appear as if the bark has been harvested, leaving behind only the naked trees. The light from above the canopy dances like it's a full moon. Beneath our feet, black sand shimmers with iridescent flecks. It's not what I expected from Bluebottle Dungeon.

I look around. "No one's here,"

"The attack," Jeiah surmises. "Everyone's life is on pause. People are grieving." She offers me a sad smile, and her blue eyes catch sparks from the shimmering sand. Somehow, seeing her in this new place is like seeing her for the first time. She just fits here.

"Never been here?" she asks.

"No, but it's beautiful."

Her smile deepens at this, and I can't help but read more into it. She wants me to enjoy this, and she's found something deeply satisfying at me being caught off guard by the atmosphere of the lobby.

Rugnus clears his throat. "Jeiahlir, which way?"

"Up."

I scan the canopy but it's too dense.

"Surprised?" Jeiah asks me.

"Continually."

Rugnus bends his neck to look at the canopy, tightening his grip on Icho.

"No, no, no," Jeiah says. "We've got to climb, no budging to the top. Ruins the experience."

Rugnus seems to transform back into his pre-Andalynn self— the same one that was thrilled at being almost eaten by Frrwelhst at the threshold of Wolfstaff—and he returns Icho to its place behind his back. "Lead the way."

Jeiah chooses a tree thick with bark. She scales past my head before I even find a handhold. There are so many good places to put my hands and feet that I catch Jeiah with ease. She seems happy about it.

"All that rock climbing lends ferrum?"

Lends ferrum? I know the phrase. Ferrum is money. Lends me money. Pays off. "Hey, I've probably climbed more trees than half of the people in Tungsten City."

"I think you're overestimating the people of Tungsten City."

I can't fight the grin that arrives on my face. "So why oaks?"

Rugnus grunts at my feet, pulling himself up closer to us. "It's Quercus Aluminius." When we both look down at him, he shrugs. "What? Hemdi told me about it once."

Jeiah returns to climbing. "Common cork oak."

"Not that common," Rugnus says. "Bluebottle modified these trees so they contained a fifth part aluminum in the bark. The budgecraft allowed him to bottle mercury in cobalt glass and store its power, creating bluelink."

"The cork was only part of the solution," Jeiah adds. "But an important part. The first keeper thought it would be appropriate. After he gained the keeper's key, he made this the default for the entrance lobby. Look, we're almost there."

Jeiah climbs up through the canopy balanced on a narrow, twisting oak limb. I pull myself through the same gap, and the ubiquitous moonlight from below comes into sharper focus. Thousands of shapes and icons, words and symbols, float in the air like someone cracked open bluelink and spilled its contents into the sky. The moving colors and shapes remind me of my dreams, of the canyon filled with my grandfather's memories.

"What is it?" Jeiah says. The look on my face must be more than wonder. It's strange how she can read my expressions.

"Just thinking."

"About what?" Her face softens even more in the light.

"Something I saw in a dream."

"It's so strange you have coherent dreams."

"We think they're Yinzar Mithriumbane's memories."

Rugnus comes between us. "Weird. No one being here."

I realize the usual crowd waiting to enter the dungeon is absent. "Jeiah was right. It's the attack. It's been less than a day.

Maybe people are still busy cleaning up, dealing with the fallout."

"No," Jeiah clarifies. "Cleanup is finished. It's deeper than that."

"They're afraid to come." Rugnus closes his eyes and rubs his temples. "Now what? We find the threshold icon?"

"Yes." Jeiah leads us over the canopy carefully and in silence. After a few minutes, there's a rustling sound in the canopy. A father and son climb through the canopy, and for a long moment, everyone just stares at each other.

I extend my arm to test strengths with the father. "I'm—"

He grabs my arm. "Fizzblood. Clayson Brightstorm. A pleasure to meet you. I'm Tredigfal Greatsleeve." He pushes his son toward me. "Ontrea, this is Clayson Brightstorm. He's a descendant of my champion, Erikzin Brightstorm."

Meaning his summation took place in Brightstorm Dungeon.

I test strengths with the boy. He must be about eleven. He's sober-faced, and his eyes are clear, ready for the tests that might await him in the dungeon—an initiate.

"What brings you to Bluebottle?" Tredigfal asks, taking in Rugnus and Jeiah.

They answer at the same time.

"Business."

"Security."

Tredigfal mentally chews this. "The attacks. You're here to check on something. Please. You must go before us. We only came today because of the initiation. I-I chose not to reschedule it. See, my brother"—the man's voice catches, tears spring to the rim of his eyes—"I lost him. He was killed yesterday. But he... uh, he went through Bluebottle like Ontrea will do today. It seemed..." The tears come in full force. Jeiah puts an arm around him.

I try not to think of the number of dead, but it's branded into my mind—459,341.

Rugnus takes a cautious step toward him and rests a hand on

his arm. "Taking your son for his summation is an honor to your brother's memory."

As we let the man endure this very personal grief, I glance at Jeiah. She's trying to keep her eyes open the best she can, but when she blinks, it releases a line of tears. She wipes it away quickly. She lost her father last year—I don't know how—and she lost her aunt and uncle during the attack. And the loss of Bluekeeper will change her life forever.

After a moment, Tredigfal says, "We'll follow you to the threshold, then go in after."

With the father and son in tow, Jeiah leads us higher into a cloud of symbols and icons that seems to touch the canopy. She gestures into the mist of light like she's cleaning off a foggy mirror.

"Got it," Jeiah says. Azure particles gather into a glowing form, the frame of a door. Jeiah reaches with her left hand and gestures counterclockwise. When she pulls back, the door frame fills with dull orange light.

"This is the threshold?" I ask.

Jeiah nods. She searches again in the nearby cloud of icons, drawing something physical from the sky. A blue and white porcelain water pitcher materializes in her hands. She approaches the threshold and pours a line of clear liquid at the base of the doorframe. Instantly, the orange light inside the door transforms into an inky drape of starlight.

"There. That should get us to the beginning of the path we need." To Tredigfal she says, "You'll have to wait for the effects of the paladin's key to wear off before entering."

"Of course. And... I hope you find answers in there about what happened at the festival."

"We will," Rugnus says.

Jeiah adopts a skeptic's face but crosses the threshold. Rugnus follows her.

I wanna say something more to Tredigfal, but it won't come out. "I—"

"I can see it on you." He smiles. "The weight of the world. You don't have to carry it alone. It's everyone's burden. If we share it."

I approach the door. "Thanks for that. Ide keep you."

"Ide keep *us*," he returns.

A lesser weight, that of this shared burden, comes with me as I cross the threshold of another dungeon. My feet sink into black sand, and clear crystal walls appear on both sides of me. Above my head, a jumble of stones that appear able to shake loose at any moment.

Jeiah awaits.

"Where's Rugnus?" I ask.

"I was going to ask you the same thing."

The blue rectangle of light from the threshold fades, leaving the dim light of the room.

"He came in before me."

"Strange." She sets the pitcher on the sand. It's absorbed as if the ground is hungry. When the pitcher is gone, she turns to me. "If I'm right, the paladin's key only sort of worked this time."

"What does that mean?"

"The keeper names a paladin. But the dungeon—the champion—is still in full control. It's like Bluebottle himself is predicting that we are here to take relics."

"But we're not?"

"No. Paladins can't take relics. There are rules. You gain access to places professional raiders and relic hunters can only dream of. If you were to take something..."

"What?"

"I don't think you would make it out alive."

"So, the point of the paladin's key is?"

"Investigation. Make sure there's no wrongdoing. Researchers sometimes use it, or coding artists. But a paladin can't be a raider at the same time."

"I guess that makes sense. Even Silverkeeper's key didn't protect him in Silverlamp."

"Exactly."

"And Rugnus?"

"I think—and I could be wrong—but Bluebottle is testing him to see if he's here to steal a relic. And there we are." Jeiah kneels where the pitcher had been. Something stirs deep in the sand. A hand bursts out and I jump backward. Jeiah grabs it, groaning as she pulls.

"A little help here," she grunts.

I regain composure as another hand bursts from the sand. I grab on, and we both pull. Rugnus' head emerges, and he coughs, clearing the sand from around his mouth and nose.

We sweep the sand away around his shoulders and chest. He wiggles free and plops to the side, gulping air. "This place is trying to kill me."

"You passed the test," Jeiah says happily.

"Couldn't skip that part?" Rugnus mutters. He gestures to me. "He seems fine."

"I tried. Usually, I can get three visitors in. Bluebottle must be… having a bad day."

"Good to know." Rugnus brushes sand from his pants. "Okay, let's get this over with. Shortcut?"

"Mmhm. See if you can find filament in the sand. Tungsten particularly."

They both start searching. "Why filament?" I kneel next to her to search.

"Bluebottle is like a series of circuits. To connect the circuits—get to the next room—you need a conductor. Each room has a different conductor or multiple conductors. I brought us to the beginning of a path that leads to the battery. The pattern should be tungsten, iron, mercury, gold. That will lead us to the room with the battery."

"Your key can't just take us there?" Rugnus asks.

"My key makes the challenges easier and allows us to jump forward maybe fifty, sixty rooms, to the beginning of the path."

Rugnus bends down and yanks on a wire. "Tungsten. Got it!"

As soon as the words leave his mouth, the stone ceiling above us cracks with the sound of a thousand jackhammers. Rugnus screams at me, but I don't hear his words. I know what to do, though. I scramble over to him and grab the thin wire. When the stone tumbles down, we're shielded by a hum of white energy. The crystal walls to each side glow blue. The stones turn into sand rushing off the shield, and bluelink symbols flare into existence around our heads.

"See," Jeiah says. "Circuit complete."

She chooses a red icon, something shaped like a pickaxe, which opens another door, and we step through. Rugnus is more hesitant than either of us, which is unlike him. The next room has the same shape, crystal walls but a higher ceiling, made from strange clouds. The air prickles with energy. A metal staff sits in the center of the room.

Rugnus rolls back his shoulders. "Okay. This one, I get." He walks to the center, wrapping his hands around the iron object with confidence. Without any other warning, huge shafts of lightning funnel into the staff. Rugnus growls for a few seconds, then everything goes dark.

I move forward, but Jeiah's arm finds me in the dark. "Wait."

When the same blue light from before flares up, it momentarily hovers around Rugnus, then pulses outward, taking residence in the crystal walls. More icons appear around us.

"Cool," he says.

Jeiah hesitates. "This is too easy."

But she gathers a few symbols of light from the top of his head and opens the next door. The next room follows the same pattern. Sand floor, crystal walls, but a different ceiling. This time the area above us is made of wall-to-wall incandescent light bulbs, but only a single light glows at a time, moving from bulb to bulb so fast the whole ceiling seems to glow at once.

In the center of the floor sits a pool of mercury.

"Clayson," Jeiah says. "You have the highest AMP score in timecraft. We've got to slow down the light bulbs. Stop the cycle on the bulb in the exact center. That one." She points to a single hanging light above the mercury pool.

"Wait, how am I the best?" I ask.

Rugnus' eyebrows rise. "Neither of us can beat a three."

For some reason, Jeiah stifles a laugh. She looks astonished. "How could you not—I mean, how do you not get that a three is extremely rare. You are the strangest Loamin I have ever met."

If she wasn't grinning, I would take offense, but she almost seems happy that I'm so clueless. I can see her report to the council now: *Clayson Brightstorm is a complete idiot.*

Rugnus pushes me toward the center of the room.

"So, I just hop into the pool of mercury?" I ask.

"You've got it," Jeiah says.

I shrug and walk into the pool, instantly understanding what I'm supposed to do. A lighted button appears near my right hand. The ceiling of light above me becomes more distinct. There's a pattern to the movement of the light. Instead of a large blur, I can follow the rotation of which bulb holds the light. The electricity stays in each bulb for only half a second, but it's noticeable now. I'll have to time it perfectly.

Looking back to Jeiah and Rugnus for more guidance, I find them almost frozen. Jeiah parts her lips. Her eyelids open and close in slow motion. They can't give me any more advice.

I focus on the light as it cycles through. Once. Twice. On the third time around, I begin counting the time between cycles. I breathe out, wait for the light to move around the room, and... one, two... I hit the button, capturing the light in the correct bulb. The mercury drains from around my feet, and the crystal walls turn blue with light.

"Circuit complete," I step over to Rugnus, hoping my cheeks aren't turning colors as both pride and embarrassment war inside of me. Jeiah glances at me, and now I'm sure I'm blushing.

Brick. Koglim was right. I like every girl I see. No, that's not it. I'm just nervous around girls. I stand straighter and push my feelings back down. Maybe if I hadn't been raised out in the middle of nowhere in the mountains, I'd have a better sense of these things.

She selects a golden icon next, leading us into the next room, where a single vial of blue glass with a simple cork rests on a pedestal.

"Is that—"

"Yeah, the battery. It's similar to the Bluebottle. The heart of this dungeon—or what we assume to be the heart of the dungeon. The battery has far less power than the Bluebottle itself."

We all circle it. Jeiah begins making complicated gestures I can't follow, beholder in hand. "Rugnus?"

"Was it him? Did Emberfence get more of these, farm the object out somehow?"

She shakes her head. "It appears that's not the case."

"What do you mean?" Rugnus demands.

"From what I can tell, he was the last person here over twenty years ago. He took a single copy of the relic after a successful challenge and left the dungeon. That's the best I can do."

"So, you can't be one hundred percent sure?" I ask.

"I mean... to get irrefutable evidence, we have to try to take the battery. Might as well melt ourselves. We're guests. Emberfence must have worked through the whole dungeon to get here over a few days. That kind of expertise and sacrifice... we can't duplicate it."

"This was all for nothing?" Rugnus cries. "Can't tell if he did or if he didn't."

"I'm telling you," Jeiah says, her voice still cool and collected but deeper and more menacing as well, "I'm certain he didn't take one. Sira led us astray." She raises her eyebrows, directed at me.

"She did say it would be a dead-end," I offer, earning a sharp look from Rugnus.

Rugnus and Jeiah step away from the vial talking over one

another, but I hear something. Though it's only a whisper, it drowns them out.

Take it.

I try to shake it from my head, but it grows louder and louder.

Take it.

I shake my head, but the message returns repeated faster and louder.

Take it. Take it. Take it!

I reach out my hand and lift the vial off the pedestal.

The voice is gone. In its place, a low rumble builds at the edges of the room. The pedestal crumbles to sand. Horrified, Jeiah looks from the vial in my hand to my face. "What did you do?"

"I—it's like it wanted—there was a voice."

Rugnus growls. "There's always a voice!"

The floor shakes under us. At the edges of the room, the sand begins to move.

The look on Jeiah's face is something I haven't seen from her. Disappointment? Fear? Dread? Her voice seems unnaturally low when she finally says, "We're not getting out of here alive."

WONDER AT THE WORLD

THE SAND FLOOR rises in a wave. Rugnus rolls toward me and grabs the back of my arm to steady himself. "It's always something with you!" he yells over the sound of the groaning floor.

Jeiah extends both arms for balance. "What were you thinking?"

Another swell brings us within reach of the ceiling. To keep my balance, I squat like I'm on a surfboard. The sand moves up and down, threatening to smash us into the ceiling with every crest.

The rumble of the floor forces me to shout. "What should we do?"

Jeiah grabs my hand to stabilize herself. "Keep you out of dungeons."

The sand drops so abruptly, we all fall to our knees. As the next wave comes, I jump to my feet and reach for Jeiah, but she's already moving to a crouch.

Rugnus stands. For some reason, he looks relaxed. "Everything always seems..." The wave of sand comes to rest at its lowest level. White crystal walls fill with blue light. Somehow, we've connected the circuit. Bluelink symbols and icons appear over our heads. Confused, we all watch the floor as if something will jump through and grab us.

"...to work out when Clayson's around," Rugnus finishes.

"I don't get it," Jeiah says. "There should be some challenge. That can't be it. Bluebottle wouldn't just give us this relic."

Rugnus waves two arms over me like he's revealing the prize in a game show. "I give you, Clayson Brightstorm. Prince of Whurrimduum. Peerless of Tungsten and Lead. Master of Copper. Dungeons give way."

Jeiah holds out her hand for the battery. "I guess we take a closer look."

I pass it to her.

A lemon-yellow magnifying glass icon descends from the whirlwind of bluelink odds and ends floating over us. She holds the vial up to the light with one hand and makes a few complicated gestures with the other.

Rugnus steps closer to her. "And?"

"Lagnar Emberfence hasn't been in this room for decades. No more batteries are in play. This was a dead end."

Rugnus throws his hands in the air. "Why would Sira give us the battery?"

He's not directing his words to either of us, but I answer him. "It's not like she gave it to us. We took it. But it must mean something. Especially since she couldn't tell us about it."

"I can at least authenticate this one." Jeiah gives me back the vial but takes the one Sira had given us—from her pocket. She holds it up to the same magnifying glass icon, gestures, and nods. "Belongs to Lagnar Emberfence." She gives a disgusted grunt. "They've updated his name. It's now Lagnar *Bluekeeper*. He has control of this dungeon."

Rugnus growls and shakes his head. "I'm not calling him that. How do we get out of here? Need to get this information to Andalynn and her allies on the council."

A doorway appears that can only be the exit. Bluebottle knows we have what we came for. There's no place to put the battery back down because the pedestal is gone, so instead, I set it on the ground and move toward the door.

Jeiah puts a hand on my chest, pushing just enough to make me aware of her strength. "I think Bluebottle wanted you to have that."

"I didn't come for a relic, especially not one as powerful as that. I came for information."

Rugnus' eyes widen. "But... yeah, okay. Just don't tell Koglim. He'll melt us if he finds out we could have taken it. And while we're at it..." he holds his hand out to Jeiah.

"What? Lagnar's battery? You want to leave it?"

"They used it in the attack," he says.

"We don't know that. And it's still evidence."

"If Emberfence—"

"Bluekeeper," Jeiah corrects him.

He shakes his head as if he's been slapped. "*Not* calling him that. Anyway, if he knows you have it—"

"I'm sure he does. Maybe he even recorded this very raid, but I'm keeping it. I can do some location traces on it. See if I can connect him back. Find out when it switched hands. Sira seemed to think she was giving us a clue about the attack. It's got to be connected."

"Fine. You two do that. I'll go update Andalynn."

As he reaches the door, I say, "I should go with you. Speak to the council."

Rugnus looks at the ground where I sat down the battery. "That's the least of our worries. We just need to hold the council together and stop them from dethroning your family."

He marches through the exit.

Jeiah whistles. "That's funny."

"What?"

"Rugnus—the poster boy for Tungsten City, for the Principles —trying to keep the monarchy intact."

"Hadn't thought of it."

Her mouth quirks upward. "Yeah?"

"The cities are more alike than different. At least to me. Andalynn and Rugnus seem to look past things. But... my perspective
—I don't know..."

"If you're truly a neutral party, it's more important than ever."

I risk a glance, and just like that, I'm transfixed by everything
about her. Branches of her magenta hair steal the light from the
floating icons. The brown of her perfect skin deepens. Her lips
part slightly, and she glances toward the door.

"Have you seen the exit lobby for this dungeon?" she asks.

I shake my head. "No, why?"

"I think you're going to like it. Close your eyes."

"What?"

She tilts her head and stares. "Just do it."

There's a flutter somewhere in my stomach. Koglim may be
wrong. I may not like every girl, but I'm starting to like this one
—a lot.

She takes my hand, and we walk through the door. I can tell
through my eyelids that it's much brighter here.

"Okay, take your shoes"—she pushes them into my chest—
"and open your eyes."

I had almost forgotten they were waiting at the exit. I open
my eyes.

There's always something new about this world. I should be
used to it, but I'm not. I could explore every place in the two
remaining Loamin cities, every building, every hole, every
dungeon, for the rest of my life and still find something new to
wonder over.

We're still underground, but it's like I've stepped out into an
Irish countryside—minus a sky—filled with neon magic and
strange livestock. The distant borders are made from black
stone, but beneath our feet is pure quartz, rolled out in mounds
and flats, perfect for the roaming animals. It goes on at least a
mile. Bushes and trees dot the ground, but the quartz tricks my
eyes into believing the vegetation is floating. The land is
divided by traditional half walls made from piles of stone—

which only adds to the feeling of being in a farming wonderland. In the distance, waterfalls of black sand cascade out of the walls.

Beasts—both types I can name and many I can't—roam within the partitioned areas of quartz countryside.

"Wow," I say.

"It's strange without a crowd."

Familiar disbelief comes over me. This world came under attack. So many people are dead. I can't really process it. But this, this I can process. "This place is amazing."

"I wish I had your eyes," Jeiah said. "Seeing everything for the first time."

"It's a bit overwhelming, to be honest. But it's one of the things I love about this world."

"It's interesting you have to make the distinction. Where I come from, there's only one world."

We walk from the door, shoes in hand, down a narrow road between walls. On one side, something like bison, but with iridescent horns, descend a hill and come to the edge, huffing and stamping. A few calves cling to their mothers, but otherwise the beasts wander. Many are taller than the wall, which means they're taller than me by a couple feet. On the other side of the wall, fuchsia-colored eyes follow us from a strange animal's hiding spot in a stretch of brush a stone's throw away.

Jeiah says, "It's not that typical for them to approach anyone."

The closest bison dips its head and horns over the wall. Cautiously, I set down my shoes and step toward the beast. The herd seems to grow louder at this, and a few other bison nudge their way toward the fence.

"I wouldn't—"

I rest my palm flat against the fur between the bison's horns, and it issues a low, pleasant grumble. I glance at Jeiah, unable to keep a grin from my face. "Reminds me of my goats. Bigger, but…" I draw Jeiah closer. "You try."

She takes a breath through her nose, shakes her head, and

walks over. "They seem to like you." Slowly, she raises her hand and places it next to mine. Our fingers edge against each other.

I gulp. Does she hear me? "See. They must like you too."

Her expression levels off. She removes her hand. "Why did you agree to take Sira's knife? You didn't have to. I mean, she forced me to keep her secret."

This catches me off guard. "I... it's not like I trust Sira." I test the words in my mouth. They don't seem to be exactly the truth. "Or maybe I do... somewhat. It seemed strange she wanted me to hide the knife. And she didn't wanna know where I would keep it. That says something, right? I mean, a season ago, she had this crazy idea—control everyone and everything with mithrium, and maybe she could have, but after her dad was killed in Silverlamp..."

"Something changed?"

"Something changed. She accepted it when I told her about the mithrium shield. To her, protecting and controlling are the same."

"How did you know what to do with the mithrium? Something in the dreams?"

The intensity of her question stops me in my tracks. I close my mouth, considering how much I should share, thinking all the way back to when Rugnus first told me Loamin don't dream. This is what happened with Sira. She used me to find out about the mithrium. I don't want that to happen again.

But Jeiah's reaction to my silence is unexpected. "Sorry. I tend to do that. I just need to understand... everything. I make better decisions that way."

"Brig's kind of like that. Isn't he? Except with him—"

"—he wants to understand objects. How they're forged. For me, it's—"

"—people," I finish.

"Yeah."

Jeiah's not Sira. She's not. She's Brig's sister, a kid I like and trust. And she's a paladin. They're known for their honesty and passion for the truth. But it's her reluctance to push me that strips away my fears.

I answer the original question. "At the end of the Mithrium War, my grandfather searched for a way to either destroy the mithrium or to use it to create something."

I pause here, trying to filter out parts of the story that will make me sound crazy. Jeiah's forehead creases. I can see the questions move through her eyes, and it takes an effort for her to keep silent. When I can't quite find the next part to tell her she says, "There's something else to that."

"Is it crazy if I told you he got advice from some dragon bones and an underground living mountain?"

"Dragon bone research is becoming less and less of a taboo. But an azdeth…."

"Yeah, an azdeth. A trollslayer."

She seems more eager for the conversation now. "They were an ancient race. Each one, a mass of stone and energy. They lived off lithic trolls and wormkind. Or maybe the energy from the world itself. But they're extinct."

"My grandfather must have found one. It's in his memories—the dreams I'm seeing."

She touches her lips. "You know what? I have something I want to show you. Put your shoes on. Let's get out of here." We both slip on our shoes. She takes my hand and leads me—nearly at a run—through the narrow roads. Every thought I have abandons me. Her enthusiasm fuels my sense of curiosity.

"Are you going to tell me where we're going?" I ask.

"I'll just show you."

She takes us right to the exit, where two of the stone walls come together, forming a low archway. The moment we pass under it, we find ourselves in a dark cave, lighted by groups of crystals sprouting from the walls. "We can budge now," Jeiah says. "I'll do it."

She hasn't let go of my hand and must have a budgecraft

object because I feel a weight against my calves, the added gravity, and the momentary wave of nausea.

We appear in a forest of pine trees. Their scent washes over me, dragging me back to the surface, to my cabin. But Jeiah seems fine; none of the surface effects attack her. "Seems like the surface. Where are we?"

"Back in Tungsten City, within the apex." With the same hurry in her step, she pulls me along a gravel path. At the end of the path, I can already see the glimmer of a metal and glass structure. "You *do* know what the apex is?" she teases. "Or do I have to explain?"

"It's the area directly under the brightstorm, so it gets the largest amount of light and power. Hemdi and Winta's old flower nursery was built in the apex."

"Good job, Clay."

She's teasing me. She doesn't know it, but in the few days I spent with my mom before leaving Geum Ide for good, she called me Clay. For a moment, I wanna tell Jeiah about how Dad and Ara healed the brightstorm to create a beautiful, craftless settlement in the middle of a toxic jungle.

Instead, I say, "From what I know, the proximity influences what type of plant life can grow. In Tungsten City, the citizens and years of tradition helped reserve the apex for animals and plants, coppercraft and tincraft."

Her laugh sends a thrill down my spine. "That sounds straight off bluelink."

I shrug with a laugh. "It probably is."

Light from the brightstorm reaches us as we emerge from the trees. "Here we are."

A large stone and glass obelisk awaits us, heavy with transparent, coppery bubbles frozen on its surface.

"It's a mindhive," she explains. "Have you heard of them?"

"No."

"Good. This just might work."

We follow the gravel path to the obelisk. The closer we get, the stranger the monument appears. The dark stone obelisk rests on a foundation of thick, blue glass. Geometric pieces of copper grow like fungus on the stone.

Jeiah brings me to the base of the obelisk and nods to the mass of gnarled metal. "They embed the stone with the consciousness of great animals so that we could interact with them on bluelink. This is one of the oldest."

"So, you spoke to one?"

"It's hard to tell. It's more like inspiration, whispers. Some people don't believe it at all."

"I've experienced a lot of things I wouldn't have believed until a few months—a season ago."

"That's what makes you unique."

My breathing quickens. "Is unique good or bad?"

Her eyes narrow. "You know everyone thinks of you as this mysterious person."

"They do?"

She scoffs. "Yeah, they think you're mysterious"—she twinkles her fingers—"and powerful. Some even say you're dangerous. Wraithspit, my own investigation uncovered a handful of things that aren't even possible."

"Like what happened in the dungeon?"

Her fingers find her lip again. "Yeah. But I'm not sure anyone has you figured out." My stomach flutters. "Place your hand on the mindhive. It's said to hold the consciousness of an azdeth."

Curious, I do it. But nothing happens.

Jeiah clears her throat. "They say it responds best to… strong emotion."

Before I know it, the words tumble out of my mouth. "How do we do that? I mean, uh…"

She scoots closer and rests her hand on the copper, half-covering mine.

A jolt of electricity dances through my arm. "Did you feel that?"

Her eyes widen. She nods.

"Is that supposed to—"

Arcs of blue energy flow from the obelisk into both of us. I squeeze my eyes shut to block out the light, as the ground drops beneath me. When I dare to open my eyes, Jeiah and I are floating in an entirely different place. The massive space is the shape of the obelisk, just larger.

I keep hold of Jeiah's hand so we don't float apart. "Where are we?"

"I—" The look on her face tells me this has never happened to her. "I don't know. Maybe inside the obelisk... or inside bluelink itself. This is incredible."

A voice fills the whole space. *Yes, good, good Yinzar spawn, yes.*

I know the cadence of that voice, though it's lower-pitched than the being my grandfather spoke with. Maybe it's a different azdeth. If that's a thing.

"You know Yinzar?" I ask, though there's no one direction to send my words.

Good, good. Good. Yinzar is yes and good.

"He spoke with one of your kind not long ago."

Yes. Deep and hidden is yes. Good.

"Then," Jeiah says, "there is still an azdeth alive."

Evil name. Evil and no. Azdeth sounding is no, no, no.

The room rumbles.

Spawn must not speak evil and no.

Jeiah lets go of me. "How do I name you?"

We are GOODYES.

"Is there still a Goodyes under the mountain?" Jeiah asks.

Good are far. Yes, and yes, almost beneath the ice. Yinzar was good, and yes, to find the deep and hidden. That Goodyes shared this event with me.

I'm still looking for some source of the speaker, but if Jeiah is right, that this ancient beast only uploaded its consciousness to bluelink, I won't find its physical form. "Yinzar asked the other Goodyes questions about the mithrium, and—"

The light. The creation. The connecting of all and of one. Neither good and yes nor no and evil.

Jeiah looks as confused as I feel. "What do you mean?"

I tire. Good, good to speak again. But to sleep is good, and good, and good and yes, and yes, and yes.

Pulses of electricity crackle from the interior wall toward us, blinding. The hair on my arm tingles with energy, and suddenly we're back on the outside of the obelisk.

Jeiah is breathless. "What was that? I mean, I know it was the azdeth, uh—Goodyes—but I've never... this has never happened. How did you—"

My whole body is buzzing with power. "I don't know. That was... intense,"

She squeezes my hand.

"That voice. It was just like from my dream, from Yinzar's memories. The Goodyes told Yinzar the mithrium couldn't be destroyed. It could be used to make something."

"Have you asked your sister or another silvermage to help access the dreams directly? Is that what a dreampick is?"

"It didn't work. But yes, I was trying to access my dreams. I've tried everything. I think Yinzar wanted me to find Mithriumbane, but I don't know what I'll find there. Part of me thinks I shouldn't look. But it seems like the right thing to do."

"I don't know. Maybe you are the only one that can be trusted with the mithrium. If it's in that dungeon. And if he didn't destroy it. If decoding the dreams can help you track it down..."

Something warm stirs inside at her faith in me. I wanna hold it in my hands, like a physical object, a relic that could light my way forward, but as quickly as it comes, the light fades. "Sometimes I feel like—I don't know— like this world is not mine, and I'm going to mess it up."

"Here's a clue for you, Clay: it's already messed up. If you haven't noticed, we've been misusing the mithrium since we found it. And even without mithrium, well, look what we just did to ourselves at StoneYoke. Maybe there's no one better than you to figure this all out. Sometimes I can't solve an investigation because I become too close to it. Having an outside perspective can be good."

There's a noise in the forest, and we turn to look. A dozen figures in thick woolen uniforms step from under the trees. Behind them, my sister's royal guards in their lead vests stand at attention. A single mech swivels its arm upward in a greeting, Winta in the cockpit.

"Brick!" Jeiah says.

"It's just my escort to Whurrimduum."

"No, you don't understand." She drops my hand. "I-I gave the council everything I found about you. Everything. I had already been investigating you for months. They could use it against you."

I run headlong into her fear like it's a stone wall. What did she tell the council? "Like what? You could come with me? Put things in context."

"It's not that I couldn't... but I need to keep working our leads about this battery. And if I stay around you much longer, I won't be able to be as objective about you either."

"No, that's... good." The second I say it, I feel like an idiot. Good? As in good she turned over a bunch of surveillance on me to the council. Good I make her feel less objective? What's wrong with me?

"Good and yes," she says in a low voice, then grimaces. "Sorry, not funny."

"Sure it is," I say with a laugh, hoping she missed my stupidity. "I'll catch up with you after"—I gesture to the knights—"whatever happens in Whurrimduum."

She gives me a generous smile, and I can't help but smile back. "You can't get rid of me that easily. Check in when you can. If I find anything, I'll send an update."

"Okay." Suddenly my breath catches in my throat. She just potentially incriminated me. Why am I still thinking about her lips? And why did Koglim have to say that I liked every girl I see?

I don't. That makes no sense. But still, standing here with Jeiah, I feel like a complete idiot.

She casts a sidelong glance at the soldiers and the mech, raises her eyebrows at me. "Okay." She budges.

The sound of hydraulics and metal against metal interrupts my thoughts. Winta, atop her Behemoth mech, is grinning like she just won a supercharged sports car in a game show. The protective energy shield surrounding her drops and her heavy music—with strange hints of steel drum—blasts me.

I approach them slowly, waiting for Winta's comment about Jeiah. I'm not disappointed.

"Ooh, maybe you guys could do a double royal wedding? With Rugnus and Andalynn."

I'm about to hurl my own insult, but she adjusts her position, and I'm reminded of the imminent birth of her baby. When I say nothing in response, she frowns at me and puts her shield back up. I probably should have insulted her instead of treating her with kid gloves.

The two dozen knights stand at attention like they're prepared for a battle. A buzz of shieldcraft tingles over my skin. Something's not right. What information did Jeiah send to the council? I should have asked her directly.

One of the knights hands me an aluminum coin, and without warning, we are in the royal residence in Whurrimduum. I've only spent a little time here with Andalynn in the last month, as busy as she is with her work, but it's enough to know she has transformed the royal castlestack—or ordered others to do it on her behalf.

It's a castle in every sense of the word, and somehow more. Stone-hewn walls, suits of golden armor, hearths, tapestries, and royal banners with the Brightstorm crest hanging from the ceiling. Sections of the wall have been cut out, letting in additional light, plant life grows everywhere. It's a transformational signal that my sister is in charge.

I give the knight back the coin and ask about my sister.

"Her Highness, Queen Everbloom is in council with the keepers. You are to await instructions in her suite." We turn a corner,
and oaken doors block the way. "Here you are."

Winta snaps open her shield. "I think Hemdi's in there somewhere. He'll update you about the... situation."

"You make it sound like things have gotten worse."

"Much worse," she glances at the knights, and I get the
sudden impression I'm not here as a guest. This is a show of
strength.

I march through the line of knights and pull open one of the
oaken doors. The room speaks even more of Andalynn than the
hallway. A light mist covers the floor. One vine-covered wall leads
away to the balcony. White flowering plants rest in large silver
pots. A metallic mirror spans one section of the room, made from
an alloy of silver and gold called electrum. It's the same craft
Wolfstaff's son used to lure me into the party during my summation. I pass it quickly but catch shadows moving about and
bluelink messaging icons floating around in the shadows.

Someone calls my name from the balcony. It's Hemdi. I find
him watering a plant by hand. Vor, the council's Dura servant, is
with him. "Don't they have tincraft that can..." I trail off. "Sorry, I
didn't mean to—"

"It is fine, Clayson, my friend. Everyone is being very careful
around me. It would make me happy if things could go back to
normal. And as for this plant"—he holds up a watering can made
from tungsten— "it needs special watering using shieldcraft,
which I still have a decent rating for."

"I know I've said this to you, but I feel like—"

"It was your fault I lost my tincraft? I know. But you are
wrong. Let's move on. I have important news."

Vor steps aside as I move toward the balcony. The castlestacks
of Whurrimduum look more like a city-sized collection of children's blocks, towers upon towers, stone upon stone upon stone.
The uniformity only gives way at the tops of some of the towers,
where the white light of Whurrimduum's brightstorm plays over

pyramid roofs and—in the low-lying market areas recently restored to new life—reflective fabric tents and glass awnings.

"There's a certain beauty to Whurrimduum," I say. "I see why my sister loves it."

He nods absently. "Clayson, this morning, Emberfence has been accepted as keeper and earned a place on the council of ten."

"I'm aware of that."

"That's not the worst part. You've been summoned to come before the council."

I glance at Vor. Was he able to get my request to the council? "Vor did you..."

Vor deepens his stare at the ground. "I *did* speak with members of the council on your behalf, but—"

"It's not what you think," Hemdi says. "You're not here to make your request about the mines. There's talk about a cast to end your sister's time on the throne. They could strip her of her title."

I shake my head. "Of course."

"That's not all. Rugnus and Andalynn said Emberfence—Blue-keeper—has evidence that you caused the attack. They're bringing you before the council sometime after daychange."

CAST THE TRUTH

An hour later, the brightstorm abruptly switches to night. I could get word from the keepers at any time—Andalynn is still deliberating with them over the details of our meeting. Vor will be my escort, though for the moment, he and a few caterers busily set out a table of steaming food. Automated serving trays hover in the corners, ready to serve us, laden with more food than we can eat, even after Koglim gets here.

"Vor," I say, "this is a lot of food. I don't know that we can eat all of it."

He keeps his eyes glued to the floor. "This is the traditional variety of food for an evening meal. Many of your friends are here."

"Well, you're making it feel like my last meal."

Hemdi shrugs. "They set a meal out twice a day, no matter who eats it. Whatever isn't eaten Andalynn has budged to the nullhouses."

"At least that's something."

Koglim and Winta push through the large doors to the main room. I sense something off with Winta. She moves behind Koglim, her eyes darting to Hemdi. Koglim's resting smile is gone. In its place, his jaw is slack, and tears threaten at the brink of his eyes.

Hesitant, I step toward them. "Hey."

Koglim only nods, his eyelids half-closed.

"Koglim," Hemdi asks, "what is it?"

I've seen Koglim excited, angry, giddy, awed, but never this. The angle of his mouth speaks of desperation and shock. "Three of my team..." It's all he manages to say before his face clenches in grief. He turns to the reflective wall, but the second he finds his reflection, he angles away.

Rugnus and Andalynn appear on the other side of the room in mid-conversation.

"...that could work. We—" Andalynn freezes.

Rugnus scans everyone's faces. "What happened?"

My eyes stay fixed on Koglim. The only thing I can think of is his raiding team. Three of them must have been killed in the attack.

Winta rests a hand on Koglim's beefy forearm. "This sucks, Koglim," she says. And what else can any of us say more than that? Sorry? It will be okay? None of those things can bring any of us comfort. We need to find the people behind this and bring them to justice.

"I'm okay," Koglim tries. "Everyone's lost someone. I'm not special."

Andalynn moves to his side next, then Rugnus. "It's okay to mourn our friends. How's the memorial coming together?"

"It's gonna be beautiful," Koglim says through tears. "Rugnus, your mom's work on the pillars is gonna have people dropping bricks. Whole place looks peerless, to be honest."

"She's good at these kinds of things." Rugnus jerks his head toward the food. "So... Vor's got food set up. Could you..."

Koglim sniffs. He wipes his eyes. "Is that pork roast?"

In the next room, we find seats on tall palm-woven stools under an aluminum dome. Vor hands us each a serving plate and sets the food trays suspended in the air between us. Koglim uses tongs to gouge a chunk of pork roast from the sizzling slab of meat hanging in the air.

"So, what are we going to do about Clayson's inquisition?" Koglim asks.

Rugnus hesitates, glancing at Andalynn. "The council holds three types of meetings. A Casting is used for typical day to day things. An Inquisition is where they sit in judgment. Your meeting *was* an Inquisition, but Andalynn...convinced them to change it to a Gathering."

"Isn't that good?" I ask, taking a slice of pork roast from Koglim. I try to ignore the slight tremor in my hand.

"Maybe," says Andalynn. "These are more open, but..."

Rugnus sets his plate down on his lap. "Potentially more dangerous."

Something about his tone makes me wish it had stayed an inquisition. "What do you mean?"

Andalynn shifts in her chair. "There's no one agenda. Only a topic."

"The power of the Brightstorm family," Rugnus adds.

The table goes quiet as we process the implications. Andalynn stuck her neck out for me, but now we're both on the chopping block.

Andalynn fixes her gaze on the ceiling. "Past Gatherings have led to some major policy changes—usually for the worst. They could review my status as queen; they could banish you to the surface or sentence you to Keelcrawl; they could declare war on Tungsten City. Who knows? When there is a consensus among them about what to vote on, they will vote."

"But," Rugnus says, "in an inquisition, you're not allowed to speak in your own defense or have anyone with you. That's what Lagnar wanted. In a Gathering, you can both speak and have council—meaning I'm going with you, Clayson. They will present evidence about your powers. I can't address the council, but I can give you advice and answer your questions."

Rugnus looks pale like he's in a cold sweat. He is the poster child for Tungsten City. How much can he even know about council politics? I turn to Andalynn. "Can't you do it?"

"Brick," Rugnus says, "thanks for the vote of confidence."

"Sorry, Andalynn has more experience with—"

"She's the queen, fizzblood," Winta adds. "She can't be your council."

"Winta's right," Andalynn says. "Besides, I will already be there."

Rugnus pushes a few yellow tomatoes around on his plate. "By my count, this could end with Andalynn off the throne permanently and Clayson sitting frozen in Keelcrawl prison."

Winta scoffs. "They haven't even charged him with anything. Just because Lagnar says he has some evidence against him—"

Andalynn holds up both of her hands. "A Gathering of the council can turn from a friendly discussion into accusations very, very easily. And lately, they've agreed enough to cast their opinions over my objections. With a few new keepers in the mix, I can't predict what will happen."

A wave of nausea rolls through me. "Jeiah said she turned over all her research."

"Ide keep you then," Winta says. "It's bound to be thorough."

Rugnus drops his plate on one tray and takes a steaming broth bowl from another, scowling. "Let's just hope we stop you from getting yourself incarcerated."

"Rugnus," Andalynn says. "That doesn't help. Clayson, tell the truth and don't do anything rash. The best we can hope for is that they don't move toward any decisions. They like to hear themselves speak. Let them. And I don't care what Lagnar presents; you didn't cause this attack. The council will see at least that much. Most of them have no love for Lagnar."

A bell chimes.

Koglim swallows what he's chewing. "Is that the summons?"

Andalynn nods. She's gone pale. "Vor, can you take Rugnus and Clayson to the council room?"

"It's my pleasure." Vor places a hand over his heart.

Andalynn looks me in the eye, takes my hand. "I won't be able to speak during the council, but I'll be there." She budges out of the room.

Vor sweeps a long arm toward the doors to the suite. "This way, young sirs. The rest of you are invited to remain here."

As we leave through one of the suite's many doors, a weight settles on my chest. My mouth goes dry. I must find a way to turn this council in my favor. Whatever hope I had to ask them about getting access to the mines is gone. Everything is focused on finding the person responsible for this attack.

Vor leads us down a hallway and up a set of palatial stairs. It's a wing of the castle I've never been in. After another few turns, we come to a wall made of a gray, flaky rock. A million tiny chips have fallen to the base of the wall leaving the hallway looking like it needs to be swept.

Rugnus issues a deep sigh. "The Knight's Wall."

"It's shale?" I ask.

"Indeed," Vor says. "Present yourselves."

Rugnus rolls back his sleeve and presses his forearm and his open palm against the shale. The flakey rock crumbles around his arm. He leverages his body against the wall to keep his arm steady. After a few seconds, his whole arm is engulfed in the shale.

"Your turn, Prince Brightstorm," Vor says.

The knot in my stomach tightens. What if the council sends me to Keelcrawl? Or what if I accidentally incriminate my sister? Or my friends? I would rather have the inquisition; the council could only vote on *my* fate.

"Clayson, come on," Rugnus says. "It needs both of us."

I roll up my right sleeve and press my arm against the shale. Sharp barbs of cool stone press into my skin until my arm is wholly contained. It occurs to me that it's a very literal way to test strengths.

Rugnus grits his teeth, and I'm about to ask what's wrong

when a sharp prick shoots the length of my forearm. I try to pull free, but I only manage to strain my elbow.

"Please restrain your reaction," Vor says.

"A little warning would have been nice. What's this for?"

"The council room is maybe the most impenetrable place under granite," Rugnus says. "And you know Whurrimduum's love of tightened security."

"Not as well as you."

He shoots me a look that I don't respond to.

The center of the wall splits, and a passageway opens. Our arms are released.

Vor bows slightly. "Now that your strengths have been verified, I will guide you through the wall."

The passageway is narrow, cut from the same shale. Grit and dust crunch beneath our feet. There are dozens of turn-offs, but Vor moves quickly through the hall and down a flight of stairs.

My insides are tied in knots. I could read my heart rate from a breath. Rugnus places a hand on my back. It's a very Andalynn thing to do. She must be softening him a bit.

I shake my head. "What should I... is there anything I can say to them?"

"Forget Emberfence. Just tell the truth."

"Transparency barely works in Tungsten City. This is Whurrimduum."

"I hear you. That's why we can't let them cast their voices to end the monarchy. Andalynn's the only thing holding this world together right now." We turn another corner, and Rugnus' breathing deepens into a steady growl. "If Emberfence wasn't on the council, we could call for an inquisition against him. Council immunity is a bunch of trollbrick."

"Which members of the council still support Andalynn?" I'm trying to be logical, but my head is pounding.

"Chainkeeper, Tinkeeper, and Brightkeeper usually cast in our favor. Hardkeeper, Sternkeeper, and Emberfence—I hate calling him Bluekeeper, but technically that's how we have to address him in here—those three will definitely cast against you or her no matter what."

I stop walking for a second. I might know how to get out of this and save Andalynn at the same time.

"What is it?" Rugnus says.

"The council members gain their positions as a result of the difficulty of raiding their dungeons, correct?"

"Right,"

"So, like Chainkeeper. He's the highest of all the dungeons and the strongest of the ten Council members, so he gets to cast ten votes. Then the next guy nine, then—"

"Right, right. And?"

A grin reaches my face. The knot in my stomach loosens. "I have an idea."

"What do you mean? Run it by me."

Vor stops ahead of us. When his face comes into the light, he's smiling and blinking. "We have arrived. May Ide keep you in truth and justice."

"Trust me," I whisper to Rugnus.

His expression says he'd rather kiss a wraith.

We step past Vor and into a large chamber. My sister sits on an alabaster throne at the far end. The throne is flanked by two great armadillos, rolled into protective armor. These are the council guardians. They supposedly never leave the room, which makes me wonder how they keep them fed. I'm not sure I wanna know.

In a horseshoe shape, descending from Andalynn's position, each keeper stands or sits upon a lighted dais. There are no desks or other obstructions to prevent them from jumping down and attacking me, and most hold a single relic—probably as some form of intimidation. Below each of them, hanging from the stone, are the flags of the dungeons they represent.

Emberfence, representing Bluebottle, stands in blue light. The keeper of Shatterkeg, in orange and brown. In purple light stands the keeper of Chainbearer Dungeon, the man who ignored our incursion into Keelcrawl prison to free my mom. The last time I saw him, we were standing in the wreckage of the StoneYoke, when he charged Jeiah to investigate the attack. The man who lost eight minutes.

I've heard my sister say all their names, I've seen their pictures on bluelink, but I have never seen them all together. Across the top of the horseshoe, washed in green light, the keeper of Tinseer sits either meditating or asleep. Even sitting down, she's one of the shortest Loamin I've ever seen. Sira had introduced us at the Keeper's Social. Tinkeeper had thought I looked like Dad, though I had been trying to stay hidden at the time.

I recognize the young keeper of Brightstorm Dungeon. Like me, he is a descendant of Erikzin Brightstorm, but his lineage— the second-born—keeps Brightstorm Dungeon, while Dad's descendants have cared for the kingdom. He looks nervous, sweating, and pale, hair tied back in a long blonde braid. Slight bags under his eyes make him seem older, but he's younger than me and one of our allies on the council.

Somewhat center, on opposite sides of the horseshoe, I find the two swing votes—Ogrekeeper in golden light and Foilkeeper in dark brown. These dungeons don't always cast with my sister, but she tends to win when they do. But both have been replaced with new keepers. Wildcards.

Rugnus and I ascend a few stairs, not quite coming to the level of the keepers. But we face them. I don't like having the armadillos at my back, and it must be by design to make visitors understand their place before the council. Behind me, Andalynn's clear voice echoes across the room. She sits on a balcony opposite the council.

"I lend the floor to the Council of Ten Keepers. May Ide keep you in the light of justice, truth, and compassion." There are murmurs from some of the keepers.

"She added that last word," Rugnus whispers. "Not a good time to break tradition." The soft smile on his face gives me a sense of his approval of her small rebellion.

The lighted platforms dim, but a strong spotlight settles over the two of us. It's bright enough to transform the room and its occupants into silhouettes. I squint against it. We're on stage now. A voice I recognize emanates from the top left of the horseshoe. It's Chainkeeper.

"The council recognizes Clayson Brightstorm and Rugnus of Tungsten City as his council. These are weighty times. Strange times. Suspicions abound concerning your powers, Clayson Brightstorm. You are called to defend yourself. As it was Bluekeeper and Hardkeeper that called this Gathering, I leave it to them to present evidence for our review."

Somewhere to the side of Lagnar—a voice pierces through the darkness. It's the keeper I offended at the festival. I hear the accusation of his tone the moment he speaks. "Thank you, Chainkeeper. Clayson Brightstorm represents a grave danger to this council and to all Loamin. He and the Queen continually engage in a campaign of secrets and misdirection about the reality of this boy's power. Last Gem, he created a shield using mithrium, a shield thought to be powerful enough that the combined strength all the Knights of Shale could not break through."

I shake my head. "The information about the mithrium shield was already presented to the—"

"The insolence of this boy," Hardkeeper snaps. "The fact that you think it reasonable to interrupt a member of this council is astounding. Keep your mouth shut until it is your turn to speak."

A few of the other keepers to my right—Lagnar among them—call out something about formality and process.

Hardkeeper speaks again. "I yield the floor to Lagnar Bluekeeper. The evidence he revealed to me earlier today is so shocking that it must be heard. Lagnar."

"Thank you kindly, Hardkeeper." Emberfence drawls. "Y'all got the large quantity of info about Clayson Brightstorm from the office of the paladin, Jeiahlir. The sheer volume was so much that

I doubt anyone has gotten all the way through it. I'll try to sum up.

"Basically, this young man—well, he's intent on destroying our way of life. His power is unmatched. I'd wager that's the kind of person who could have attacked the StoneYoke festival. Bunch of us saw *some* of his recorded exploits in Silverlamp. His incursion into the dreamwell is... well, unsettling. It pushed Silverlamp Dungeon out of the council. The first time in seventy-five years. I believe that right there should cause us to ban him from every dungeon under granite."

"Outrageous," one of the keepers—Sternkeeper—high on the horseshoe shouts. "There must be a cause to ban someone from the dungeons."

Emberfence is undeterred. "Let me just finish, please and thank you. We all saw what happened in Silverlamp. But as I've said, Jeiahlir inundated us with info. Let me just highlight something that you maybe haven't yet seen. If I may, this is from Clayson's summation. And while I know that such a thing is prohibited, we gave authority to the paladin, and she used it to great effect. Watch."

The spotlight falls away from us. Inside the horseshoe, a massive hologram blooms from the floor. It's me inside Wolfstaff Dungeon. This is the moment in the dungeon last year when Landred Wolfstaff tried to attack me—and failed.

That's what Lagnar wants everyone to see, that I'm immune to the effects of wraiths. I swallow hard. This is one of the things that makes me stand out from every other Loamin.

The wraith takes its full form and races toward me. One of the council members gasps as the cloud of dark vapor and rainbow lights rolls over me. The display shifts to the moment from Silverlamp days later when I charged through the three wraiths in Silverlamp Dungeon.

The keepers are as silent as a mausoleum. I feel a strange chill. This is everything I've feared. I'm somehow different from every other Loamin. Not just strange. Not just the son of the king or an outcast. I am fundamentally different.

"As typical, both of his wraith encounters were buried," Lagnar drawls. "As if the dungeons themselves were keeping this a secret from us. Mind you, the first example is during his summation. The record is blank for hours after that. And he lost no craft—from highest strength to lowest weakness.

"That can't be true." Ogrekeeper folds her massive forearms in a defensive stance.

"If you want more evidence of his unusual power," Lagnar continues, "I've got more. We know that during the Keeper's Social last Gem he healed his friend with dragon scales. Dragon scales! And it's purported that Therias' son prefers life on the surface. In fact, I have it on good authority that he doesn't experience any of the side effects of the surface."

Sira. It must be her. Though she never revealed this to the council during her investigation after Silverlamp Dungeon.

One of the keepers from my right murmurs, "Not possible."

"And more recently," Emberfence continued, "he and the paladin Jeiahlir and Rugnus raided Bluebottle. Watch."

The hologram changes to a recording of me entering the mercury pool in Bluebottle, slowing down time to complete the circuit. We enter the next room. When I take the battery, the murmurs and whispers grow louder.

I turn to Rugnus for help.

He leans in again. "It's the furthest anyone has been in Bluebottle in generations, even with the paladin's key. It's overpowered for you to be able to take the battery like that. And there was basically no response from the dungeon. Taken together, it doesn't look good. It could even make the council reevaluate the position of Bluebottle Dungeon next season."

With the spotlight down, I can see Lagnar more clearly. He's gloating. His eyes hold danger, but something else. Fear. He's afraid of me.

He speaks again. "We're all out searching for someone who

could have been responsible for the attack during the festival, but Clayson Brightstorm is the most powerful and dangerous person to ever enter a dungeon. And I have one final piece of evidence—one we all know. Ergal, the ring he was granted in Wolfstaff. He combined it with mithrium and survived. How?

"I submit—with the utmost respect—that this young man should be locked up in Keelcrawl until we learn the truth about him. If not, he could end up taking every one of our dungeons from us—or, if he is behind the attack, destroy what's left of Loamin civilization altogether. I yield back to Chainkeeper."

Chainkeeper takes a moment to look at each of the other keepers. He's judging their reaction to Emberfence's information. The fact is, I'm still judging my reaction to it.

This isn't the revelation that I thought it would be. He didn't have to fabricate evidence or make up something about the festival to make people fear me.

I feel guilty, even though most of those things were out of my control. All the terrible things happening in the world seem to come back to my presence here. But I can't think that way. It's Jeiah's words about this world that steady my mind: *it's already messed up... there's no one else I would trust to fix what is wrong with us.*

"Do you refute any of this, Clayson?" Chainkeeper asks. "Now is the time for you to speak."

The spotlight remains off, and I don't know if it's part of the process, but I'm thankful I can see his face. Chainkeeper is on my side. He's giving me a chance to answer. I scan the council in search for encouragement, but find only concern, anger, and fear.

"I-I had nothing to do with the attack at StoneYoke. The mechs almost killed me, and to be clear, Bazalrak came after me directly. So, I don't see how anyone can believe I had anything to do with causing it. I understand more than anyone how different I am, different from those who grew up in this world. But I can't tell you I understand what's going on any more than you."

The hologram plays on a loop, and Tinkeeper, who had been asleep or meditating, is watching the display closely, not listening to me. I try not to think about it, but it's more than a little annoying. The keepers have to hear me.

"This world fell apart before I even knew there were Loamin." No matter how hard I wish, I can't stop the words from coming out. If they're going to throw me in Keelcrawl because they think I'm too dangerous, I'll make sure they understand who I truly am. "The first day I got here, you wanna know what happened? Rugnus brought me to his vault, and I accidentally took a budge to Thiffimdal. That's where I saw how well this world of yours has been guarded."

Rugnus grips my elbow, but I push forward.

"And yes, I did create the shield from Ergal, which I found in Wolfstaff Dungeon. I did it because Silverkeeper's daughter would have either killed everyone by mistake when combining the mithrium with her own relic. Or worse, she could have succeeded in doing exactly what I did, but instead of a shield, you would have an object capable of controlling the minds of an entire population. I—"

A green light flares to life at the front of the horseshoe. Tinkeeper's platform overflows with green-gray ivy. The young keeper of Brightstorm Dungeon skitters to the other side of his platform, face white.

"Something is happening in the distance." Tinkeeper's eerie feminine voice swells.

Hardkeeper fires a worried look to Emberfence, who only shakes his head.

Chainkeeper says, "What have you seen?"

A painful mask of consideration transforms Tinkeeper's features as if she's about to cry. She nods to herself. "I must not speak of what I saw. The vision itself is perhaps unimportant, but I can offer a new point of view on behalf of this child."

Rugnus says, "I think the child is you."

"I get that."

Chainkeeper urges her to continue. "Please, illuminate us."

Tinkeeper gestures toward the hologram of Bluebottle, and for a moment, I am afraid she will add more to the evidence against me, but she stops the footage the second I place the battery down on the sand. "I met Clayson Brightstorm at the Keeper's Social. He was hiding behind a lie. Glintwheel was it? No matter. This moment"—her finger extends to the hologram— "should be the seed of our trust for the child."

Emberfence interrupts. "This moment shows exactly why he's dangerous."

"Not seen in the correct light." She continues. "He returns the relic. He doesn't seek power. He rejects it. The very relic you sought and took, *Bluekeeper*, he turns away from it. Why?"

I watch the understanding dawn on a few of the keepers, and even Hardkeeper—seemingly Emberfence's strongest ally—looks at me with new, curious eyes.

The ivy around Tinseer stretches further in toward the middle of the room. "Child, what is it you want from us? A weight hangs around your neck. A burden. I sensed something in the way you moved from the moment you stepped to the dais."

A lump rises in my throat. I think of my mom. There was a moment in Keelcrawl where not only did she see me, but she remembered all the times she *didn't* see me. The effect of the mithrium shield is wider, but Ergal's power was diffused over all Geum Ide. Restoring all her memories of me is an impossible task.

I think of Dad living without craft in Geum Ide, tearing apart an engine, working the land under the healed brightstorm, and within the protection of the mithrium shield. I wanna spend my time there, but fear keeps me from doing that.

I can't sleep down here. I'm plagued with dreams or memories. I want relief. I wanna bring Andalynn down from her throne —though I know it will upset the balance of power in Whurrimduum. I just want her to be my sister. To hang out at the cabin and goof around at the lake this summer. And even though I know it's foolish, I want Dad to leave Geum Ide. I wanna break this curse on my mom. We can be a family.

My mind wanders to Jeiah. There's a spark I can't explain between us, and maybe if the world wasn't a hot pile of trollbrick right now, I could see where that might lead. Finally, Brig's request bubbles to the surface of my thoughts, and I'm faced with exactly what I need to do. What I thought to do the moment I walked into this council room.

The whole council waits for me to speak.

"Finding those responsible for this attack is my focus right now, but..." Rugnus tightens his grip on my arm. I know this is not why we came. Maybe if the council can understand my real intentions, they will know I wasn't involved in the attack.

"I need access to the mines. If there are answers about why I am different, I think I can find them in the dungeon of my grandfather, Yinzar. I believe I would qualify as keeper of Mithriumbane. And if a keeper is rated by how difficult it is to raid their dungeon, then Mithriumbane is the hardest—no one can even find it. That means I should have a seat in this council."

The chamber erupts in a riotous sea of shouting. Members turn to each other, finger-pointing. A few council members are yelling directly at me. I hear a few Loamin swear words I've never heard before.

I turn to Lagnar. His face is red. He's huffing breaths from his nose like a wild animal. But it's Moburan Hardkeeper who surprises me. He's looking to the side, eyes flashing in calculations. His fiery pupils and hair appear bright instead of deadly. He shouts down the whole cacophony with the aid of some voice-amplifying craft.

When the room is quiet, he turns to me. "Could you do such a thing? Find Mithriumbane Dungeon?"

"I believe I can."

Tinkeeper claps her hands. "A true request. Honest of what the young man seeks."

"Perhaps this was not the intention of the Gathering, but I sense the need for a cast," Chainkeeper says. "Allow Clayson entrance to the mines. Yinzar was a friend—strange as he was—

to many of us. The most skilled craftsman I've ever known. Uncovering his dungeon would add to the legacy of this council."

Ogrekeeper leans forward, bunching up the muscles in her shoulders. "We can't set aside Bluekeeper's case so easily. It seems the boy's power and finding Yinzar's dungeon are connected issues. I would add two conditions. First, he returns to Wolfstaff to obtain more information about the ring called Ergal. This visit will be privately recorded and made available to the council alone, though we should notify Tarden Wolfkeeper of this raid."

There are murmurs of agreement and nods from the other keepers.

"And looking at his exploits into the dungeons, I don't want him entering Orgebelt... ever. The damage to my dungeon's reputation may be irreparable. We need no more evidence than Silverkeeper's fall from this council. Therefore, the second condition is this: after Wolfstaff and Mithriumbane—if he can even find it—he will be barred from entry into the other dungeons, permanently."

The keepers murmur. Rugnus shakes his head. "Don't, Clayson."

I shake him off me. "I would submit to those conditions." This silences them. "With one condition of my own: the council drops the matter of removing the monarchy for as long as my sister lives."

Lagnar's laugh reverberates off the walls. One of the giant armadillos shifts behind me—I can hear its armor against the stone. "Well, is that all?"

Chainkeeper quiets the keepers. "I do not see—this would not be out of the ordinary. If we strip all power from the son of Therias Brightstorm, it stands to reason we would balance this with maintaining the power of his other heir, his daughter. Keeping balance is our way. It is what guides our casts. So... I move to cast on this immediately, and the cast begins with our lowest member. Shatterkeeper?"

Lagnar reels back as if he's been physically struck. "This is ridiculous!"

"Silence, Bluekeeper, you must learn your place on this council. Now please, Shatterkeeper, what do you cast?"

Her answer is quick. "One against."

From the other bottom side of the horseshoe, another voice. "Two against."

The cast continues like a tennis tournament, volleying back and forth from one side to the other. Lagnar, three against. Foilkeeper, four against.

When the cast comes to the Hardkeeper, it stalls. After a moment, he finally says, "My second daughter awaits summation in the dungeon of Mithriumbane. I cast five in favor."

Lagnar is enraged. "Wraith's blood and fizz! Ide curse you Moburan, you fool. How dare you?"

Hardkeeper offers only a smile in return and passes the cast on to the next keeper.

Ogrekeeper shakes her head. "The monarchy must come to an end. This is too high a price. Six against."

"Seven in favor," Brightkeeper nods in my direction, his face earnest. I promise myself to thank him personally as soon as I have a chance.

Sternkeeper, who has been silent until now, seems more bored than anything else. "Eight against."

Tinkeeper is next. "Nine in favor,"

"And ten in favor," Chainkeeper says. "Thirty-one in favor and..."

Rugnus mutters some profanity. I didn't keep up with the math, so I hold my breath.

"...twenty-four. The cast is forged. Clayson will visit Wolfstaff Dungeon and obtain more information for the council. He will continue his search for his grandfather's dungeon, but he can no longer enter other dungeons. And this council will hold to its word to sustain the monarchy. We are yoked together. If either side violates this forged cast, justice be done upon them"—he stares at my sister across the room—"not compassion."

RETURN TO WOLFSTAFF

Back in the suite, Rugnus recounts the verdict for everyone.

Hemdi and Winta sit together on a small pink loveseat, stunned. Koglim, his eyes glazed over, mindlessly strokes an iguana that has found its way into the room. Where did that come from? When he pushes the thing too hard, it hisses and snaps at him. "I'd have asked for Keelcrawl instead. We could have broken you out."

"What's done is done," I say.

Rugnus, who has busied himself with something at the other side of the room, refusing to acknowledge me, finally shakes his head and speaks. "What if our investigation leads us into other dungeons? This has to be the stupidest thing you've done yet."

"Really? I just saved my sister's throne. I thought that's what you wanted."

"Not like this. You gave the council control over our search for Mithriumbane."

"A search you could care less about. Who else can open the mines?"

"If it's even there. Or worse, what if there *is* another piece of mithrium in there. What if he didn't destroy it? You want to lead the council straight for it? I can barely look at your stupid face right now."

My breath quickens, and my chest tightens. The impulse to reach out and grab him by the collar arrives like something slowly burning across the atmosphere. I haven't told him about seeing the Cradle in my visions. Now, I don't think I want to.

Koglim looks at me, then Rugnus, then me again. He clucks his tongue. "Don't you guys have friendship bracelets for Ide's sake?"

Rugnus runs a hand over his hair. "That's not... Koglim, just shut up."

"Your boy just saved the monarchy. You're acting like he spit in your beard. And he's carrying a lifelong ban on dungeons." Koglim's voice grows increasingly high-pitched.

Rugnus starts to pace. "We need to find the person who caused the attack. Instead, we're dealing with... this." He gestures to me.

Andalynn appears at the door. She takes everything in at once. Sending Rugnus a sharp look, she squints at me, concerned. Something about her eyes makes me turn my face away. I don't know what I'm feeling.

But Andalynn comes to my side, offers an embrace, and absorbs some of my thoughts and feelings through the silver tendrils in her hair. I try not to let her in this time. I don't want her to see how I'm feeling. But it doesn't work.

She draws her head away and finds my face. "Is that what you think? You don't belong? That couldn't be further from the truth. Clayson, the oath you made today? No one else would have ever done that. And the people of Whurrimduum will have you to thank. I can still be their voice against the council."

"Yeah, I know. And they're going to open the mines. Honestly, when I think about it... I don't know. It's a relief not to have to go into any more dungeons."

"Except Wolfstaff," Koglim says. "Which you may or may not live through."

"Right. True. Thanks for that."

"What about the attack?" Rugnus says. "Finding the person responsible? Are we just going to go on this errand for the council... we have to—"

"Both." Andalynn glances at a shadow on the reflective wall. "We need to check into Wolfstaff with Clayson and keep looking for the attacker."

"Maybe that's what Emberfence wants," Rugnus says, "to keep us sidetracked. Look, Clayson. I know what I said about helping you look for Mithriumbane, but with everything that's going on—"

"He's gotta find it," Koglim says, dismissing Rugnus altogether. "There's no question about that. Not the best timing, but it keeps Andalynn in place. Besides, a little raiding will help clear my mind."

Rugnus weighs Koglim's words with a tilt of his head. "This is the dumbest...."

I hold up my hands. "Look, there's no timetable on my agreement with the council. Rugnus is right. We continue the investigation. Wolfstaff can wait."

"It's late." Andalynn places a hand on Rugnus' leg. "We can make some decisions in the morning. Clayson, you should go back to the surface and get some rest."

A wave of anxiety washes over me. I want nothing more than to sleep in my own bed in the cabin, but Yinzar's memories are open to me again. "I'll stay down here. I need to see what else I can find in Yinzar's memories while I can."

Koglim scratches his pecks. "I thought they were kind of on repeat."

I open my mouth but, Hemdi answers for me. "Clayson was able to see a different memory after his injury."

"You sure it's not just brain damage?" Winta asks.

Rugnus gives a short laugh. "Suit yourself. You've got the armband. You know your own limits. I'm heading back to Tungsten City."

"I'll come with you," Koglim says. "Brude and I are trying to help get ready for the memorial ceremony in a few days. By the way, Rugnus, your mom is quite the organizer."

Rugnus stands and removes Icho. "No surprises there." Without saying anything else, he and Koglim budge.

Andalynn sneaks another quick look at the mirrored wall. "Get some rest. Go to the surface if you need to. I'll wrap up my business with the council. See you in the morning."

After they all leave, I find a massive bed in the next room. I stretch out on top of the covers, but my eyes won't close. I know what happens when they do. Mindlessly, I open bluelink.

When a message from Jeiah arrives, I forget everything else. I gesture the icon open. It's a recording.

She's standing in her office in bluelink tower. "Hi. I-I hope everything went okay with the council." There's a nervous smile on her face as she waits for a second longer. "I found two new leads. First..."

She gestures as if she's asking me to stand, but a new video replaces her. It's Bazalrak. It must have been sent right after the attack. From his bruised and bloodied face, I would say, right after Rugnus buried him in the ground.

Bazalrak snarls. "None of this was part of the plan. What happened? Find me."

Jeiah's face replaces the video, and I smile. She's really good at what she does. "Thought you'd like that. This may have been sent to Emberfence. I need to dig a bit more, but... maybe this proves that connection. And second..."

It cuts to a video of StoneYoke as the first glass buildings fell. She zooms in on the brightstorm in the background. The second the attack begins, the smallest flare of energy blossoms from the brightstorm.

"Strange, right? Everyone's focused on the mechs, but this can't be a coincidence. There's a connection between the brightstorm and the attacks. Anyway, I'll, uh, catch up to you guys maybe tomorrow. Gonna keep following this lead. Let me know how things are going on your end. I can't get a straight answer from the council about the information I sent. And Clay, I didn't mean...I'm sorry if it caused you any problems. I understand you now. I didn't when I sent my work over to them."

She must have sent this during the meeting, which wasn't public. If I've learned one thing in Whurrimduum, it's that the council can hide anything they want from anyone they want.

I record a message to her that will get delivered in the morning. I don't wanna wake her if she's asleep. "Jeiah, you genius. That's awesome. And I've got my own news too, but I can talk to you tomorrow."

The smile stays on my face for a long time. My mind swirls with thoughts. The flare of the brightstorm. The Cradle. Stone-Yoke. Emberfence. Wolfstaff and my promise to the council. Mithriumbane. All these separate things are jumbled in my mind, but it's like they want to be connected.

It takes me what feels like an hour, but eventually, my eyes start to droop. The darkness and quiet steady my breathing. A swarm of multicolored light bleeds through my eyelids. I drift into muted colors and soft voices. When my feet touch the stone and water, my eyes open. As expected, I'm back in Yinzar's memories.

When I speak, my voice echoes off the walls, mixing with the sounds of a thousand water droplets. "If you're going to keep dragging me here every night, at least show me something clear. I need to find your dungeon."

A soft voice—not Yinzar's—emanates from an orange butter-fly. "...always loved..."

It's my mom, but she sounds more like Andalynn, filled with hope and determination. I creep toward the orange light, making every effort not to scare it off. But I'm not watching my feet as well as I should. My toes find a divot in the rocks, and I stumble forward. The orange light takes flight.

"Come on," I tell Yinzar, or his memories, or maybe just the walls.

The orange butterfly circles high above me. I'm never gonna get it now. But when I stretch, the orange glow simply expands into an orb of light. My mom says, "...beautiful any time of year..." The light settles on top of my head gently, and the memory opens like someone's parted a curtain.

I did it. I controlled the dream. Maybe Hemdi was right.

My mom and Yinzar sit on a bench in Everbloom Garden. She's older than Andalynn, maybe in her early twenties. Which would mean she's married, and Andalynn has already been born. My birth would certainly not be far off.

"It is, of course. But that's not why I sent for you, my dear Bena."

Her face falls. "I-I know. You went down there again."

"I did."

"If the council—"

"They're too consumed by their affairs to notice an old man's wanderings. In fact, they may not even notice if something went missing from the royal vault."

Standing quickly, my mom hushes him. "You can't speak like that." She moves to a large bush with fire-red leaves and plucks one from the top. The bush shivers with a gust of wind.

Yinzar follows behind her as she continues along the grassy path. Not in a hurry, not desperate, but calculating. "The mithrium is too dangerous in its current form. I... I've discovered a way to transform it. Change the mithrium into something useful, something that can neither be destroyed nor destroy anything else."

My mom stops walking, glancing up at the brightstorm then back at her father. "Can there truly be a way?"

"Yes, my dear. There is." He gazes out over the city. His orange hair a shade darker than hers. Hope and fear and wonder all seem to muddy the clear emotion on his face. "I was convinced that the energy needed for the forge would be the opposite energy, an active energy. But I'm sure now, yes, that it must be potential energy."

My mom's face is awash with concern. "Potential energy? Where would you get that much potential energy?"

Yinzar gives her a knowing look.

She shakes her head, chin firm, lips pinched together. "No. The mines alone are restricted, and you want to go... it's not possible. You would have to find it first."

"I did."

The vision starts to peel away at the corners, pulling back into darkness. The conversation is drawn out like a stream of water. The world blurs, and my mom's words are swallowed.

There's a sharp pain on my cheek, and I wake up. Koglim standing over me, like he just slapped me. In fact, I think he *did* just slap me.

"See, awake," he says to Rugnus.

"Now he is." Rugnus leans over me and adjusts the gold armband. "Are you okay?"

Light from the brightstorm streams through the long glass windows. Koglim and Rugnus are standing by the bed, looking down at me with confusion. Andalynn and Winta come through the door toward the bed. I sit up.

I rub the sleep from my eyes. "He did it. Yinzar found the Cradle." I tear the sheets off me and swing my legs off the bed. "My mom was in this one. She guessed he was going down to the mines. She was afraid of this place he found. Said it had been lost, but Yinzar found it. It... there was tremendous potential energy there."

Koglim whispers reverently, "He found it?"

Winta says, "I just want to point out that Clayson has been hit on the head recently. A few papers short of a card deck."

"It's a few cards short of a deck," I tell her.

I see her catalog the human phrase in her mind. At least she's stopped arguing with me about human phrases.

"His dungeon must be there."

"It would make sense," Andalynn says. "He must have

thought he could make something with the mithrium in the place
our ancestor made the brightstorms."

"But if it killed him…" I don't have to finish the statement.

"I could check with Quilgist."

Now I'm confused. "Who's Quilgist?"

"Brightkeeper," Koglim says. "You must have seen him at the
council meeting."

I don't even know his name. Another reminder of how little I
have engaged with this world.

"One thing's for sure," Rugnus says. "Yinzar was wrong about
the type of energy he needed. The energy from the Onthratia
worked. Clayson, you made it work with the shield. So, whatever
he tried to do with potential energy… maybe that's why he failed.
That's how he died."

Andalynn says. "Yinzar was able to destroy the mithrium. He
lost his life doing so, but he destroyed it. And became a champion when he did."

For a long minute, no one says anything, but Koglim clears his
throat. "Okay, for us to even get there, the council has to open
the mines. Which means we need to raid Wolfstaff and get info
on Ergal."

"Right," I say. "Wait, Jeiah's message! You guys gotta see this."

I open bluelink and cast the video on the nearest wall. Winta
winks at me as Jeiah stumbles through saying hello. At the
mention of Emberfence, Andalynn and Rugnus trade looks mixed
with shock and excitement.

"This is it," Rugnus says. "This is what we needed to prove
his involvement."

"It's not enough to send to Chainkeeper," Andalynn says. "But
she's good. Maybe she'll find the connection."

Koglim put both hands on his head. "Keep Ide. That Jeiah is
something else."

"Told you guys," Winta says. "Clayson, you have my permission to get yoked."

"I—" The words don't quite come together in my mind. I feel a flare of red in my cheeks.

Koglim rescues me. "So... what's next?"

When I realize everyone is staring at me expectantly, I pull up the clip of the brightstorm. "There's more."

Rugnus asks me to play it again, and we watch the brightstorm flicker at the time of the attack.

"I don't understand," Koglim says. "What did we just see?"

Rugnus balls up his fists. "Someone messing with my city."

"More than that," Andalynn says. "The craft they used to attack StoneYoke was connected to the brightstorm."

Winta zooms in on the frozen image of the flaring bulb of energy. "Then there could be a connection to the Cradle. The mithrium, the attack, the craft battery. I just don't see how to piece it together."

Rugnus sits down roughly. "You were right, Clayson. It could all be connected."

Koglim smiles. "So, our raid of Wolfstaff is back on. We need to get to the mines and figure out how the Cradle and the Brightstorms might be involved in the attack."

Andalynn frowns. "Maybe. That's still a stretch."

With another look at the image, Rugnus says, "With Clayson involved, there's no coincidence. But this no longer feels like were searching for information. It feels like..."

"Like someone is laying a trap for us."

"And yet," I say, "Lagnar was dead set against me entering the mines. So, we're back at square one with him."

Koglim brushes his hands with finality. "So Ergal..."

"If I could find Wolfstaff's son..." I volunteer. "He gave me the ring."

Koglim whistles low, then laughs. "Guess you could use wraithbait."

"Sounds dangerous. I'm in," Winta says.

Andalynn glances at Winta. She shakes her head. "The baby's

imminent. You should be making preparations with the healers and goldmages."

Winta's jaw tightens. "I still have time. I'll make my own choices, okay."

"Little latchmage nearly popping out," Koglim says.

My sister swats his arm. "Ide keep us, Koglim. It's a baby."

Winta stretches her back. "He's not wrong. Little thing is wiggling all over the place. For now, I'm keeping them in here."

"I don't think that's how it works," Koglim counters.

Andalynn crosses her arms, but her face remains kind. "You should be with Hemdi. That's—"

"Fine," Winta says, "Fine." She blows out a breath. "You guys, go. Enjoy. Hope a wraith eats your soul."

"Hey, don't joke... be cool to watch, though. Too bad for you."

Winta storms from the room, and I hear the door to the suite slam closed.

"Okay," Koglim says. "So, wraithbait?"

I ask the obvious question because I always do. "What's wraithbait?"

Rugnus strokes his chin, his eyes as big as brightstorms. "Pretty much decorate you with as many high power direct-use relics as we can find. Has to be every craft, or it won't work."

"So, I'll be like a Loamin Christmas tree."

"What's a Christmas tree?" Koglim asks.

For a second, I wish Winta hadn't left. Her explanations of human traditions are always bad enough to make me laugh. "It's, uh, used to celebrate the birth of a baby, a baby boy. People put lights and ornaments on a tree and... it's a lot to explain."

"Seems fitting. When that wraith comes for you, you'll be crying like a latchmage in no time."

Andalynn gets my attention. "So just us four? Do you want to message Jeiah?"

I consider it but shake my head. "She'd wanna come, but it's dangerous enough for you three. And she's working to find that other connection."

"Okay," Rugnus says. "Give us a minute to grab some relics from my vault."

Koglim and Rugnus disappear, and Andalynn moves out of the adjoining room into the living space. I refresh my body and clothes with a quick clean. It scrapes the stubble from my face. As I exit the room, I find Andalynn standing before the mirrored wall I saw the night before, sending a few messages. Every once in a while, she presses her palm against the surface of the mirror, causing the shadows inside to hover closer.

I check my newsfeed. There will be a memorial event at the festival site in two days. Hosted by the professional raider's union. That must be what Koglim has been working on. The body count from the attack hovers within my peripheral vision.

Koglim reappears behind us talking about a video he watched from a few years ago where three professional raiders used wraithbait in Ogrebelt Dungeon. It didn't end well.

Rugnus isn't listening to him. His face is puckered in anger. While Koglim has me test a few objects, Rugnus stands by scowling, his arms folded across his chest.

Andalynn notices too. "You alright?"

"Me? Fine." But the look he gives me could cleave my head in two. He produces Icho, and we budge to the corridor leading to Wolfstaff lobby.

We walk in the darkness into a rectangular hallway leading behind a massive waterfall. When we emerge from around it, the lobby is empty. We follow the massive stairs down to the entrance. The energy field that lets us in one group at a time immediately dissipates, and we enter the final pathway to the threshold. The walls slowly close around us until we must squeeze through.

No one speaks. Whatever anger Rugnus brought back with him from his relic search hangs over the whole group. He marches straight to the door and bangs a fist on the gilded surface. The threshold opens, the stone doorway swinging wide, light pouring out to fill the room.

A cautious Koglim moves next to Rugnus. "You got something on your mind?"

"Just go through the door."

"Not smart to go in angry. Probably oughta—"

"Get in the dungeon," Rugnus says, blowing out a frustrated sigh.

"Alright. Don't get me killed, though."

He proceeds through the door, but Rugnus hangs back. Andalynn squeezes Rugnus' hand and follows Koglim.

As I try to walk past him, his hand comes up. His furious eyes nearly bore a hole through my head. If there were a gold object that could give him laser eyes, I'd be dead right now.

Finally, he speaks. "When were you going to tell me? Assuming you would have."

"Clue me in. What are we talking about here?"

Rugnus takes two rings from his pockets and yanks my hand toward him.

"Don't know?" He laughs. "Really? Then maybe it was Jeiah. You two are the only people who have been in my vault lately. The vase? Who put it there? Did Sira have it?"

I finally connect the pieces. He went to get relics and found Sira's knife hiding inside the vase where I put it. I try to formulate words, but nothing comes out. A strong itch at the back of my neck and the sensation I've forgotten something. Then I remember: I swore in silver not to say anything.

The skin on my index finger pinches hard as he tries to jam one of the rings into place.

"Watch it!" I readjust the ring on a different finger. "I don't think I can even explain if I wanted to."

He looks me over. "And you don't feel used? Like this is all a trick again to lead you to more mithrium? Ide keep me, Clayson! Of all the fizzblooded things... why did you do that? You did, didn't you?"

He takes a lead choker from the bag and pushes my face upward, exposing my neck.

"I did." I test the limit of the silvercraft I swore by. "She... she was afraid of it. I think she was afraid that someone else would take it from her." A twinge of pain ripples across the back of my mind. It must be the effect of the oath I made.

Rugnus' hand slips on the clasp of the choker. He squints at me. "You didn't? You made an oath in silver. Well, don't try to go against it. Just... can you tell me if she knows where you put it?"

"She didn't wanna know."

"Wait, *she* didn't want to know?"

The choker in place, I step backward, trying to put some distance between us. "I think that was the whole point. You didn't bring it, right? You kept it there?"

"Of course. I—keep Ide, Clayson. Why would I move it? It's as safe as it can be."

I nod. Rugnus walks past me, his chin up, his eyes still simmering with anger, but I can tell he's trying to process what I did and why I did it. And that's enough. He crosses the threshold, and I follow him.

Inside, Andalynn and Koglim have their heads craned upward, following a rock wall all the way up to the ceiling. The threshold seals us in. This room is like what Wolfstatt presented me the first time I entered the dungeon. Except, this time, instead of three smooth walls and one climbing wall, each of the four walls can be scaled all the way up to the ceiling. There's no metal birdbath, but the floor itself is the same dark metal. I shudder to think what will try to prevent us from reaching the top.

"I think we're supposed to climb this," I say.

Koglim rubs his hands together. "Awesome. We should—"

"That's not how this is going to work," Rugnus says.

We all look at him.

"Put the rest of the relics on Clayson. That's the plan."

Koglim scratches his head. "In the first room? Usually, have to get in a little way. What if we—"

"No. Right here. Right now."

Andalynn tilts her head to one side. "Rugnus, did I miss something?" She can sense his mood without craft. "Wraiths don't normally visit the edge of the dungeon."

"Well, Clayson here is the exception. I'm sure of it. Let's get this over with. And remember, the council will be recording this."

Koglim hands me a thick silver necklace and a tin lunchbox.

Finally, I take a titanium and cobalt crown from Andalynn.

"Before you put that on," Koglim says, "maybe you should climb a bit. I'm just now thinking that Rugnus is right. The wraith might actually come out this far to get you. And this first room is very, ah, narrow. I mean, I don't want to seem like a latcher, but..."

I nod with understanding. "You don't wanna risk getting touched by a wraith."

"Correct, sir."

There's a spot to stand maybe twenty feet up the rock. "Will that work?"

Koglim looks up skeptically, but Andalynn says, "We'll be fine. The only registered wraith in this dungeon is Wolfstaff's son. Besides, Clayson can protect us."

Koglim shrugs, still squirming a bit. "He had Ergal in Silver-lamp too."

Rugnus shoves me toward the wall. "We'll be fine. Get up there. I'll throw you Icho, and you can put the crown on."

The hand- and footholds are so generous that I scale the wall without any difficulty, even balancing a few objects in my hands. Rugnus yells up to me and throws Icho. Once I have both Icho and the lunchbox in one hand, I place the crown on my head with the other. A visible ring of mercury spins above my head like an oversized halo.

"I feel pretty stupid with all this stuff. I can't seem to focus on using any of them."

Koglim giggles. "Don't forget, after the council screens this, the recording goes out to everyone. You'll look as fizzblooded as ever, but all over bluelink. Anyway, that's the thing. Direct objects don't do well together. You can only use one or two at a time. They say it's the confusion that draws in the wraith. Speaking of which"—Koglim raises his voice—"Here wraithy, wraithy. Here wraithy. Come on."

Nothing happens.

Koglim shrugs. "Maybe we *will* have to get through a few rooms before—"

A pool of cloud and light spills over the wall.

"There it is!" Rugnus points.

"Champion's bones." Koglim scoots against the surface of the rock and curls into himself.

The wraith heads right for them. I try to command it as I did in Silverlamp. "Stop!"

The swirling cloud gathers to a halt, morphing into a flat cyclone. At the center, a figure of light takes shape. I recognize Wolfstaff's son in the long, gaunt face. The brightest two sources of light become sunken eye sockets. The wraith shrieks, first at the other three raiders I've brought with me, and then, even louder, at me.

"I-I need to speak with you?" I try.

The cloud becomes tighter and tighter around the figure until it is no longer a mass of particles but the outline of a person.

"The ring Wolfstaff granted me, Ergal, can you tell me about it?"

It was dangerous to lure me here. His mouth doesn't move.

"I understand that, but I don't have a choice. Where did it come from? Is it the heart of this dungeon?"

Do you know so little to ask such a thing? The staff is the heart of this dungeon. Ergal was—

His head jerks toward the side, and for a moment, his ghostly face sharpens, an undead reflection of the man I saw in the mirror the first time I came here. But the cloud swallows the details of his face again. He can't affect me, but my heart is jumping out of my chest.

Andalynn shouts, "What's happening?"

"Give me a minute," I shout.

The wraith redirects its glowing stare at me. *We will tell you the story of Ergal for a price.*

"A price?"

A gust of wind crashes against my back, and a bright pink light appears behind me. It's a doorway. "Am I supposed to go through?"

In answer, the wraith bursts forward, engulfing me for a brief second, and disappears through the doorway.

"I think we are supposed to follow it," I say, only to discover Rugnus is already halfway up the wall, followed by Andalynn. Koglim bounces on his toes below them, preparing for a fight. When they reach the landing, Andalynn checks me over. "Are you okay? It flew right through you."

"I'm fine. I think."

Koglim ascends the last few handholds. "Three attempts, three failures by the wraiths. It's official. Clayson's immune."

"What's through the door?" Rugnus' face is stony in the pink light.

"We'll have to pay a price. That's what he said."

"It spoke to you?" Andalynn's voice swims with disbelief. "I didn't see that. Did anyone else?"

Rugnus and Koglim shake their heads.

"Great," I say. "Let's hope I wasn't hallucinating."

After reclaiming all the relics, Rugnus rounds his shoulders, pushes past me, and enters the door without a word. We follow him into a long rectangular tunnel.

"My bag!" Rugnus' voice is shrill. He pats himself down. "Icho! Cursed dungeon took my club. Took all my stuff."

My Tungsten bracelet remains, but it's not a relic. It's useless here.

Andalynn shakes her head. "Strange."

"But without relics..." Koglim says.

"This doesn't feel right," Andalynn echoes my thoughts.

The dim pink light fades as we move deeper down the tunnel. The floor declines until we're pitched forward slightly. It won't be easy to come back the way we came. At the end of the tunnel, the unmistakable outline of a cave appears. Darkness spills from its edges.

Rugnus glances at Koglim. "You heard of this place before?"

For once, Koglim answers with a single word. "No."

His response cools my blood down to Thiffimdal levels. "But Koglim, you know everything… about every dungeon."

"Not this place." His voice is like the whisper of a ghost.

Enter the cave. It's Landred's voice again, speaking to me alone. *Your presence in the dungeons has awoken something. Wolfstaff is restless. Seize the heart of her dungeon and hear the story of Ergal.*

"It's the heart of the dungeon," I say, somewhere between a question for him and a statement for everyone else.

The three others stop walking. "What?" Rugnus says,

I ignore them, focusing back on Wolfstaff's son. "What will we face in there?"

This is the den of the feral wolves my mother tamed. They guard the staff against thieves and raiders. No one else has stood before this entrance. You know Frrwelhst, their leader. But as guardian, she can never enter the dungeon, never rejoin her pack.

"What's happening?" Rugnus asks, "You can't be serious."

I hold up a hand.

Landred's words grow soft and dangerous. *In her absence, the wolves have grown restless and hungry. You have been warned.*

MELT THIS DUNGEON

T HE MOUTH of the cave breathes cool air, but Koglim is visibly sweating. Andalynn places a hand on his back. "You okay?"

He takes a moment to swallow. His tattoo glows softly. "All I see is teeth and fur." He draws in an uneven breath. "We're doing this, right? Into a den of feral wolves, without any relics, and then we find the heart of a dungeon. The champion's staff. No, uh, no big deal."

Andalynn rubs his back in slow circles. "If this is Wolfstaff's desire, we will make it out of there."

It's a nice thought, but her words can't shake Landred's solemn warning from my mind:

We will tell you the story of Ergal for a price.

He takes another deep breath through his nose and lets it out slowly, finally nodding. "They do say, a few raiders have reached all the way to the heart of a dungeon."

"There you go," Andalynn encourages him. "We've got this."

"What happened to those raiders?" I ask.

Rugnus and Andalynn glare at me.

"What? It's a valid question."

Koglim frowns deeper. "No one knows. They never came out."

"Come on, Koglim," Rugnus adopts a hesitant smile. "Think

about it? Who won during the War of the Wolves? Wolves or Loamin?"

"Yeah," Koglim says. "Yeah, true. Okay. We'll be smart."

As we push into the darkness of the cave, a strong acrid smell rises in an invisible cloud. Rugnus and Koglim share a look of disgust. This smell is multitudes worse than the winter I waited four months to clean out the goat pen. They were holed up in the barn so long that—after I let them out for the day—it took me an hour to coax them back in.

I shorten my breaths. "Not so bad."

"Okay, farmer Clayson," Koglim says.

We come to a fork and Andalynn stops us. "Which way?"

To the left, the floor continues to slope downward. Straight, the floor begins an incline. Either way, the walls are distant from each other, and the vaulted ceiling reminds me of Frrwelhst's massive size. You could fit two of her side-by-side in this corridor.

"Follow the decline," Koglim says. "You know what they say..."

I look at Koglim. "Actually, no."

"Bigger the trap..." Rugnus starts.

"...bigger the treasure," Koglim finishes

We take the declining trail.

Something crunches under my shoe, and we all look down as I lift my foot. Half of a small, winged skeleton blanched and broken. We tread deeper into the cave. When there's a choice between incline or decline, a bleak determination puts us on autopilot.

Downward.

Massive scratches rake the walls on every side. My shoulders draw as tight as a bowstring. Here and there, where the ceiling meets the wall, I can spot smaller openings, rough and oblong. Some are no bigger than my head, but they all reveal other possible directions.

At one turn, Rugnus stops us. "What's that sound?"

I hadn't noticed anything over the shuffle of our feet. Koglim, who had been breathing the loudest, sucks in air and holds it. A soft, almost calming noise pulses through the corridor. I incline my head to listen closely. Where is it coming from? There's another opening near the ceiling, empty and dark. But the sound comes from further in, around the next turn.

"Something like snoring, maybe?" I ask.

"No," Andalynn says. "Listen, it's getting closer."

"Not snoring," Koglim whines. "Sniffing."

We all tense. Rugnus squeezes his wrist just below his bracelet. Too bad it won't work. The sound only grows louder. "Get ready."

Koglim is dancing on his feet, ready to fight. "Spit. Spit, spit, spit, spit."

My eyes fly back to the opening high on the wall. It's got to be a tunnel. "I don't think we should stay in the main tunnel. There. Look."

They follow my finger to the wall and to the rough oblong opening just out of reach.

"Go in those tiny tunnels?" Koglim scrunches down a bit as if he's trying to figure out if he'd even fit.

The sound grows. How can sniffing be so loud? But I know the answer to that—a feral wolf is the size of a semi.

Rugnus flees toward the wall. "Better than waiting here." He interlocks his fingers and gestures with his shoulders for me to climb.

"I'll go last," I say. "I can scale that easily."

Koglim gulps. "I'll go." He moves past me and, with our help, grabs the lip of the tunnel. The second he does, the hair on the back of my neck prickles. We all turn toward the end of the larger tunnel and freeze.

The wolf's white pelt glimmers in the soft light, marble gray eyes focusing on us. The beast's ears go back and its tail wags, slapping against the stone.

Koglim cocks his head to one side. "It looks..."

"Happy?" Rugnus says.

But I know exactly what it means. Our dogs. Nox acts the same way every time he hears the can opener. "Koglim, get up there—fast. We're probably the biggest meal it's seen in a long time."

"No, no, no. I'm like a juicy butt roast. We're melted." Koglim's only halfway inside. His voice is swallowed by the smaller tunnel. Rugnus and I hoist Andalynn up, and she clambers into the hole.

Andalynn motions for us to move. "Faster!"

The great wolf gallops toward us as I push Rugnus upward. I back against the wall, expecting its canines to sink into my flesh, but it skids to a stop in front of me, its tail still wagging, ears back, eyes narrowed. I see nothing of Frrwelhst's intellect. It will eat me.

"Clayson," Rugnus hisses, "get up here!"

It's one jump away from pinning me to the wall and scarfing me down like a small potato. The wolf sniffs the air, bares its teeth, and paws the ground. I can't make it before it gets me. As slowly as possible, I grab a rock from the ground and hurl it behind the wolf. The beast's eyes follow it, giving me a split second to reverse grab upward.

The wolf lunges as I execute one more grab and pull myself into the hole.

I'm safe.

Wait. Did it get me? My legs feel wet and cold.

But dragging myself deeper into the narrow tunnel, I don't feel any pain. Are my feet numb? Are they gone? No. The others are moving ahead of me. I feel for my legs in the dark, expecting to find them gone, but instead, I find a pool of liquid. Behind me, I hear a soft whining. We've disappointed it. Something wet slaps against my legs.

"Clayson, what is it?" Andalynn calls from ahead of Rugnus. "Did it—"

"I'm fine. It got its tongue in the tunnel. I'm covered in slobber. It's"—I wipe my sticky hand off on the rock beneath me—"really disgusting. Keep going. It's still licking me."

"Aw cute thing," Koglim says. "Deadly, terrifyingly cute little puppy."

Rugnus scoffs. "It almost ate us."

"I wonder if I could train one?" Koglim murmurs as we crawl forward.

I can breathe more easily as Rugnus moves ahead, following Andalynn deeper in. We can hear the wolf sniffing the opening behind us, but we're too far in for it to reach. After a minute, we stop.

"Another fork," Andalynn announces.

Both Rugnus and Koglim say, "Follow the decline."

"Right." Andalynn leads us to the left.

As we move forward, Koglim asks, "How are we going to do this? We failed against one wolf. Just think how many there will be when we find the staff."

"We got away," I say. "We didn't fail."

"One problem at a time," Rugnus adds. "We need to find a way through this place."

After we crawl ten feet or so, the opening widens on all sides. We can stand, but we have to crouch. Andalynn and Koglim walk forward shoulder to shoulder. Rugnus moves next to me.

A familiar feeling of guilt finds me. "I should have told you about the knife." I whisper.

Rugnus only grunts and changes the topic. "If we do reach the heart of Wolfstaff, what will happen... I can't see ahead to the consequences. Koglim."

Koglim sniffs. "I saw fur and teeth. We probably all die. Wolves will get a good meal, though."

"Normally, I would agree, but Clayson's presence gives us an advantage. He's anything but normal."

The tight space becomes impossibly quiet. I battle against his statement. Being forced to find the mithrium in Silverlamp. The attack on the StoneYoke festival. It all seems to be my fault. And if not my fault, at least so connected with me that it might as well be. What will Landred say or do if we reach the heart of Wolf-staff? Will he really give me information about Ergal? Or is this all some sadistic trap? I tend to walk right into those.

Andalynn stops. "It's not fair to place all of this on Clayson. The whole world is at fault, and we don't know the outcome of this raid anyway. We have to trust each other."

Rugnus squeezes around me, and next to Koglim. "Tell that to Clayson."

Andalynn falls back in the near darkness. "What's he talking about?"

I wanna tell her about the silver knife, but the oath prevents me. I can't fight against it. "Couldn't tell you."

"It's not your fault... the attack."

"I know that. After Bluebottle, Jeiah said basically the same thing. Well, that and that she gave the council all that damning information about me."

"That was her job. Still... Jeiah." A grin comes to her face.

"What about her?"

"Don't get defensive. I just—are you two... like a thing now, or—"

I can't hold in a groan. "No. We... no. I mean, I don't think so."

Ahead of us, Rugnus and Koglim are forced back to their hands and knees. They fit side by side and squeeze through. We follow suit.

A little way in, Andalynn says. "She seems to... I don't know. She's very interested in you."

"I guessed that much." Saying this out loud makes me wanna see her again. "It's an investigation. She's... I don't know, attentive."

"One way to put it," I can almost see Andalynn's smile. "I've seen her kind before. A lot of paladins are like that."

"Like what?"

"Focused. And in this case, focused on you."

The way forward becomes larger. Rugnus and Koglim slip out. This is the biggest part of this branch yet, rounded and high enough for us to stand straight, facing each other. The floor is no longer rock but a rough black metal, pock-marked with water-filled dimples. Koglim's looking at me, grinning.

"Been listening to our conversation?" I ask him.

Koglim shrugs innocently. "Pretty echoey in here." He lightly shoves me. "It can't hurt to bring her the heart of a dungeon." He pauses. "No. Don't do that. I think that would be bad. Uh, which way are we supposed to go?"

Andalynn pauses. "Dead end."

"Wait." The stones shift at the other side of the small cavern. "Right there. Is that—"

Beady eyes send back a reflection. The world is suddenly filled with flapping wings, thousands of them all heading toward us, bringing a wave of paranoia and fear. The same bats from the cliff during my summation.

I can't keep the rapid thoughts from entering my head.

Hatred boils under my skin. Everything is my fault, and I can't fix it. I scratch the flesh of my arm, trying to get to the muscles, make myself hurt. This is punishment for being so stupid, so incapable. My family can't trust me. My friends can't trust me.

A splash of cold water bursts across my face. "Keep it together," Koglim orders. He's crouching against the ground, slapping water up at me. "Use the metal at our feet."

He's right. It's the same black metal from the birdbath last year. I kneel and touch the metal. It's much stronger than the birdbath. I force the bats out the way we came in.

When the last few flitter by, a new way opens where the mass of bats had been blocking it. We all stand. Everyone had been trying to use the metal, but only I was able to actually control the bats. A thrill of satisfaction washes over me. I've come a long way since my summation.

Koglim rubs my head. "That was trippy. Nice work. At least we're not totally without craft. The dungeon provides."

"After you," Rugnus nods to Andalynn. His mouth still looks like he ate something sour.

At the end of the tunnel, a soft grayish outline waits for us, growing steadily into a clear light—an exit.

"I don't like this," Rugnus says. "That probably means we're almost there."

He's not wrong. The tunnel ends abruptly, and below us in the center of a large room a dull black light lays under layers of something dark. For a second, I think the whole cavern is carpeted in fur pelts. But one of the pelts rolls over onto its back and scratches its belly. At the far edge, one of the wolves tries to pounce on a bat, but the rodent dodges the beast's paws. The dark gray wolf barks and howls at it.

Another wolf rolls away from the black light, revealing the source. A glowing staff, as long as my wingspan. Dark energy pulses around it, filling the cavern with strange shadows.

"The wolfstaff relic," Rugnus whispers. "I can't believe it."

Koglim rubs the tattoo on his arm nervously. "Be cool to take one of these guys as a pet. These wolves would be so cute if they didn't want to eat us."

Andalynn asks the obvious question "How are we going to get down there?"

"No clue," Rugnus says. "Is there no possible way to command them? The guardian—Frrwelhst—listened to you, right? Even came to you on the way to Geum Ide."

"Landred—uh, the wraith—he said Frrwelhst couldn't enter the dungeon. I think she was their alpha. Without her... I don't know... they must think like regular wolves. It really wanted to eat us back there."

"Stupid, adorable guys. I bet I'd be tasty," Koglim flexes his biceps.

Rugnus rubs his hands together. "We need a distraction. Big enough to get them to move out of the way."

"If they will," Andalynn says.

The wolf that had been chasing down the bat slinks back to

the group, climbs on the heads of a few others, and plops down at the top of a pile. My eyes drift up from there, following the walls. They don't look hard to climb. Patches of the black metal are interspersed through the rock. Coming to the edge of the tunnel, I dip my head over the lip of the rock and find an area of metal.

I could reach it with a quick climb down. "The bats. If the wolves want a bigger meal..."

"Brilliant," Koglim says. "One thing. How do we control them?"

I point downward. "Same black metal."

Rugnus crosses his arms. "You're the only one who could get the bats to do something, so you're up."

I move to the edge and sit, ready to swing my legs down, when Andalynn rests a hand on my arm. "The metal is embedded in the cliff. You can distract them for a bit, but... you'll still have to make a run for it to reach the staff."

"They'll be busy with the bats," Koglim says. "We can make a distraction if you need one."

Andalynn hesitates but releases her grip. "Okay, just be careful."

The climb down isn't difficult. The strip of metal, easy to reach. But I can't quite find a place for both of my feet. I balance on my right toes and reach for the metal.

My skin crawls with energy, alive with goosebumps. I start with the bats high on the cavern ceiling, extending outward to find as many as I can. I compel them to swoop down on the wolves. The moment before the wave of flying rodents reaches the tallest pile of wolves, regret washes over me. I'm sending a lot of these bats to their death.

But remembering how they made me hate myself, how they filled me with doubt, I unleash them on the wolf's den. The wolves clamber to their feet. The fur on their backs prickles, and many of them slap their tails against the stone. The frenzied wolves have a bounty they haven't seen in a thousand years.

I force the bats to stay low to the ground but drive them out of the den through a large corridor. The wolves bound after their supper. It worked.

"That's it!" Rugnus shouts. "Now finish this."

The second I begin my descent, Koglim calls out, pointing his beefy hand toward the staff, where two wolves have already caught a few bats and are making short work of them. They didn't go out far enough.

I look up at Rugnus. "What now?"

"I don't—"

Koglim comes to the edge of the ledge and scrambles down. He hits the floor of the cavern. "Hey, wolfies. Wolfies!" He calls out, waving his arms. "How 'bout a big piece of meat. You like meat. Bats are gross. Come on."

The two remaining wolves adopt the same focus as the wolf from the hall. They gulp down their bat appetizer and bound for Koglim with dangerously happy faces.

Rugnus jumps down next to him, and they sprint to the other side of the den. The wolves continue after them.

"Go!" Andalynn screams at me. "It's our only chance."

I jump the rest of the way, landing on the rock below. The staff calls to me, and I rush forward. It floats at the top of a pile of stone like a prize. I scramble up the rock pile. A howl urges me forward. A group of wolves re-enters the den, apparently unsatisfied now that the bats are not under my control. Another five feet, and I'll have it.

As I reach out, a yowl of pain echoes off the rocks. I glance toward Rugnus and Koglim, but they're surrounded by wolves. Andalynn is no longer in the tunnel where we came out.

This is all wrong!

The pack howls triumphantly.

I pull the staff from its place. Instantly the howling stops. An incredible charge of power flows through my veins. Everything seems so insignificant and fragile. As I hop my way down from the rock pile, wolves hang their heads, letting me blur past them toward where I last saw Rugnus and Koglim. I still can't see Andalynn.

I speak to the minds of the wolves using the craft in the staff. They move out of my way. I feel my body growing larger. Hair prickles against the inside of my shirt. Fur sprouts on my legs and arms. Rough pads form on the palms of my hands. Andalynn comes into view. She's safe.

I'm half-man, half-wolf.

I can almost breathe easy, but my friends are in danger. Rugnus backs away from me in fear. "It's me." My voice feels like gravel.

Rugnus looks up to me. "Clayson?"

One of the wolves remains in my path. It growls. I smash the staff, the heart of the dungeon, over its head. "Heel." And it cowers before me.

I grin as they all let me pass. Koglim cries out in pain, blood staining his shirt. He can't get his legs under him. Andalynn is already moving to hold him. Rugnus looks from Koglim to me and back to Koglim.

The wolves stand around us in a circle, the heat of their breath palpable.

"I can't—ow," Koglim grimaces.

"Don't try to talk," Andalynn cautions.

"Rugnus." I look at him. Suddenly, a hunger for his flesh bubbles inside of me. It must be the staff. If I let it go, the wolves will be free to attack us.

"The price... this is..." Koglim trails off into a groan, almost weeping now.

I swing the staff over my head and pound it on the ground. "Where's the wraith?" My voice is deeper, gravellier. "We have the staff. Where is he?"

Rugnus' bag, our relics, appear near Koglim's body.

Andalynn strokes Koglim's forehead. "Rugnus, the gold bandage."

"That's not going to heal him!" Rugnus' hands grip the bag so tight they blanch white.

I start to ease back on the power of the staff—they need my help—but the wolves growl and take one step closer to them. Instead, I growl at Rugnus. "The bandage. Take away his pain."

Rugnus opens his mouth to speak but can't. His words catch in his throat. He pulls the bandage from his bag and kneels next to Koglim. The more he wraps around the wound, the calmer Koglim becomes. Koglim's side and leg are soaked in blood, but he sighs with relief and smiles.

He looks up. "Fizzblood. That's so much better."

He stands, but the moment he does, he collapses. After that, Andalynn can't get him to open his eyes.

A mass of cloud and light materialized over our heads. The wolves scatter, clawing past each other as they flee the den. The form and shape of a man appear in the cloud. Something falls, landing next to Rugnus.

"Icho!" Rugnus snatches his club from the ground.

"He's still breathing," Andalynn says. "Can you get us out of here?"

"Yeah. If the dungeon will let us budge to the exit."

With the wolves gone, I drop the staff, immediately returning to my normal self. I put one hand on Rugnus and one hand on Koglim, but Andalynn pushes my hands back.

"No. We came for a reason. Find out about Ergal. We'll take care of Koglim."

"I—no, this is my fault. I have to—"

Rugnus pushes me away. "Then, get what we came for."

I step to the side, and they vanish.

The cloud swirls in on itself, descending as it takes shape. Landred's features appear stronger this time, less ghostly and decaying.

"All things come to an end." He stands right next to me, and together we look out over the den. "I thought I would guard this place for eternity."

"I don't understand."

"The price. My mother wants—"

The cloud becomes an agitated mass. A few of the colored lights inside become bursting firecrackers. A rumble of thunder hits me like I'm standing next to a rushing freight train.

I yell over the din. "What's happening?"

Landred's head and torso suddenly appear in the cloud again. "She's coming!"

The mass swells, and in a single burst of light, dissipates like morning fog. I'm left alone in the den, the staff in my hands. Dozens of wolves watch from the shadows, but they are low to the ground, ears pressed flat. A hiss of breath causes me to whirl around, but there's only empty space between me and the wall.

I catch the large shadow on the wall. It takes the form of a Loamin, except stretched at the head, elongated at the feet, hands more claw than finger. It moves, and I catch layers upon layers of shadow as if there are a dozen lights projecting the shape onto the surface all at once. It moves again, and the hiss of words bleed from the rock, almost as visible as smoke.

"What are you?"

The shadowy projection billows out from the wall. "I am what you think I am."

"The champion. You're Torlina Wolfstaff."

"The burden is over. Take the staff."

I glance at the black metal in my hands. "What will happen if I do?"

"I will be free. Everything that has been trapped by this illusion will fade into the darkness of stone."

"What will happen to you? The dungeon, will it be... gone?" What would Rugnus think if he knew this was the outcome of our raid. Could Torlina actually leave this place? Is that what she's talking about?

"Perhaps I can remember my life again."

Something's not right about this. "You don't remember your life before the dungeon? That makes no sense. I saw Landred—"

"All of his thoughts, your thoughts, all of the minds of those who have entered here. I have had to peice together who I am, who I was. Even then… it does not matter. After this, I move on."

"To where? To what? I don't understand."

The hissing turns to laughter. "Nor do I. But no one else could take the heart. All who have touched it have died."

"Died? I could have died?"

"You didn't."

"Why not? What makes me different?"

"Shadows…" The layers of darkness against the wall form something larger. They curl and bend into a mass on four legs. The hiss becomes more of a growl.

"I-I don't know what that means."

"Shadows. This is why I gave you Ergal."

I look down at the staff on the ground. "And Ergal is-is what? Tell me. Landred promised me the story of Ergal."

The hiss-growl swells to a bone-rattling roar. "Ergal was not here to begin with. It was brought by a man named Exralt Blackmug. Do you know this name?"

"No."

"The relic was beyond his power to control. Blackmug wanted to leave it here."

"Why?"

"Safe."

"And he did? You let him leave it in your dungeon?"

"For a price."

My body involuntarily shudders. "What price?"

The shadows on the wall become a story. A man runs, falls. As he gets up, wolves swirl around him until he's gone. Torlina fed Blackmug to her pets. I hang my head.

"Did he know where Ergal came from?" I ask.

"Shadows," Torlina hisses.

"I don't understand. What else can you tell me about the ring?"

"Another came for it but was not worthy."

The shadows on the wall transform into the shape of another man, but this time a smaller shape stands near him—a girl. "Is that a child? I thought they weren't allowed to enter the dungeons?"

The man, and what I can only assume to be his daughter, run for their lives. They climb over stones, hide in a river, but the pack of wolves stays on their trail. The man hides his daughter in something, maybe mud. He faces the wolves, a knife in his hand, his daughter peeking out. She watches as they take one of his legs, a foot, then an arm. He drags himself into a different puddle of mud, opposite the child. When the wolves leave him behind to die, the girl crawls out and comes to his side.

"The knife," Torlina hisses, a shadow curling around an object inside the misted story art.

Inky tendrils snake from the knife into the man. The man forms a new leg from the mud, and they walk toward a door in the stone. This is their escape from the dungeon. Torlina let them go. The reality—this secret—hits me so hard I nearly topple over.

"When did this happen?"

"You already know."

Disbelief swirls inside my mind. "This is Theridal Silver-keeper, and th-that's Sira, his daughter. This is where his accident happened. No one knew what happened. That's the silver knife. He came in with it, looking for Ergal."

"Silverlamp's spawn were not worthy of the ring, even though they had its equal."

"The knife and the ring are equals?"

"Yes. Now... your promise. The story is told. The price. Take the staff and leave. Free me!" The shadow swells, appendages peel away from the wall and stretch out over the cavern. The wolves howl as one. The staff quakes on the ground.

"I don't want this!"

"Take it or die!"

Snarling, anger coiling my muscles into a viper ready to strike, I lift the staff again. In front of me, the blinding white of the threshold door appears, and the copper embellishments crack along the seams. The door swings open.

The shadows grow closer to my feet. The writhing mass herds me toward the door, and just before I exit, I hear the hiss of Torlina Wolfstaff. "Yinzar awaits you in his dungeon."

I open my mouth to speak, but the light from the doorway swallows me.

The world grows instantly colder. There's only light. Cool stone under my hands and knees. When my sight returns, I find myself in the entrance lobby, at the opening behind the waterfall. I take a few steps until I can see the cut in the rock below that leads to the threshold.

Strange. I expected the exit lobby. What will happen if someone tries to enter the dungeon through the threshold again? Is Torlina Wolfstaff free?

In answer, the entire room shakes, the disrupted waterfalls splash torrents beyond their bounds. With a loud crack of stone, one of the massive chandeliers breaks free from its mount and comes crashing down into the river below, pulled under the churn and eaten up by the edges of the tunnel.

A new power rips through my blood. I can't explain what it is. Maybe it has to do with the heart of the dungeon. Or maybe it's something else—the soul of Torlina herself taking possession of me—but it causes a smile to bubble to my lips. I feel free.

The thought passes quickly. I shake the smile off my face.

Strange. Terrifying and strange.

As the other chandelier frees itself from the stone and drops to the floor, I run for the tunnel behind the waterfall, cursing myself. When the council sent me to Wolfstaff, I don't think they wanted me to destroy it.

"The council's gonna melt me."

GATHER THE PIECES

THE LEADMAGES GIVE Koglim a fifty percent chance of living through the healing process. I watch through a slotted window, bordered with hard rivets of iron, as they affix some contraption to his side and upper leg. Long screws drill down into the marrow of his bones—drill down and reverse back, drill down and reverse back. Six separate gears, varying in size, made from a copper-lead alloy, spin on the screw heads. I don't hear his screams until the door opens briefly and Rugnus steps out.

Feral wolf attacks are rare. These leadmages are specialists, housed deep in the belly of Tungsten City, in a cave dripping rust-tinged water. I don't know much about Loamin sanitation laws, but this doesn't seem to pass the grade.

Rugnus stares at Torlina's staff, shrunken by half somehow and lashed to my bag with a leather strap. "The leadmages can't figure out how to keep him sedated. The expert on this type of stuff... she was killed during the attack on StoneYoke."

"But he's alive," I say.

Rugnus smiles softly. "And if he lives through it, he'll never stop telling everyone how awesome it was. He'll still probably want to try and tame one of them."

I bring up my arm and shake the bracelet on my wrist. "Peerless in shields, and I still couldn't stop this from happening."

"Not your fault. Takes a special type of craft to heal wounds caused by a feral wolf. Leadmages say they haven't used tooth gears in decades, but the injured are always out of Wolfstaff when they do."

Andalynn pushes through the door next, and Koglim's screams reach me again.

"Well, they won't have to worry about that anymore," I say.

Andalynn frowns. "Worry about what?"

I take a deep breath. "Whatever I did, when I took this staff out of the dungeon, I think I destroyed it. The lobby came tumbling down around me. Wolfstaff said... she'd be free."

Rugnus eyes the staff again. "Can't be possible. Are you sure?"

"Yeah, it's gone."

From around a corner, Hemdi and Winta duck into this branch of the cave. Winta struts toward the window and looks down at Koglim. "Idiot." She spins back to Rugnus and me, hands hanging away from her midsection. "Spill it. What happened?"

"Wait." Andalynn puts up a hand, sorting through something on bluelink. "Jeiah sent me a message. Clayson, are your notifications on?"

A knot of fear twists in my stomach. Jeiah had been chasing that lead on Bazalrak. I open bluelink, scan my notifications, and find a few messages she's sent me. Before I can read them, a video chat pops up. It's her.

I smile. "Hey, what's—"

She breathes a sigh of relief. "There you are. I have some news."

"Yeah, so do I."

She squints. "What's wrong? Never mind, where can we meet?"

"You look—are you okay?"

"Sure, besides being followed through the city and having my paladin's access revoked by the *new* Bluekeeper."

"Brick."

"Yeah."

I peer through the video to the rest of the group. "I'm going to head to my vault. Jeiah has news."

Rugnus looks between the tiny window and me. "The nurses said we couldn't stay here anyway. We'll come with you."

Winta shakes her head. "We just got here. I want to check on—"

"Leadmages said it would be a full day. There's not much we can do," Rugnus adds "He'd want us to keep pushing ahead."

I add, "And, I think everyone needs to hear about Wolfstaff."

Rugnus scrambles for his club and holds it out. "Ready?"

Winta turns back for only a second to look at Koglim. "Yeah, okay. But we'll come back to check on him?"

Rugnus smiles. "Never crossed my mind we wouldn't."

In a blink, we arrive at my vault. The news feeds along the wall offer the only light. I programmed the vault to play music when I enter, so a cerebral electronic mix overlays a chill beat in the background.

I give Jeiah permission to budge into the vault, and she immediately appears.

"Hey. Um..." Her sudden appearance triggers my self-conscious mode. "Let me find you somewhere to sit. I—"

"I just saw the news," she says. "Clay, what did you do? What happened in Wolfstaff?"

"Is this it?" Hemdi's pointing to an icon in the newsfeed. It's Wolfstaff's logo, but instead of the silver and gold wolf head, it's flashing red.

"Open it." Rugnus glances in my direction.

I snatch the icon from the air and throw it in the middle of our circle. The light from the recording glares as we watch Wolfstaff come to an end. The gargantuan chandeliers fall from the ceiling of the lobby and crash into the waterfall. The stone walls thunder down to the floor. It loops a few times, and then Rugnus reaches up and pauses it, zooming in on the staircase. There I am. Unmistakable. In the shifting lights, smiling.

"Are you..."

"I... Wolfstaff, or whatever it was, kind of settled on me for a second. I felt satisfied with everything. Th-that's not me."

"If you're going to destroy a dungeon," Rugnus says, "the least you can do is be upset about it."

"I was. I-I am."

"Maybe it was gas?" Winta jokes. "Wait, did you say *destroy* a dungeon?"

Hemdi shakes his head. "That is not what he means. Dungeons are indestructible. He means the lobby."

Jeiah removes her blue glass rod, and a blue light passes over my face. "The video is authentic. How can that be right?"

Winta grabs my shoulders and whirls me around. "Sacred bones. Is this... wraiths melt me. You did it this time. This is Torlina Wolfstaff's staff."

"So Wolfstaff is... gone?" Hemdi's mouth twitches. He sits down roughly on a nearby stool. "This is awful. I can't... this is too much."

The pained lines at his mouth and eyes deepen. Winta moves to his side with a sigh. She puts an arm around him. "This is hard, but neither of us have dealings with Wolfstaff for the most part, and—"

"I'm not thinking of myself," Hemdi snaps.

Hemdi never snaps.

"There are thousands of people who are connected to Wolfstaff! Tens of thousands. There are people whose lives will be permanently affected by this. Scholar raiders, summation leaders, representatives, coppersmiths. The list goes on and on and on. Think of others for once!"

Winta's jaw flexes, and her hand comes away from around Hemdi. She smooths back the wisps of her dark hair and opens her mouth to speak.

Rugnus intercedes. "There's more at stake. People will think Clayson destroyed the dungeon on purpose, and if he did that..."

Andalynn picks up the thought, "...then he may be powerful enough to attack the festival. It's what Emberfence has been saying this whole time."

"That's ridiculous!" Winta says.

"It might not be true, but it's *not* hard to believe," Hemdi says. "People are hurt, looking for answers." He goes silent, but his body language is defensive.

"People are stupid," Winta says.

Rugnus throws his hands in the air. "The people are not the problem. It's the council! And it's... it's Clayson. Running around, breaking everything under granite. Ide keep me, Clayson, this... I knew this would..." He growls in frustration.

"Clayson didn't cause the attack on StoneYoke," Jeiah insists, and there's something about her voice that both draws me in and quiets the whole group. "And I have proof."

"Then you know who—"

"Maybe. But more importantly, I know what happened." Jeiah places an 3D map next to my newsfeed. She zooms in on the now-familiar image of StoneYoke district. With a quick gesture, she flips the map vertically so that the hanging glass skyscrapers are right-side-up and the giant terraced volcano containing the amphitheater is upside down.

At the base of the skyscrapers, the construction drones appear more like vultures than hanging bats. Jeiah zooms in further on one of the drones, and the image advances to the second, where the skyscrapers come unglued, and gravity takes over. Complicated letters, symbols, and numbers appear in a spider web pattern. Waving her blue glass rod, another image snaps into place beside it. Lagnar's battery.

"Is that what powered the mechs up?" Rugnus says.

Andalynn blinks. "It wasn't Bazalrak? Rugnus was right about Lagnar?"

Jeiah shrugs. "In a way. Every object contains a unique craftprint, and every use of that object augments that craftprint just enough to be distinguishable. In fact, you could use the same object thousands of different times, and it would create a different craftprint each time. But here's where it gets weird. The craftprint on every mech is identical, like someone copied and pasted instructions to each one."

Winta pushes me out of the way to get a closer look. "Unreal. That's not even craft. Did you try to find a match in—"

"Yes. There is a print that matches—exactly matches."

"Impossible," Winta says.

"This craftprint is from a raid of Chromewall Dungeon," Jeiah continues. "Thirty years ago, Lagnar used the battery during a raid to power up a suit of armor. Foilgrips, mechcraft, and blue-craft connection. Everything that appeared in the craftprint during StoneYoke festival."

Winta taps her fingers to her lips. "Are you saying someone is stealing craftprints and finding a way to magnify them?"

"More like multiply them," Jeiah says, "but, essentially yes. This is new. There is no kind of craft like this. Anywhere."

"Could the mithrium be involved?" I ask. What they're saying sounds impossible, but since when is anything around mithrium normal? "And what about the flare from the brightstorm during the attack?"

Jeiah shrugs. "As far as mithrium... any guess is as good as another. And the flare from the brightstorm seems to be some strange aftereffect. I haven't found the connection. The only thing we really know is—"

"The craftprint is from Lagnar's history," Rugnus says. "He did this."

"Or, more likely," Jeiah says, "it's being made to look like he did this."

We fall quiet as we process this information. Who would frame Lagnar Emberfence? Who even could?

Andalynn clasps her hands. "What about the video from Bazalrak you sent us. Could you trace it?"

Jeiah shakes her head.

"That settles it," Winta said. "There's only one person that could bury message data so deep inside bluelink that neither of us can find it."

"Lagnar," Rugnus says.

"What about Sira?" I ask.

Rugnus' lip curls. "What about her?"

"Well," I start, "she showed up at the festival. She had the battery. And... there's more. Something I learned in Wolfstaff before..."

Jeiah touches my arm. "What happened in there?"

"I know where Ergal came from. Well, no. I know how it got into Wolfstaff."

Hemdi, who's been sitting by quietly, levels his eyes on me. "Tell us."

"A man, Exralt Blackmug, a raider, I guess, came into Wolfstaff trying to hide the ring from the rest of the world. It worked, but Wolfstaff killed him. Years later, guess who shows up? Silverkeeper and Sira. He was looking for Ergal, but instead—"

"The accident," Andalynn says with a start.

"The accident. The wolves attacked. Torlina let them escape, but Sira had to keep him alive, control him, force him to live. But they never got the ring."

"Wolfstaff bestowed it on you," Rugnus says. "Did you find out why?"

"Something about a shadow."

Hemdi looks up sharply. "You spoke directly to the champion?"

I nod. "She wanted me to take the staff. She said she would be free."

Hemdi mulls this over. "She was a prisoner? Is that how all the champions feel?"

"I don't know." I rub my hand across the day's growth on my chin. I need another quick clean. "But they're connected. Plus, Ergal and Onrix fit into all this somehow. Torlina said they were equals. And remember, before he died, Silverkeeper mentioned a third relic. Something just as powerful as the other two. Which I've been thinking about. What if it's Icho?"

Rugnus scrunches up his face like he's tasted something disgusting. "What? No. My mother presented it to me after my summation."

"It's the most powerful budge I've ever seen," Hemdi says. "Maybe Clayson's right."

Jeiah looks like someone just dumped cold water over her. "So Silverkeeper mentioned three objects."

"Yes."

"Ergal and Onrix, I understand," she says, "but Icho, even knowing how powerful it is, that is simply conjecture."

As the thought cycles through my mind, Winta replaces half my news wall with a picture and text. The man floating in front of us wears a long beard braided with aluminum foil. A cap of iron plasters his long hair to his head, and beneath that, covering his eyes, he wears a pair of orange-tinted sunglasses. His clothes place him sometime before the Mithrium War began.

EXRALT BLACKMUG
10TH TIER RAIDER/POET

"He's nobody," Winta says.

"Poet?" I ask.

Hemdi says, "I bet Koglim would know him. Even a tenth tier."

Rugnus disconnects the text, moving it closer to his face. "Huh." He clicks on the highlighted words Zal Kakraja, which leads to another text. "My mother's family comes from Zal Kakraja."

"They couldn't have known each other," Winta says.

Rugnus brings our attention back to the text. "Says he's famous for searching for protodungeons. And for the loss of his shieldcraft after being—"

"Wraithtouched," Hemdi says, reading over his shoulder.

Winta scoffs. "He ever find a protodungeon?"

"Doesn't say."

"What's a protodungeon again?" I ask. "I mean, I think I've heard of that, but..."

Jeiah answers. "There are ninety-three known dungeons. The first one, Runearmor, opened after his death in 3282 anteprimus. Before that, the Rimduum mountains were held by dragons, lithic trolls, feral wolves, azdeth, lizards—the creatures of the ancient world.

"Protodungeons were made long before Runearmor and the First Age. They say Loamin used to occupy the mountains here. That there was an exodus of sorts. Loamin didn't come back to these mountains until the First Age."

I nod, some of the pieces falling into place. "So Ergal could have been made before the First Age when Loamin originally lived in these mountains, uh, before their exodus around the world."

"I suppose it's possible," Andalynn says, "but that would make it more than five thousand years old."

Winta whistles. "I've never seen a more powerful object than Ergal or Onrix... or Icho for that matter."

Jeiah shakes her head. "It's a theory."

"But it makes a lot of sense," I add.

"Clayson," Rugnus says, "I just don't think it's my club. I mean, the attack on the festival used mechcraft and bluecraft."

Andalynn's eyes open wider. She understands something I don't. "But if this third relic comes from before the first age..." She looks at me. "Bluecraft, mechcraft, and time craft weren't discovered until the end of the First Age."

"So," I say, "a relic with the power to destroy the festival couldn't have been found in a protodungeon."

"And," Jeiah says, "there's the battery and the craftprint to justify. I'm not seeing the connection to the protodungeon myths."

Hemdi clears his throat. "Myth is the right word for it. And if they did exist, who's to say they didn't have mechcraft or bluecraft long before the Loamin exodus? History and time have a way of forgetting."

Rugnus throws up his hands. "So, we're back at square one. We don't know what type of object was used. We don't even know for sure who did it."

"Sira gave us the bottle as a clue," I say. "Emberfence has to be involved somehow."

"But it's not true craft," Jeiah reminds us. "It's duplication."

"So, what do we do now?"

Andalynn says, "We need to face the council, tell them about Blackmug, Silverlamp, and Ergal. That's why they sent us to Wolfstaff in the first place."

"I'll go. I'll tell the council what happened in Wolfstaff, and—"

"No way," Rugnus says. "They'll throw you in Keelcrawl prison before the day is out."

"Talking to the council is the only way to get access to the mines." Everyone waits on my next words. "We locate Mithriumbane. Stick with the council's original orders. Wolfstaff said Yinzar was waiting for me."

Winta's eyes nearly bug out of her head. "Now, there's a plan. First, blow up a dungeon everyone likes. Next, find a dungeon that everyone in all Rimduum has been looking for for over fourteen years. After that, it's a chunk of cake, just grab a bit of mithrium and make something special for your new girlfriend and call it a day."

I ignore her girlfriend comment, but I can't help glancing at Jeiah. She returns a curious glance at me. I aim my words at Winta. "Chunk of cake? You mean piece of cake."

She growls at me.

"And there's no mithrium in that dungeon," I add. "Yinzar destroyed it."

Rugnus angles away from us, scanning the news for a brief minute but then closing his eyes. Andalynn maintains her place in our circle but scoots closer to him. On the far side of the wall, a media stream about the upcoming memorial service scrolls slowly upward. Koglim had been helping to plan the event alongside the professional raider's union and Rusela Whitechin—Rugnus' mother. Rugnus watches the comments spool by.

His attention is drawn back toward the newfeeds. An icon I recognize blinks yellow. It's the logo for Kel's Lounge. I know it well. We go there pretty much every week to watch raiders compete in the Hundred Dungeon Games. It's where I first met Koglim.

Rugnus fiddles with the icon. "Weird."

I stand next to him. "What is it?"

"Koglim had this alarm set up—called it the awesome alarm. It goes off when a large group gathers at Kel's. Usually means some event or just a good size crowd that will make for a fun time."

"The dungeons are at a standstill," Hemdi says. "What else would draw a crowd?"

Rugnus takes Icho from his side. "Should we check it out?"

Jeiah gestures to the icon. "I've been to that place. Has good soup."

Rugnus nods approvingly. "Yes, it does."

"Is this really a priority?" Andalynn says, not so much impatient, but confused.

Rugnus smooths down the hem of his shirt. "Something seems off. Let's just check."

No one argues, so Rugnus produces Icho, blinks, and we leave my vault behind.

Kel's Lounge sits on the fringe of Tungsten City. The budge lands us at the edge of a loud, swelling crowd. One man tries to shove Rugnus back, but he sees Andalynn. His mouth drops open, and he lets us pass.

"Excuse us," I say.

He murmurs my name, and the crowd catches on. After another second, a wide lane has been cleared. I'm not sure if they honor us or fear me. Knowing what's in the news, maybe a bit of both.

We stop at the edge of the crowd, gaping. Kel's Lounge is covered in Bazalrak's shadowcraft. Drapes and tendrils of gray shadow hang over the normally green-gray desert landscaping. Even the bright cactus flowers are cloaked with a ghostly film.

My heart is in my throat. I've seen Bazalrak use this power, but the effect has never been this widespread.

"Keep Ide," Hemdi whispers.

"Bazalrak," Andalynn hisses.

Jeiah begins scanning the air with her blue glass rod, gathering forensic details. "Careful not to touch the shadows," Jeiah says, but no one needs reminding.

Rugnus surveys the landscaping and the building. "It's like a shadowcraft bomb went off. Can Bazalrak's ax do this?"

"Maybe he just exploded," Winta mutters. "If we're lucky."

"Wait," Jeiah says, and the urgency in her voice stalls our methodical trail forward. "Wraithspit! This shadowcraft comes from a multiplied craftprint, just like the attack."

Everyone has the same reaction. "What?"

Hemdi says, "Maybe Bazalrak used the same object that Lagnar used, something that can magnify—"

"Multiply," Jeiah corrects, stepping back from an encroaching shadow.

"—Multiply craft. The third object."

"The third object," Rugnus agrees, "Not Icho."

Jeiah nods, but her face keeps an edge of skepticism. "I scanned Icho's effect. It's frankly not like any craftprint I've seen before—extremely powerful—but if it was like the object we're looking for, I would've noticed. No multiplier."

Winta cuts to the front of our group. "Do you think Bazalrak is in there?"

The whole scene pushes me back to the night we fled the cabin, the night I met Bazalrak for the first time. I grit my teeth. "One way to find out." I extend my shield around the front of the group, and the shadow fights against the circle of light I've projected. It's not lightcraft, but it's the best I can do under the circumstances. "I'll lead the way. Hemdi," I call back, "can you cover the back with as much shield craft as you can?"

"Certainly."

We make our way past a tall barrel cactus oozing with deep shadows. Half of the flagstone path leading into the restaurant is covered, and to avoid it, we move through the landscaping in a single file path. When we reach the doorway, we freeze.

Two men block the entrance. They're covered in pools of darkness, their mouths half open, jaws pushed forward in a soundless scream. Their eyes look soulless and hungry.

"Ide keep us," Rugnus whispers.

I extend the ring of shieldcraft outward, but the shadows rise from their bodies like venomous snakes, testing the shield with strike after strike.

"I'm not sure we can get through here," I say.

Behind us, I hear the crowd gasp. We all turn. Eddies of living light, like the rays of a July summer day, radiate in streams over the landscaping. The shadows flee before this new power. It's so bright our whole group has to avert our eyes as it approaches.

"Lighthealers." Hemdi's voice is thick with relief.

Andalynn calls out to them, "Over here, quickly. These men need help."

Two silent lighthealers appear at our side. They push past us, eyes closed, arms extended. Pure tungsten rings, each topped with an oval of white quartz, glow on their pinky fingers. One of them places his hands on the men guarding the door. The shadows dissipate, and the two men collapse to the ground.

"Will they be okay?" Hemdi calls after them, but they continue into the gloom of the restaurant without answering.

Two more lighthealers approach from behind us. One of them stops when he sees me. I recognize him. Where do I know him from?

"Clayson Brightstorm." I can read the surprise on his face. "Are you here to help?"

I remember where I saw him. He's the seer of Lighthealer Dungeon. I met him during the Keeper's Social last year when I healed Rugnus. He'd offered me a job. "What can I do?" I ask.

He looks at my bracelet. "Crude. I'm not surprised it works for you to some extent. Here"—he passes me a pinky ring— "use this."

The moment the ring touches my pinky, a powerful burst of light explodes from the front of my fist. I surge forward into the restaurant clearing huge swaths of shadows. The effect makes me yearn for Ergal. It could do this and more. Somehow, I doubt this ring can do more than eradicate shadowcraft. As I clear one half of the restaurant of shadows, I wonder if the ring is a relic from out of Lighthealer Dungeon itself.

The restaurant had been packed at the time of the attack— what else can I call it? Though Kel's patrons are free from the shadows, we can't wake them.

"Where's Kel?" Rugnus shouts.

We find her wrapped in the thickest shadows, in the far corner of the kitchen, and though I can free the area around her from shadows, they won't leave her body. Maybe it's because she's Dura, but the ring has little effect.

None of us dare to touch her in this state.

"Help her!" Rugnus yells. "Why isn't the ring working?"

"She's Dura. I-I don't—"

Kel's eyes open, and she takes in a breath. Maybe clearing the area of shadows around her body had helped somehow. Her voice is clear. "The first, the second. The first, the second. Between them. Not free, lost. Didn't work. Lost, lost, lost. Connection."

Aiming the ring directly at her chest, I blast her with light. The shadows writhe and stretch, but when I pull my arm away, nothing has changed.

Kel continues the same strange words.

"It's nonsense," Winta says.

"No. I've heard it before," I say. "From Tas, the other Dura in Geum Ide."

Rugnus sniffs. "Who did this to you? Was it Bazalrak?"

"The first. The first. The first. Ice and fire."

Hemdi finds a clear spot on Kel's forehead and tests her temperature with the back of his hand.

They're not listening to me. "She's not talking about temperature. Tas says this, connection."

Rugnus grasps desperately for someone to help. "She's not herself, though." He leans even closer to her. "What happened to you?"

The volume of Kel's voice increases, but she repeats herself.

"This has to be connected to the attack," I say.

"Forget about that!" Rugnus says. "Help! We need some help in here!"

The other lighthealers find us quickly, but even combined, only a few more strings of shadowcraft are broken. We need something more powerful, something to counteract the craft that was done here.

Craftprints. Why would Bazalrak or Lagnar attack Kel? I've seen so much disregard for Dura—treating them like servants, calling them vacants—could it have something to do with...

An idea, hot as wood ash, burns through the fog that's been my thoughts. The attack on the festival. The sheer power of it. I've seen it before. I try to shake the horror of the idea from my head, but it won't dislodge. Not Ara. It couldn't be. She doesn't do anything unless Dad—

"No." A whisper comes from my mouth. "No, no, no."

Loamin have no gods, only champions, or I would pray to them, beg them. Please don't let Dad be connected to any of this. To StoneYoke. To craftprints. Silverkeeper had left him a leaf containing something. What was it? They were friends. Did he know about Ergal? About Theridal's knife? Why didn't Dad wanna open that leaf?

Concern is written on Jeiah's face. "Are you okay?"

"I-I think I figured out who would have this kind of power. It's not a third object."

Rugnus is so concerned with Kel he barely looks up at me. "Figured what out?"

"Why didn't we see it? We should have known. The attack on the festival. It was a Dura. Maybe… it was Ara."

Now I have his attention, but his eyes are narrow in disbelief. "It can't be. Dura aren't like that. They're like children."

"Not Ara," I say. "You know that."

"Wait." Jeiah blinks rapidly. I can hear her brain making a dozen connections at once. "You know a Dura that can use craft as strong as Loamin?"

"Stronger," Andalynn says. "But Ara… she wouldn't."

"Maybe not, but if the attack on the festival was done by a Dura…"

Andalynn starts spinning more connections. "It explains how it could be so powerful. Maybe when Ara uses craft, it's like copying it from the Loamin she's borrowing from. And… and…"

"Multiplying the power," Jeiah whispers.

Kel has stopped talking. She pierces my mind with a look. *Connection.*

Rugnus sighs, nods, and turns back to me. "If we can get Kel to Geum Ide… maybe Ara can heal her. We need to go now."

"But—" Winta starts.

Rugnus cuts her off. "We go now. Take Kel."

He starts to draw Icho to budge us there, but Andalynn nudges his arm back. "What if they don't let us leave this time? Glaris warned us—"

"Kel's gonna die!" Rugnus is frantic now, looking from face to face, trying to find support.

He's right. "It's worth the risk," I say. "Let's go."

Andalynn takes a step away from us. "I can't go to Geum Ide. If I don't come back, the council…"

It's as if Rugnus has lost his footing. He shakes his head, blinks, and stammers. "I, well, but Kel. I need to…" Something in his eyes changes, hardens. He places Icho in my hands. "Take it. Take Kel. Figure out if Ara is involved. Figure out what your dad knows about the three relics. About protodungeons. Tell him what you learned in Wolfstaff. Everything. Tell him everything! I'll stay with Andalynn. And Clayson... bring Icho back to me. You hear?"

I don't know what to say. "Okay." I look around the group and swallow hard. What if I can't leave Geum Ide after this? Will I not see my sister again? Before I can close the distance between us, Andalynn pulls me toward her for a hug.

"Okay, okay," Winta says. "This isn't a funeral. Besides, Hemdi and I are coming with you."

"You are?" I ask.

Hemdi's mouth falls open. "We are?'

"Let's just go," Winta grumbles, "before I change my mind."

Jeiah's eyes find mine. She doesn't look away. "I'll keep working on Bazalrak's video. It must lead somewhere. Andalynn, I'll share my findings about the attack with the council."

Andalynn inclines her head. "That will go a long way."

The seer of Lighthealer Dungeon gestures toward the ring. "Keep it. This is a dangerous time. You can bring light where there is shadow."

Jeiah lightly shoves me. "Find a way back, okay."

"I will. I have to." I grip Icho and find a place on Kel to contact her skin. Winta and Hemdi grab on as well. "You sure this will get me through the mithrium shield?"

"It will," Rugnus says. "I just hope it's not a one-way ticket."

I swallow again and budge us to Geum Ide.

We appear in the town square, near the fountain, surrounded by pillars of red granite. Light from the brightstorm soaks the dark green brush and shimmers off the surface of the pond. A host of people moving through the square jump back in surprise.

I yell for my parents, Ara, or my grandmother, but no one comes to our aid. There must be ten times as many people living here as when we last came, but the sudden appearance of craft has them scared or angry. An ominous feeling sinks like a weight in my gut. We shouldn't have come here.

Within a half of a minute, we're surrounded by guards, each with handmade rifles. One guard whispers to another, and the first one slings his gun back over his shoulder and disappears into the crowd.

"You were told not to return," he says.

"Kel's dying, you idiot!" Winta shouts.

"Where are my parents? Where's Ara or my grandmother?"

A tall figure squeezes through the people. It's Tas. "The first and second. The first and the second."

"Connection," Kel groans.

"Connection?" Tas squints at me.

Kel squirms under the cloak of shadow. "The first? The first and the second... and the third."

"And the fourth." Tas smiles oddly.

"Connection," Kel groans again.

I open my mouth in question, but I hear my mom's voice in the distance.

"Clayson?" She bursts through the guards, Dad trailing behind. "Clayson!" She rushes to me.

When they see the shadows over Kel, they both stop short.

For some reason—maybe it's all Dad's other secrets—my mouth hardens into an accusation. I look right at him. "Where's Ara?"

CONTEND WITH CONJURERS

MY MOM STARES wide-eyed at Kel. "But she's Dura. Who would do this to a vacant?"

Kel's teeth are clenched, eyes shut. Her right hand, unencumbered by shadowcraft, tightens and releases over and over.

The crowd swells with the commotion of our arrival. Loamin of all backgrounds and ages surge into the square. Most of them look curious or surprised, but a few look angry—really angry. I hear the roar of a few engines in the distance, and I know my grandmother, Glaris, or her right-hand-man, Nasur Lavalock, must be on their way.

"Ara. Quick, Dad," I prod him again. "Where is she? We can budge to her if we have to."

But when I move toward him with Icho drawn, Dad drops to Kel's side. "It's Shadowcraft."

My mom's hands are shaking. "Bazalrak?"

Dad stands and faces me. "Why didn't you call a lighthealer?"

"The lighthealers did all they could. We need Ara. Where is she?"

"What do you mean they did all they could?"

Winta huffs. "Meaning they couldn't do anything. Now, where's Ara?"

"The wound isn't the same as normal craft," I say. "It's like someone took a single craftprint and—"

Dad's head snaps back to me. "Multiplied. That's why you need Ara. You think... no. No, she couldn't have done this. How bad was th-this shadow attack?"

I can read the expression on his face. The same thing I've seen every time some secret comes spilling out. Hurt feelings? Guilt maybe. "You know something, don't you? Ara's power. She can multiply craftprints."

"Keep your voice down," Dad hisses, scanning the crowd.

My mom looks bewildered. "What is he talking about? How Ara heals the brightstorm?"

The crowd parts, and two trucks with armed Loamin toss up gravel at the edge of the square, skidding to a halt. Nasur jumps from the first truck, spits on the ground, and unholsters a heavy pistol from his belt.

Hemdi gulps. "I think our arrival has upset Lavalock again."

"Dad," I say softly. "This can't wait. I can give my lighthealing craftprint to Ara. I know she can heal Kel."

The conflict on his face seems almost painful, like someone's peeling back his skin. "I-I can't."

"Then I will," My mom steps over to me, holding out her hand. "Come on."

Nasur levels his pistol at me. "Nobody mo—" His face freezes. Winta's twirling a wheel of mercury in front of her. She's holding them in place with timecraft.

"He won't be happy you used craft against him," I say.

"Just go." Winta breaths heavily. "Hurry."

Hemdi watches his wife with worry. Timecraft shouldn't take this much out of her.

My mom takes Icho from me, and we budge someplace dark, water covering our feet, surrounded by red stone on three sides. The fourth side is made from iron bars. It's a prison cell. I jump when I hear Ara's voice.

She steps down from the only surface not submerged in water, splashing toward us. "Hello. Is that, Clayson? What are you doing here?"

A single column of light illuminates the center of the room. Ara steps under the bright column, looking toward me but not right at me, like a toddler trying to catch a glimpse of something frightening but filled with too much fear to look directly at it.

We must be on the lower level of the settlement somewhere.

"They're keeping you here?" I ask. "How long have—"

My mom answers for her. "About a week. The conjurers are afraid. They think she can affect the shield somehow."

"The shield?" My mind spins. This thought will have to wait. Ara was here during the attack. It wasn't her. I grab her hand. "We can talk about that later. We need help."

She doesn't hesitate.

My mom budges us back to the square where Winta still faces off against Nasur and several frozen guards. "Hurry up!" she growls at me. "None of them have craft, but if there's enough of them, one could slip through." As if to highlight her words, one of the men unfreezes briefly and swings his gun toward me, only to freeze again, his finger on the trigger.

"Right." I pull Ara toward Kel. "Take my lighthealing."

"Kel?" Ara says, dazed. Another squeeze of her hand, and she snaps out of it. "Okay."

"So, what do I need to—" All at once, I feel empty, naked. She's stripped away my shieldcraft. It's gone. A chill runs through my blood. I grasp my bracelet but its doesn't work. Is this what Dad felt each time she took his craftprint on the surface? Like an exposed nerve?

Dad edges over, placing an arm around me. My mind flashes to the night Ara came to warn us of Bazalrak. Dad had seemed invigorated when she drew his ironcraft from him. He'd been able to breath more freely, run past me even. Did taking his craftprint also remove the effects of fizzblood? I add this mystery to the sea of unknown things I'm currently dealing with.

Sunlight pours from Ara's hands in a huge cone, spotlighting

Kel's tall frame, so bright everyone looks away. In slow motion, Nasur and the conjurers stare in shock, but then, Winta lets her mercury band draw back around her wrist. She stumbles, but Hemdi is there to steady her. Still, the guards and Nasur don't move.

When the light recedes, the shadowcraft is gone. Kel sits up, and, more clearly, she states the same message as before. "The fourth. I am the fourth. Below fire and ice. Deeper. The first and the second and... and..." She scans the bewildered crowd, finding another figure. "...the third."

Tas emerges from between two startled Loamin. "The third. Connection?"

"Connection," Kel says. She sweeps toward Tas and embraces him. With lucid, wide eyes, they turn and look at Ara.

They speak as one. "Connection?"

Ara makes direct eye contact with them. With a small gesture, she nods.

Dad blinks disbelievingly. "What is happening? Ara, what is the connection?"

"I..." She looks down at her hands. "I can hear them. With Tas, it was so slight, but now... Something is happening."

My mom crosses the distance to her, gripping her shoulders. "What's happening?"

"It's like they're half awake. I need... I—"

Nasur Lavalock's nasally voice rising into the air. "Grab her! She's going back to her cell. And those three, take any visible object from them, and get them in the truck."

Nasur's men move to subdue us. But this I expected. I knew we would have to give up our objects and relics while here. Lowering Icho, I nod with reassurance to Hemdi and Winta, but they're already dropping their objects.

Ara's words are so soft, I barely hear them. "I won't."

"Ara, wait!" Dad's too late.

Blinding light fills the square, rushing outward. It feels like standing too close to a brush fire. Nasur roars with indignation, pushing past me even in the scorching light, heading for Ara. But the light continues to move until it's far enough, dim enough to open my eyes. I search the square for Ara, but she's gone.

Nasur's voice is as cold as Thiffimdal. "Find her. All she's got is light, and she'll burn through the craft eventually."

A few of his men jump in one of the trucks and peel off in the direction where the light had lingered. He steps over toward me and yanks Icho from my grip. He hefts the wolfstaff relic from its place at my back. Shaking his head, he shouts into my face. "How dare you come back here!"

"Kel was dying. We—"

"That's not our concern." He passes our objects to a subordinate and shakes his head. "Glaris will return from the shield wall by daychange. Until then, we need to take you to the Great Barn, divest you of all of your craft objects."

"Then back here," Dad says.

Nasur rolls his head back with his eyes. "Do what you want, Therias. But hear me: this time, the consequences will be much worse for you and your family."

Dad ignores him. "Let's get you three up to the Great Barn, so you can change while you're here."

Nasur Lavalock, huffs, holsters his gun, and climbs behind the driver's seat.

Hemdi and I help Winta climb up into the truck bed. My parents sit across from us. The rest of the guards climb in around us, gunmetal shining.

The winding path leads away from the red granite settlement, through the terrace farms, and uphill to the Great Barn, a massive building of stone and glass. We pass crowd after crowd.

"So many new people," Hemdi shouts over the roar of the truck.

Dad offers a genuine smile. "All vetted. Friends or family of those who live here, or just nulls who want a chance at a normal life. In fact, that's where Glaris is. She went up to the wall to bring back this week's newcomers and collect messages. There has been a lot more interest in our lifestyle since the shield went up, but she wants to make sure everyone that comes in is committed to the conjurer lifestyle."

"Any changes since the attack?" I ask.

My mom blinks. "Attack? I thought... wasn't that today? At Kel's?"

They don't know about StoneYoke. This realization drops a stone into my stomach. I don't wanna be the one to tell them. "When was the last time you went for messages?"

My mom shrugs. "About this time last week. Why?"

Dad puts a hand on my back, concern in his eyes. "What attack? Is this about Kel?"

Winta, Hemdi, and I trade looks. Geum Ide really is sealed off from the world. Whatever process they have in place for keeping out the influence of either of the remaining cities must be working.

"Andalynn's festival... StoneYoke was attacked."

Dad's face is unreadable.

The trucks jerk to a stop in front of the Barn. Nasur swings down from the driver's side and gestures for everyone to get out of the truck.

But the five of us stay seated, tension like a taut string suspended in the air.

Dad holds a hand up for them to wait. "Can everyone give us some space?"

Nasur squints at us. With a signal, he sends the rest of the guard toward the Barn. He leans against the lip of the truck bed.

"What happened?" Dad asks.

With a deep breath, I explain everything: the disruptions, seeing Sira, the skyscrapers falling into the festival, bluelink and budges being blocked, and finally, our suspicion of Emberfence and the death of Bluekeeper. The evidence about the craft battery.

Dad shakes his head. "Ara was here." But there's another secret behind his eyes.

"Don't keep anything from me, Dad. What is it? What are you thinking?"

"Nothing." He waves a hand. "Just... she didn't do this. She's been locked up for almost a week."

When he tries to stand, I push him back to his seat. He can't brush me off this easily. "I know when you're keeping things from me, Dad. What am I missing here?"

"I... we need to find Ara. But trust me, Clayson. She didn't do this."

Winta tries to stretch her back. "I thought she was, like, sacred to the conjurers. She helped heal the brightstorm. Why do they have her locked up?"

My parents both speak. "The shield."

"Ara has felt drawn to it," my mom continues. "No one knows why. But the conjurers fear she could disrupt it somehow. She agreed to be moved to the cell as a preventative measure."

"Has she disrupted the shield?" Hemdi asks.

"No," Nasur says. "But we won't risk it."

I make sure Dad's looking at me. "If Ara could absorb even more craft from you—like the type of craft in the battery..."

Reluctant, he nods. "It would be exponential. Multiplying a multiplier."

Nasur stands by scowling. "StoneYoke. How many dead?"

There's a long sigh from Hemdi. Winta answers. "Almost half a million."

A cloud of grief settles on Nasur. "Ide keep us."

My mom looks to the brightstorm, and Dad looks at his feet. Eventually, Nasur forces us from the truck bed and into the Great Barn.

We follow the same process as last time; they already have our objects, so we each find a changing stall and switch to the simple linens of the conjurers.

I keep seeing Dad's knowing look. There's something he's not telling me—as always.

My thoughts float before me in pieces. I can only connect a

few of them. The attacker from the festival used the battery with craftprint from Lagnar. But then Sira gave us the bottle. Gave me Onrix. Why? A day later, someone used Bazalrak's craftprint to attack Kel, a Dura. Did Kel begin talking in riddles before or after the attack? Was she involved somehow?

Ara. Tas. Kel. They must be connected to this. If it wasn't Ara… did Kel attack StoneYoke? Maybe Emberfence and Bazalrak were using her? But that's not right. Tas can't use craftprints like Ara. Ara's the only one who can do anything like that.

"Hey!" Dad's shout echoes from down the hall. I yank on my shirt and dart out of the changing room.

A dozen guards have Kel and Tas at gunpoint.

"They didn't do anything wrong!" Dad growls. "Stop this."

Nasur fiddles with his revolver. "If the type of craft Ara used to heal the brightstorm can be used by other vacants, I'm not taking the chance. Where was Tas a few days ago? Do we know?"

Tas and Kel mumble to each other. Something in their words is important. I just don't understand why. If I can get back, maybe Jeiah can see how everything fits together.

Nasur whistles shrilly, and guards move to the three of us. "You've come here without any authorization. You were told not to come back. So, this is what we are going to do. You're going back down to Geum Ide with your father." Disgust poisons his words. "And you'll stay there until Glaris gets back."

He turns to the guards. "Half of you can escort these people back to town, including Therias and Azbena. The other half stay here. No one gets access to this building for the next twenty-four hours. Even me. Keep these *vacants* under close guard, give them dinner, but otherwise don't interact with them."

"You're making a mistake," I say, but an uncertain feeling gnaws at me. Maybe he's right to detain them.

"No, you've made the mistake in coming here uninvited! We don't want anything to do with the outside world. We live simple lives here. Just look what craft can do in the wrong hands. Half a million people. It's horrifying. I had friends…" With an abrupt grunt, he strides past us, head held high, moving down the hallway with Tas and Kel.

The guards usher us back to the trucks.

We loop around the side of one of the terraced farms, where new shoots of wheat poke through black earth. Along the road, the ditch is filled with water. It could be the timing or just seasonal, but last time we were in Geum Ide, the harvest was coming out, and water was scarce. The shield must have repaired the damage to the brightstorm and to the city—a massive water supply from the jungle joined the ecosystem.

Surrounding the whole settlement now, instead of a mithrium poisoned jungle-city, there are rolling green plains and structures of red stone, leading to even higher stacks in the distance.

Geum Ide itself, resting on both sides of a deep ravine, is the clearest evidence of the renewed strength of life under the healed brightstorm. Trees and bushes of every shade of green sprout between, even on top of the clusters of red granite dwellings. Newer buildings hung with wooden shingles have popped up at the edge of town and near every terraced farm property.

It's beautiful, and I could make a home here with my family if circumstances were different. But there's Mithriumbane to find and a dangerous madman on the loose. Not to mention so much I don't understand about myself, about the dreams and the curse my mom and I share. I don't know how long my quest for answers will take me. Or if I ever will find answers.

As we park, my mom breaks the silence. She's been watching Winta closely. "How about a trip to the garden? Something relaxing. I've planted so many different things. Hemdi, you'll love it. The rows of tomatoes are starting to bud with little yellow flowers. What do you think?"

Hemdi agrees right away. Winta shrugs and lumbers out of the truck bed, using a step welded near the tailgate. "I think I'll go hunt down a few of the pit crews. See if there is anything I can do to lend a hand. More my thing."

My mom watches her retreat, frowning.

The guards order the rest of us out, and leave us there in the square.

"I'm going to head back to our place," Dad says.

"Maybe I'll go with you." My mom looks disappointed, and to be honest, I would rather spend my time with her, but I need to see if I can get more out of Dad.

As Hemdi and my mom move around a corner, something like contentment crosses Dad's face. "Like old times. You and me."

I know I can't jump straight into asking about what he's keeping from me. I need to take some time to soften him up. That's how it works. "How are the goats?"

"Good, adjusting well to being under granite. How are the chickens? Didn't you say you bought some layers?"

We move deeper into the town, under archways, around a cluster of buildings.

"Rugnus has me automating their production. Their eggs get delivered to a few restaurants and shops in Tungsten City. Spangler Eggs. They're selling well, or they were before the attack. Now I don't know. A few of my distributors... they didn't make it out of StoneYoke."

Dad's quiet for a second. He looks away to the horizon. "Spangler Eggs."

We descend to the level of town just below the surface, walking along a ravine path. Light filters through gaps in the stone ceiling. Under these wide spotlights, trees and bushes grow.

Water roars below us. Last time I was here, the ravine was full of industrial metal garbage. Now the stream is a river, and vegetation grows intertwined with the garbage, covering most of it.

"Dad, I wanna talk to you about something else that happened."

"Okay." His feet slow a bit.

"Did you know Silverkeeper's accident happened in Wolfstaff?"

His spine stiffens. "No. I didn't. We used to meet in secret after I left the kingdom, but one season I went to the crossroads where we would meet... he didn't show up. It was only when your mother told me about his antagonism toward her that I learned of his accident."

We pass under an archway swirled with ivy. One of the light-falls drops over their yard. Raspberry bushes line the stones on one side, heavy with fruit. Lilies have sprouted around the cobblestone path leading to the doorway, mixed with iridescent plant life. Inside rests a simple wooden table, a few chairs, an oversized feathered beanbag, and a workbench cluttered with greasy machine parts. A circle cut out of the stone leads to another room.

Two orchids, one orange and one pink, sit inside a cubed flowerpot on the table. Dad pulls a chair out and gestures for me to sit. "Please, I want to hear about the accident. How do you know it happened in Wolfstaff?"

"Silverkeeper went to Wolfstaff looking for Ergal."

He scrunches up his face, confused. "Your ring? Why?"

"I don't exactly know. Did he ever talk to you about Ergal? Or maybe other relics that were as powerful? We think Ergal and Sira's knife might be from the protodungeons. I mean, it's a guess but... everything seems to point to the three similar objects."

He's thoughtful for a long moment. "Protodungeons. That *was* Theridal's interest. Sure, we shared relics all the time, we were inseparable, but he never said anything about Ergal. Maybe it's something he started looking into after I left. He was always the one talking about getting a world without craft. Returning to Ide. He would have fit right in here if he... that's just wishful thinking, though."

"Why did he wanna end craft?"

"His wife was a null in budgecraft. Worse than Rensira. Not that he believed it should be taken from everyone. But given a choice..."

"There's something else I should tell you; we went into Wolfstaff on orders from the council to find out more about Ergal, a- and Wolfstaff's son sent me into the heart of the dungeon."

"What?" His face drains of color.

"Wolfstaff wanted to be free. And apparently, only I could take the heart out of the dungeon. Something about the dreams I have... about shadows."

"The staff you brought here, that's—"

"*The* wolfstaff."

He blows out a breath. "Well, don't tell Nasur. He'll drop a brick. So, what happened when you took it out?"

"I don't really know but Wolfstaff Dungeon is, well, gone."

A mix of emotions plays over his features. At first, its disbelief, but sorrow and shock bleed into that. He shakes his head, rubs his hand across his face, and relaxes. Soft laughter comes from his lips. "That could be it."

"Could be what?"

"People are tired of being defined by the dungeons, by their weaknesses and strengths. This could be the end of craft."

I shake my head. "Dad, that would be terrible. You can't want that. This whole world is based on craft. All the beautiful places and impossible things I've seen. They would cease to exist. Besides, destroying Wolfstaff didn't change anything. Craft is more than the dungeon's right. It's a way of life, connected to Ide."

"You sound like your mother." He says it like a compliment.

"Craft doesn't define people, anyway," I add, wondering if she believes that, too. I've had so little time with her.

"Perhaps not. But some say it's a reflection of who you are. Others say it shapes you into something that it wants, like forging a tool. Ide controls you."

"But look at Hemdi. He lost tincraft in Silverlamp last year, and he's..." I trail off thinking about his change of mood and behavior. The optimism he once held was replaced by a sense of hopelessness.

Dad looks at me knowingly. "Different, now."

"But that's not because of tincraft. That's because he lost a part of himself. It's trauma."

"I think"—he pauses and settles his hands in his lap— "we will all have to give up craft one day to truly connect with Ide."

These are a radical's words. A revolutionary's words. My heart races. "Dad?"

He scans my face. "What is it?"

"Did you... did you and Ara have anything to do with the attack?"

He bends forward, the hurt on his face visibly painful. "I-I... how could you even... Clayson, no. I could never."

"But there's something you're not saying."

"I had nothing to do with the attack. Clayson, please."

I rub the back of my neck. If only I could truly trust him again. Standing, I rest my palms flat on the table. "I wanna believe you, Dad." One last idea comes to mind. "Open the leaf for me."

"What?"

"The one Silverkeeper left you. It could have the information we need."

He looks at the ground, catching me with a quick glance. "I-I destroyed it."

"What? Why?"

"No one else could use it."

"There could've been important information on that."

"I guess we can't know. I'm sorry."

Standing, I pound the table harder than I intend to. How could he do something that stupid? When I move for the door in frustration, he grabs my elbow. "Not using craft can cause some problems, I get that, but I have to do what I think is right. Can't you understand?"

I don't understand. Sure, even on the surface, we lived differently than most, isolated, hidden in the mountains, making our own fuel and food. But still. Here we could have a different life. And I know he did it for me because of my dreams, but there must be something different now. I wanna reach down inside him and shake all his secrets loose. But I know him. He's a sealed vault, and I'm done begging him for scraps from his table of secrets.

So, without another word, I leave. Whatever answers are out there, I'll have to find them without his help.

As the brightstorm fades from burnt orange to a deep red-violet, I find my way to the town square. The smell of campfire and grilling goat meat welcomes me. A small crew of workers moves metal racks of meat from three huge pits, dumping the contents directly onto long wooden tables. I think about eating, but I'm too tired, too upset.

Somehow, I find myself at the edge of the settlement, looking out at the ruins of what was once a city as long and deep as Whurrimduum. I notice again that this citybarrel is a pentagon, five distant walls framing the city. That's as far as the mithrium shield protects the conjurers. No one can get through it without someone from the settlement escorting them.

Two squat muscle cars barrel toward me, sailing over a snaking gravel road. Just when I think they'll roar past, one of them brakes hard. Human rock music blasts from inside.

"Winta?"

She stumbles from the passenger seat. I step over, lending my hand. "What are you thinking? Can the baby—"

"Yeah, maybe I'm over doing it." It's so uncharacteristic I need an extra second to process it. For the first time, I catch a hint of worry on Winta's face, but she scrubs it out quickly and straightens her back as well as any pregnant woman can.

"If Andalynn—"

"Don't finish that sentence or I will get back in the car and run you over. Have you ever been pregnant?"

"I—"

"Then shut up."

The girl in the driver's seat says, "All done, girly?"

"For now." Contentment. That's what I'm sensing from her.

As the cars speed off, I narrow my eyes in disbelief. "You like it here?"

She cocks her head to the side. "There's just something about it. No craft, just work. But don't tell Hemdi I said that."

"Why?"

"He'll think I want to stay." She pauses, and we look out at the deepening darkness. "Ever since he lost tincraft... I don't know. He fits here. He likes the garden as much as I like the grease."

I hear two things at the same time: a body of conjurers gathering behind us from the settlement and engines in the distance. My mom and Hemdi part the crowd and come toward us.

"Glaris," my mom says. "She's back from the shield's edge."

Three trucks and two large passenger vans that looked like they've survived an apocalypse enter my view. They cut toward the settlement, finding the gravel road. The crowd retreats until the five vehicles come to a halt. At least fifty people tumble out of the vehicles. A moment of confusion rolls through the crowd.

Someone behind me whispers, "So many."

Another, "It's because of the attack."

The news we brought from Tungsten City has spread.

A man in the crowd calls out, "Ponris? Ponris!" He rushes over and pulls the woman into a bear hug. A similar scene plays out over and over until the crowd is awash with excitement. We find Glaris by her truck speaking with Nasur Lavalock.

"Clayson," she says. "I told you never to come back here."

"We had to come. We—"

She holds up a hand. "Nasur filled me in."

"Mother," my mom says, and as always, it's strange for me to hear that title used for Glaris. The woman who wouldn't let my parents stay in Geum Ide after my birth. She's about as motherly as a stone wall. "So many. What happened?"

"There are thousands of them. Lined up at the shield. After the attack at the festival, well, people are afraid. They're apparently willing to give up craft to be safe."

"Thousands?" Winta says. "But you've brought in only a few dozen."

"The others didn't have any connections here." With her matter-of-fact tone and callousness about these refugees, I think Rugnus might have melted her right here in front of all the other conjurers.

"Let me get this straight," Winta says. "You left them outside the shield because they don't know anyone here?"

Glaris turns a shoulder toward Winta but delivers her verdict to my mom. "Those people have tents, food, and budges to take them back to Whurrimduum or Tungsten City when they get tired of waiting. We can't take in everyone." Then with some finality, she says, "The people of Geum Ide will meet in the square tonight."

"To decide what to do with us?" I ask.

She nods.

"Well, don't worry. There's a memorial service in Tungsten City tomorrow. We'll leave in the morning."

Her jaw tightens. I know I've touched a nerve. "Ide keep me, child. It is not that easy. You can't come and go from here without consequences. We will debate what is to be done with you and decide. Return to your parent's home. We'll have dinner sent to you."

"I wanna be there. We deserve—"

"Your father and I will represent you," my mom says.

"Come on," Winta says. "There's no convincing this brittle bone old hag."

Glaris grabs Winta by the wrist. "Watch yourself, girl."

Hemdi surges toward her. "Let go of my wife this second."

Glaris huffs as Winta pulls free. Winta wheels back an arm to throw a punch, but my mom steadies her. Glaris walks into the crowd.

Hemdi shakes his head. "Let her go. She's not worth it. Besides, she's as afraid as anyone else. If something happened to the mithrium shield, they would be overrun. People would bring craft in here."

I know Hemdi means well, but something about him defending Glaris' lack of compassion gets under my skin. In this way, he's a little like Dad. I can see his growing passion for this life, and as I glance at Winta, I see her mind moving between disdain for Glaris and something else—something more thoughtful.

My mom rests a hand on my shoulder. "I'll make sure you have a voice tonight, Clay." Then she chases after Glaris.

We find our way back to my parents' place, through the underground, oil lanterns casting shifting shadows in the ravine as we cross the walkway.

I breathe some relief when I realize Dad is already gone. He must have prepared the place for us. A single oil lamp lights the room, and a few cots have been set up for us. I can't help seeing the similarity between the conjurers' voting and the council's Casting, though I don't know much about the power dynamic here in Geum Ide, just that Glaris is firmly in charge.

Last year, Dad had some leverage because of his relationship with Ara. They healed the brightstorm, so they were allowed to stay. But for Dad, living here has always meant more. It's a life without the pressures of kingdom and craft.

Dinner arrives and we scoot the heavy square planter with the orange and pink orchids off to one side of the table and sit. After we eat and clean up, none of us feels like sleeping.

The conversation swells and ebbs a half dozen times: Mithri-umbane, the festival, the memorial service, then the festival again. Koglim's recovery and Wolfstaff. The council. Andalynn and Rugnus. Jeiah. Emberfence and Bluebottle Dungeon. The festival. We have no purpose for the conversation, but we circle the danger in the world. What will it be like for their child?

"Was it Ara?" Hemdi asks.

I shake my head. Dad is keeping some secret, but Ara didn't do this.

"Kel or Tas?" Winta says. "They're the only ones who have changed. I'm not even sure you can call them vacant anymore."

I cringe at the word. "I never did."

"Do you think the conjurers will find Ara?" Hemdi asks.

Winta scoots forward in her chair the best she can. "Maybe she went to the shield."

"Dad said she felt drawn to it, so that will be the first place they look."

Eventually, Hemdi's eyes start to droop, and he leaves the table. Winta follows him. To the cots, she gently lays on her side, and Hemdi drapes a second blanket over her before he slides another cot as close to her as possible, lays down, and drapes an arm over her side.

I stay at the table thinking. It must be for longer than an hour because, by the time I snub out the oil lamp and spread out on the remaining cot, there's only a little oil left.

Sleep. I close my eyes, wishing it would only be sleep.

And of course, it's not. Every night I spend under granite Yinzar finds me.

The canyon looks new tonight. The bright colors, the butter-flies, the moonlight, and the way the memories whisper to me softly as from out of a dream long forgotten. Somehow the familiarity calms my anxiety, and it gives me the patience to search for just the right memory.

I catch a neon-yellow butterfly that brings me side by side with my grandfather. This is the most vivid memory I've seen. His shock of orange hair, his brawny frame. A film of mercury clings to his boots. We're near a crucible on top of a metal knit floor. The room around us is shaped like a massive bowl—a summator.

All the same ingredients from his first forgeside cluster the metal-woven ground around a pool of molten lava carved into the metal. The pure mithrium bubbles inside the crucible. He's close to the end of the recipe.

"You know," he says. "They think I talk to myself."

"You do," I joke to the vision of my grandfather.

His back straightens. From under his characteristic orange eyebrows, he almost looks me in the eye. "After all this time haunting me, you choose now to speak?"

"Are you talking to me?"

"Haven't I always. You're the silent one." He glances at the shinning crucible.

"I—wait, this is a vision. I don't understand."

"A vision? You have haunted me for many days. Today is just the clearest. I can almost see you before me."

I try to process what's happening, but it's impossible. Could I really be speaking with him? But that would be in the past. I thought these were only memories. If I can talk with him in real time, then I can prevent whatever he's about to do.

"I'm your grandson. I—you need to listen. If you're doing what I think you are doing, it doesn't work. You can't create anything from the mithrium in this place. You destroy the mithrium. You'll die here today. You will become Mithriumbane and forge a dungeon."

My words break his staring contest with the crucible. "Impossible. I'm no champion. You would fill my head with lies."

"No, listen to me. The lake. Onthratia. The recipe will work under the lake. Don't do this."

"You look like my son-in-law. But I know a trick when I see one. You're a wraith, or s-some abomination sent by the champions to stop me."

"No, please. Listen to me. I'm with Glaris. She wouldn't want you—"

"Invoking that woman's name does you no favors. We've been on different paths for many years. She wants to destroy craft. I want to create a new type."

"And you can. The recipe works in your other forge, under Onthratia. I created a shield. It-it can protect a whole city, heal a broken brightstorm."

His face contorts in rage. "Get out of my head! You serve the great smoke. I—"

A far-away, almost hollow voice cuts him off. "Hello?"

"Who is that?" he asks. His eyes dart to the cube of mithrium. "You're stalling me? It's a trick." He scrambles for the crucible. "Be gone!"

The voice grows closer. "Are you there?" It echoes off the walls, but there's something familiar about it. It could be Anda-lynn's voice but for a ring of something timid—no, worried. It's my mom's voice.

Removing a pendant from his pocket, he holds it above the mithrium. "I won't be tricked."

"Don't—"

He drops it into the mithrium.

HASTE TO STONEYOKE

My muscles are sore. I fight the groggy effects of restless sleep and force my eyes open. My mom's strawberry blonde hair falls around her face, a halo framing individual strands, turning them to rods of light. "Clayson?"

The concern in her voice doesn't have the same hollowness as the voice from the memory. But it sounded so much like her.

"Mom." I grab her hands. "I... did you... Yinzar he—"

"The visions?" Her voice is a low whisper. "Are they getting worse?"

I shake my head only to find it muddy and aching. I need that armband. Looking around the room, I find Winta and Hemdi are already gone. "No, clearer. Listen, did you ever go into the mines to find your father? I just... I thought I heard you there."

She guides me to the table. "Never. Glaris forbade me. All the time he spent away from us... it was an obsession. It wasn't until the mithrium went missing and his name entered our minds that anyone learned what he had done, or guessed it rather, from the new name he received—Mithriumbane."

"Wait, so I kinda get this, but people *heard* his new name?"

"When someone becomes a champion—reaches sixty-three

AMP score—their new name is spoken into the minds of every Loamin, unless they're on the surface. In his case, it was most likely the same moment he died."

"Weird. What was it like?"

"Hearing it? It woke me up. I was in the castlestack at Whurrimduum. I'll never forget it. Terrible way to learn of the death of a loved one. Just terrible. A voice in my mind—and I still remember it exactly—said: *Yinzar Copperoath is gone. There is only Mithriumbane.*"

"How did you know he was dead and not just at sixty-three AMP?"

"The phrases heard are common knowledge. Records indicate it's always the same. If the voice would have said: *Yinzar Copperoath has become Mithriumbane,* that would have meant he was still alive."

"That's why people think destroying the mithrium killed him."

"And accelerated his AMP to sixty-three. Imagine what that was like for him?" She shifts her attention from me to the table, focusing on the cubed vase, her mind wandering into the unknown.

"Your AMP score, Mom. It's sixty-one."

She turns her face back to me. "Yes. Another reason to stay in Geum Ide. I don't think I would ever want to die like that. If I were to gain any more strength, in any of the crafts... I guess I don't like to think about it. Some people would love to reach the level of a champion—their souls living forever in a dungeon of their own making."

"I've heard Koglim say that before, but Wolfstaff couldn't even remember her real life. She wanted out."

She was thoughtful for a moment. "I'm sorry Koglim got hurt. You know it's not your fault, right?"

It is my fault, but I don't say that. Instead, I stand and cross the room, thinking. I could have sworn that was my mom's voice. "So, you never went to the mines?"

"No. Why? You thought you heard me?"

"I guess not. But someone else was coming through the opening of the Cradle."

"Then you were right? The dungeon is in the Cradle."

"It's like a giant summator, right?"

"Yes. And if what you're saying is true, whoever was there..."

That's it. I shake my head. "Of course! They would've become a wraith. I could find them in Yinzar's dungeon. They would know what else happened that day. This could answer so much." I give her a peck on the cheek and move toward the door.

"Clayson, wait." She gestures for me to sit back at the table. It takes her a while to form her next sentence. "I just feel like I'm struggling to catch up. I want to know more about you. I want to hear your opinions about the world. Sometimes you seem so much like your father I—"

A sudden, hot anger floods my veins. "I'm not like him."

She holds up her hands. "That's not exactly what I... I'll start over. I want you to know that I'm here for you. That's all. I wish I could remember all the times I didn't see you. If that makes sense."

"I wish that too. I thought Ergal could help us."

"It did. I can see you now. And at least I can get to know you."

There's a long pause. I try to think of something to say, but everything sounds stupid.

"Your father keeps things from both of us, you know. He thinks it protects us. Even after everything, he still thinks like a king, hoarding the world's secrets. I know it bothers you. I wish I had a solution, but I don't. Please know I would do anything to help you."

I feel the desperation behind her words. I push all thoughts of Dad to the side and let her in. This is my mom. This is the woman who taught Andalynn compassion.

"Okay." What else is there, but acceptance of her offering.

A second later, Winta, Hemdi, and Dad enter the room, all with sullen faces.

"This doesn't look good," I say. "What's the verdict?"

With a sigh as deep as Whurrimduum itself, Dad says, "The conjurers are a peace-loving people. We value freedom and choice. It wasn't hard to convince them that you should not be kept here against your will."

"Th-that's great. Why do you all look like you've stepped through a wraith?"

Hemdi winces.

"Sorry, poor choice of words. I didn't mean to—"

Hemdi raises a hand, cutting me off. "Honest mistake. And you're not wrong. Geum Ide"—he glances at Dad— "They're willing to let us stay, but if we leave, they're keeping Icho."

The breath goes out of me. "Wraithspit! Rugnus is gonna kill me. They can't do this."

"Don't swear, Clayson," my mom chides. "It doesn't... you lived your whole life on the surface. You don't even know how to use profanity correctly, anyway."

I laugh softly at this. She's not wrong, but I shake my head. "I-I can't go back without Icho."

Dad's face is firm. When I catch Hemdi stealing another glance at him, I understand. He did this. He doesn't want us to come back here. Not by craft, at any rate. "You'll have to," he says. "Nasur is waiting with a truck. He'll take you to the wall and give you a box to open once you're through the shield. After that, you can budge back to Tungsten City. Tell Rugnus... tell him I'm sorry about Icho."

"No, you're not," I snap. "It was your idea—taking Icho from us. I can see it on your guilty face. You keep doing this, Dad." I swivel to my mom, looking for support. "He keeps doing this"— then back to Dad—"ignoring the fact that craft has a point, has a purpose in people's lives. Just because you think craft screwed up your life doesn't mean you can deny it to everyone else."

His chest expands with a response, but his mouth is sealed shut. Growing up, we didn't have many confrontations. Maybe it was because he was sick. I feel my closeness to him slipping away, and it makes me even angrier.

Hemdi gestures for me to lower my voice. "Clayson."

My emotions swell up in a wave, and I push my thoughts out like someone is using silver against me. "You know, Rugnus is right. Geum Ide doesn't deserve the mithrium shield. If I had created it at the center of Tungsten City, I... It could have protected everyone. StoneYoke would've been... it would've—"

I flinch as my mom's hand reaches up and brushes my face. "It's okay. It's okay. You're right. There is so much that is broken and unjust in this world. I'm not sure any one of us can fix it alone. Maybe after a while, Geum Ide will—"

"Allow craft?" Dad snorts. "No. That can't happen. Not ever."

This effectively ends our conversation. Dad stuck in his conjurer attitude and me defending a world and a life I barely chose for myself. "Come on," I say to Hemdi and Winta. "Let's leave this place. There's work to do."

Winta stands, but she has to pull Hemdi up. "Clayson, wait," he says.

My blood is simmering with frustration, but Hemdi's hesitance flips a switch in my mind. Something is different with them. Winta is being suspiciously non-abrasive.

Hemdi's eyes shift to my mom. "We're thinking about staying."

Winta drops his hand. "No. That's not...we're *thinking* about coming back. Just... let's go. We're not dealing with this now."

I'm caught by a wave of genuine surprise. "Winta... so... wait, what? Would Glaris—"

"Any of you are welcome back here," Dad says, "if you are willing to forsake craft."

"Not a chance," I say, surprised to find that I mean it. The words stick to my bones, become a part of me. But Winta's eyes avoid mine, she's looking downward at the expectations to come —she's considering a life here. What about her child? Would they raise it without craft? Rugnus lost Icho today. I can't take away his two closest friends. "We're leaving."

"I'm not making any decisions today." Winta draws a long, steady breath. "There's... time. We need to get back to Tungsten City. Immediately."

A small movement appears in the corner of my eye—Hemdi nodding to Winta, though barely perceptible. I say goodbye to my mom, and they follow me from the house. We walk alongside the ravine, its peaceful waters stubbornly cutting the stone deeper and deeper. When we reach the surface level, Nasur is grinning so wide I wanna punch his face in until I can't feel my hand.

Two guards wait in the back of a truck sitting on a large chest filled with our objects.

As I help Winta and climb in after Hemdi, Dad catches up to us, resting his hand on the lip of the truck bed. He's out of breath. "I'm sorry, Clayson. I wish my life could be different. Our lives." He swallows. "Be careful. Craftprints... I... just promise you will be safe."

Nasur turns on the truck, and I bang on the cab window. "Let's go!"

The truck lurches forward, leaving Dad in a wake of dust. He calls my name one more time. A goodbye. My emotions are like an exposed nerve, rattled with every bump as we fly through the settlement— apparently Nasur is eager to get rid of us. I'm just as eager to leave.

Under the stark light of the brightstorm, we travel quickly from the settlement to the farms to a brief wilderness dotted with groves of trees. We pass rivulets and streams as they cut their way down toward the ravine. It's beautiful. In minutes this gives way to the ruins of the former city—Gythanstyan. But even the maze of pentagonal buildings, like a beehive long forgotten, has a sense of structure and order. It's a place that could be restored.

Thousands of Loamin could clear away the debris, sweep off the dust, and resettle the entire place. With craft, that work would be done within days. I can't wrap my mind around the selfish choices the conjurers are making. Especially when the shield could protect everyone from being harmed by craft.

In the distance, the radiance of the mithrium shield shimmers, a film of white energy lining the inside of the citybarrel. It would've protected everyone. It still can.

As we approach the edge of the city, Winta shifts once again in her seat. "Your father is trying to build a better life. You shouldn't be so brittle boned about it."

Of all the people who would accept the ideals of the conjurers, I didn't think Winta would be among them. But I don't wanna debate with her. "It's fine. Where should we meet up with Andalynn and Rugnus?" My heart sinks into my stomach when I imagine Rugnus' reaction about Icho.

"Let's check with Jeiah first," Winta says. "See if she's made any progress finding who Bazalrak sent the message to."

Jeiah. The thought of seeing her thaws a small piece of my frustration. I shouldn't have left Dad standing there without so much as a goodbye. It could be the last time I see him in a while. It doesn't escape me that my emotions rest on the edge of a knife.

The truck brakes hard, making Winta clench her teeth.

"You okay?" I ask. She pushes away my concern with an eye roll.

"We're here!" Nasur shouts. "Get them out and get them through the shield."

The guards in the truck drag both the box and us out of the truck bed. They heave the box through the shield and push us forward. Winta and Hemdi don't hesitate, though I catch Winta glancing back to the valley.

Behind Nasur I catch a glint of light from a distinct point in the ruins. There's a certain rhythm to the pulse of light, but it fades quickly. If I didn't know any better, I would say it was Ara, trying to remind me that she's out there somewhere, but with everything that's been revealed about her powers, I can't determine if it's good or bad that no one can find her. I want to say it's good; I want to believe that she and Dad weren't involved in the attack. And yet, my dad's secrets sit like a heavy boulder.

Nasur scowls when I pause before crossing through. "I don't want to see you again."

"Yeah." I'm unable to keep my eyes from rolling. "Feeling's mutual."

I turn back toward the shield. Once I pass through the sheet of white energy, the world becomes heavier. Where there had been grass under our feet, there's stone. Where there had been a light in the sky, there's only awaiting darkness. Hemdi already has the box open and hands me the armband.

I slip it on and sigh with relief. "This thing's like pure adrenalin." I take the the wolfstaff relic and nestle it on my back, adjusting the leather strap. And last, I place the aluminum-cobalt slap bracelet around my wrist. A comforting glow of news and information fills my view. I budge my real clothes back on and send the simple conjurer linens to the garbage where they'll be dropped into the lava pits.

Winta rolls her mercury band into place and breathes a sigh of relief. Is there shieldcraft in it? I thought it only allowed her to slow things down, and I'm distracted for a split second by why she would find so much comfort in something that's not healing or protecting her. But my focus returns to Jeiah. She hasn't sent me any news. Her location marker floats around her workspace in bluelink tower.

"I thought she lost her paladin status with Bluebottle," I say. "Can she still work from bluelink tower?"

"Clayson," Hemdi says, but I don't look up from the news.

I scroll through the feeds and find a video of my sister explaining what happened in Wolfstaff. Every word is the truth from my own mouth. There are still calls from the council to locate me, but Chainkeeper is working to soften the rhetoric, which I appreciate. Maybe they won't throw me into Keelcrawl for destroying a dungeon. It was the council that sent me there in the first place.

"You guys see this?" I ask.

"Clayson." Winta is trying to get my attention.

A mass of waiting refugees press us closer together. "What's going on?"

Hemdi holds his hands up to the crowd.

Someone shouts. "Are they letting more people in?"

"Where's the truck going?"

A woman ten feet away can't peel her eyes away from me. "Are you... you're..."

Whispers of my name ripple through the mass of bodies, and the people press in to get a closer look.

"Time to go."

Winta grabs her budge. "No argument from me."

This won't be as smooth as using Icho, but we link up through bluelink's budge controls. The moment we arrive before the Bluelink building, my skin prickles, not with craft but with the feeling that something is off. I wait for the sense of nausea from the budge, for the pull of added gravity on my lower limbs, but there's nothing. Winta and Hemdi both look like they connected with a moving vehicle.

I didn't feel the effect of the budge. Even Icho can't mask all the physiological effects of budging. I open my mouth to say this, but something's wrong with Winta. Her hands and fingers make complicated gestures scanning bluelink. No, not scanning. She's digging into the code. The ruby-brown of her face goes dull.

"What is it?" I ask.

"Clayson, you absolute latchmage. How could you miss this?"

A fog settles over me, my mouth suddenly dry. "What's wrong? Is it Jeiah?" The ground at my feet seems to slip away. "Wh-what are you—"

Winta bolts for the lobby of the Bluelink building. A few people milling about scatter as she flies through them. She calls back to us. "Come on! Quick!"

We follow Winta to the budgeports inside the building. I still don't feel the effects when we budge. My thoughts are centered around Jeiah. Her location beacon points to her office, but when we arrive, we're greeted by an empty room. The map of the building hangs between us. Winta makes another complicated gesture in the air, grabbing a corner of the building and pulling, shaking it like a can of spray paint until suddenly the dot representing Jeiah vanishes.

"Where is she?"

Winta moves straight into the pentagon of clear blue rectangles in the center of the room, opening up Jeiah's workstation.

"Winta, answer me. Where is Jeiah?"

"You need to let me work. Can't believe you didn't notice the hack on her location data. It's like you're a bluecraft null sometimes, Clayson."

I step back. Someone faked her location data. Why?

"Where is she?" Hemdi says.

Winta winces, making a gesture like nails scrapping over a chalkboard. "Working on it."

"Work harder," I say.

Winta glances at me. Her eyes say something like *don't test me*.

Hemdi places a hand on my shoulder. "It will be okay. Winta can track anyone. Breathe."

He touches my armband, using the goldcraft to force me to breathe. It helps. "Right. Okay, how can I help?" I search Jeiah's bluescreen stations for anything that might give us a clue about what happened. All five are open this time. I stop dead in front of the fifth display, the one that hadn't been open when I was here last.

"It's all about me," I whisper. "This is what she must've sent to the council. She said she'd been investigating me, but this is, this is…"

"She's thorough," Winta says over her shoulder.

Hemdi steps to my side. "That's one way to put it."

Surveillance pictures and video of me clutter the screen. Biographical information scrolls on one side: family history, likes and dislikes, a calendar of days I've spent in Tungsten City, my known AMP score—everything. Recordings show my highlights from various dungeons. I know all of this is public record, but I haven't seen it all gathered like this. There's even a list of videos by the ClaySlay girls playing on a loop, muted in the top corner. I blink in confusion.

Winta cheers. "Got it! Or close as we're gonna get. And, uh, yeah, that's gonna be a problem."

I whirl around. "Where is she?"

Winta opens a map of the StoneYoke district and zooms into the site of the memorial ceremony. I catch Jeiah's name highlighted in pink, but it blinks out, only to reappear a second later in a different place, but still at the ceremony. She moves over a dozen times in half a minute.

"Why is she—"

"She's not moving anywhere. Her location data is being scrambled. I mean, she must be at the festival, but... wait a second." Winta spreads her palms open, and a few hundred similar icons appear, all staying in one place for a few seconds, vanishing, and reappearing somewhere else at the memorial. There are hundreds of them. I'm about to ask who they are, but Bazalrak's name blinks to the forefront.

"Bazalrak," Hemdi says. "And these others... I'm not sure."

Winta uses an erasing gesture, and the names shift and glimmer.

"Wait," Hemdi says.

Winta issues a low whistle. "Jeiah's got them all tagged. Known darksmiths. A lot are aliases. This is not a good group of people. And... well, they would all know Emberfence from his days running the black market. Plus, the fact that Bazalrak is with them."

Winta's explanation crystallizes my thoughts. "They're going to attack the memorial service. We've got to stop them. And find Jeiah. I'll get Rugnus, and we'll—"

"No need," A voice comes from behind me—Rugnus. "We already know. Winta connected us the moment you arrived."

Andalynn moves from his side and hugs me. "We're getting Jeiah out of this mess."

Rugnus' shoulders are in knots, defensive. "I tried to update my mother, but someone's blocking the message. Winta?"

She grabs something invisible next to his head and tries to pull. She strains, but her hand doesn't move. She growls. "I need to be closer."

"Then let's go," I say.

"Are we sure about this?" Rugnus says. "No offense, Clayson, but we barely know Jeiah. What if this is a trap? Like last time."

"Last time meaning..." I know what he's thinking.

"Meaning Sira. Meaning a girl you liked, or who liked you, leading us to our doom."

"For the last time, I didn't like Sira. I—"

Winta snaps. "Get melted, Rugnus. We're wasting time. Jeiahlir is *not* Sira. I approved of her days ago. No need for a council on this one."

"I agree," Andalynn says. "Jeiah's with us. Let's go."

"Okay," Rugnus says. "Just wanted to make sure. I—" Rugnus looks around empty-handed. "Wait, where's Icho?"

"Before you get upset," Hemdi starts. "You should know our trip to Geum Ide was a success. Ara was able to heal Kel."

"Yeah, Winta messaged us already. Where's Icho?"

"Just remember how difficult and secretive the conjurers can be."

"And that you insisted we go there," Winta adds.

Rugnus' face turns purple. "Not. Helping. Where is it?"

I need to take the blame on this one. "To prevent us from returning without permission, Glaris, and Nasur—and if I'm being honest, my dad—convinced the people to let us go only if we left Icho behind."

Rugnus stumbles backward, clutching his chest. "Spit. Are you serious?"

Winta taps her foot. "Rugnus, stop being such a latchmage.

I'm going to the memorial. Catch up with me." She walks out of the room.

"What are they even going to do with it?" Rugnus says, his rage conforming into something desperate, almost pathetic.

I blow out a breath, shake my head. "Sounded like they were going to purge it, but... I don't think it's possible. If it's like Ergal and Onrix, it's indestructible without mithrium."

"But it's not. I got it from my mother as a summation gift. It has nothing to do with Ergal or the protodungeons. It's going to be purged. They're going to turn it into truck parts." Tears prick his eyes.

"I'm sorry, Rugnus. This is awful." Andalynn leans over and kisses his cheek. Her hair brushes against his face, but he steps away.

"Don't try to make me feel better with silver. I don't need that. I need Icho." He jabs a finger at me and steps within striking distance. "Ide keep me, Clayson. I've had about enough of your inconsiderate actions screwing everything up for everyone. I-I can't believe you let this—"

Hemdi steps between us. "There's no time for this. And you're not listening, Rugnus. There was nothing we could do about this."

Rugnus locks eyes with me, "Did you even try? Did you think about what I would lose if—"

Hemdi places a hand firmly on Rugnus' chest. "Slow down. Kel was healed. Besides, we all are dealing with loss. All hurting. Craft is not more important than your friends. It's not."

Rugnus' shoulders slump. "I-I... Hemdi, I'm sorry. I didn't... I'm not thinking."

Hemdi drops a hand on his shoulder. "It's okay to be upset, but we really need to leave before Bazalrak can hurt anyone else."

Rugnus nods.

As we make our way out of the Bluelink building to a budge-port, I can't help but think of Hemdi's true powers. Kindness. Empathy. He's our rock. He lost his strongest craft in Silverlamp last year, but he didn't lose himself. My dad is wrong. Craft doesn't make Loamin who they are.

Outside the building, we link budges and find the memorial on the map of Tungsten City. When we budge, I still don't feel the effect. Something must be wrong—just another thing that's different about me. Did Ara do it when she touched me?

We arrive on the cavern side of the memorial site. From this angle, impossibly tall, uneven pillars molded out of hundreds of substances spread out across the space: cement, stained-glass, crystal, granite, cooled lava. It's as varied and strange as Tungsten City itself. Thousands of people throng the turf paths wrapping around the pillars. Even more hover above us, like a kaleidoscope of butterflies searching for the perfect flowers to land on.

I turn back to Rugnus and Andalynn. They're as wide-eyed as everyone else.

"Who created the pillars?" I ask.

Rugnus tugs at the hem of his shirt, straightening it. "As soon as the buildings fell, people reacted. It's like the father you helped during the attack, the one from the video everyone saw, where he gathered the dust particles into mud and dried it. Same thing happened all over the place. The wreckage of the attack was turned into a million objects, as fast as ironsmiths and others could clear up the debris."

Andalynn adds, "The architects only smoothed things out a little. A thousand pillars, soon to be filled with thousands of memorials."

For the smallest moment, it's as if the dead speak as one in approval of what was made to honor their memory.

"Your mother organized this?" I say to Rugnus.

Rugnus, a little embarrassed, says, "She's really good at throwing parties."

"That's an understatement," Andalynn says. "She's a peerless social planner. She understands what people are looking for. Friends and families of those killed can mold a leaf, filled with memories of their loved ones, into the pillars so everyone can see and hear their stories."

"It's beautiful." My voice is a whisper.

"It is," Rugnus says. "Let's make sure Bazalrak doesn't do anything to melt it."

The crowd absorbs us, and for once, no one seems to be paying attention to me. We wander deep into the memorial, around a dozen pillars, following Winta's location. I watch the people above me soar through the air. Two teenage girls press a thin silver square against a crystal, producing wisps of light, tendrilling outward to touch their faces.

When I lower my eyes, a boy with pink hair, harvest moon skin, and a bolo tie blocks my path. Brig.

"Ho, finally decided to show up. Did Wolfkeeper find you? He's not happy. And where have you been? Ten minutes ago, Jeiahlir's location data shifted, and I got all kinds of readings."

"Slow down. You didn't notice the loop either?"

"If I had, don't you think I would have found her by now? She tells me not to bother her at work. So, I don't, but—"

"Brig," Rugnus says. "We don't have a lot of time here. We have to find her."

"But her location signal is jumping all over the place. First, I get an update that her data was tampered with, after that I—"

"Brig." I hold up a hand. "We're dealing with it."

"I'll follow, and you can tell me what's happening."

Andalynn and Rugnus move ahead of me, and I tell Brig as much as I know about Jeiah's disappearance, though he interrupts me so much it is hard to provide any details. When I mention Bazalrak, he stops trying to speak over me.

Close to Winta's position, the crowd becomes a dense knot. There are raised voices. As we approach, I hear dogs barking and growling. Rugnus cuts a path through the pack of people, and we follow in his wake. I grip the staff out of instinct.

A large burly man in fur pelts has Winta and Hemdi pinned

against one of the pillars. It's Tarden Wolfkeeper. "Where is he?" Wolfkeeper growls.

Rugnus motions for me to move back into the safety of the crowd, but I step forward. "I'm here, Wolfkeeper. Leave them alone."

His dogs bound toward me. The mastiff takes my left and the Alaskan husky center. I swing the staff from my back. It extends to its full height as I jam it into the ground. The dogs heel, hanging their heads.

"What have you done? Th-that... It can't be." Wolfkeeper's voice rises in pitch, his face contorting. "You had no right!"

My shoulders and arms prickle with energy. My frame begins to swell, and the whole crowd shrinks back. Fur sprouts on my arms. I can smell their fear, taste it. My voice comes out angry and low. "Wolfstaff gave me the right!" A soft noise from a Loamin baby reaches my ears, and I show my sharp teeth to the tiny woman who holds the thing. I could eat it in a single bite.

What?!

No, that's... why did I think that? I have to be careful not to become more wolf than man.

"Clayson!" Andalynn calls. "Clayson, back down."

Her words have a bone of craft behind them. A breath escapes through my teeth. Then another. I scan the faces of the surrounding people and catch the glimmer of blue in some of their eyes. I'm being recorded. I shrink back down to my normal height, thankful not to have gone full feral wolf in front of hundreds of people. I'm already strange and dangerous enough.

"Sorry," I say. Wolfkeeper has fallen to his knees. I pull him to his feet. "Please, I'm sorry. Torlina—it's what she wanted. I didn't mean for—"

"If it was her will, then I can accept it." His whole demeanor has changed, his head slightly bowed, his hands at his side.

"Accept this as well," I say, extending the black metal staff to him.

He finds my eyes, thinking for a long moment. His hands

reach out, but they cover my own hands. "It was well earned. Ide keep it—and you—safe for many years."

Wolfkeeper strides past me, collecting his dogs, who still crawl along close to the ground, casting quick, fearful glances at me. Wolfkeeper disappears around another pillar.

"Okay," Winta says. "Stop messing around and get ready."

"Ready for what?" Andalynn says.

"I don't know, but the way I figure, the moment I expose all these darksmith idiots, they're not gonna like it."

"You have a way to do that?" Rugnus says.

Winta glares at him. "While wolf-boy over here was settling his business, I found a way around their craft. It was easy. Told you. I just had to be at the location."

"Okay. Do it."

Winta straightens her left arm in front of her like she's about to karate chop Rugnus' face. It's a gesture I've never seen before. With her right hand, she reaches over the top of the straightened arm. Her right arm shakes. She strains with the effort, pushing her hand further out and pinching something, wiggling her pinched fingers like she's trying to loosen a knot.

"Got it!" She holds up something invisible.

I open the icon Winta gave us all with the scrambled location data. It worked. None of the hundreds of dots change location again. They're spread out evenly across the memorial, almost too evenly. Jeiah's pink dot pulses a half-dozen pillars toward the center of the memorial.

"I've got her," I say. "Lets—"

A construction mech, just like the ones during the festival, budges in front of me. It swings an arm, and one of the memorial pillars explodes, scattering debris over the grass paths. Before I can even reorient myself, two things happen at once: Rugnus captures the things' legs with rock and fire, and I hear hundreds of people scrambling to flee. A teenage boy in a silver jacket budges. He's gone. Safe. People all around us budge to safety.

This won't be like the attack on the festival. And Winta

confirms it. "They're not using multiplied craftprints. I disabled the foilgrip. Take that thing down."

After only half a minute, everyone in our proximity has fled. This is how it *should've* been at StoneYoke. The people should've been able to budge, to protect themselves. Andalynn has half of the mech covered in barbed ivy before I can get myself unglued. Rugnus shouts something at me. I shake my head.

"Clayson!" His words come into focus. "Find Jeiah!"

"Leave it to us." Brig drags me in the wrong direction.

I shake my senses loose. "Brig, wait. It's this way." My feet are moving under my own power now. We snake around the pillars. We have to get to Jeiah. A dark shape passes on my left, burnt flesh, and shimmering silver. Brig skids to a halt.

"Ho, this is bad. Darksmiths."

Three half-burned corpses with gleaming metal weapons in their skeletal hands rush us from the side. Behind them, a blood-eyed girl rushes forward with golden gauntlets. She's controlling these bodies. I should switch to my shield bracelet. They're about forty feet away. Thirty feet.

I shove the staff toward Brig. "I need to switch to my shield."

Twenty feet.

"Are you crazy?" Brig shouts, his voice a high pitch squeal. "Use the staff."

Ten feet.

Rage bristles to life all along my skin as I swell to three times my normal height and length. I let the staff take over—fully this time. Pads shape under my feet and hands. I bend forward now, more the shape of a feral wolf than the shape of a man. The staff becomes part of me. The smell of burnt flesh tickles my nose, tempting me to bite into the closest of the three burning bodies. But at the last second, I smell the rot eating away at them under the fiery flesh.

With a giant paw, I bat the three flaming bodies away from us without a second thought. I'll wait to find something worth eating when this victory is behind me.

The girl with the golden gauntlets stutters to a stop. The smell of confidence has evaporated from her bones. Good. The marrow of the fearful has the freshest taste. I growl at her, ready to pounce, but she flees. Another tiny Loamin figure sneaks into view near my right paw.

"Ho! Don't stay a wolf for too long. That would be bad."

This is Brig. The little one I knew when I was also inferior. I could warm up on his flesh before moving to the main course. I growl.

"I swear. If you try to eat me, I won't let you work for me when I'm famous."

It takes me a second to reorient myself, but my body shrinks. The fur retracts into my skin. I examine the staff, shaking a little. "I could barely control myself that time."

"Awesome though. Come on."

Our momentum carries us around another few pillars. Jeiah's pink location label is just ahead of us. The way is clear of dark-smiths, but I continue to peer around each corner.

"I don't wanna use this thing again." But Brig was right. It's the most powerful object I have. I won't hesitate to use it to save Jeiah.

Brig cuts into my thoughts. "Are you seeing this?" He's scanning something in bluelink.

I glance at the map still floating in my view. Jeiah's location is in the pillar right in front of us. And that's what's strange. Without getting this close, we couldn't tell.

My heart thuds. "Bazalrak captured her inside the pillar."

Brig melts into a hot rage. "I'll kill him. If she's... I'll kill him myself."

"It's okay," I push down my own panic. "We'll get her out of there."

"It's *not* okay. She's... she's..."

"She's what?" I change the location data to a 3D model to see how far up she is.

"Doesn't like tiny spaces."

I stop scanning the pillar and look at Brig. Her vitals pop up. Her heartbeat and breathing look normal. Still. "She's claustrophobic? I thought Loamin couldn't be—"

"It's rare, but it really affects her. I..." Brig's eyes become watery, but he shoves his chin out.

"We're getting her out right now."

A new location dot appears in front of me, and I freeze. Bazalrak stalks out from around the pillar and glares at me, gloating.

His lip ring moves as he smiles, but his face is twisted and red, his cheeks drawn in. Rugnus was right. His time in Keelcrawl prison has driven him to madness.

"You will have to postpone your rescue plans." His usually smooth voice has become more of a growl. "In fact, maybe it would be advantageous to cancel them altogether."

HIDE NO LONGER

Brig tightens his fists. "Give me the staff. I'm gonna eat this guy."

Ignoring him, I plant the staff in the lawn between my feet. "Bazalrak, I'm gonna send you back to Keelcrawl where you belong."

He sneers. "What a rare and beautiful relic. Heart of Torlina Wolfstaff's Dungeon, if I'm not mistaken. But it is not made of mithrium, nor are you. There's a limit to its power, and plenty of my associates know how to take down a feral wolf."

Location dots overload my map, forcing me to gesture it off. A hundred darksmiths stand in a loose circle around us, all with eyes as dead as Bazalrak's, all brandishing dangerous-looking objects.

"No use trying to outrun us," Bazalrak warns. "And don't try to budge. Runecap here..." One of the darksmiths—Runecap presumably—edges forward, his lips smeared with metallic balm, his breath a visible fog of aluminum dust. "He assures me that if you were to try to escape, it would be very painful."

My skin prickles with energy, and before I can stop, the power of the wolfstaff relic transforms my body and mind into an ancient, feral monster. Slapping my tail on the ground, I leap toward Bazalrak, only to be pulled backward by cold hands. I try to spin around, but a large Loamin with thick gold hands hoists my tail above his head.

A growl comes from deep in my chest. I lift my tail and fling him beyond the crowd of darksmiths. I sniff the air for the smell of his blood that's sure to rise into the air, but more of the filthy creatures come forward. I smell their vain hope to ensnare me.

I will not be captured.

I let loose a howl so magnificent it will call all my allies to me at once. And I'm not wrong. The tiny Loamin I know—Rugnus— appears at the edge of the crowd in a ring of fire and a rumble of stone. His mother Rusela is beside him, her skin hardening, a bone-spiked nose growing on her face. I issue a low growl to them in greeting.

The darksmiths spring into action, swarming around me before I can find my other friends. A carpet of greasy bug machines cascade over me, pinching and poking. The grass under my feet turns to burning acid, and though my paws give me more protection than Loamin skin, it begins to sting.

The wicked little flesh bags take the boy Brig from my side, binding him in mercury chains. Dozens more darksmiths swarm me, and soon I too am overwhelmed and immobile, covered in strange crafts of every kind.

I howl at Bazalrak, who hasn't moved from his place in front of me.

"See," he says. "Outmatched. There's a few hundred of us and a handful of you. The arithmetic is on our side. Now return to Loamin form so we can converse in a fashion to my liking." With a flourish, he produces his ax.

My friends are dragged through the crowd under a hail of hisses and jeers. One of the darksmiths has Winta contained inside a cube of shieldcraft. She lashes the inside of the shield with angry tendons of mercury. The woman controlling her orders someone else to rip the mercury band off her wrist. They force her to kneel before Bazalrak.

I shrink down, the staff reappearing in my hands. One of the darksmiths starts forward to rip it away, but his skin sizzles on contact, and he drops it. I scan the crowd again. A hundred, maybe two hundred. If we could get the attention of Tungsten City, we could have ten thousand people here in the next five seconds.

I gesture open bluelink, turn on recording, making a plea with one word: "Help."

As Rugnus and I are brought to kneel in front of him, he switches his ax from hand to hand. The air hisses around the blade, and shadows creep from the hilt. That's when I realize how sharp the blade is and how I've never actually seen it cut through anything.

Andalynn is the last to kneel before Bazalrak. She refuses to lower her head to him. "This is foolish, Bazalrak, even for you. Working with Emberfence gets you nothing."

"Means to an end, dear. Lagnar allowed me this final distraction, but I don't care about his cumbersome plans. I just want what I want, and I don't care what happens to anyone else. That's why I fit in so well with these fine individuals." He salutes the darksmiths with his ax. Their cheers echo through the columns.

My mind grabs onto Bazalrak's words. Something's not right.

Rugnus scoffs. "Then you *are* working with Emberfence."

This attack is different from the attack on the StoneYoke festival. Even his appearance during the festival to attack me, now—in context—seems disconnected and ill-planned. He's a distraction, a deadly one, but still meant to draw us away from something. The attacks had been planned, calculated.

"He's telling the truth. The only thing he wants is revenge." I glare up at him, my neck straining against the heavy hand. "Who freed you from Keelcrawl?"

"So clever." Bazalrak's lips twist into a smile. "Chainkeeper of course."

"The eight minutes," I whisper.

"You may not be helping Emberfence," Andalynn says. Her

words are diplomatic, but I can hear the tremor under them. "But you know what he's trying to do. Tell us. How did he attack the festival? How did he prevent people from leaving? Who else is involved?"

Bazalrak lets his ax drift to our eye level. "You misunderstand what this is. This is not a council, Queen. This is an execution."

At his words, the darksmiths line up Brig, Rusela, Hemdi, and even Winta next to us, removing any crafted objects from our possession, tossing them behind us. Torlina's staff lays on the ground where it fell. My bluelink recording is still going, but I can't access any controls to see if anyone has responded; if anyone is watching.

Bazalrak's tongue swipes across his bottom lip. His eyes narrow on my sister, and suddenly I understand. This wasn't an attack on the memorial. This was a trap designed for a single reason. Murder.

I try to stand, but rough hands force me back down. "Who attacked Kel's? You couldn't have done it, but it was your craftprint."

Something flickers in Bazalrak's eyes, but he shakes his head and raises his ax.

This is the last moment before our deaths. Bazalrak can't be reasoned with. He has nothing left, and murdering us is the last thing on his bucket list.

He nods at Andalynn, and two darksmiths drag her forward with morbid excitement and anticipation. Hopeless desperation floods my body with nervous energy as her head is forced low, a few of the woven strands of metal hair touch the ground.

"Andalynn!" Rugnus cries.

Bazalrak has nothing but a distorted motivation to kill. He raises his ax higher, his chest bulging outward like he's gathering in all his hatred and resentment.

I strain against the two darksmiths holding me down. Rugnus struggles next to me, cursing.

This can't be happening. I shout a guttural roar against his madness, but more and more hands force me down until my cheek is pressed into the ground. We're powerless.

The moment the ax falls, chains lash out from above him, grappling the neck of the ax before the blade can reach my sister. Bazalrak whirls around in a fury.

Chainkeeper hovers in the air in a ring of mercury. Purple light ripples out from him. A pulse of energy streaks over the metal, and Bazalrak's expression freezes. All around us, the darksmiths stare slack-jawed as more defenders arrive to aid our rescue, blazing in neon light and metallic hues. I recognize two of Koglim's teammates, professional raiders. The darksmiths slacken their grip, and I catapult to my feet, pulling Andalynn away from the execution block. Tears shimmer down her cheeks, but she wipes them away.

Hundreds of Shale Knights, alongside a thousand citizens of Tungsten City, surround the group. In a heartbeat, the darksmiths take flight, some budging instantly, others physically bursting through the crowd to get free. Rusela mounts up and slams one of the fleeing darksmiths into the dirt. Then she brushes off her hands and helps her son to his feet. Winta struggles on her hands and knees but refuses help from Hemdi.

"This is awesome," Brig whispers.

Chainkeeper descends. "Your terror is over, Bazalrak. And if you don't answer my questions with complete satisfaction, the only execution that will take place here today will be your own."

Frantic, I look toward the pillar of glass and cement holding Jeiah hostage. Before I can think, I leave Chainkeeper to deal with Bazalrak and rush toward the pillar. It's riddled with bumps and knobs. Ten feet into climbing it, and I hear Bazalrak call out to me.

"I wouldn't do that," he chides.

I freeze, but I can't help sending him a worried glance.

"Now there, there, baby Brightstorm. You can't just free her from the pillar. There's a lock. Ironcraft. If you tear away the stone, the girl's heart will stop, and if her heart stops... well, let's just say she's the pin in the grenade. Wouldn't want the whole place to explode again, would you?"

He's lying.

Andalynn grabs Bazalrak by the shirt. "What did you do?"

"We disguised them like leafs. Pressed them into nearly every column throughout the whole memorial. A bit of a perversion of what a memorial should be but—"

Rusela charges forward. "How dare you!"

Chainkeeper yanks Bazalrak back to his knees. "Undo the lock. I give you one warning only." The words are so flat and emotionless that even Bazalrak swallows. Chainkeeper means what he says.

Bazalrak strains against his bindings. "The Queen will not let you execute me without a meeting of the council."

Andalynn shifts uncomfortably by my side. Chainkeeper doesn't blink an eye.

"With all due respect to our beloved Queen, this is an issue of an escaped prisoner, and as warden of Keelcrawl, I can do whatever it takes to protect the integrity of my prison. Even if that means killing you."

Bazalrak sneers. "Go on. You think I care about living? I have nothing left."

Chainkeeper lowers his eyes, and he fixes Bazalrak with an icy stare. "If you do not defuse your trap, I swear by Ide itself, by all the silver under every mountain in the world, Keelcrawl will be the least of your worries, torturer. I will drag you into Chainbearer Dungeon and hide you in a hole so deep and dark, no one will ever find you. Your body and mind will be frozen until the great brightstorm among the stars winks out and obliterates all of Ide."

Bazalrak's shoulders sink, and for the first time, a flicker of fear crosses his face. "Timecraft only traps my body. I was in Keelcrawl for months. It's supposed to be merciful"—he spits this word out— "but I remember every second. You c-can't do that to me again."

It's a fate worse than death if Bazalrak's mind truly can't be frozen with his body.

Chainkeeper loosens Bazalrak's chains. They fall at his feet. "Defuse this bomb, and I will consider a kinder alternative."

Bazalrak stands, marches over to the pillar, head held high. He places a hand on the cement. Veins of gold and red light streak toward Jeiah's location. About a half-block up, the stone melts away. We wait for what seems to be an eternity. No one blinks.

When nothing happens, I continue my climb.

A second later, Jeiah leaps from the pillar, catching a sudden updraft someone sends to catch her fall. She lands in the grass and rolls forward, the neon magenta of her hair dazzling in the light from the brightstorm. I leap down from the pillar to go to her, but her eyes narrow on Bazalrak, and she charges him. Tears push their way to the surface, but her face is flushed with blood, her mouth clenched with anger.

Winta steps between them. "Easy there. The warden has his punishment covered."

She un-balls her fists, takes a deep breath, trembling. "They have the battery again. That's what this was all about. Sira wasn't supposed to take it. And this... it's a distraction." She whirls on Bazalrak. "I told you Clayson would find you. Now, tell me about Emberfence, about the battery."

Chainkeeper leans in.

Bazalrak's normal sneer resurfaces. "I will not give you the satisfaction of—"

"Do it." Chainkeeper's word holds another warning for the torturer. Either Bazalrak will comply or spend eternity in Chainbearer Dungeon where he can contemplate his choices.

His jaw trembles. "It's not that I won't tell you, it's that I can't. I don't understand how Lagnar could have used the battery like that. He won't tell me what's going on."

"And the craftprints?" Jeiah says.

Bazalrak struggles for words, glancing from face-to-face. He's not the type for subtle manipulation. He simply doesn't know.

Chainkeeper shakes his head, gesturing the knights to take Bazalrak away.

"Wait! Wait. Emberfence, h-he works with someone, a shadow. He won't speak of it. Even Emberfence didn't know about the attack until it was too late. Now he's trying to cover up his involvement. He blames the prince, deflecting the eyes of the council away from himself."

Rugnus laughs. "Partial truths. There's no way Lagnar didn't know."

"No, it makes sense." With a bit of wolf behind my voice I glare at Bazalrak. "Did you attack Kel's Lounge?"

Confusion, or maybe dismissal, is readable on his face. "What? You're talking about the attack on that vacant's restaurant?"

"We know you attacked her," Andalynn says. "It was shadow-craft. Why did—"

"It wasn't me. What dealings would I have with a vacant?"

Rugnus blinks. "But the shadowcraft—"

"I pledged my craft to Emberfence using the battery. That thing is filled with all manner of powers. From there..." He turns to my sister. "Queen. I make a request. Do not let my sentence be cruel. I will pay the price in time, but I haven't taken a life. Consider that. The attack on StoneYoke was not of my creation."

Andalynn considers this. "We must weigh all matters, but we will stay our judgment until we have all the information."

Bazalrak exhales, and for an instant, he almost looks relieved.

Chainkeeper harshly adjusts the binds on Bazalrak's wrists. "I make no such deal with you, traitor. Knights! Take him to my personal lobby in Chainbearer and place him in stasis. I've made my judgment; you will live forever under a seal of quicksilver until time ends." He hands one of the knights a budge key.

Bazalrak fights against the chains, yelling at the knights to release him. One of them pushes him to the ground with a boot against his back. "No. No, you can't do this. Queen Everbloom! We have an agreement. Mercy! Please! Don't—"

When the two knights vanish with Bazalrak, the torturer's yelling echoes over the memorial. Chainkeeper smiles. "Queen Everbloom. It's clear that Lagnar Bluekeeper is involved. We need to return to—"

Chainkeeper's eyes suddenly bulge. His neck tenses, and he tries to speak. Brown light snakes up his legs. I step backward, surprised, but Jeiah steps forward, her glass rod flashing.

"Someone's trying to forcibly budge him to the council room!"

Rugnus looks to his empty hands, desperate. "Don't let them."

A band of mercury blasts from Winta's hand, wrapping around his torso. The tan light creeps upward past his waist, bucking against the thin line of mercury. Winta grits her teeth. "Add more craft!"

I grab Winta's hand, focusing on the timecraft she's using, trying to aid her. Rugnus' face floods red with effort. Tension pulls tight against me through my contact with Winta's band, but it holds. The tan light flickers like a fuse shorting out. In a flash, it's gone.

Winta's mercury band curls back toward her. I let go of her hand. "What was that?"

Jeiah answers. "It was the craftprint of the budgecraft used during the attack. Someone was trying to budge him to Whurrimduum."

Chainkeeper glances in concern at Winta. "That was an impressive use of timecraft, slowing the budge like that."

She nods.

He looks her over cautiously. "I must return to Whurrimduum and apprehend Bluekeeper."

'We're coming with you." Rugnus says.

"All of you?" Chainkeeper raises an eyebrow.

Brig straightens up. "Yep."

Jeiah stares him down. "Brig, be quiet."

"Come on. I helped Clayson fight off a goldsmith. You should have seen these reanimates we faced down. And who talked him out of his wolf state?"

She pulls him away from the group. He protests as they walk away.

Chainkeeper points to Winta. "I'm glad you were here, but young lady, your other use of timecraft... it's extremely dangerous." He looks to the Queen for an extra second and vanishes.

All eyes fall on Winta, who's breathing heavy, eyes closed. Hemdi reaches out to support her but slowly draws his hand back.

"Hey, uh, Winta," Rugnus says. "You okay?"

Winta manages to straighten her back. Hemdi lets his arm balance between them. She shoves it away but has a second thought and accepts his help. "Wait, okay."

Rusela marches toward our group. She opens her mouth to speak but stops when she sees Winta. "That looks forthcoming."

Andalynn switches a ring from her gloved finger to the one where it will contact skin. "Is it the baby? What was Chainkeeper talking about? What's dangerous?"

There's a slight grunt in Winta's response. "No. Just... ooh, tired all of a sudden. Headache."

The four of us share a quick glance. Normally Winta would have already pushed everyone away, yelled at her husband, and left to fix something.

"Okay," she says. "Okay. I may have been using my mercury band to slow this thing down."

"The baby?" Hemdi says, a tremor in his voice.

"Yes the—what else would it be!"

Andalynn stares blankly. "Winta, why would you—"

"I'm scared, okay. I don't... I won't... I won't be a good parent. I'm rude and mean, and I just... I don't want this thing to come out. And with everything else going on... Then we went to Geum Ide a-and..."

It hits me. "And you didn't have craft. Okay... uh, you should really—"

"Yes, I know, Clayson: slow down, change my pace. All that. But I just want to find who's responsible for the attack. I want..." A great roll sigh tumbles from her mouth. "Who am I kidding. I need a nap."

"Winta, *we* can take care of this," Rugnus says. "With Chain-keeper helping..."

Andalynn adds, "And I'm sure after hearing Bazalrak's accusations against Emberfence, we can finally get down to the bottom of this. We'll see this through."

"Okay, Queeny." Winta releases an enormous sigh. "This is just... hard. I don't-I don't want to leave. Not yet."

Something in the way she looks at Hemdi says we've all missed something important.

Rugnus shrugs. "We'll be back."

Winta takes a breath like she's going to speak but stops herself.

"What is it?" I ask her.

"I'm going back to Geum Ide," she looks at Hemdi.

"You are?" Hemdi asks.

Winta tightens her grip on Hemdi's arm. "If you want to come too, that would be great."

When Hemdi smiles, it's like the world itself lights up. He doesn't need craft when he has Winta. She's like the roots of some great plant around his heart. "I would follow you into the brightest pool of lava."

Rugnus squeezes his eyes shut like that will keep them here. "But Geum Ide—"

"We talked it out with Azbena," Winta says. "There's a place for us there, and our child. Even old Glaris agreed. Azbena will be checking for us at the shield every evening. We could make it there tonight. But once we're there, we're there for good." Another long breath.

This sobers the whole group. Winta and Hemdi were the first two people I met in Tungsten City. If they go to Geum Ide, it will be a long time until we see them again. "Geum Ide—despite my grandmother—has the protection of the mithrium shield. You'll be safe there."

Jeiah reappears next to me. Brig is not with her. She waits quietly at the edge of the conversation, but I can tell she wants to say something to me.

"May Ide keep you." Andalynn takes Winta's hands in her own. "And your son. Winta, you'll be a great mother."

"Son?" Hemdi says, a grin spreading across his face.

Horrified, Andalynn drops Winta's hands. "I'm so sorry, Hemdi. I knew you were waiting. I don't know what I was thinking."

Winta waves a dismissive hand. "He was being dramatic. It's good he knows."

"I—a son?" Hemdi is dazed. "Well, I—does Geum Ide have a place? No, I suppose…well, wait, there's no craft. Without lead-mages or goldmages, what will—"

A glimmer of danger passes over Winta's eyes like she's getting ready to race again. "I don't need craft to have this child. They have these beautiful mudbaths where—"

"Mudbaths? You can't birth a child in—"

Winta's face sends a warning. "I can, and I will. Now—if he's awake—let's go say goodbye to Koglim before we leave this city for good."

"Very well. But I'm not going to be the one to tell him we're joining the conjurers and swearing off craft."

They say their goodbyes. When Winta gets to me, I hold out a fist—that has become our agreed-upon form of recognition, though uncommon in the Loamin world. Instead of a fist bump, Winta draws me into an embrace. "Don't get all excited, Clayson. A hug from a girl just means a hug from a girl."

My face must turn bright red.

Hemdi tips back his head and laughs, large and loud. I look to him for help, but he shrugs. "I cannot blame you for having a crush on her at first. I felt the same way the moment I saw her."

"It wasn't a crush."

Winta pats my arm. "Okay, Clayson. Just do me a favor and take care of this one. She's a keeper." Winta acknowledges Jeiah with a nod and a fist bump.

But Jeiah doesn't look at me. All the images and videos from her investigation flash through my mind. Maybe it was more than an investigation. I'm not sure whether to feel excited, flattered or something else entirely. But I don't feel awful about it. She grew up here in Tungsten City. There's a lot less personal space here than in the Blue Ridge Mountains.

Winta and Hemdi budge, leaving a wake as deep as the city itself.

"We ready?" Rugnus asks.

Andalynn nods and scoots next to him. "I just hope Emberfence doesn't try to put up a fight. We've had enough of that today."

"Agreed," I say.

Rugnus dusts off his hands. "Speak for yourselves. If he was behind the attack, I hope he does put up a fight. I'll melt him myself." Rugnus looks at his empty hands. "Too bad I don't have Icho."

"Don't have Icho?" Rusela says. I hadn't realized she had been paying that much attention to us. She had been ordering people to spread out and find the rest of the fake memorial leafs. But now, her attention is on us.

Rugnus casts his eyes to the ground. "About that. Been a lot going on."

"That's my fault," I say. "We took Icho to Geum Ide. They didn't appreciate us budging in without their permission."

It's as if Rusela doesn't hear me. "Rugnus, could we speak privately?"

Andalynn and I might as well be sharing thoughts. We both scoot closer to Rugnus. "Does this have to do with Icho?"

"It's between my son and—"

"Does it have to do with Blackmug?" I add.

Now she looks directly at me. "Where did you hear that

name?" She looks away. "This is a private matter. If he chooses to tell you later, that is between you and him."

Rugnus' eyes don't leave his mother. "I'll meet you all at the castlestack."

Andalynn nods, and then to Rusela, she says, "Sorry about the memorial service. I will help to reorganize it when things are straightened out."

Rusela brushes the comment aside, staying focused on her son. "Plenty of days left of the memorial. Besides, I've had worse events."

Andalynn steps away from Rugnus, but I shake my head. Ergal, Onrix, and Icho. If I'm right about Icho, Rusela could know more about them. "Rugnus, I wanna hear this. If it's about what I think..."

He turns to me. "Need some space here, Clayson. I won't keep you in the dark."

Andalynn tugs on my sleeve. "Come on."

I reluctantly accept the budgeport invitation. There's still no pull of added pressure in my muscles, no nausea, and we're transported directly to the large throne room, which leads to the shale passage. There's physical energy in the air, like a charge of lightning.

Andalynn's expression of shock stops me. Where the shale wall once stood impenetrable, there's a giant, burned-out hole. Shards and powdered rock form a rough semicircle outward from the wall.

"Did someone blow it up from the inside?" Andalynn's voice is a whimper.

A layer of burning shadow lies over the rubble.

"The wall," Jeiah says. "Isn't it protected from attacks like this?"

Andalynn rushes toward the rubble, avoiding the deep shadows fading from the stone. We follow her the best we can.

When Vor led me and Rugnus through the wall a few days ago, there were a series of narrow passages and multiple flights of stairs to bypass. It must have all been craft. The council room is wide open as we move through the door.

It's dark as pitch. Chainkeeper stands alone on the dais where I faced the council's inquiry. He looks back at us slowly, mournfully, as we approach. The council members visible from the door, rest lifeless near their daises. Their bodies are cut with deep, bloody wounds not made from shadowcraft.

"What happened here?" My voice is as dry as firewood.

Anguish rolls from Chainkeeper in a rush of words. "Rensira Silverlamp is free from the Keeper's Prison. Bazalrak's attack was indeed meant as a distraction. Though I believe I was designed to be here. Your timemage saved my life. Silverkeeper's daughter must have... must have attacked. Or maybe it was Lagnar. But I don't... I don't understand how any of this is possible."

Only when I stand next to him, do I see the black-shadowed outlines of the two massive armadillos who had acted as the second layer of protection for the council. The beasts are dead, unrolled from their corners, claws glistening. Shadows burn through them.

A light on one of the dais flickers on and off. It's the pale green light of Tinkeeper—she's moving! Blood flows from a wound on her chest.

Chainkeeper flies toward her. We scramble after him. But Tinkeeper's body falls forward, her arm dropping limply to one side. She's clenching a relic.

I pour healing craft from my bracelet into her body, but nothing happens. She's dead. What's the use of having a peerless rating in protective craft if I can't protect anything?

"She's dead." Chainkeeper's voice is flat. "The council is destroyed."

Jeiah sweeps the beholder over the room. Her vision flashes with blue light and she pushes a graphic overlay out to us. "Not all of it." It highlights the bodies of six of the council members in infrared, along with the two hulking forms of the armored animals. Splotches of heat lay on the ground in vivid colors—the blood of the victims. She's analyzing the whole scene.

The wall of shale was destroyed from inside the room. Emberfence had been here. Shadowcraft had been used to destroy the shale wall. Bazalrak's craftprint. After that, it had been silvercraft. Sira. But I would've never guessed her capable of something like this. Besides, her knife is locked away in Rugnus' vault. She couldn't have overpowered the keepers without it.

Jeiah's readings are clear—the minds of the council members had been paused before their murders. Ogrekeeper was forced to order the massive guards to stand down. The shadows burned through their shells with necrotic venom. No member of the council resisted the silvercraft. The outline of the offending party is disrupted, just like the bluelink data that led us to Sira. Whoever did this did it quickly, viciously. Could Sira or Lagnar do such a thing?

Chainkeeper says, "The new Bluekeeper's location marker was here, but his body is not. That confirms Bazalrak's account."

"And two others are not accounted for," Andalynn confirms. "Hardkeeper and Brightkeeper."

"I am messaging them now," Chainkeeper adds.

Jeiah nods. "From the information I've collected, it looks like they weren't here at the time of the attack."

"Yes. Even more reason to be on guard. Here they come."

When young Brightkeeper and Lagnar's friend, Hardkeeper, come through the doors, they look devastated, shocked.

A purple light grows around Chainkeeper, and he rises from the ground balanced on two chain stilts. "Prove to me you have no part in this!" His words thunder around the room.

Brightkeeper cowers in fear, his frame trembling. It reminds me of a baby goat trying to take its first step on wobbly legs. Brightkeeper clearly wasn't involved in this.

Hardkeeper is more calculating. "Prove the same to me. You're the one who's missing eight minutes of his life. The only one who could have opened your prison before the attack. And now you're standing here with the forgotten prince, the destroyer of dungeons." He gives me a scathing look. "Ah, but I forget myself. Chainkeeper, this couldn't be your work. There's always a few layers of protection between you and those you murder."

"How dare you—"

My sister inserts herself between them as Hardkeeper reveals a rough, cast-iron sphere—some type of craft. "Enough. It's clear neither of you were involved. Emberfence, however, was." Turning to Hardkeeper, she asks, "Did he say anything to you?"

Begrudgingly, he tucks the sphere away. "No, though a couple of minutes ago, someone tried to forcibly budge me to the council room. I prevented it."

"As did I," Chainkeeper says. "I was dealing with Bazalrak at the memorial."

"Did the general have anything to do with this?"

"A distraction, I believe. But taken care of."

"Taken care of?" Hardkeeper narrows his eyes. " Did he say anything about the attack on the festival?"

"Emberfence was involved," I say. "We came back to question him."

"And he's nowhere to be found," Jeiah adds, at last lowering her beholder.

Chainkeeper moves toward Brightkeeper. "And you, young council? Why were you not budged?"

Brightkeeper swallows with difficulty. "I was. But into Rensira Silverlamp's cell. She stole my budge and left me there. Took me a while to get the guards to let me out." Brightkeeper tries to keep his eyes on Chainkeeper, but they drift to the bodies around us.

Andalynn notices. "Can we have someone's help to care for the bodies of the council members? Our discussion can continue elsewhere."

Chainkeeper swivels his head over the room. "I called for Vor the moment I arrived; he should be here."

A clue tries to push itself out of my subconscious. Some

single detail I've overlooked but tucked away in the shadows. Something about Ara. Something about Sira and her knife. About Silverkeeper. My father's friendship with him, their time here in this very castle together. A connection I should have made by now.

The pendant drops from Tinkeeper's grip. I pick it up from the stone. The moment my fingers touch the tin, a branch of plant life grows up my arm, and a barb pricks my scalp just below my ear. A recording begins to play in my mind.

I'm seeing things from Tinkeeper's perspective. All the council members, including Emberfence, stand at attention on their platforms. They're arguing. Emberfence brushes his hands off, hangs his head, and steps away. The others shout him back, but he refuses.

A crack of stone rips through the room, shaking the pillars on the outside of the chamber. The thick muscles under the armadillo's shells tenses in anticipation, their heads retracting from the bodies. An earthquake of sound continues to shudder through the room until the wall of shale splits down the center and explodes away from the chamber, dripping with festering shadows.

A figure rises in the wake of the explosion of rock, particles raining down from the ceiling. From out of darkness, a voice, clear and deadly, echoes over the room. "I need to know what's down in the mines. Unseal them."

Every council member obeys. They open bluelink, making difficult unlocking gestures I can't follow. Tinkeeper, for a brief second, seems to break out of the figure's control. From my perspective, it's me grasping the pendant, me speaking.

"I see you, Vor. Come into the light."

The Dura servant of the council of the Brightstorm family steps up to the dais where he can no longer hide. Behind him, a girl waits in the half-light. It's Sira. It was always Sira with him. I can almost imagine it. Vor raising her after the death of her father in Wolfstaff Dungeon. Keeping her hidden in Whurrimduum.

Setting her loose in Tungsten City. Helping her manipulate me into the Silverlamp Dungeon last year, like a piece on a chessboard.

As the council's servant, he has seen hundreds of years of mistreatment. He knows all the intimate history of the Brightstorm family going back generations. How long has he been self-aware like Ara?

Vor doesn't smile. His expression is flat but filled with inquisition. "The light? That's exactly why I'm here. Answers. Reasons. Tell me what I am? What *Dura* are?"

"You think I have knowledge of something so ancient? I do not."

"I suffered hundreds of years under the mistreatment of the council."

"Not by my hand."

"Then, I will kill you quickly."

As Tinkeeper sits down, I watch helplessly as Sira's eyes fill with tears. She looks away as Vor raises a jagged sword and leaps forward.

SEE MANY THINGS

WHEN THE RECORDING ENDS, my mind slips away from the council room altogether. He murdered them. He used Sira's craftprint to trap their minds, to bend their wills, but he murdered them. He took a cruel, plain sword and cut the council to pieces.

A pair of hands guides my body to the side of the room. My feet move, but my thoughts are racing. Someone is saying something to me, but I can't process it. How could it be Vor? He's not like Ara. My dad had said that she was the only one capable of using craftprints. Had he lied, or did he not know about Vor? But I know the answer. He lied.

I feel someone shaking me, but I don't respond until Jeiah rests a hand gently against my cheek and finds my eyes. "Hey! Snap out of it. You okay?"

I blink. "It was Vor." My senses return slowly, but I find myself standing outside the council room beyond the shale wall. The three remaining keepers, Andalynn, and Jeiah all stand, waiting for me to speak. They must have pulled me from the darkness of the council room. Light pours through the long stone-framed windows at either side of the room.

My mind whirls with thoughts. "It's been Vor all along."

Chainkeeper steps in front of me. "Explain this. Vor couldn't have—"

"He could have," Andalynn says, eyes wide. "We've known of a Dura woman with similar powers since Silverlamp. Her name is Ara. Before the mithrium shield, she helped my father heal the brightstorm in Geum Ide. My father gives her his craftprint, and she multiplies it to do impossible things."

Now it's Hardkeeper who speaks, head tilted, eyebrows raised. "And you kept that information from the council?"

"We hadn't connected it to the attack." Andalynn raises her hands, palms outward. "She's not important right now. We need to understand what Vor is after."

Her comment surprises me. I don't have to use my imagination to know what he's after in the mines. "You don't know?"

"I—" she considers me for a moment. "Of course. Mithriumbane."

Hardkeeper whispers the name, almost a reverent question. "Yinzar Mithriumbane?"

I nod. "Yinzar tried to forge the mithrium in the Cradle."

Brightkeeper speaks. "The Cradle." I had almost forgotten about him. He's younger than me. Probably only a year out from his summation. "Where Erikzin forged the first brightstorm with the twelve peerless."

"But my grandfather's death destroyed the mithrium."

"I'm not sure you believe that," Jeiah says.

And she's right. I'm not sure I ever truly believed it.

"Dura cannot enter the dungeons," Hardkeeper says.

Chainkeeper mindlessly unwinds the chains around his forearm. "Maybe yesterday that seemed true."

"No, he's right," I say. "Last year, Ara broke through the foilgrips Silverkeeper placed around the lobby of Silverlamp, but she couldn't go in. The way I see it, whatever's true for her must also be true for him. They interact with craft the same way. It must be given to them willingly, and the craftprints they do use can be used up."

"Then we wait," Chainkeeper says. "He'll run out of power. We tell the whole world what he is. Expose him. No one will give him their craft."

Hardkeeper narrows his eyes, shakes his head. "Lagnar's helping him. He could keep putting craft into the battery."

"And Vor will find a way into that dungeon," I add. "Sira will follow him willingly. If he's had access to her craft, it's even possible that he's been controlling the council's decisions. That he forced you, Chainkeeper, to open up Keelcrawl prison."

"Wait," Jeiah says. "No one's been in the dungeon yet. It can only be opened by a person who's been called for their summation. So even if they wanted to, Vor, Lagnar, Sira—they can't go in. Not without..."

Jeiah's face goes pale, her eyes wide. I steady her, but her hands dig into my arm.

Brig.

I swore to help him find Mithriumbane, complete his summation. I made it public. Vor must have seen it, seen Brig's connection. I squeeze Jeiah's hand. "No. He won't need Brig or any of the other initiates. If I'm right, my grandfather—Yinzar—will let me cross the threshold without that. I'm the keeper of that dungeon. If Vor's after the Mithrium, I'm sure I can find it first. Even if he's already found the Cradle."

"Stupidest idea under granite." We all spin around to find Rugnus standing near the rubble. It's clear from his wide eyes that he's been in the council room. He descends the stairs slowly and joins the circle.

What did his mother tell him about Blackmug? I wanna ask, but I'm not sure that's information we want out in the open. Besides, he looks ready to burn a hole through someone.

"Can you elaborate on your reasoning?" Jeiah says, though I detect a hint of annoyance.

Rugnus huffs. "Sure. Clayson's thinking—or maybe not thinking—about running down to Grandpa's dungeon and... what? Opening it up for Vor? Grabbing some mithrium? And if I know him, he's thinking about how he could use it. You know, make something like the mithrium shield. I mean Vor can't use craft directly, just the craftprints of others, so if Clayson makes something untouchable, like the shield, Vor can never get it. And we can all go back to our regular lives. The world is a happy little place filled with smiles and stormshine."

Something's boiling inside of him. I take a step back out of pure instinct.

Hardkeeper chuckles, but it sounds more like he's choking. "Finally, someone with sense. If Vor is trying to drive Clayson to this dungeon, the trap is obvious. And Lagnar is calculating and dangerous. We should send a legion of knights to the mines to—"

"He'd kill every single one of them," I say. "He has the battery. Meaning Sira's craftprint from the knife, Bazalrak's craftprint from his ax, and the craftprint he used at StoneYoke, Lagnar's craftprint. He is dangerous. But maybe Sira will help us. Maybe we can—"

A trail of fire flickers to life along Rugnus' arms. "This is how it always works with you. It's like you spin a wheel in that thick head of yours and just do whatever it lands on. So, not today. I'm not letting your recklessness make decisions for the whole group."

Andalynn steps toward him. "Rugnus."

Hardkeeper's hand drifts toward his aluminum belt buckle. What craft does it hold? "Rugnus is correct. Young Brightstorm's naïveté could have terrible repercussions."

I know he's right. I'm reckless sometimes, but that doesn't mean I'm wrong. "I might be naïve, but I'm not going to stand by while—"

The floor rumbles at my feet. "No," Rugnus says, "Come on, Clayson. Think! For a Brightstorm, you're not very bright. Why can't you see things in front of your face? Huh?" He waves an angry hand close enough to my eyes that I flinch.

"Vor manipulated all of us," Hardkeeper says.

"And there's no way to find the Cradle anyway," Chainkeeper adds.

Jeiah's beholder shines against her clothing, and she readies it in front of her, sweeping over the group. "Brightkeeper's heart rate is elevated. There's something he's keeping from us."

Chainkeeper only needs to nod at the young council member.

Brightkeeper clears his throat. "I wasn't keeping anything. I... it's an old secret, passed down from keeper to keeper. I know the way to the Cradle. Vor serves the Brightstorms. He must be aware of that somehow."

Rugnus' dark laugher turns my stomach. "Great! See? Vor left Brightkeeper alive for a reason. It's. A. Trick." He pronounces every word so I can understand. "Get it?"

"Stop!" A single word from Andalynn snuffs out the fire along Rugnus' arms. She drops her gaze to Jeiah, and I freeze. Jeiah's eyes are brimmed with tears. She's frozen in place, mouth open in horror, head slightly shaking.

I reach for her. "Jeiah, what's—"

Her mouth closes, her jaw trembling. Tears escape both of her eyes. "Brig is gone. Won't message... h-he's not in Tungsten City anymore. Vor has him. I know it. I just know it. Clayson, it's like he's been watching us. He knows you will come for Brig."

Jeiah has never jumped to conclusions that I know. She must be right. "We'll find him. He'll be okay." The whirlwind of thoughts in my mind swirls into a final knot. I glance at Rugnus. "Vor has to be stopped. If there is mithrium in my grandfather's dungeon, we don't know if it's safely hidden like the one in Silverlamp."

"Yes, we do," Rugnus says. "It will be the heart of the dungeon. Get it? Mithriumbane. That's the object most important to him. The heart. Why do you think Vor wants you? Why do you think he's waited this long? He couldn't get it. But which one of us can reach the heart of a dungeon?" He gestures to the staff at my back. "Give you a hint: none of the rest of us. It's you, Clayson! I'm not going to be a part of this."

He scrambles in his bag for a budge. He hasn't found something to wear that can replace Icho. I grab his wrist. He forms a fist out of his other hand.

"You're right. You're right about everything. Everything. But Brig's in danger, and Sira's always been in danger. You know what she gave me. Why would she do that? She's protecting it. Sooner or later, we'd have to face Vor anyway. But if we don't do something..." I glance at Jeiah.

Rugnus rips his arm free. "Stay away from me."

He budges.

Jeiah wipes a few tears from her face, straightens up. She grabs my hand. "It is a trap, Clay. I just don't know what else to do. Brig is all I have. I can't lose him."

"You won't." I turn to everyone else. "Look, I know this is a trap, and I don't have any right asking, but I..."

Andalynn wraps an arm around me, adds courage to my mind with silvercraft. "I'm with you, Clayson."

I have a sudden idea. "Is it nightfall in Geum Ide?"

Jeiah opens bluelink and scrolls through something. "Almost, but not yet."

"This will work. Jeiah, can you send Winta a message? Tell her where we're going. Tell her we need Ara's help. We'll keep our location data open to her."

"That could work." Jeiah says. "The craft between them may be equal."

Hardkeeper shakes his head. "You trust this Dura?"

My dad and Ara are keeping something from me. But I don't know what it is. "Right now, we'll have to."

"If they can even find her," Andalynn adds.

I nod and turn to Brightkeeper, trying to remember his first name. "Quilgist, right?"

He swallows hard. "Yes."

"Can you really get us to the Cradle?"

"Uh, I memorized the correct pattern." His hands are shaking.

"But the minesmiths tore out all the budgeports when they left after the war. It would—"

"But you can get us there?"

"Theoretically."

"Good. Who else will come?"

Chainkeeper unwinds the links of the metal chain around his arm. He inclines his head to me. "It's an invitation to death, but you'll need all the help you can get."

Jeiah clenches my hand harder. "Let's find him."

Hardkeeper looks from Chainkeeper to Quilgist, then back to me. He shakes his head. "Someone needs to stay to manage affairs here. But I'll rally the Knights of Shale and send them to the mines."

"Make sure they understand the risk. Vor could kill them all," Andalynn says.

Hardkeeper crosses his arms. "It is the knights' duty to protect Whurrimduum. They must help face him. I'm sending them. But I'm staying here in case none of you come back from this fool's errand." It's an abrupt decision, and he punctuates it by turning and walking away from us.

Chainkeeper calls out to him. "Coward."

He raises a dismissive hand. "Enough keeper's blood has been spilled today."

"Hemdi got the message. They'll pass it on." Jeiah says. "And I have the budgeport for the mining control hub. Are we ready?" There's no fear in her eyes, only resolve. She must save Brig.

Everyone nods.

"Let's go."

The budge deposits us at a port on the edge of a large hangar bay, filled with hundreds of bean pod shaped machines with open baskets on their backs. Behind us, a myriad of blue lights assaults us from long, angled windows the moment we arrive. The windows look out over the Foundation, an impossibly massive sheet of ice that makes life under granite possible for all Loamin, filled with energy beyond anything even a brightstorm could rival.

Jeiah catches me looking at it. Her eyes, still slightly reddened, scan my face, pausing, I think, on my mouth. "Have you seen it before? The Foundation."

I scan the Foundation as far as I can see, but I don't find the black, obsidian wall that borders the flow of lava from the earth's mantle. The Foundation must stretch at least the width of the Rockies themselves. No wonder I can't see the edge.

"Twice. We went through Edium Fiarie to get to Whurrim-duum last year. And... we came to Silverkeeper's funeral, after..." I can't say it. Last time we went to a dungeon to protect my parents, someone had been killed. But Jeiah knows this.

The others move deeper into the hangar, and Jeiah takes my hand, helping me to follow them. My heart must be pumping faster. I can feel it against my rib cage. A hungry sensation fills the pit of my stomach. Can Jeiah read my emotions? This is not the time to be trying to figure out my feelings for her.

We stop in front of one of the giant bean pods, and she presses a palm against its flat porcelain surface. The clear shield on the inside bend opens, and a step swings down. "What's your mechcraft score?" Jeiah asks, eyeing what I can only call a cockpit.

"You don't know it?" I say, surprised.

Her eyes widen. "I-I mean..."

I intercede, unable to watch her embarrassment. "It's average. Three."

She pushes me up the step. "Other seat. I'll fly."

"Fly?"

"Yeah. The mines stretch on forever. It may take a while to navigate them."

The two seats angle away from each other at forty-five degrees. Both have a view through the shield, which remains flipped open above us. I stand near my seat, looking out over the fleet of pods. The rows are neat, each with exactly twenty white mining pods. Andalynn and Quilgist have already climbed into one, Chainkeeper another, but now, from my higher vantage point, there are two more missing. Jeiah follows my gaze to the empty spots.

"Vor must have come this way already," she says.

I try to comfort her. "We know Sira is with him. Emberfence could be as well. We don't know if he has Brig."

She hangs her head. Her jaw firms. "Vor might be guessing you'll protect my brother."

This time I squeeze her hand. "And I will."

Andalynn's voice crackles through a small speaker between the two seats. "You two ready?" I look further upward and find two pods hovering in the air like banana-shaped hummingbirds.

Jeiah takes the controls, seals us behind the shield, and we lift off, forcing me into my seat, where I clip into the harness. We fly straight upward into a dark shaft, and Jeiah flips on the pod's headlights. After a minute of upward motion, we coast to a stop.

"Here we are," Chainkeeper says over the speaker. "The door is already open."

Jeiah angles the pod slightly, and we move through the opening, where I get my first glimpse of the door that has blocked the mines for centuries. Somehow Yinzar had found a way around or through it. This is what Vor killed the council for.

It's a clockwork of gears and smoke. Here and there, slates of the open door look almost flesh-like. I see pieces of nearly all the types of craft. Each council member had unique keys. From what I know, it takes at least six of them to open the door. Vor controlled all but three.

The scene beyond the door is like no other place I've seen in all the Loamin world. Vast and as deep as the night sky, the chamber glimmers with gossamer threads of craft, rippling along the distant, uneven walls of the chamber. Waves of smoke and heat vapor swarm from place to place. A thousand strange sounds compete for attention.

"This is Wyzal's Chamber," Quilgist says, his voice rising softly through the speaker. "The first of nearly two hundred chambers."

"Two hundred," I say. "How do we find our way to the Cradle?"

Chainkeeper's voice rumbles over the speaker again. "That's why the great Erikzin Brightstorm hid the Cradle here in the first place. The mine is vast enough to conceal perhaps even an entire city. Brightkeeper, what is the pattern? What should we be looking for?"

Quilgist's voice is tentative. "Uh, mirrors and lilacs and threes, uh, and fours.'

Chainkeeper chuckles. "That's it?" A deep sigh rumbles over the speaker. "Okay, Use the pattern. Keep in communication."

His pod zips to the left, disappearing into a fog hanging within the chamber.

"Okay," Jeiah says. "Mirrors, lilacs, threes, and fours. Keep your eyes open."

But our pods stay back-to-back. Jeiah and Andalynn put them into automated search mode, scanning the air and the surface of the rock. We pass through what seems like a rain cloud, and I catch the smell of sulfur. The air almost tingles with energy.

The moment we reach a wall and move upward, the rumbling sound of animal hooves clatters against the windshield. What is this place?

"Why did they abandon the mines?" I ask Jeiah.

"It's easier to get craftable metal in the dead cities," she says. "Isn't Rugnus a surveyor?"

"Yeah," I say. "But can't they just dig up more metal here?"

"Craftable metal is different from metal in the human world. They must find places where there is strong potential energy. Like that cloud we drifted through or the sound of that stampede. Did you hear it?"

"So, craftable metal could've been in that cloud or in that noise?"

"Couldn't you feel the potential energy?"

"Yeah, I guess. And potential energy is what brought Yinzar here."

"Once they find the right potential energy, they print out the metal."

"Out of nothing?" I ask.

Jeiah's laugh is more of a breath. "I've never thought about it before. But I guess from Ide itself. The mines sit only a few tens above the Foundation. But the energy of the Foundation is too wild. The craft just rolls off it, impossible to capture. But enough of it rises upward, getting trapped in the stone. That's where it stays."

A ripple of green flame cuts through the air out in the void. "Potential energy."

"Look," Quilgist says excitedly. "Our reflections."

I gaze over to the other pod and find Quilgist pointing to the wall. This section is hard obsidian, like the wall separating the Foundation from a sea of lava. Our pod's reflection bounces back to us from the surface of the stone.

"Mirrors," I say. "What now?"

"You think this is what was meant by mirrors?" Quilgist says.

"Chainkeeper," Andalynn says. "Are you following this?"

For a second, there's no response. Then, "I am. Back up. See what you can see. I'm coming over."

"Zooming out." Jeiah moves our pod a further distance from the wall. We scan the reflective surface. "Are those—"

"Shapes," I say. "I think so."

There are dozens of polished surfaces, each a different shape. "Threes and fours," Quilgist suggests. "That could be triangles and rectangles."

We hover from side-to-side scanning for that combination. There's a circle inside a star, a rectangle inside an oval, dozens of combinations of shapes but no rectangle and triangle. As we float to the upper right corner of the reflective surfaces, I catch something in the air. Not sulfur like last time, but something sweet.

Jeiah's head snaps toward me. "Lilacs." We both recognize the scent at the same time.

I open the speaker. "Got something."

In response, the speaker crackles in between us. A few seconds later, Andalynn says. "Chainkeeper is that you?" Andalynn's pod swivels around toward a growing cloud of darkness. Jeiah angles us in the same direction, and we wait.

"Chainkeeper?" I ask.

His pod bursts from the cloud, its porcelain surface beaded up with water. "Keep looking."

Jeiah adjusts our position, following the scent of lilacs. By the time Andalynn finally floats next to us, we've found ourselves in an overwhelming fog of lilac scent. I scan the wall and freeze—an opening.

"There. A rectangle inside a triangle. We couldn't see it without being in this position."

"Threes and fours." Quilgist sounds awed.

Chainkeeper joins our group, looks down at the new opening, and waves us forward. "Okay, next step."

The scent of lilacs links us like a chain right to the opening. The moment we cross into the rectangular maw, I know we've budged, but I still didn't feel the physical effect.

Our headlights shine over a much smaller place. Finding nowhere to move forward, we set the pods down. Chainkeeper is the first out, hovering using the chain he always keeps at his side. Jeiah pops open the shield, and I follow her.

"Where are we?" Quilgist pulls the question right out of my mind.

"Look." Chainkeeper points to a narrow opening in the rock guarded by a wrought iron fence. Andalynn wastes no time. She moves toward the fence and opens a tall gate. We follow her inside the tunnel.

It's wide enough at first to fit us two by two, but soon we come to a massive hole in the ground, and we must skirt around it. We're forced into a crouching, single-file line. Chainkeeper leads us. Quilgist, Andalynn, Jeiah, and I follow behind. Ahead of me, Jeiah's breathing becomes uneven.

"You okay?" I ask. "It's a pretty small space."

She turns her head back slightly. "Brig cannot keep a secret."

"It's okay."

Andalynn says, "Good thing Bazalrak didn't know. He would have used that against you."

"He did know. The moment I heard where he was going to put me, I lost it. I begged him not to do it."

"And?"

"It's weird. I know his reputation. But, when he saw how afraid I was, something changed. He promised I wouldn't be awake. Started talking about Keelcrawl prison, that it's supposed to freeze people's bodies and minds. But it didn't work."

"I've heard of rare cases like that," Andalynn says.

"It was the invisible hand of justice," Chainkeeper adds ahead of us.

Jeiah tries to steady her breathing. "Whatever it was, it made him sympathetic, if only for a second. I'm sure I looked pathetic enough."

"It's nothing to be embarrassed about."

"It's a silly fear."

"Well, most Loamin are afraid of water, so don't be too embarrassed."

She tries to laugh, but it comes out somewhat hysterical. "You're not?"

"No. I swim in the lake all the time above granite."

A moment of disbelief hangs in the air. Quilgist scoffs. "I'm afraid of everything." A nervous laugh escapes him.

We all laugh. Everyone except Chainkeeper. But for a minute, the tension is lessened, and Jeiah's breathing becomes more rhythmic.

"A second pit," Chainkeeper says. "Watch your step."

The narrow hallway becomes a bit wider, and the ceiling lifts enough for us to stand upright. We edge around a circular hole, wrapping our way toward the other side—another tunnel. We move through the next tunnel at a quicker pace, reaching a final gaping black hole.

"Number three," Quilgist whispers.

"Threes," Chainkeeper says. "Maybe the pattern could work in Brightstorm's dungeon. Something to remember next time I go on a raiding party."

"Three times four is twelve. Twelve peerless Loamin created the Cradle."

"I'll go down first," Chainkeeper says. "I have a mobile budgeport. I'll set it up when I get down there. Then you can join me."

He drops into the hole without another word, plummeting into the darkness.

We wait for just a minute until Jeiah says. "Budgeport is up."

We budge.

I stare in disbelief.

This is the exact chamber from Yinzar's memories. Loose rock litters the ground around a hundred drill holes. Each hole is roughly the diameter of two Loamin back-to-back. The pit entrance that was at our feet is high above us. I step toward the center of the chamber, trying to discern which of the drill holes looks the most like the one from the dream.

It's not hard to find.

"Here it is." I point out the same hole I saw in Yinzar's memory garden. A layer of dead plant life erupts from the dark open circle."

"Brightkeeper, is that right?"

Brightkeeper looks up from staring at a rock near the toe of his boot. "How would I know?" He reaches downward, a curious expression on his face. The moment he touches the rock, both he and Chainkeeper yell out at the same time.

"Ah!"

"Wait!"

Quilgist retracts his hand, investigating the rock that's stuck to his skin like a burr. "Something's wrong with my arm. It—it's tingling. Wh-what is this?"

"Trollshards," Chainkeeper shouts jumping to the side.

I freeze. "What's that?"

Jeiah backs away from him. "Not good."

"Wait. I'm confused. Are trollshards like trollbrick? Are we in trouble or—"

Chainkeeper spreads his arms out, palms toward the ground, head lowering. It's like he just noticed we're standing in a minefield. "Everyone, stop moving. Clayson, shield your feet from the shards. Get the Queen. She's closest to you. Don't step on them."

"What are trollshards?" I shout.

Andalynn points to a rock at my foot. It has the same black and red coloration as the one attached to Quilgist's hand. "Lithic trolls don't die; they just shatter into hundreds of tiny poisonous pieces."

The rock rolls to one side, exposing what looks like rough flesh or skin. "Gross." I craft a layer of white shielding around my feet and legs and nudge the thing to the side. It sizzles when the white light touches it like cooking meat.

I move to Andalynn, grabbing her arm and extending the shield around her feet as well. I gather the whole party, me at the center, all connected by shieldcraft.

"What now?" Jeiah asks.

"Anyone else seeing this?" Quilgist asks. "I think the light is attracting them."

I spin in his direction. He's right. Hundreds, maybe thousands, of trollshards scramble out from the drill holes. I can't help but think of the trollbrick jokes Koglim would make if he were here. I shake that from my brain. Maybe if we can make it back to the correct drill hole, they won't follow us.

A rockslide of trollshards rushes our feet, wave after wave burning against our shield until they've hedged us in.

"Enlarge the shield!" Chainkeeper shouts.

I do, but I can feel it growing thinner as the tiny shards tower on top of each other, trying to reach us. "It's not going to hold much longer!"

Suddenly the shards on one side squeal in pain. Red molten streaks of magma superheat them, and they scurry away.

Rugnus appears outside of the shield. "You gonna let me in, or what?"

I briefly drop the shield on that side, and he slips between Jeiah and Andalynn to join me in the center. "Let's nuke these littles shards," he says.

"Idiot," I say.

Rugnus nods in agreement. "Yeah, fine."

"How'd you find us?"

"Explanations later." He covers the outside of the shield with magma, and inch by inch, we push back the tiny monstrosities.

CREATE TO DESTROY

QUILGIST'S FOOT and arm are paralyzed. The trollshard somehow cut through his boot and attached directly to his skin. Rugnus taps his boot against the uninfected side. "Nothing? You can't feel anything?" Next, he moves to Quilgist's arm, squeezing his fingers hard but careful to avoid contact with the other shard.

Quilgist shakes his head. "Is it permanent?"

Chainkeeper glances over and waves his hand. "Not if you get medical attention within the next, say, twenty minutes. Take the temporary budgeport I set up back to Whurrimduum. See Jenac Restshell."

Quilgist will have to go out the same way Rugnus came in.

"What castlestack?" Quilgist asks, still wincing.

"Flathand."

Quilgist hobbles toward the aluminum tent stake Chainkeeper had placed in the ground, mumbling to himself. "Why? Why did I agree to this?"

Andalynn tries to calm him with assurances. It doesn't work.

Most of the trollshards fled in fear at the combination of stone and fire ironcraft, compliments of the bracelet I gave to Rugnus. My shield didn't hurt either, though there are a few trollshards still rattling around the room, hoping to latch on to one of us.

"Does that one have an eyeball?" I squint at one of the tiny things when it dares to approach us.

Rugnus digs into the stone at our feet like its ice cream, turns it into a wad of molten goo, and hurls it at the approaching shard. "Lithic trolls were notoriously difficult to defeat. Fight them and they'd just break into smaller and smaller pieces, disgusting things, doomed to roam the darkest places under the mountains. Never actually fought one before. Or maybe that was two. The coloration was different for different pieces. Anyway, might've even raised my AMP score. So"—he shakes the bracelet—"thanks for this."

Quilgist vanishes under a brown light, and Andalynn returns to my side.

"So, what's next?" Rugnus asks Andalynn. He's trying hard to avoid talking about his meltdown outside of the council room. I have half a mind to let him so we can move on, but Andalynn— usually full of mercy in these situations—seems to be struggling with it.

She marches over to Chainkeeper where he stands at the lip of the vine-enshrouded shaft—the last part of our journey, at least according to my dream.

"It's wide enough for two. Rugnus and Clayson can go down first, back-to-back. Then Jeiah and I. Can you follow us, Keeper?"

"You may be seen as adults by the world," Chainkeeper says, "but I am the more experienced. I will go down first." A soft purple firelight flickers off his body as he moves to the edge. "I'll be waiting for you." He jumps. As his head passes the edge of the hole, his body slows down like he's going at elevator speed. He's affecting time.

Andalynn hooks my arm at the elbow, dragging me toward the shaft. Halfway there, she nudges Rugnus to follow us. At the edge, she says, "You, this side. You, this side. Back-to-back, all the way down. Jeiah and I will give you a bit of space, then follow." Andalynn grabs her tin bracelet, and the vines are renewed, becoming glossy and green-yellow.

Rugnus and I make awkward eye contact. We both know she's trying to force a heart-to-heart. But we know better than to fight against her; besides, Rugnus looks reasonable again.

"Yes, my queen," Rugnus says, lowering himself using the vines on one side of the shaft. I get in position on the other side of the shaft and we begin downward. The vines are useful as handholds, but the space is tight. We use each other's backs as support.

When Rugnus finally speaks, it's almost deafeningly loud in the small space. "Clayson, I—"

"It's fine."

"Don't do that. Don't be dismissive. I'm trying to apologize."

"Well, I owe you an apology too."

"Not just that. It's Icho. I think you were right. It's like Ergal."

"What did your mother say?"

Rugnus is silent for a full heartbeat. "Your dad. He didn't just stumble upon me in Shadowsmith Dungeon. My mother knew him. I'd been gone for a week. She was worried and turned to the person she knew could find me. Before he gave up craft, he was a pretty formidable raider."

It's brain-bending information. The way Rugnus tells it, Dad stumbled upon him. It was luck. All my frustration with Rugnus dissolves, leaving behind another of my dad's well-kept secrets. I ask the obvious question. "She knew him?"

"And Silverkeeper. They were all friends when they were our age, secretly, during the war. Never told you, but my mother is part of the royal family of Zal Kakraja. It's one of the reasons we fled to the Kingdom of Rimduum, to Tungsten City, after my father's death. I was just a baby."

"I actually read that about your family."

"Fair. It's common knowledge. My mother has a good reputation. It's why she's so good at event planning—she knows everyone. But her friendship with your dad was a secret."

"Why?"

"Her image," Rugnus says with disgust. "The highest socialite

in Tungsten City—a figurehead for the principles of democracy—
friends with the future king of Rimduum? She would have been
shunned. Him too."

I can't help but think of Andalynn and Rugnus' relationship.
So mismatched, but they work well together, balance each other
out. "They kept it all secret?"

"Silverkeeper was interested in two objects my family had
kept for generations."

"Icho?"

"Icho. And—get ready for this—Onrix. My mother gave Silverkeeper the knife for his research into protodungeons. Silverkeeper
swore there would be three objects."

"I—did you tell her about what happened to him, to Sira, in
Wolfstaff?"

"I couldn't. She would just blame herself for Silverkeeper's
accident. It was only at Silverkeeper's funeral she learned the
truth about Sira. About the knife."

I can hear shuffling above us in the shaft. Jeiah and Andalynn
are catching up, so we continue downward. The light from Chainkeeper's purple flames dies out somewhere beneath us. He's
made it to the bottom.

"Rugnus?"

"Yeah."

"I think Sira is terrified of Vor. I saw it on her face, but—"

"I know. It doesn't make her betrayal any easier. She used us
to get to you. And she tried to use you to get the mithrium.
Maybe she did it because of Vor... maybe not, but we can't trust
her."

"Do you think there's a chance we can get Brig and Sira away
from Vor?"

"Without Icho? No. But Vor wants you. He's been leading you
here. That much is clear. Maybe he'll negotiate with you. Or..."

His voice trails off for the same reason despair crystalizes over
my heart—the butchering of the council. "I don't think Vor is a
reasonable individual."

Chainkeeper's whisper stretches up to us. "Down here. There's a light ahead."

We come to the end of the shaft, swinging down, holding the vines, and dropping to a floor of sand. Dried mud cakes the walls. Not far ahead, in an adjoining room, a light flickers, waiting for us, changing color and brightness sporadically, as innocent as if I've only left the tv on in the den.

Jeiah and Andalynn drop down from the shaft. No one says another word. We all know what may be waiting for us ahead. The absolute carnage of the council room will not leave my mind. And StoneYoke, the piles of debris, the waves of powdered glass, the stacks of body bags waiting to be transferred to Edium Fiarie.

The full weight of what Vor did settles somewhere between my heart and my spine. It's a sick, grimy feeling, raising bile in my throat, turning my stomach. I want it out of me. I don't wanna think about what he did.

Everyone keeps calling StoneYoke an attack, like in one of the dead cities attacked with mithriumcraft. But the purposeful killing of so many innocent people has only one label. As a news junkie, I've read and seen the label many times, though I've never felt it caked on my skin.

Genocide.

A person who could drop a city into a festival of people can't be reasoned with.

As we approach the door, the changing lights fall on Jeiah's face.

This was a mistake.

I stop. My feet won't move forward under their own power.

Rugnus notices. "Whatever's there... it's not..."

"Brig may be in there," Jeiah whispers.

I scan the faces of my friends and my sister. We can turn around, climb out of here, find another way. My recklessness has finally caught up with me, and this isn't just a wrong turn halfway up a cliff. This is a missed grab, free-soloing a mountain. A thousand-foot drop.

Hopelessness.

I hadn't recognized the feeling, hadn't named it until now.

"There's no going back." Chainkeeper pushes us roughly to the side and marches straight into the room.

Rugnus lets out a breath. He rubs the skin under his bracelet. "Come on, Clayson. Whatever is on the other side, if Brig is in trouble, if Vor is after the mithrium... we must try."

I expect to find Vor there waiting. I expect anything but this. An unassuming, narrow room. A table at the center, surrounded by wooden benches. A door at the far end opens into the glimmering darkness of the mine. Embedded in the wall is a single screen covered in plastic. It displays a color-changing message: INCOMING.

"What is this?" Rugnus asks.

Chainkeeper passes a steady hand over the table. "It must be where the twelve peerless would counsel together about the construction of the Cradle. I never thought it would be found. Think of what this could mean."

The three other expressions in the room match Chainkeeper's.

"Could the Cradle be used somehow?" I ask.

Andalynn nods. "There are still a few places under the mountain that could be converted into livable citybarrels."

"So, new cities?"

"In theory," Jeiah says.

"Why didn't anyone come looking for this place? Why didn't Brightkeeper, or the many people before him, guide someone down here to find it?"

"No peerless were willing," Rugnus says. "The original twelve peerless lost their lives to turn off the Cradle in the first place. It would take the same type of sacrifice to turn it back on. No takers. It's been forgotten."

"Was Erikzin one of the peerless?"

"How do you not know this?" Chainkeeper says. "Erikzin Wellstone was the inventor of the Cradle, not one of the peerless.

The moment it came online, his new name was heard by all: Brightstorm."

The whole room shakes. Metal grinds against stone. The opening on the far side of the room is filled with a sheet of woven metal, scraping, sparking against the stone, but only for a second. The metal passes, and a doorway spins into view. Beyond, only a metallic glare. The word on the screen in the wall changes to: ARRIVED.

We all stare, our feet glued to the floor. No one wants to find out what's in there.

An echoing voice reaches out for us. It's Vor. "Clayson? Did you make it okay? I'm so curious to see who came with you. Come on. Come out here."

An edge in his voice scrapes against my spine. Andalynn and I share a worried glance.

Vor's volume increases. "Don't leave me wondering. Get out here." Behind his voice. An edge of silvercraft. The shieldcraft in my bracelet balloons outward almost involuntarily.

"Now!" Vor shouts.

Despite my reluctance, I step forward under the familiar power of Onrix. I'm confused at first. A shudder rips up my body. Just like Ara, Vor can use any craftprint, multiply any power. The craftprint used to reign terror down on StoneYoke had been something Lagnar had used many years ago. Vor can multiply even an echo of craft. Any hope of stopping Vor dies as my legs work without my permission, hasting me forward.

Rugnus moves involuntarily at my side. We all pass through the door.

It seals behind us.

My perspective is frozen on the ground. Vor doesn't want to be seen. Or maybe after all the years of not looking directly at anyone, it's some twisted revenge.

A thin layer of mercury clings to our feet, reminding me of the test that called me into Wolfstaff Dungeon for my summation. Rugnus had used a summator, a large metal basket filled with mercury. The summator mimics the summation basins under Gamgim forest. It seems like so long ago I first met him in that strange place.

We're standing in one giant summator. The Cradle.

Sira's voice is a groan over the air, uncharacteristically distraught. "Clayson, sweetie, no. No, why did you come here? I tried to warn you."

"None of that, Sira," Vor says. "The Brightstorms are family. I've been with them since Erikzin."

I don't see him. I try to speak, but nothing comes out. Vor has complete control over us.

His next words are so close by that my heart jumps. "I thought the other two keepers would have joined you. Hmm. No matter. Let's start with Chainkeeper."

Chains rattle behind me. I hear Chainkeeper straining against something.

"No, no, no," Vor says. I take note of how little his tone has changed. Can he really be like Ara? "No cheating. I want to see what you look like when your power fails you."

A bolt of shadows whizzes so close to my face I feel its darkness. That's when my head and upper body are freed. I crane my head around, finding Sira first, her red-rimmed eyes blinking, facing downward. But my attention is immediately drawn to Vor and Chainkeeper. That's when I lose control of my neck again. Vor's toying with me. I can only stare at the dark glimmer of the cavern above the bowl of the summator that rises on all sides. Out of my control, my head bows.

Purple flames erupt at my back. Chainkeeper's screams are swallowed up in the massive bowl. Vor adds his own scream. I need to see what's happening, but I can't turn my head. The only sound after that is a dull thud. I try not to think about what it is, but I don't have to guess as blood pools in the mercury at my feet. He did to Chainkeeper what he did to the rest of the council. That long jagged sword he carries cuts into my thoughts.

Ide keep me. Why did I bring everyone here?

Vor strides into view. His loose-fitting suit jacket is spotted with blood. "Almost done. Almost done. Chainkeeper's usefulness is finished now that I've got my Sira out of Keelcrawl. I— Clayson, you look upset. If anyone gets to be upset, it's me. You get that, don't you? We have a second. Tell me how you feel."

He gives me control of my mouth. I work my jaw open. "Wh-what's wrong with you?"

"Me? Me? I... that's a strange first question. No, 'Vor, how are you doing this?' No, 'why are you doing all this?' Really, Sira, you said he was smart. Hmm. What's wrong with me? No, no. Try again. Better questions, young Brightstorm."

"You can't do this. We'll stop you."

"Stop me? Oh, so prideful. Clayson Brightstorm, do you know how long I've known your family? How long they've trusted me with all their secrets? You have done everything *but* stop me. You're the perfect wrecking ball. No one else has ever been able to serve me like you can. You know how long I've waited... now we can make something new. I can find everything that's been hidden from me. And you'll help me do it."

"You destroyed the festival."

"Mmhm. Yes. But don't be so shortsighted. I've been forging connections long before that. You've heard of the Mithrium War? That was me. I first saw that shiny metal hundreds of years ago, and I thought, boy, that could be useful. So, a nudge here, a push there. I've had a lot of people willing to listen to my council over the years. But you Loamin are incredibly easy to kill. Like insects really, or leeches."

This new information soaks into my blood like poison. He's been like Ara for hundreds of years, slowly chipping away at the world. "For what? Why would you want that? Is it because of the other Dura? Are they like you?"

He scoffs. "Those idiots? No, they can't look up to save their lives. They're too busy serving everyone. I mean, sure, I was like them once. But something happened to me. I could suddenly think for myself. I've tried to help them, believe me, but they don't want my help. For all I care, they can serve me alongside all the other Loamin. Look at me, Clayson."

Suddenly my face is free again, but in the only form I can, I resist him. I don't look.

"Look at me!" he screams, forcing my eyes on him.

He breathes a great sigh. "Even with all this power, I still can't look you in the eye. Isn't that something strange? Why? Aren't you curious?"

Ara shares this trait with him, and for the first time, I think I understand. It's not just a trait. No Dura can look a Loamin in the eye. I can't step around this fact, and neither can Vor.

I smile at him; a short laugh escapes my throat.

His feet stop pacing. "You think that's cute. And Sira told me you were different; told me you were kind. Is it funny that I can't look at you? Huh?"

"No."

"No?"

"No. Vor, we can stop this. We can figure things out. We can—"

"Stop. You're not getting it. Just stop. I have what I want. I'm going to keep pulling the threads of this world until it finally unravels. I want to see what's next. I'm curious, honestly."

"So, you'll destroy everything?"

"Destroy. Create. Two sides of the same ferrum. And you're one to talk, Clayson. How's Wolfstaff's dungeon? See? That one, that was a surprise even to me. But boy was it shocking to watch. I mean, I could only dream of destroying a dungeon. Together, we're going to tear them out of the mountain, heart by heart. Anyway, let's get to your grandfather's dungeon, shall we? I'm wondering if we can get that mithrium out of there."

He moves my feet forward, and the lack of control turns my stomach. I find the same small forge I saw in Yinzar's memories. But next to it, a steel door rises from the mercury in the floor. It must be the threshold of Mithriumbane Dungeon. Sira stands next to it, her head hanging down.

The steel door is marred by a dozen jagged marks like someone tried to cut their way into the dungeon with a large army knife. There's no handle, and it's bolted to the floor. Abruptly, my hands and arms are free of Vor's silver grip.

"There. Gave you a little more rope. Don't play games, or I will kill..." He trails a long finger over my friends and stops on Rugnus. "...him."

Hope may have died at the door to the Cradle, but something else has filled the vacancy—rage. I don't know how, but I'm gonna stop him. I make a vow to myself, wishing that I had something silver of my own to swear it on.

Blood pounding in my ears, I move to the door, tracing fingers along one of the cuts, searching for any hint of what to do. The door itself is as cold as ice. At the bottom, an iron rod about eight inches long is welded to the steel. Is it a handle? If I can open the door, maybe I can somehow get us in. Vor can't follow us into the dungeon.

"I've tried everything," Vor says. "Only a summation will open the dungeon. When it's over, you will go back in and find the mithrium left by Yinzar and bring it to me."

"But he destroyed it," I say.

"Did he?" Vor's eyes are hollow, blank. It's an absence of something—of conscience or compassion. Something has devoured those parts of him, leaving behind an empty shell of resentment.

A familiar voice rises from the other side of the bowl. "Get your hands off of me, you bearded latchmage."

"Now just cool it, kid," Emberfence says. He strides right toward us. He's not under Vor's control. Rugnus was right—he's been helping the Dura.

Emberfence's eyes flick toward me but settle elsewhere.

"How does it feel to betray the world twice?" I ask.

"Y'know, just can it, son. I don't answer to you."

"At first, I thought you only wanted Bluekeeper's spot on the council. But Vor isn't even controlling you. So, what is it?"

Lagnar looks away.

"He knows what the world deserves," Vor says. "He's been willing to help me since I revealed your father's secrets to him—about me and Ara, about craftprints."

Tightening his grip on Brig, Lagnar marches closer to us.

"I swear on silver I—" Brig struggles against Emberfence until he sees Jeiah, who's beside herself in shock and fear. Frozen. "Jeiah? What's going on? Where am I?"

When Emberfence lets Brig go, he rushes toward the door. He scans the floor, the layer of mercury resting inside the woven basket. "This is... we're inside the Cradle. The birthplace of the Brightstorms." He looks back up to the door. "But this shouldn't be... is this..."

"It's the threshold to Mithriumbane," I say.

Brig takes a wide look around the room, pausing at each person. When he sees Chainkeeper's mangled body, he turns away, swallowing hard. "Ho, we're in a lot of trollbrick aren't we?"

"Open the door," Vor says.

Brig gulps. "You guys told him about my summation?"

"No," I say. "He knew."

Vor flies toward us, grabbing Brig by the back of the hair, dragging him to the door. "I. Know. Everything! Now, open the dungeon."

Brig sneaks a look at Jeiah and focuses on the door. "It's cold." He touches the back of his hand to it. "And these scars will have to be healed. I'll need somewhere to put these." He takes out a narrow piece of obsidian and an oblong chunk of granite—the stones from his summation—and sets them on the ground.

Tendrils of the woven floor reach out for the stones, drawing them in like a snake swallowing a couple mice. The two bumps move underneath the floor, passing the threshold.

Brig smiles, satisfied. "There we are. Now, these cuts. Ho, Clayson, did you try healing them?"

"I... no. Would that work? I can't *heal* metal."

"Ah, but the Cradle is a strange place where flesh and metal are not all that different. Where each of the mediums becomes more like one craft. I... what? I read it somewhere. Just try reaching out with your tungsten bracelet. See what happens."

"Just the door, Clayson," Vor says. "You can't protect anyone here."

The moment I even think about it, my wrist glows white. Bright smoke pours from the bracelet, chasing over the floor and up to each of the cuts, stitching the metal back together. After only a few seconds, the smoke is absorbed into the door, and the gashes are gone.

"See?" Brig says. "Now, one last thing. The door is as cold as ice. Any forger worth three spits knows how to separate two pieces of metal. One must be cold and one must be hot." He points to the eight-inch iron rod at the bottom of the door. "We heat this and then just pull."

"I need Rugnus," I say.

Vor begrudgingly frees him.

The emotion on Rugnus' face catches up, changing from shock, to anger, to resignation. He knows Vor can kill any of us. Vor has an endless supply of craft stored in the battery. Plus he's Dura, which means he can multiple its effect.

"What do I need to heat up?" Rugnus asks.

Brig shakes his head. "I just need that lapel pin, thank you. Not your summation, is it?" When Rugnus scowls, Brig scolds himself with a murmur, then says. "Though this is a terrible way for things to happen, it's just terrible." He holds out his hand, waiting for the pin. Rugnus relents with an eye roll.

Brig superheats the small iron rod and pulls it free. There's a click and the grinding of gears at the side of the door. Two small holes appear in the bolted frame. Slipping one end of the super-heated metal into the lower hole, Brig bends the rod into a half loop, attaching the second end into the upper hole. He stands back as the rod shapes itself into an ornate cast iron door handle. He feels the door with the back of his hand.

"Room temp. Okay, so who's the surveyor. Rugnus right?" He hands him the pin back.

I turn to Rugnus. "Can you walk him through his summation?"

Rugnus begins to nod, but Vor says, "Unnecessary. Clayson will go."

"I'm not a surveyor."

"Really, Clayson, it's not that hard. Just do what I say." A hint of shadowcraft dances over his fingers.

"Fine. But after the summation. I'll need help in the dungeon to find the mithrium. That's how it worked last time. My friends will come with me."

"No," Vor says with finality.

Sira tries to speak, but it comes out as a dry hiss.

Vor frowns at her. "What is it?" For the first time, consideration tightens Vor's face. He's weighing something, calculating.

Sira tries again. "If you want to find the mithrium, it's your best chance. Clayson is a tool in this, but a tool must be sharp. It must work properly. Without his friends, I'm afraid he's a bit dull."

Vor nods slowly. "Fine. Sira has yet to be wrong about you. Summation first, then a few of your friends can help you get the mithrium. Doesn't matter to me."

Brig clears his throat and holds up a finger. "Ho, that would be an honor, Clayson, but do you know what you're doing? I mean, this is my only summation we're talking about."

Rugnus shakes his head. "He'll be fine. Honestly, there's not much to it. The summator will do most of the work." He shrugs. "And in this case, this whole place is a summator. Mithriumbane will make its assumptions through your thoughts, Clayson, so stay focused on the types of craft Brig's using. Afterward, my guess is that the kid's AMP will appear somewhere in the mercury."

Brig rolls his shoulders back and faces the door. "For a very frightening situation, this is pretty exciting. Come on, Clayson. Let's see what Mithriumbane left behind for us."

He pulls the handle, and the door swings open. I follow him into a long hallway where the walls are made from a thousand bones, from something so large, I don't wanna think about it. It reminds me of something my mom said in the memory of her and Yinzar. He'd been searching the deep places. Our shoes kick up an impossible amount of dirt.

Behind us, the steel door swings shut.

At the end of the hallway, we find what can only be described as an industrial warehouse, shelves cluttered with hundreds of unimaginable objects. The shelves themselves are twice our height, ladders can be seen leaning against a few places.

"Where are we?' I ask.

"Ho, the largest store of forging materials anywhere."

We pass row after row of strange materials and enter a low-ceilinged room. In the center, there's an anvil, molds, and a stream of bubbling lava. The other side of the room completes another half circle of shelves with the same odd instruments and ingredients.

"It's the most beautiful forge I've ever seen," Brig says in wonder. "I think I'm supposed to make something out of each metal. That's my test." He scrapes his hands over his face in pure disbelief and joy. "I'll never leave this place again."

RAISE A DUNGEON

BRIG'S SEVENTH RECIPE—A decorative ornament made of copper wire and red glass—releases the souls of ten fire beetles. Their copper shadows crawl over the forge, spilling ingredients and eating our coal.

"Smash them!" Brig yells, grabbing a large skillet he used in the fourth recipe. He swings for one of them, but the thing flattens out before Brig can whack it. Brig tilts the skillet back slowly, only to have the copper shadow launch for him, biting down on the fleshy part of his palm.

I react, dousing the little monster with a bucket of water. It sizzles and fades into a single copper ferrum.

Brig shakes his hand out. "Ho, brick! That hurts. Get the rest of them."

As I start baling water from the basin near the forge, I watch in horror as Brig's hand swells like a balloon. He looks at it and shrugs. "At least it doesn't hurt anymore." He runs the other one through his pink hair.

Once the last fire beetle's soul is quenched, Brig starts cleaning up. "Reorganizing."

His hand is a balloon, and he's worried about an untidy workspace. Who is this kid? I shake my head and help him.

The swelling abates, and his hand becomes the size of a cantaloupe instead of a watermelon. I follow him back to the shelves in his search for ingredients for his next recipe. After a moment, a light bulb must go off in his mind, something like the ah-ha of silvercraft.

As he gathers another armful of ingredients and heads back toward the forge, I struggle to follow both his quick pace and his rapid explanation of what he will be making this time.

I've been slowly learning how to forge objects over the last two months, but he knows an impossible amount about every ingredient. And he's following ancient recipes he's apparently cataloged in that filing cabinet of a brain.

"You remember about means and ends, right?" he says, risking moving his gaze to me instead of the precarious number of bottles and boxes in his arms. I keep thinking his hand is gonna pop like a blister.

This is basic forging. Means are ingredients you put in the fire. Ends are ingredients you put in the metal. "I—"

"Of course, you do. You forged the greatest object in the history of, well, everything."

We reach the forge again, and he's still explaining everything as he sets down his findings. "...river stones as means for this, but these have been buried in wool and sawdust for more than a decade—though I don't know how time functions here because some ingredients are much, much older than Mithriumbane's dungeon would technically be. It's the greatest, though. Right? Ho! And this is powdered crab shell from the coast of E'thrishia Lake—that's on the surface above the Kingdom of Dashen. That's where Winta's family is from, right? What's Geum Ide like, I wonder? How do all those people..."

Brig doesn't expect answers, and I'm content listening to him ramble on as he finishes another recipe and then another. I watch which metals he uses and which ones have the strongest reaction to him. All I can say is that he's good with every type. As of yet, everything he's forged has worked, though he didn't expect the beetles to crawl out of that glass ornament.

"How are you going to get us out of this one? Vor he's crazy and"—Brig rubs his fingers together—"what he did to Chain-keeper? Shadowcraft and then... yeah, that jagged sword of his. Then there's the mithrium? The dungeons? Do you think he will let any of us live?"

"I'll keep you and your sister safe."

"Keep us safe?" He laughs, his eyes squeezing shut. "More like Jeiah's keeping you safe. You know, from all the stupid stuff you do. I... oh sorry, I mean no offense. I do risky stuff all the time and—" He grins at me. "So... my sister, huh?" He's going to ask me about my feelings for her, so I distract him with a question about the gems he's using as means in the coding. It works, but his words don't take my mind off Vor.

He's still out there with my friends, waiting for us to exit. Did Sira really convince him I would work better with their help? I have the unnerving feeling that Vor has no intention of keeping any of us alive after we've outlived our usefulness. A wrecking ball. That's what he called me.

Brig is scratching his head, trying to plan out the next— perhaps final—recipe he will put together when a familiar flitting shape appears glowing in the ingredient library a few rows back. A neon butterfly. Curious, I come around the forge and watch as it flutters between the open space between columns of shelves.

It's Yinzar's doing. It's got to be.

Brig sets his tools down and steps behind me. "What is it?"

"There." I point to the neon blur as it ducks behind a row.

"Ho, shiny."

We follow the butterfly as it meanders over bottles, hunks of rocks, ornate boxes, and dozens of other ingredients. For about half a minute, it settles on the skull of what must be a crocodile, balanced near the thing's eye sockets. Is it Yinzar, trying to communicate? The insect lifts off from the skull, whizzes past my head, and banks to the left.

I follow it, and Brig follows me. When we turn down the row after the butterfly, Brig skids to a halt. "Ho, man. Jackpot."

Light glimmers from a thousand polished surfaces. Leafs. The books of the Loamin world. I reach out and graze the surface of a few of them like dragging my fingertips across the spines and titles of physical books. They're forging guides. If I were to leave my hand in place on one of them, I would start to absorb temporary knowledge about the recipes. If I were to take one and wear it against my skin for a month it would be like studying the same book for the same amount of time. Not instant knowledge, but the potential of knowledge.

"How many leafs do you think there are?" Brig says. "With these recipes... I mean, I've been doing great, don't get me wrong, but if I can find one that's more complicated, I... ho, what's the butterfly doing?"

The insect's wings beat as it hangs from a shelf in the middle of the row. Rainbow light begins to drop from its worm-like body, and the wings themselves dematerialize. Just below it, a light begins to gather into a square, flat shape. When the whole insect is gone, all that remains is a single glistening square of light reflecting tiny rainbows around the room like a prism.

It's a leaf.

I reach out for it, but Brig nudges past me and pulls it off the shelf. After only a second, he squints and holds it out to me. "It's locked. Maybe...you have to open it."

"Locked?" I can't help but think of the leaf Silverkeeper left my dad. I take it from Brig, and the title is clear in my mind. "A Guide to the Keeper's Key."

This is the recipe to forge a keeper's key for this dungeon. Somehow, I understand how to unlock it for Brig. I trace a circle over the flat surface and tap Brig's forehead right between the eyes with my middle finger. He takes the recipe, tilts his head to the side to think, and looks up at me.

"Am I supposed to make this? It's a really challenging recipe. I've done everything else leafless. Ho, do you think the dungeon wants me to be keeper? No, that doesn't make sense. Oh, wait. Of course. It must be for you. What do you guess they'd call you? Mithriumbanekeeper? No, maybe just Banekeeper? Yeah, that sounds flawless!"

"I hadn't even thought of that part. So, wait, do I need to make this key then?"

"Never. The keeper usually has an expert make it. And I know you're good, but—"

"You do it. It wouldn't be present during your summation if I was supposed to make it."

A huge smile erupts on his face. "You know, if I make this key for you—if I remember right—it might prompt you to start designing the tombscapes. The entrance and exit lobbies. Wait, that's it! What if you could change the area surrounding the threshold? We could—"

"Change it? How?"

"As a keeper you oversee the tombscapes, around the dungeon, you know, like the waiting area with the waterfall in Wolfstaff or the rainbow glass corridor in Chainbearer. You'll get to choose symbols, structures, challenges for the outside of the dungeon—like designing a vault. Set the whole tone for—but that's not important right now. What I'm trying to say is—"

"If I can change the area around the threshold, it could affect Vor."

Brig's wide smile is entirely mischievous. "The perks of keep-ership. Designing tombscapes, hiring paladins, mapping out the place—as best as you can—documenting wraiths."

How could I forget? Somewhere in this dungeon, there's a wraith. The person who had been approaching the moment Yinzar tried to forge the mithrium. The voice I heard. The one that sounded so much like my mom. If I'm the keeper of this dungeon, it should be easier to communicate with the wraith and gain their help... maybe even figure out who they are. The key can help me find them.

I drag Brig back to the forge and press the leaf into his hand.

"Okay, we're making this thing."

"It's levels above what I've been doing so far, but I've got this."

He sets out among the shelves, leaf in hand, returning with a bucket filled with large balls of aluminum foil, holding the bucket away from himself at arm's length like it might explode.

Brig clarifies. "Foil-wrapped black liana, gloomvines, nasty creatures."

Each time he returns, he explains the growing list of ingredients, adding extra details like whether they're used as means or as ends.

A velvet bag filled with diamonds and emeralds. Means. In the human world, they would be worth millions. I'm not sure about their value in a Loamin market. Two jars, one filled with white powdered lime, the other with dark powdered zinc. Ends. A bottle of what looks like black wine, made from the grapes of gloomvines. And last, cubes of new craftable metal, aluminum, iron, cobalt, and a bronze one made from nickel and copper.

Brig is meticulous, measuring everything to exactness. Filling the foundry with the gloomvine parts, lowering it to three and a half inches above the flow of lava and the balls of foil start to leak steam. He examines each diamond and emerald before putting an exact count in with the glowing gloomvine coals. He fills the crucible with the craftable metals and sets it into the glowing foundry.

"Just let that get nice and melted. Now to mix the lime and zinc."

He weighs small amounts of both the white and black powders on a hand scale and places a pair of yellow-tinted sunglasses on his face. With a soft laugh, he sprinkles the two powders onto the surface of a tin plate, forming an intricate flower pattern.

When he finishes, he wipes sweat from his forehead. "Ho, that's the hardest part, but I think I got it right." He watches it through the glasses for a moment. "And six, five, four, three, two... oh yeah. That's cool."

A single chrysanthemum with white and burgundy petals shoots up from the center of the tin plate. Brig plucks it and drops it in the crucible with the metal. A flare of brown-red light loops into the air, fizzling into tiny particles of glowing dust.

Brig smiles, brushing something invisible from his shoulder. I feel suddenly protective of him. If our plan doesn't work, what will Vor do to him?

He sprinkles both sides of the silicone mold with more lime powder and clasps it together, standing it upright. A long pair of tongs hangs from a leather strap next to him. He retrieves them and pulls the crucible out of the fire. With a cautious hand, he pours the molten metal into the mold.

"Missing something." He grabs the leaf again. "Hmm. Oh, that's it." He finds the black wine, unstops it, and pours the bubbling liquid over the same hole he poured the metal. It sizzles and pops and fills the room with the smell of summer grapes. "That should do it."

Brig dances in place, but his understanding of forging outweighs his impatience. We wait a few more minutes as the metal cools. When he finally unclasps the mold, we both stare down at the skeleton key resting in the silicone. He knocks it into a barrel of water to cool but only waits a few seconds before he takes it out. A strip of dull light bleeds into the room from behind us, and a hot wind swirls in around my legs.

"The exit is open," Brig says, stunned. "I did it. I completed my summation. We'll have to go back out to the threshold to get my AMP. Oh, here. I think you'll want this."

He hands me the keeper's key, and Yinzar's voice enters my mind, but it's a tinny recording. *Keeper's access granted.*

A half dozen bluecraft icons pop up around my head. Titles float under each icon: WRAITH MAP, RELIC MAP, SECURITY, VISITOR HISTORY, TASKS, RECORDS.

The TASKS icon is flashing, so I open it first.

Do you want to begin lobby construction choices now?

I minimize the TASKS icon and open the WRAITH MAP. The glowing blueprint of the dungeon in its current state doesn't show any data for wraiths. That's not right. There must be one. I try zooming out, but the dungeon is only the forge and the surrounding shelves. There's no wraith in sight. Maybe they're only on the map when they get close to someone? Rugnus would know.

"So?" Brig says. "Can you change the lobbies? What does it say?"

"Hold on." I open the TASKS menu again. A large holographic stone casket with a jackhammer at its side floats at eye level. "Can you see these?"

He shakes his head. "Probably best if you keep it private for now."

"Right. Um, and"—I tap the icon— "looks like I can do it."

The air fills with model walls and model rooms made from every stone imaginable. The first one I notice is a replica of the room we're standing in, but the shelves are empty. There's an option of requiring a sacrifice in order to enter and setting the default first room for summations with a tag that says NOT RECOMMENDED. I swipe back, revealing a host of garden objects and themes. I can also allow animals or disallow them. The options are endless.

I choose a garden for the entrance lobby and a forge for the exit lobby. I increase the number of rows to fifty and uncheck the box that requires people to leave an ingredient as a sacrifice before crossing the threshold. My hand hovers over the hologram of a switch.

"Should I do it now?"

Brig cast a long look through the shelves toward the threshold. "Depends on the plan."

"Well, we can't all budge away. I'd say our best option is to confuse Vor and slip back into the dungeon where he can't follow us. Then regroup."

"That could work. You'd want to time it perfectly. Ho, and you don't want to tip him off that you have the keeper's key."

"What if..." I move back in the menu a bit and find an icon of an hourglass. "I set it to go live in, like, three minutes. The moment it goes off—"

"—everything will transform, and we try to get back into the dungeon. In theory, that could work. Though..." Brig trails off, frowning.

"What is it?"

"I think the changes are permanent. You only get to set up the lobbies once. That would mean it would be stuck like that. What will the Raider's guild think?"

Resisting the urge to slap my forehead, I say, "That's the least of our problems."

"Right. Just that they take these things really seriously."

"Clayson!" Rugnus' voice is a soft echo this far into the dungeon. "You there?"

The threshold door has been reopened. I give one more thought to the plan and start the timer, stashing the keeper's key away and leading Brig past the long rows of ingredients into the light from the Cradle. Rugnus' figure blocks the doorway, Jeiah standing next to him. They're still alive.

"Clay?" Jeiah calls out.

"We're here," I answer. "Everything's okay."

The moment we exit the dungeon, it's clear that everything is *not* okay.

Rugnus' left eye is puffed and green-black. His limbs are frozen, his hands balled into fists. Andalynn and Jeiah stand close to him, but their bodies are also frozen. Sira looks as though she's been crying. And Lagnar's wearing a face so smug it's more of a caricature, a mask trapped in a single expression. He taps a pair of tongs mindlessly against the small forge at the center of the Cradle. Vor allows him to move. I know he's responsible for the assassination of my dad's parents, I know he hates our family, but I can't wrap my head around why any reasonable person would help Vor.

I don't ask about any of this. We have less than three minutes. I make eye contact with Rugnus, willing him to catch on to my urgency.

"That was entirely too long," Vor says. "Now, choose two of these people and go back in there. Find the mithrium, bring it to me. If not…" he gathers a bit of shadowcraft in his hand.

Rugnus' pinkie finger twitches. "No one can go back in until we find Brig's AMP. That finalizes the process. Should be here in the mercury."

Brig says, "It would usually be waiting in the quest agent, but—"

Rugnus keeps his eyes on Vor. "Whole room is the quest agent. It's gotta be here in the mercury."

This could work. Vor is yards away from us, staring past impatiently. "Vor," I say, "This would go quicker if everyone could look."

"I've been waiting for hundreds of years. You think I can't wait a bit longer?"

I look to Sira for help.

Even without being able to make eye contact, Vor understands this. "She's in enough trouble as it is, Clayson. Losing her knife, stealing this." He waves the blue glass battery at me. "She can't help you, but fine"—everyone's bodies come unglued— "find the boy's AMP."

I glance at the time still in my view—Two minutes and forty-seven seconds.

Vor barely watches as we spread out, searching the mercury at our feet.

The time ticks away as we search, but after twenty seconds, Brig shouts, "Got it!"

Rugnus completes the formality with the same words he used at the completion of my summation. "Stone upon stone. Wisdom upon knowledge. May this guide you to self-illumination and clad you in the understanding of your place under the mountain. Take your record."

I'm drawing my hand from the liquid when my thumb grazes something warm and angular. My hand closes around another AMP. I pull it from the mercury. It's pure crystal, translucent, etched with marks of light that show the scores.

Whose AMP is this? I turn it over. I find only my first name printed there.

A shock goes through me. The scores on the AMP don't match the AMP I received in Wolfstaff. Every single mark is higher—much higher.

Everyone is focused on Brig's scores until Jeiah looks over to me. Her eyes settle on the crystal AMP in my hands. "Clay. What is that? Is that…"

Rugnus bends around Brig to look. His mouth drops open.

Andalynn hands Brig his AMP and steps toward me. "It's a Champion's AMP. Where did you—"

"I found it. It has my name on it. Can that be right?"

Lagnar stops his incessant tapping on the forge and stares at me. "Cards on the table, huh?"

Brig crinkles up his nose. "Is that a human expression?"

"You're a champion," Jeiah says, hushed.

"That can't be right." I look to Rugnus for help, but he's still standing, mouth open, shaking his head. "My AMP score would have to be sixty-three."

Rugnus shakes the confusion from his face. "I don't know. Wouldn't we have all heard his new name? That's how it works, right?"

"Yes," Brig adds, "but usually, the person must learn his name after getting notification through a new AMP score. His score must have gone up. Once they learn their name, that's the point when everyone will hear it. Unless it happens at the moment of their death. In that case…"

Rugnus' face is blank. "Right. Of course."

Brig squints at me. "Experience any changes in craft effects?"

I blink. "Yeah, actually. Since Wolfstaff, I can't feel any budges."

"You're peerless in budgecraft now?" Rugnus' voice is a little strained.

I look back down at the crystal AMP to find my rating in budge craft. A sideways diamond to match the other one in shieldcraft. "I guess."

"Do you know your Champion name?" Jeiah asks.

"I-I... no. I have no idea."

"Ho, this is the coolest thing I've ever seen. Congratulations, Clayson. Best of luck trying to learn your true name. Let alone deciding on a Keeper name." He looks at everyone else. "I think it should be Banekeeper."

Everyone is too dazed to absorb his ramblings.

"It's weird," Rugnus says. "I always thought if I ever came in contact with a real champion, that I would..."

"Run away like a little latchmage," Brig says, eyes wide.

"Pretty much. He could turn us all into wraiths."

"We're not running," Jeiah says.

Rugnus nods slowly, "If he's killed anywhere close to us..."

Andalynn locks eyes with me. "That won't happen."

This is what it felt like to be Wolfstaff. To be a pariah. My mind takes me to her isolation, to her son sitting by her bedside, saying the exact things my sister and my friends are saying. That he would never leave her. But I remember her response as well. I remember her wishes. She wanted Landred to live a normal life. To flee from her before she died. He refused.

A minute left on the clock.

"No, this isn't right. I'm putting everyone in even more danger."

"I always wondered why some people choose to become wraiths," Brig says. "Besides the crazy worshippers, I mean."

Andalynn grabs my hand. "Love."

I feel Jeiah look over at me. Would being trapped as a wraith inside a dungeon be like an eternity of claustrophobia for her? I can't let that happen.

"It's all so irrelevant, isn't it?" Vor says with a shrug. "Even as a champion, you're nothing. So, back across the threshold. Find the mithrium. Bring it back to me. Understand my instructions? Choose two of your friends. I'll keep the rest as… an assurance."

Thirty seconds.

Lagnar takes a step forward. "You waitin' for something, young Brightstorm?" A strange glint in his eyes makes me pause. He's thinking through something. How to kill us, I bet, before Vor does.

"No," I say. After a quick calculation, I choose the two people furthest from the threshold. "I'll take Rugnus and Jeiah." We move toward the door. The two of them slow down, picking up on my slow, deliberate steps.

"Move!" Vor says.

A burst of grass cuts across the threshold. Grass.

Suddenly bushes, alight with yellow fire, erupt behind us. The weave of the floor, the mercury, transforming into a pine bed floor, soaked with water. The whole area is transforming into an entrance lobby. It worked!

"Run for it!" I push Rugnus and Jeiah toward the door. Andalynn is already halfway there.It's gonna work.

Andalynn hooks an arm into Brig's and drags him toward the door. Rugnus flies across the threshold. I see a flash of brilliant silver to my left, but I don't stop.

Jeiah gets through. It's gonna work.

Vor appears between me and the door, one hand on the battery, drawing in energy through a large intake of breath, siphoning it toward him. The other hand has Sira pinched like a vice. I charge, smacking right into both of them. Sira tumbles through the doorway, but Vor falls to the side. I rush on.

"Now!" I call. Andalynn and Brig are at my side. The threshold accepts me. I breathe a sigh of relief. We did it. I try to pull Andalynn with me, but my hand slips. I turn back. Through the doorway, Andalynn and Brig stand frozen a breath from the threshold.

Not thinking, I reach my hand out to grab Brig. My fingers wrap around his wrist, but as I pull, my hand freezes.

"No!"

A satisfied sneer comes to Vor's face. "Might be fast, but... I expected this. You're the keeper. Think I didn't walk through this scenario? So now... I get to kill two of your friends. Really dumb move, Clayson. And you're still trapped in there. Get the mithrium. Now!"

In a flash, an earthen light bleeds into the world in front of Vor. He stutters backward, confused.

Lagnar appears in the light. I barely have time to gasp before he plucks the battery from Vor's hands. With a guttural roar, he smashes it to the ground. Vor crumples to the floor, groping at the pieces. Lagnar touches Andalynn and Brig, and the two vanish. He strides through the threshold, pushing my hand aside. Vor struggles to push himself up.

"There," Lagnar says. "Problem solved. Let's just get those other friends of yours and be on our way. Find something strong enough to kill this son of a brick."

CARVE OUT A NAME

When the door seals shut, a cover of midnight darkness settles over us. I reach out to grab Lagnar by the shirt, but the area next to me is empty.

"Lagnar! Where are you? What did you do to my sister? To Brig?"

"Take it easy there, Brightstorm." His voice is close, but he's moved further out into the darkness. "I budged them out of there the second Vor lost his control. You're welcome, by the way."

My hand is still on the iron door. I hesitate to remove it in the darkness, but the second I do, pinpricks of light appear like grains of salt in the air. Prickly outlines become visible all around us.

"Where are we?" I ask.

Lagnar reaches out for one of the shapes. "How would I— ouch!" He draws his hand back. "Spit, what is this?"

The grains of light float upward. The whole inky sky lights up with a fever of stars. The shapes around me form into cacti. Blue-black shadows cover the dirt at our feet. A cold, panoramic view unfolds around the horizon. I've seen places like this before on TV. It's like a postcard from the Arizona desert. We're inside the dungeon, but since when have dungeons been concerned by little things like time and space? A chill rises in the air around me, not like winter in the mountains, but something dry and deadly.

Lagnar's holding his hand out, grimacing. A bulb from a jumping cactus is attached to his fingers with needlepoint barbs. Something satisfying about that.

"Explain yourself, Lagnar."

"Keep Ide, boy! Just, can't we deal with this first?" He waves his hand.

At my feet, I find a piece of gnarled deadwood from some scrubby plant. "Fine, start talking." I break the wood into two and use the pieces to squeeze the bulb, yanking it out of his hand.

"Spit and bones!" He reaches for what's left of the needles but jabs his other fingers.

"Stop it! Hold still while I get those little ones out. And talk."

Lagnar growls. "Okay. Fine. Look, I get it. You assume the worst of me. How could you not, knowing that fizzblooded father of yours? But this is how it went down. I'm a calculating kinda guy. I wanted my dungeon back from my cousin. We share a mutual hatred for each other. And he wasn't gonna give it up. Everyone knew that."

"So what? You attacked StoneYoke as cover? Killed half a million people!" I pull three more barbs from his fingers at once.

"Youch! No. And take it easy. That was Vor. The way I see it, he must have kept just enough of Sira's craftprint after she went into Keelcrawl. He guessed he could use my battery—draw the craftprints from it. I'd been stockpiling my own craft in it for years. So yeah, it was powerful. Vor used what he had of Sira's craft to force me to imprint the craft battery to him. Couldn't add to the battery himself, but he sure can drain it. How was I to know what he'd do! I knew he took the bottle, but..."

Two more barbs remain, but my hand freezes. "So, you weren't helping him?"

"Of course not. I... you bearded latcher. How could you think—"

"Then why accuse me before the council? Why—"

"The way I figured, I'd keep my reputation and you may well lead me to another piece of the mithrium. If I pushed you."

"Mithrium?" I pull the last two barbs out.

Lagnar presses his fingers into his palm. "You that thick? If we can find the mithrium in this dungeon, we can combine it with another metal, ironcraft maybe, and bam!"

"You wanna make a mithrium bomb!"

"Blow that Dura to kingdom come. About the only thing I think can stop him."

"That won't work. He'll see it coming. And it will take us with it."

"Do you have any bright ideas? Cause I'm all ears."

"I don't know."

"He doesn't know," Lagnar yells to the cactus. "Hear that universe? A Brightstorm shooting from the hip. Surprise, surprise. We follow my plan then. Come on." He starts walking down the path toward the looming outline of a mesa in the distance. "And take that keeper's key out. I know you got it because you set up the lobby. Smart move, by the way—for a Brightstorm. Check for your friend's locations."

The second I grip the key, the icons pop into view.

I open the map. Three yellow triangles appear in the distance, hovering inside the lone mesa ahead. The mesa is marked with the words: THE BANE OF MITHRIUM.

Lagnar stops ahead of me, waiting. "You got it open?"

"I'm supposed to trust you?" I hiss.

"Keep Ide, boy. Just open the thing so I can help you."

Grudgingly, I change the settings so he can view it. I grab the smaller overhead map and toss it between us, zooming in with a gesture.

"There they are," he says. "But they ain't moving."

"So, the dungeon put them there? They were right ahead of us."

"Kinda how these things work."

"Right, so—"

A message flashes above us: WRAITH ENCOUNTER IMMINENT

I scan the sky, expecting to see a cloud of dazzling light pooling above us.

Lagnar's hands fly to his pockets in search of relics. He spins on his heels watching, waiting for the wraith to appear. I search the map for any visual icon, but there's no obvious indicator of the wraith. After another tense minute, Lagnar turns back to me.

"Nope. I do not like that one bit. Where is the thing? I feel like it could just pop out from behind something and drain my bluecraft. If I can see it, I'll know what direction to run."

"Or maybe it will tell us what to do next."

Lagnar's jaw drops. "You'd take advice from a wraith?"

"Faster than I would from you."

He stops in the middle of the trail, grabs my arm, and moves me in front of him. "By all means, you first. To the mountain." Lagnar sweeps an arm out toward the mesa.

We hike along the path. Each step closer, I feel the place seem more and more familiar until I realize where we are or what this place is supposed to be a copy of. There's a mountain in Arizona where legend has it, a group of men once hid Spanish treasure. I saw it on the travel channel and made a whole poster about it for school. I thought it would have made a great place for climbing.

Yinzar wouldn't have known anything about it. But this is unmistakably the same place, or at least built out of my recollection of the same place. It's another reminder that the dungeons worm their way into your subconscious and build things out of your dreams and fears.

I can only hope that Yinzar isn't trying to kill me.

The trail leads to the foot of the mountain. Lagnar seems unimpressed as the sheer cliff rises above us.

"I think we're supposed to climb it. Look for a way inside," I say.

"I ain't climbing that. Got to be another way."

Something moves in the brush near my feet, and I jump backward. A scaly lump of neon orange can be seen through the bristling twigs. The next visible movement is the flick of something slick and pale. A Gila monster emerges, searching the ground with its tongue.

Lagnar takes a step back. "Lizard!"

It hisses at Lagnar as it crawls behind a barrel cactus for a second, then scrambles up a pile of rock, coming face to face with me. I sigh. "So, what do we do?"

Lagnar gives me a look. "What's your score in Coppercraft? Do you have a relic that allows you to communicate with lizards?"

"I don't think I'll need it."

The lizard paces in a circle for a second. It skitters off the pile of rock, heading down a narrow offshoot that could have once run with water.

"See? We follow the lizard."

I keep the Gila monster in view as I wind my way around a dozen types of cacti. I steer clear of the type that jumped onto Lagnar's hand. They overflow onto the narrow path like bunches of evil grapes.

Lagnar trails me. "We better not have to climb this thing."

A tall cactus, with its arms held to the sky, shades the path as we move into an inlet of sorts. The rock rises on both sides. The lizard stops where a brown-painted, wooden post juts from the earth. It circles the post a few times and slowly crawls back into the brush.

A pouch of climbing chalk rests on a hook at the center of the post.

"Trollbrick," Lagnar says.

"Looks fun." But as I scan upward, my stomach sinks. The only path to the top involves a vertical incline with a large overhanging rock. But Rugnus, Sira, and Jeiah are in this mountain.

When I take the pouch and move toward the wall, Lagnar

shakes his head. "Nah, I'll scout around. Look for another way up."

"You think I'm gonna let you wander around down here while I'm climbing this thing? I'll be a sitting duck."

"Of all the—Jimmy Christmas, Clayson. I just saved your neck back there. Could you give me just a teensy bit of trust and respect?"

I shrug because honestly, how would I know if I can truly trust him.

"That's *your* problem," he says, turning away from the wall and stalking off around the mountain.

I wait only another minute, take a deep breath, and start up the cliff.

The first twenty feet are easy until I have to transfer from one wall to another. I swing the left side of my body around, catching a lip of rock with my foot, bringing my legs apart, empty space beneath me. Once I transfer to the other wall, it's easy going, and I get a rhythm, hanging here and there, dusting my hands between holds.

The desert is cold, but I've worked up a sweat. The next ten feet is a vertical incline leading to an overhang. I find a place to wedge my right leg in a gap to steady myself. I take a few cleansing breaths about to begin, but a hissing starts to my right. Below the overhang, hidden in shadow, the lizard's beady eyes glow. It retreats into a large hole. It's as good a place to hide Spanish treasure as anything I've seen so far.

"Okay, follow the lizard."

I do another wall transfer to reach it, but I'm glad I didn't have to try to jump for the overhang. At this point, it's a long fall to the base of the cliff. I shimmy my way into the hole, nervous the lizard will crawl in beside me. Could it be a trap? But the hole opens, and soon I'm standing in a narrow passageway, torches adhered to the rock every few feet.

Misted light plays over the surface of the tunnel walls.

Droplets of water ping and echo through the air. "Hello?" My voice echoes off the walls.

Using the keeper's key, I pull up the map. I'm near the edge of a maze of tunnels. Right or left, the tunnel will lead me circuitously to a larger cavern if I make all the right turns, but I'm not focused on that. Sira's location indicator sits a few tunnels away, a steady yellow light. Rugnus' another few tunnels away. And past the larger cavern, Jeiah's indicator. None of them are moving.

My legs move before my brain makes a choice. Left, then around the next curve, through another tunnel, this one slick with water. The ground remains hard. My feet slap against the stone, through a puddle, over wet sand until I'm standing in front of what should be Sira's location indicator.

In the center of the tunnel, a statue of pure silver looms over head. It's Sira. Her arm is stretched out as if reaching for me. I get close enough to catch a warm, somewhat playful smile on her face. There are even burnished freckles along her cheeks, but her eyes are empty sockets.

I stumble back, but once the shock passes, I crawl closer. It must be her. The location data can't be wrong. I touch the cool surface of her face. "Sira?"

No answer.

I grasp her hand, but she makes no response. A search of the statute reveals nothing. In case she can hear me, I say, "I'm going to go check on the others."

A few tunnels further, I find Rugnus in the same condition. Except he's not made of silver. His hands, feet, and legs are made from dense aluminum, his torso and face are iron. This statue is just as lifelike as Sira's. Again, the eye sockets are empty.

I stand in front of him. "If you can hear me, say something."

Another minute passes as I wait for anything to happen.

"I'll try Jeiah."

I sprint through the next few tunnels. The map overlays reality. The shortest way leads me through the central room.

Again, the message flashes: WRAITH ENCOUNTER IMMI-NENT. I don't slow down. If a wraith comes, I can deal with it. In fact, a wraith may improve my shortage of information. When I pass into the room, the light shifts almost like a brightstorm.

Instead of the orange torchlight, the cavern opens to the sky. The night is so packed full of stars it doesn't look natural. A billion tiny spotlights instead of a steady light source dazzling against the rock floor. It imprints an unsettling feeling on my mind, like being watched over bluelink.

The room has five noticeable features: a huge crucible and furnace; a solitary wooden table cluttered with power tools; a massive prickly pear cactus with limbs shaped like tennis rackets; walls formed half with massive bones, like I'm inside a monster's rib cage; and a frozen pond, under which I catch glimpses of swirling neon colors, reminding me of Yinzar's memories, the butterflies from my visions.

The crucible is suspended from two chains over a giant furnace, radiating with vapors of heat.

Sitting on the table of heavy oak are a dozen oversized power tools for breaking metal and stone and a stack of stone blocks. My stomach lurches—the statues. The answer to the puzzle is obvious. Tear apart my friends with power tools and offer them to the dungeon by melting them in the crucible.

I leave the room hurriedly, finding the statue of Jeiah as easily as the last two. Jeiah is made of copper and titanium along her joints, but her body is pure cobalt-forged glass, shimmering blue. Her face is crystal, but I can't look at her without her eyes.

I shake my head. "What am I supposed to do?"

Yinzar was known for his wisdom and kindness. If I'm supposed to destroy these statues, that would be another example of how terrifying the dungeons are. Was Wolfstaff this sadistic during her lifetime?

Rugnus and Koglim make the dungeons out to be as essential as water. Dungeons are a way of life, a means of worshiping Ide itself. I'm supposed to believe in the champions, to find purpose from their lives and from their tombs. To Loamin, the dungeons are a malevolent force meant to hone your craft and life into something meaningful—to me, they are more like forces of nature, like hurricanes, floods, and fires.

Returning to the cavern, my focus returns to the table, to a protective mask and a handheld circular saw, sharp and glistening in the orange light. Cold fingers run their way over my heart, claw down into my stomach, searching for my decision. Without thinking, my hands reach out for the table. I squeeze the edge and push the whole thing over.

I flee the cavern before the sound of clattering tools and stones even settles, running through the tunnels. Ignoring the map, I fly through tunnel after tunnel, but after a minute, I find myself back with Rugnus. I sit with my back to the wall, facing the statute staring at the empty eyes.

My face falls into my hands, and I press them against my flesh, push and feel at my temples and along my cheekbones. I rub my eyes, burying my head into my knees. Hide. I just wanna go back to the surface. I wanna rewind the days and months and return with my dad to the cabin. I preferred life before I knew all his secrets. Though even now, after everything that's happened, I doubt I know them all.

Something inside of me refuses this, pushes back against the hopeless feeling. There has to be a way out of this that doesn't involve tearing down statues of my friends. This world is messed up enough that they could really be in there. "This is complete trollbrick."

"That about sums it up."

Lagnar leans against the opposite wall. How long had he been there?

"You found your way up?"

"Wasn't fun. Involved a bit of shieldcraft—which ain't my strong suit. Eagle picked me up and dropped me at the top of the mountain. And boy do I mean dropped me."

"You see the other statues?"

"Sure have."

"And?"

"And I saw the power tools. Bet you're just cut up about it too. No pun intended. But the way I see it, should be fine and—" He squints at Rugnus.

Following his gaze back to the statue, I see two wide eyes.

"Rugnus?" I say, a grin coming to my face.

The eyes blink. Dark eyes. Eyes I know. It's him.

I whisper a silent thanks to the ceiling. "Ide keep me, Rugnus. I-I need help."

He blinks firmly. Yes. He's saying yes.

Rugnus' eyes dart to Lagnar, then back to me.

"Believe it or not, he's not the worst part of this situation right now."

"Hey," Lagnar says. "That's offensive."

"You, Sira, and Jeiah are statues. There are tools to cut you apart, and I think... I think we're supposed to melt you down— maybe. To get you out."

Lagnar steps to my side. "That's the way I see things."

Rugnus closes his eyes for a moment. When they open, he blinks once.

"One blink is that—"

He blinks once again.

"—yes. So, okay. One blink for yes. Two for no. So, yes? Yes, to what? To melting you down?"

He blinks.

"What if it kills you?"

Another blink, only one.

"You think it will kill you?"

Two blinks.

"You're not sure?"

A single blink.

"But you think it's worth the risk?"

One more fierce blink.

"Well, ain't this fun," Lagnar says.

I ignore him. "Rugnus, if you're awake, maybe the others will be too. I'll check on Jeiah and Sira. Lagnar, stay with him. And don't... do anything."

"Hey, I'm not the notoriously rash prince out there breaking dungeons."

"I... forget it." Shaking my head, I rush back through the tunnels past Sira's statue. Her eyes haven't returned. I cut through the room where power tools and stone blocks clutter the floor. When I come to the tunnel with Jeiah's crystalline form, her blue eyes send a shock through me. She's there.

I can't do this. I can't risk her life.

"Jeiah, blink if you can hear me. One for yes, two for no."

Her lashes fold together.

I shake my head. After a deep breath, I tell her about the other statues and the furnace and tools.

"I can't do this," I tell her. "I can't risk..." my voice catches in my throat. Her eyes hold questions like an endless pool of water. "I'm not sure there's another way."

She blinks, meaning a thousand things—acceptance, compassion, trust.

"Okay. Okay. Give me a minute. We'll work on Rugnus first."

She blinks.

As I go, I don't take my eyes off her until I pass into the next tunnel. In the cavern, I find the face shield and the reciprocal hand saw. I depress the trigger. The saw growls to life. Once I fit the mask to my face, I find Rugnus and Lagnar again.

Lagnar's eyes widen when he sees me. "Well now, here we go. Very sensible."

I ignore him and speak to Rugnus. "Jeiah agrees with you."

After a second, he blinks once.

I bring the saw up. "I'll cut off, like, a finger to start. Maybe it will be enough."

Lagnar chuckles softly, but with a quick look from me, wipes the smile off his face.

Rugnus blinks again.

The saw comes to life in my hand. Rugnus' eyes don't leave mine. When I bring it close to his fingers, he clenches his eyes shut. The saw tears through his aluminum hand like its paper. The piece clatters to the ground, and I pick it up. I look back at Rugnus.

"Did it hurt?"

Two blinks.

"That's a shame," Lagnar says. "Oh, should I go get the other tools? Cut Sira up. That'd actually make my day, I think."

"Just hold on. One at a time."

"Sure thing." I catch the disappointment in his voice.

With another deep breath, I take off Rugnus' whole hand. Still no pain. The iron of his arms proves more difficult to cut through. Sparks pour to the ground, but eventually, I have both of his arms removed. His eyes haven't registered pain or fear, only determination. I place the blade near the statue's throat.

He blinks one final time, and I remove his head. When it drops to the ground, his eyes stare back at me, glimmering mischievously. "You can't think this is cool?"

Blink.

For some reason, laughter erupts from me. Maybe it's hysteria. Rugnus' eyes smile at me. I cut his torso in two, dismantling the rest of the statue until it's in small enough pieces to carry back to the crucible.

Lagnar helps me haul the chunks of metal to the central room.

Once I have Rugnus in a pile near the furnace, I lower the crucible. Rugnus' eyes show he's still alive. When the crucible begins radiating heat, I toss in the first finger I cut from the statue. Rugnus eyes well up with pain.

"Rugnus, are you—"

Two blinks.

"Well, this is just awful," Lagnar says.

"Rugnus, should I stop?"

Two more blinks.

"It's hurting you. I can't—"

His eyes become something like steel, determined.

"Okay. Okay. I'll be fast. Lagnar, help."

We dump everything in the crucible as quickly as possible until only his head remains. I lift it up to meet his eyes. "This will work. If not—it will work."

His eyes are dangerous. He blinks. I swallow hard and throw his head into the pool of gathering metal. In less than half a minute, the molten metal begins to convect. A large bubble swells to the surface and bursts.

"Clayson, can you—" Rugnus' voice escapes in the vapors but fades.

As the liquid boils, more bubbles gurgle out Rugnus' broken voice. "...fine... I think... where am I? What's... can you—"

I follow his voice as it bounces around the room against the large animals' bones and the glowing, frozen pond. After a minute, Lagnar comes to my side, a look of concern on his face.

"Should be working." He glances in the crucible. "I'm no smith, but that looks like it's burning. Don't we need something to draw them out?"

Draw them out. I scan the debris from the table. The stones. "Like the dreampick recipe."

"What?"

I sprint to the table and grab one of the square stones from the ground. I throw it into the crucible and start stirring counterclockwise. Rugnus' voice cries out, rattling against the bones. The stones absorb a pink color, and slowly, the liquid metal somehow evaporates.

Lagnar clears his throat and points next to the prickly pear tree.

Rugnus stands there smiling. "If I ever tell you to get melted again..."

I clasp my arms around him and slap his back hard. "It worked."

Rugnus nods and gestures to Lagnar. "And what's with him?"

"Let me sum up," Lagnar says. "Vor used what was left of

Sira's craftprint on me. Forced me to give up the battery. I played along until we got here! Now we can find the mithrium and use it to turn Vor into trollbrick."

Rugnus scowls. "Just don't get in the way."

"That's funny. You think you can dictate to me. But what do I care? Just get us out of here with the mithrium and we can take down Vor. I smashed the battery, by the way. You're welcome. And I budged the Queen far away from this place."

Rugnus doesn't take his eyes off Lagnar. "Which way are the others?"

"Jeiah's in the next room"—I point left—"and Sira is a ways back."

"Get Sira. I'll grab Jeiah."

Rugnus grabs a chop saw, but I snag his arm as he turns to leave. "Wait, she's mostly glass. Be careful. Maybe—"

Rugnus trades the chop saw for a pry bar. "I won't break the glass. Wouldn't want anything to be out of place." His smile widens, but it dips almost immediately. "Lagnar, you're with me."

Sira's statue was made of pure silver, more malleable than Rugnus' iron and aluminum. I grab a pair of metal cutters and a reciprocating saw just in case as I leave the room. When I reach her statue, her eyes are finally visible. I didn't even ask Rugnus anything about what happened to him before his eyes showed up. Now, seeing Sira's reddened, tear-filled eyes, I wonder if there was a challenge involved to get into the statue. When she sees me, tears spill from her eyes.

"Hold tight. I can get you out of there."

She sees the tools in my hands and starts to blink rapidly.

"It'll be okay. It worked on Rugnus' statue. He's free. Trust me."

She closes her eyes once more, and I almost sense her acceptance.

The same as with Rugnus, I start with a finger. When Sira makes no complaint, I take off a hand and quickly work the statue down to manageable pieces. The metal is thin and not hard to carry. I bring her back to the chamber in three trips, but there's no sign of Rugnus. I hold Sira's face up to look at her.

"Once I melt you down, you should return to normal."

Her eyes remain wide, darting from side to side.

"It might be painful."

The crucible is still hot, so I drop in the silver as fast as possible. It melts quicker than Rugnus' statue. As it begins to pop and bubble, Sira's voice erupts into the room. No. Not her voice. Her cries.

"Hold on, Sira," I throw in another stone and stir the liquid, watching as the metal liquid evaporates and the stone becomes pink. As it does, her crying focuses into a single location. I look behind me and find her sitting facing the wall, her hands wrapped around her knees, head buried. The moment I rest a hand on her back, she springs upward and throws her arms around my neck.

She sobs into my shoulder. "I can't do this anymore. I need... I need my dad. He always... I just need him. Vor's too powerful. Keep me safe. Please, Clayson. Keep me safe."

I let her bury her face in my neck, but I'm otherwise numb. My mind collides with the idea of her innocence. Everyone else believes it had been her doing. She controlled her father, manipulated the council, and tried to get the mithrium from Silverlamp. "Sira." I peel her away from me, look directly into her eyes. "Did Vor make you control your father, go after the mithrium?"

Her face sours. "Why are you asking me that? Of course. Don't you trust me? I kept my father alive. I kept him safe. And... well, I just can't tell anymore. I gave Vor my craft sometimes. And there were times he used it to make me hurt people or trick them, but I thought I was doing good. I-I can't sort it all out. Clayson, you have to believe me."

My heart tightens. Sira may have had some choice in what happened, but she was young, impressionable. Her life is wrapped up in his lies. Vor used a child to do his dirty work. The thought drops like a stone colliding with the nerves of my spine. Anger heats my blood. We must stop him. Make sure no one else listens to him. No one gives him any more power. With the battery destroyed, maybe we have a chance of doing that.

"I do believe you, Sira. I'm sorry about what Vor did to you."

She draws me in for another hug and weeps even more freely.

Rugnus and Lagnar return with armfuls of metal and blue glass. Lagnar sets a large glass piece of Jeiah's statue next to the crucible, nods to me. Rugnus passes me her head.

"Sira's back then, huh? Does she see what she did wrong?"

"I don't think it's like that, Rugnus. Vor raised her. Point your anger at him."

"Oh, I will."

I look at Jeiah's eyes. She's staring at me unblinkingly. "Okay, Jeiah. Cutting you down didn't hurt, but I think the part where we melt you does."

When she blinks, it's with the same precision and scrutiny she does everything else. Rugnus and Sira stand back as I carefully slip the largest piece over the lip of the crucible. Some of the pieces crack as they collide. I wince as I let the last piece go but complete the rest of the process and stand back.

I don't hear her voice until she appears on the other side of the crucible. "That was a unique experience. One for the record books."

I cut over to her and hug her, only to realize how attached I'm becoming. My face flushes, and I try to pull away, but Jeiah leans into me a second longer, as if in approval. I take a deep breath and turn around.

Sira looks completely crestfallen, but only for a second. She rounds back her shoulders. "Okay, cuties—besides you, Lagnar— what's next? And what do we do about that lizard?"

The Gila monster has reappeared on the floor between the frozen pond and the giant prickly pear tree. It looks at me.

"Is he..." Rugnus glances between me and the lizard.

"Right?" Lagnar says. "Clayson has a weird connection with this thing."

"Is it saying anything to you?" Rugnus asks. "Like Frrwelhst."

The Gila monster clicks its way across the floor closer to the large cactus. It twists its neck around and stares at the gray-green limbs.

Everyone edges forward.

"I don't get it?" Lagnar says.

The lizard twists its head back to me. I crouch down, holding out my hands. "What do I do, huh? What are you trying to—"

I can't react fast enough. It skitters at me and bites down on my fingers. Sira cries out. Rugnus jumps forward, but the Gila monster gnaws at my hand. Pain ripples up my arm, neon venom seeping into my veins. Rugnus stomps on the lizard's tail. It hisses and backs away.

But its beady, reptilian eyes find me. Something in them seems wise and kind.

What is your name? Yinzar's voice draws me in—not the artificial one from the keeper's key, something deeper, more at odds with the dungeon.

It's the lizard. He's the lizard.

"Clayson. My name is Clayson Brightstorm."

No. Your name is Wraithking.

BREAK THROUGH SHADOWS

Clayson Brightstorm has become Wraithking.

The whole world hears this. I'm a Loamin champion. Rugnus and Sira both whisper the name. Jeiah looks as though she's doing a complicated math problem in her head.

"What does it mean?" I ask.

Lagnar laughs. "You're asking us? Craft is wasted on the young."

Jeiah takes the question as a challenge. "Well, let's think about this. We know that wraiths can't affect you. This was true in Wolfstaff with Landred and in Silverlamp with Challozil's brothers. You have an uncanny ability to move quickly through dungeons without some of the consequences most raiders typically face—which, to think about it—sounds very wraithlike. But what's your connection to the wraiths?"

"I don't know."

"None of that answers the important question right now," Rugnus says. "How do we get out of this dungeon?"

"Maybe Yinzar wants me to find the connection. Wait, where did he go?"

"He," Jeiah says. "You think the lizard was Yinzar Mithriumbane?"

"I take it that means none of you can hear him."

"Nope," Rugnus offers.

I shake my head, turning my attention to the rest of the room. "There's something weird about the cactus."

Lagnar is already looking it over. "Just a cactus. A big one, but I don't see anything special about."

Jeiah produces her beholder and circles the large plant. As she emerged around the far side, she stops and points. "There. One of the limbs is fake."

The limb she points to is discolored. It's not the green of cactus but of copper pipe. "Copperoath," I say. "Wasn't that Yinzar's last name? He was peerless in coppercraft."

Lagnar circles the cactus. "That he was."

"What do we do with it?" Sira asks.

Jeiah casts her eyes around the room again. "It's coppercraft so—"

My hand moves out, and I pull the whole head-sized piece of fake cactus off the plant. Jeiah's hand reaches out to stop me a second too late. I bend it just a bit to test, but there wasn't any reason to. It's copper. The small hairs at the back of my neck prickle, goosebumps rise on my arms. It's the strongest copper-craft I've ever felt. Even the the wolfstaff relic was an alloy of silver, gold, and copper. She places a hand on the copper and the craft siphons between the two of us. Her hair stands on end.

"Wow. That's strong."

The click of Yinzar Monster's claws can be heard across the small pond of ice. We gather closer to it, watching as the lizard claws its way through the ice, down to the swirl of lights.

"It's kinda cute for a lizard," Sira says.

Rugnus rolls his eyes. "Really, Sira?"

She shrugs innocently.

"But what's it doing?" Lagnar says.

Jeiah still has the beholder out. She waves it over the ice, then back to the cactus for a second. "Why would that one be fake?"

"Not sure," Rugnus says.

"Does ninety-five mean anything to anyone? The beholder keeps pointing out the number of real limbs on the cactus."

Rugnus is thoughtful for a second. "That's a beard's breath from ninety-three."

"The number of dungeons?" Jeiah says. "Interesting. But plus two?'

I turn the fake limb over in my hands. "Three. If you add this one back in, it makes ninety-six. So, plus three."

Rugnus snaps his fingers. "What if you count the three relics? Onrix, Icho, and Ergal."

The hair on my head tingles. Ninety-three dungeons, plus three protodungeons. "The connection with the protodungeons. Could there be—"

The whole cavern fills with rainbow neon light. A cloud of vapor billows out from the pond, where Yinzar Monster has cut through. The lights inside the cloud sparkle and pop, until all at once, the mass of cloud and light collapse in on itself.

Everyone stumbles backward. To her credit, Jeiah only steps back a foot, scanning the cloud with the beholder.

The keeper's key buzzes in my pocket: WRAITH ENCOUNTER IMMINENT

The closer I look, the stranger this wraith becomes. Its features are finer, more distinct. Its physical form doesn't have the same undead quality I have seen in other wraiths. As the face becomes more distinct, I gasp.

"It's you," Rugnus says.

"It's me."

We all stare. The figure doesn't move, but its chest rises and falls. Strong shoulders, dimpled cheeks, tousled hair. It stares through me or at me. There's a look of expectation on my duplicate's face.

The second I step toward it, three sets of hands pull me back.

I try to shrug them off, but they won't let go. "I think I'm supposed to connect with it."

"By all means," Lagnar says. "Maybe that's how we get the

mithrium out of here."

"Is this how you make every decision?" Jeiah asks, her jaw set like a cut sapphire. "Just reach out, grab the unknown object?"

"Sometimes I feel like I know what needs to be done."

Her blue eyes dig in deeper. "Melt the consequence?"

"Yinzar *wants* this."

"You keep saying Yinzar," Rugnus says, "but in this place, your grandfather doesn't exist. There's only Mithriumbane. We can't know what will happen if you touch that thing. And Koglim would probably want me to remind you of Ringgiant's son—killed in his own father's dungeon."

"Fine. Then it kills me. And Vor is down one wrecking ball. But we have to get out of this dungeon." I look down into the pond. The surface is cracked. Yinzar Monster is gone. Beneath the thin layer of ice, the swirl of neon light—no, neon memories—invites me to find all my answers. "Yinzar cursed my mom and I... the meaning of that curse, the key to it, is right here. I have to do this."

"Do it," Sira says, her hands move from my arms to my face. "I trust you."

Rugnus, Jeiah, and Lagnar trade looks. Lagnar shrugs.

"Okay," Rugnus says. "Just don't get melted." He lets go of me, but his hands stay in the air as if he's trying to pass all his craft and luck to me.

Jeiah is the last to let go. Her eyes bore into mine. "Whatever you find in there, remember what makes you unique."

Sira clears her throat. "You're one of the strongest Loamin in the world. You're a living champion, and you're immune to wraiths."

"No." Jeiah shakes her head. "That's not what makes you unique. You see the world differently. You see the wonder in it. You're courageous and brave. And you're good."

This catches me by surprise. Jeiah sees past all the things that make me dangerous. All the things I wish weren't true about myself. I hold her gaze for as long as I can. "Thanks."

In two quick steps, I'm facing a light-filled reflection. "What's next?"

He reaches out an arm. I take a deep breath and reach out to test strengths. A jolt of craft rips through my skin. Revelation fills every synapse of my brain. My muscles all feel suddenly bruised. Goosebumps. Nails on a chalkboard. Sunshine. Déjà vu. Static electricity and the hard press of gravity against my calves. All the sensations of the elements of ironcraft, wind, and stone, and fire, and water, and light, and shadow.

The ice cracks under my feet, and I fall through into cold liquid.

My mind opens to the world of the dungeons, the world of the champions. Like the experience I had in the dreamwell, I'm connected to all of them, as they are connected to each other. The world is a swirl of light and thought. I'm floating in the vastness of Ide itself.

Until my feet touch the ground.

I'm back in the Cradle with Yinzar. It's the moment just after I left him in the last memory I saw. The object in his hand falls toward the bright, liquid mithrium. The light from the adjoining room becomes brighter, the voice becomes clearer. A figure appears, but I don't understand. It *is* my mom. But it can't be. She heard his name far away in the castlestacks of Whurrimduum.

She enters the room. Her eyes are red from crying.

This is impossible. She wasn't here.

"Dad," she says. "Wait!"

As the light from the mithrium combination fills the room, Yinzar's face blanches. "Bena? No. Why? Get away from—"

A sound like a percussion grenade fills the room.

Then we're all in the void of Ide together. Yinzar stitches together a dungeon from the mithrium and the recipe he perfected. But his AMP score was never sixty-three. He was never a champion. The dungeon he makes with the recipe is fake. The fake limb from the cactus.

But how can a dungeon be fake?

In the same moment of creation, his bright intellect fights to shield his daughter from becoming a wraith in his falsely made dungeon. I sense my mom's consciousness searching for a way to escape her fate. Both her thoughts and Yinzar's thoughts settle on the mother's unborn child, forming inside of her. I was there that day. The day Yinzar became Mithriumbane.

My mom and grandfather spin craft together out of mithrium and shadows. Yinzar protects his daughter, and my mom protects her son. The mithrium fractures. A small part creates the dungeon around Mithriumbane, but the larger part enters the tiny body forming inside my mom.

Me.

Suddenly, the other champions become aware of the intrusion within Ide. They rage. Howl at the audacity of Yinzar's plan. He has forged a dungeon from craft alone, hiding the mithrium at its heart. No one will ever find it. The other champions can't stop him. And when the craft has been woven together, Mithriumbane's intellect begins to focus. With one last force of will, he budges his daughter back to the comfort of the castlestacks. Her memory of the event and her child becomes a weight around her neck, like a sealed locket.

She forgets her unborn child. She forgets me.

I am the wraith that should be in Mithriumbane's fake dungeon.

Part of his craft, the secret to making dungeons—perhaps destroying them—resides in me.

All my breath leaves my body. My sense of the physical world returns. Somewhere in my mind, a word—no, a name—repeats itself over and over and over.

Wraithking.

Wraithking.

Wraithking.

The world is made entirely of light. I flex my hands and reach out for the outline of a bright cube. I reach, and the dungeon reaches back.

I have the mithrium.

The world is still. Until it isn't.

The world shakes. Until it doesn't.

"Clayson?" Rugnus' voice pulls me into reality.

We're standing between two bookshelves—the type from the forge Brig and I had been in—sand at our feet, stars above. No, not stars. Lights made to look like stars. Which seems fitting, knowing that Mithriumbane itself was a fabrication. My heart rate is still running, ten blocks on ten blocks.

The bookshelves. This is the exit lobby I created. I'm outside of the dungeon. We all are. Rugnus, Sira, Jeiah. I take a deep breath. I'm alive. Safe. In my hands sits a bright cube of mithrium.

"It worked." My voice crackles like fire. I clear my throat and the ground beneath rumbles. "It worked, right?"

Jeiah smiles. "Yes."

Sira hugs me. "You did it!"

Light behind the stars begins to bleed through, a million tiny holes tear the fabric of the inky sky. The room shakes again, and blacklight flakes flutter down on top of us.

"What's going on?" I ask.

Jeiah scans the sky, then the shelf. They tremble again. "I think you were right. The mithrium was the heart of the dungeon. It's destroyed."

"Fake dungeon," I clarify, earning me confused looks all around. "I'll explain later. Where's Lagnar?"

"Ran off," Rugnus says.

Another quake, this time stronger. A fault opens across the sky.

"Let's get out of here!" Jeiah shouts over the rumbling stone.

"Can we budge?" I yell. Shelves break apart around us. The sky is no longer there. The black façade peeled back to reveal plain brown stone. I dig out the keeper's key. Mists of digital fuzz swirl over the lobby map. A disruption. The last time I saw this was at StoneYoke. The battery. "We're being blocked. It must be Vor. Jeiah, can you—"

"We can't let him find us!" Sira yanks on my arm, her eyes begging me to turn and run.

The beholder is already in Jeiah's hand. She traces the invisible edges of the digital fuzz and taps the keeper's key in my hand, making the map clear, though our location is still not. She shakes her head. "Can't break the foilgrip."

"Brick!" Rugnus tightens his empty fists. "I thought Lagnar said he broke the battery."

"Right, but Vor must still have the craftprint. The battery combines them all. I think he can use them at the same time. He's throwing everything he has left at us."

"We need to find another way out."

Pushing the key back into my pocket, I scan as far as possible past the shelf. There's a difference in the light in one corner. Less firelight, more silver. "There."

Jeiah grabs my hand and pulls me. We scramble over broken shelves and large chunks of rock. Rugnus vaults a smooth boulder.

We sprint down one row, and another, and another, passing through a small grove of green barked, green stemmed trees with leaves like pine needles. Half of them lay demolished by fallen stones. The smell of green wood fills the air.

At the base of a rough stairway of sandstone, a massive segment of the ceiling comes crashing toward us. My bracelet flares to life, shoving the wall of stone a few feet out where it crashes to the ground. The whole shape of the wall darkens like clouds passing in front of the moon.

Not clouds. Shadows.

Vor.

Rugnus leads us all around a sharp right turn, and the exit appears, a vaulted sandstone vee cut out of what's left of the wall. "There it is."

We must reach it.

"Faster," Rugnus yells. "We can make it!"

I push my legs to go faster, but behind me, Jeiah yelps.

With a quick glance over my shoulder, I realize she's stopped entirely.

She tries to wave me away. "Go. Get the mithrium out of here!"

"Is that what you found in there?" Vor appears behind her. In only that second, the shadows swarm around us, saturating the whole world with a layer of gray-dark blurred edges. In the second before shadows close off the exit, two wary eyes stare at me. Lagnar. But the darkness swallows him.

Jeiah pulls herself up. "You shouldn't have turned back."

"We wouldn't leave you," Rugnus says.

An alert blinks on the security icon of the keeper's key.

Yinzar's automated voice speaks from the key to my mind. *Connected to bluelink. Security breached.*

I glance at Vor, but he focuses on the shadows, on finding a way through my growing shield. The keeper's key echoes its words. *Security breached.*

I gesture the security icon open and find a message, but before I can open it, Rugnus spins me back around. Vor shakes his head, impatience bubbling under the surface of skin, erupting in jittery motions in his hands and neck. He looks toward the ceiling and sighs.

"Sira, come here," he says. When she doesn't immediately move, Vor shouts. "Now, child!"

"No." Her voice is soft. "You can't hurt me. Not with Clayson around. And... and you're running out of power."

Vor's anger almost brings his eyes up to meet her. His lips curl, and his fists tighten into hammers wrapped with shadow. "Is that what you think?"

The message blinks with urgency. With Vor's attention on Sira, I quickly gesture it open. It's from Lagnar.

Toss the mithrium toward the exit.

He's gonna make his bomb. If he does, it will kill us all, but it will take Vor along with us. A second's breath and another message chimes. The whole cavern settles, the rumbling stops. Whatever Yinzar's dungeon was, it's gone.

Only way.

My hands move before my brain fully decides.

I hurl the blazing cube of light toward the exit, hopefully in Lagnar's direction. The light of the mithrium cuts through the shadow. And I see him. The mithrium sails over his head, but he's already turned around, through the exit, sprinting the rest of the distance, grabbing the glowing block from the air like a wide receiver. As the shadows knit back together, Lagnar smiles, winks at me, and budges.

Everyone looks at me in shock. It takes Vor longer to realize what I've done.

He almost looks me in the eye. Almost. But no. It's against his nature. It's as impossible as—but what's impossible anymore.

Vor crosses his arms and begins rubbing his gangly elbows hard, rocking to his heels and forward, heels and forward. He squeezes his flesh as if he's trying to keep his anger inside. It doesn't work. His mouth opens briefly but smashes together so tight I think he may have bit himself. "This is what you get, people. Give them one ferrum and they want a hundred."

The shadows all around us claw their way closer. I send out a wave of brightness from the ring the lighthealers gave me at Kel's Lounge. It tears through the shadows near our feet, but it's not enough.

Even if he did use up Sira's craftprint—which I'm not even sure about—he still has a hundred times our craft. Rugnus opens fissures of earth all around us, trying to keep the shadows at bay with fire. The slick, gray-black ribbons merely ooze over the flames. As darkness enwraps us, I search for any other way. Anything. But only a patch of the fake stars above remains in a sea of black.

I send out wave after wave of light.

Rugnus responds. "There's not enough of us."

"That's it!" I know what to do. Scrambling, I open bluelink and record a single word. A message can get past a foilgrip. "Help."

"No one's coming to help you," Vor says. "The people are running scared."

"You're wrong." I saw it on my first day in Tungsten City—how the people worship at the thresholds of the champions. Millions of people—everyone left under granite—heard my name echoing through every stone in every city, reverberating off the glass of a hundred skyscrapers. Wraithking.

They are the stars themselves. The millions of people who watch, and watch, and watch. They come for their summations, for research, for sport, crawling out of every hole and rock in the world. And they will come at the call of the Wraithking. If they all push against him together, the foilgrip will snap like a bowl of glass. Because no matter how strong he is, Vor isn't made of mithrium. Multiplication succumbs to exponents.

Everything in this world happens in an instant. And this moment is no different.

Light and sound, rock and fire, bleed out from the tiny exit. A hundred, then a thousand Loamin flood the lobby. The first wave seems almost engulfed in shadow, but quickly the light overtakes it, as bright as the morning. I look away. The homespun garments of the knights appear in the haze, alongside the X-ray shielding of the royal guard. A thousand plus a thousand forms of craft burn away at the shadows, chopping down the tendriling hands and arms that had reached for our flesh.

The next vision must not be real. My mom, charging from the middle of the group. Her body glimmers in golden light. Have I seen her use craft before? Only once, to cover my identity. I can't find my dad in the fray, but I don't know why I would expect him.

In a sheer panic Vor stumbles away, but the swelling crowd of Loamin—eyes and hands full of the tools of revenge—are already behind him. My mom is chief among them. Vor might die here.

A hand drops on my shoulder. "Looks like everyone got your

message," Hardkeeper says. Andalynn and Brig are right behind him.

My whole body is still tense. Hardkeeper scoffs at me. "Relax. He's all used up."

I follow his eyes back to Vor. All the shadows are gone. If he has any craft left, it won't be enough. With so many people pushing toward him, there's nowhere for him to put his eyes, but his head snaps my direction, and he tries. He wants to look at me. His head shakes with effort. He can't do it. He snarls. With a flash of tan light, he's gone.

The whole crowd stumbles back. Hardkeeper leaps forward, grabbing one of the knights. "I said to block him!"

The young woman stammers to answer. "Sir, we did."

Hardkeeper releases the knight. "He won't get far. He's drained. Send out an emergency message to every Loamin in both cities. I want him found. The moment he shows up, we attack again." When the knight doesn't immediately respond, Hardkeeper shoves her toward the other knights. "Go. Now. Not another single person gives him craft. We have to keep him in the light."

From that moment, the chaos begins to recede like a wave. Thousands upon thousands of Loamin move for the door. Not even one misses their chance to look at me. To them, I'm a spectacle. A living champion. They keep a healthy distance from our group.

Emerging from the crowd, my mom searches our group with desperation. Her thoughts somehow radiate from her eyes. Love. And the hope that everything can be fixed, that everything can be made whole, sealed up together, and held in the palm of her hand. I know the look because I see it so often in my reflection.

She takes two more steps forward, and our eyes meet. At this moment, I know the curse is broken. Whatever I did in Mithriumbane has healed us.

"Clayson," she places a hand on my face, drawing me in. Her arms stay on my back, and she rests her forehead against mine, whispering. "It's over. Gone. And it's more than being able to see you."

"You could see me after the shield."

She nods emphatically. "Yes, but this is more. The curse is broken. I can see all the times where I didn't see. All the times you tried to reach out to me, tried to speak to me. I'm... it must have been..."

Every shield I've ever held between us shatters. My heart swells to encompass everything about this woman. She's my mother. Mom. And had her craft with the mithrium not protected us, we would have both become wraiths in Yinzar's dungeon. "You're healed."

Andalynn slips through everyone and hugs Rugnus.

"Do you think you'll be able to sleep now?" Rugnus asks. "Down here, I mean?"

Andalynn adds. "And Yinzar's visions?"

Soft footsteps sound behind me. "Is that what they were." It's a voice I recognize more than if I could see him. Yinzar Copperoath stands on the brink of our little group, alive.

At this point, every synapse inside my head misfires. I stumble against what my eyes are trying to show me. He's aged, but he's here in front of us, as Brawny as before. Every rough scar from his years at the forge is clear—no clearer—than any vision. How is this possible?

Mom opens and closes her eyes. "Dad?"

The aged skin around Yinzar Copperoath's eyes crinkles in sorrow. Tears brim his eyes. His hands run through the shock of white-orange hair ordaining his head. His muscles flex in every movement. "My sweet Bena. I'm sorry. I'm sorry I left you. I thought I could hide the mithrium for good. I thought—"

"Ide keep me," Rugnus says. "You were... and now... how?"

"I was never a champion. I simply found the right code, a set of ingredients, to use the mithrium for something useful for once."

"But how?" I say. "You just, what, found them?"

"Exralt Blackmug knew the recipe. Each ingredient is connected to a protodungeon. I—" His face falls on his daughter and he shakes his head. "None of that matters now. There are more important issues. Bena, I'm so, so sorry."

Mom shushes him, and suddenly we're all holding each other, Mom, my grandfather, and my sister. When we part, I notice a tear trapped in Rugnus' eye as well, not for us, but because in her haste to free her arms for additional family members, my mother passed him Icho.

Rugnus whispers its name and smiles.

She must have used it to leave Geum Ide. Now I understand the sadness mingled with the joy in her eyes. She left my dad there, betrayed her own mother. Had she heard my new name? Had Hemdi and Winta reached her with our plea for help? "Jeiah's message found you?"

Her slow nod tells me there's something else. "Clayson," she leaves a long heavy feeling in the air. "I think your father knew."

It's like she passes me a boulder to carry. "Knew what?"

"Not about StoneYoke, at least I don't think so, but when Winta gave us Jeiah's message... he knew. He knew Vor was like Ara."

Andalynn shakes her head. "Of course, he did. I don't think there's an end to that man's secrets."

I take the weight she passes me and drop it on the ground. I couldn't care less about my dad's secrets. Nothing surprises me anymore. "Where's Ara?"

She's still staring at her father, so I repeat the question.

Mom shakes her head. "The conjurers haven't found her yet. Maybe she even left Geum Ide altogether. We don't know."

Yinzar speaks now, and it's strange to see the connections to his world from fourteen years ago come to life. "I knew there was something about Ara that Glaris didn't tell me. She and Therias must have gone through with establishing Geum Ide. How many people? Did they find a way to fix the brightstorm?"

I rub the stubble on my chin, nodding. "Ara helped restore a

Brightstorm with my dad's craftprint. And now it's surrounded by the mithrium shield I made with your recipe. They won't let anyone in unless they swear off craft."

A cold exterior suddenly grows around Yinzar's skin, around his eyes. "That's a shame. Withdrawing from the world that way. Sounds like Glaris."

"You didn't agree with her?" I ask.

"Giving up craft, trying to bring it to an end? Never."

Mom's face tightens. There's history there, shared experience. All at once, she appears more childlike than I've seen, more like someone's daughter than someone's mother. "We don't need to talk about that. But there's more you should know."

A million secrets spill out into the world in this single moment. A heavy burden for a few minutes. And as happens when secrets are unleashed, the world is muted, judgment suspended as the facts are gathered into clumsy piles, and we're left with even more to wonder about.

When I reveal the meaning of my name as a champion, about having become part wraith outside of the dungeon, Brig smiles, and my heart lifts from its position. He doesn't seem upset about the end of the dungeon. Maybe it's because his champion is standing in front of him in the flesh. Or maybe he sees it as something unique and strange, a thing that will bring him popularity and fame.

"Ho," Brig says, "that makes complete sense. It's a wraith's cradle."

"What do you mean?" I ask.

"A wraith's cradle. You know—"

Something clicks in my mind. "Difficult because it's impossible to understand."

"But there's more to the phrase."

"Of course," Jeiah adds. "Because information about people who become wraiths, those trapped in the dungeon, becomes blurred. You could try to read a record about their life, or a recording they left behind, but after you do, it's like..."

"Like you never did," Andalynn says. "A wraith's cradle. I didn't think of that."

"Because you couldn't," Brig says. "None of us could."

The conversation moves forward like a beast sniffing out something important, something that could provide sustenance against an oncoming winter. After a long while, I turn to Sira.

"Why does Vor want the mithrium?" I ask.

She seems almost glad, maybe relieved, to be free of him, but something like grief still hangs from her like invisible chains. "I'm not sure he did," she says. "I think it was you he wanted, what you could do with the mithrium."

"Make a weapon with your knife?"

She nods. "That, and he kept talking about you pulling out the heart of Wolfstaff, like... he was proud of you. The destruction you left. The answers it could provide. He's kinda like you in that way—endlessly curious."

I force her words off me, let them roll like water to the ground. I'm aware of my own power for destruction, but will it be the same now that Yinzar is out of his dungeon? I don't feel any different. Will I be able to sleep?

"There's only one way to put the mithrium out of his reach," Rugnus says.

"Like this shield, you were speaking about?" Yinzar says.

"Your recipe was right," I say, "but the dragon bones were wrong. I made the shield from a ring. We think it might have been from a protodungeon. I used Lake Onthratia to cool it down."

His fleshy eyes widen in realization. He reaches out toward me as if accepting the information. "Opposite energy. I was so close to doing the same, but I didn't trust the Great Smoke. Wait! Did you say a ring? Protodungeons? Not the one Silverkeeper was looking for?"

Sira peeks her head through our circled group. "You knew my father?"

Scrutinizing her face, Yinzar says, "Rensira. Yes, of course. I—

he was so curious about those objects." A new spark fires in his eye as he puts more together. "You," he says to Rugnus. "You're a descendant of Blackmug. I'd bet on it. Your mother is—"

"Yeah." Rugnus holds up Icho. "This is one of them. Clayson made the mithrium shield that protects Geum Ide with Ergal. And there's the knife. Onrix."

"You have it?" Yinzar asks.

Jeiah and Rugnus nod.

I sew the ideas together. "Three objects. Three pieces of mithrium. Are they connected?"

"Not that Silverkeeper and I could figure out. Exralt Blackmug and Erikzin, they have something to do with it. We could never put the pieces together."

"We need to keep the knife hidden," I say.

Rugnus shakes his head. "It's too dangerous. We need to combine it with a piece of mithrium so it can never be used directly. It will be out of Vor's reach. Out of everyone's reach."

"We'd have to find Lagnar."

"General Emberfence?" Yinzar's face darkens.

Jeiah weighs this in her mind, searching the air near her face. She must have full access to bluelink again. "That's going to be difficult. I don't think he wants to be found. He's not anywhere."

"Has to be on the surface," Rugnus says. "He was banished there for years. Fizzblood is tough on him, but he can survive and stay hidden with the humans for as long as he wants."

I relax my shoulders. Let out a breath. "Then the mithrium is out of Vor's reach and ours."

Sira shakes her head. "But Rugnus is right. We have to make Onrix impossible to use."

Mom speaks so quietly I barely hear her. "So, we take the last piece of mithrium your father has hidden in Geum Ide."

WIN AGAINST TRUTH

THIFFIMDAL'S SUBZERO winds howl against an orb of shieldcraft extending fifty feet in every direction. Andalynn, Mom, and I stand huddled close together, watching as Rugnus affixes an aluminum flagstone in the central square of the plaza, and Jeiah continues to adjust the automated shield.

"Budgeport is up," Rugnus says, as a tan light blooms into the deathly cold air.

The shield is made of a Tungsten cup linked to a small mechcraft machine amplifying the effect and putting the craft on autopilot. Rugnus circles us at the edge of the shield, placing a half dozen protective torches along the circumference of our work area to keep the mithrium fallout at bay. Beyond that lies the world of Thiffimdal: ice-packed trees, slick buildings, and a handful of frozen upright bodies.

Above us, in the ominous night, the brightstorm lashes the air with wild energy, uncontrollable and violent.

With a final adjustment of the shield, the temperature reaches somewhere closer to freezing, instead of deadly. Jeiah cuts back toward us. "We're risking an awful lot."

Andalynn nods in agreement. "Even if we *can* get the last piece of mithrium, there's no guarantee this will work."

"If your grandfather says it will work," Mom says, "it will work."

"That I believe," Jeiah adds.

The opposite energy from Lake Onthratia helped to stabilize the mithrium shield. All the dead cities are filled with opposite energy, but this one is coupled with the temperature we'll need to cool down this object when it's complete.

A flash of tan light and Yinzar appears, Brig at his side.

Yinzar took one look at Brig's very respectable, very balanced AMP score and claimed the kid as his new apprentice, much to Jeiah's dislike.

They've brought my ten-gallon furnace and the forgeseed, along with all the same ingredients from Yinzar's recipe. Apparently, he kept seven other hidden forges stocked from floor to ceiling spread out in secret places throughout the kingdom. Though Sira and Vor must have discovered one of them last year as they prepared to make something from the mithrium. Yinzar said it had been raided. And it explains how they knew the right ingredients to make something from the mithrium.

Yinzar directs Brig to set up the forge, then walks over to us. "So, I've been thinking."

"This won't be good," Rugnus says.

"Clayson was peerless in shieldcraft, and he was the one to add the ring into the mithrium." He stops there with a look of expectation.

Jeiah connects the dots first. "You need someone peerless of silver to fully duplicate the recipe from the lake."

Andalynn wags a finger. "Absolutely not."

Yinzar raises an eyebrow. "We want this to work, correct?"

He means Sira.

"Silverkeeper's daughter would be the best choice," he adds. "She's a Silverlamp and she has a connection with the knife." A flicker of something like grief crosses his worn face. "Her father's death... such a loss, such a loss. He helped create this recipe. And

why are you against her? I thought you said she had been manipulated by Vor?"

Rugnus pulls at his collar, frustrated. "And that makes her a
good choice?"

"I'm merely being objective. Clayson was peerless in shieldcraft and had a connection to Ergal. Rensira is peerless in silvercraft and has a connection to Onrix."

"Sounds good to me!" Brig calls out from the forge.

Andalynn shakes her head but says, "I'll go get her from
Whurrimduum."

"We'll get the mithrium, while you do that," Mom says.

She says this like we're running down to the store for something. "You think it's going to be that easy to take the most
dangerous substance known to man from the most secretive
person on the planet?"

"Hopefully, we'll be able to talk him into this."

"Not likely."

Mom frowns. "I'll use his weakness to get what we need."

"Weakness?" Andalynn says.

Mom smiles. "Me. He will listen to me."

"Well, let's get this over with." I stretch my hand out, waiting
for Rugnus to give me Icho. Instead, he pulls it back and hands it
to Mom.

"I'm giving this to someone responsible," he says. "Last time,
you didn't bring it back."

"Fine with me," I say. "Ready?"

Mom grabs Icho from Rugnus. "No sense waiting."

Yinzar hugs his daughter. "Keep Ide."

Jeiah's eyes linger on mine. "Good luck."

I blink, and we're standing at the table of my parent's home in
Geum Ide. It's the middle of the night, but the warm air is a relief
after the bitter cold of Thiffimdal. Mom steps over to the table.
Slowly, she draws the planter with the orange and pink orchids
toward the edge of the table. It scrapes across the stone.

A soft murmur sounds in the next room. My dad's stirring.

Mom hefts the planter into her hands, presses her fingers into the stone. The loudest possible click echoes across the room. The mithrium slips from the bottom of the planter illuminating the room in a brilliant display of stark white light.

It was here the whole time.

Mom reaches for my hand. "Do we wait to talk to him or…"

My dad appears at the door. "Melt me. What's going on? Who's there?" He holds an arm against the brightness and spots us. "No." I'm not sure if the color drains from his face or if it's a trick from the stark light of the mithrium. "You can't."

I level a final accusation against him. "You knew about Vor."

Mom seems frozen for a second, long enough for my dad to leap from the doorway toward the mithrium. In another step, he will take it from us, and this will be over. I throw my shield around us with so much force it knocks him against the wall.

Mom sucks in a startled breath.

"We need to go," I yell.

She shakes her head. "We owe him an explanation."

"He owes us an explanation. But we can't wait for—"

"Clayson," my dad says, "please don't. Please don't bring that out into the world again. You don't know the consequences. You don't know how hard it was to keep it hidden."

I shake my head. "We're taking it. We need to make it so Vor can never reach it."

My dad closes his eyes, almost as if he's praying. "Clayson, I *did* know about Vor, but I didn't know he would… He refused to help us heal the brightstorms, but he was peaceful, kind. He never—"

"But he did, Dad. Whatever you saw of him was an act. He was right under your nose. You can't tell me you didn't know."

"I didn't know. You can believe me or not. But this… whatever you think you're doing with the mithrium… the shield is more dangerous than you think."

"Said from behind its safety. I'm done listening. Mom, we have to go."

She looks between the two of us, pain in her eyes. "Therias, you have to trust us. The shield keeps anyone from getting the mithrium. And... Therias, Yinzar is alive."

The color drains from his face. "What?"

"It's a long story, but—"

"Did he have his piece of the mithrium?"

Mom nods. "But Lagnar has it now."

"Lagnar? What?! How did—"

"We're wasting time," I say. "Despite what you think, the mithrium isn't yours. We have Yinzar's recipe. We're going to make sure this piece is out of his reach. Out of anyone's reach."

"That may be your intention, but there's more to it."

"Therias," Mom says. "What does that mean?"

His face freezes. "It's just... I can't..."

The part of me able to cling to his every word, absorb all his instructions, that part of me is dead. I reach for Icho, drop the shield, and in a flash of tan light, we are back in Thiffimdal. The end of the word *sorry* tumbles from Mom's lips into the frozen air. We left the other half in Geum Ide with my father.

Everyone has gathered around the glowing forge, watching Yinzar prepare the ingredients. Andalynn isn't back with Sira yet.

Mom looks at me as sternly as she's capable. "That wasn't how we should have handled that. We needed to hear him out."

"I'm done listening to him."

She closes her eyes, clearly holding back tears. "Even after all his secrets, I love him. He took care of you, gave up everything, and he never stopped hoping we could all be together. He didn't have any craft. We were safe behind your shield."

I swallow the part of me that wants to make her happy. "I just couldn't listen to him."

A well of tears falls from her eyes, sending them spilling over her jawline. They begin freezing almost instantly, and she hurries to brush them away. "Okay."

The light from the mithrium has drawn everyone's attention. I move toward the warmth of the forge to give Mom a moment to compose herself. I try to feel something of what she's experiencing, but I'm too angry at him. Or more like I've passed the point of being shocked, or sad, or angry. I'm done caring about everything he keeps from me.

Jeiah slips the beholder out and scans the mithrium. "Whoa."

"I can't imagine what that's showing you," Rugnus says.

"Good stuff?" I ask her.

There's something mischievous behind her eyes. "Good and yes," she says, impersonating the deep mystic voice of the azdeth.

Yinzar looks up. "You're impersonating a Goodyes. How did you find it?"

"We didn't. We used the mindhive," I say.

He starts to point at me but rubs his chin. "The experience was that clear for you?"

"Can we focus?" Rugnus says, gesturing to the forge.

They've already started the process. The bucket that had been filled with slimy pieces of oak sits empty, the chunks sizzling like steak in the bowl hovering over the forgeseed.

Yinzar blows into the furnace in a strange pattern of whistling and half-humming, and the light brightens into an intense white.

"I don't know that trick," I say.

Brig wipes sweat from his forehead. "Ho, don't feel bad. Even I don't know half of the things he's doing." He gets a bit starry-eyed. "I'm going to be the best smith in Tungsten City."

My grandfather's eyes focus on the forge. "It's ready for the next step."

Brig grabs the lambskin bellows and pumps until the pieces of oak are glowing.

I ready the gypsum, and we work in a slow rhythm, constructing the recipe step-by-step.

As I sprinkle the oak coals with gypsum and peat, Andalynn flashes next to me, Sira at her side. Sira's hopeful eyes try to find mine, but I ignore her. The coals morph into translucent diamonds. The change seems almost miraculous.

"How did you discover the right ingredients, the right process?" I ask Yinzar.

"It took me years to catch the ends and means in Blackmug's poetry. Even then it was obscure. Many of the noble beasts of the world helped me figure out the coding itself." He glances at Sira. "Silverkeeper helped me make the connection to protodungeons. The best I know is that each of the ingredients is associated with a protodungeon somehow." He gestures to the mithrium in my hand. "Time for the real test."

"It worked under Onthratia. It will work here." I set the mithrium inside the crucible and lower it into the furnace. Andalynn and Rugnus lean in, mesmerized.

It melts like any other metal, just brighter. Strange that it can be so powerful. When it's fully melted, I add the onyx. The molten mithrium takes on a slight silver coloration. The next step is the amethyst dust, and Brig's ready with it.

Sira watches intently as Rugnus hands me the knife. I almost feel her body tense. The silver knife has been a part of her for nearly all her life. And we're going to destroy it. I gesture for Sira to step closer to me, and after a moment's hesitation, she does.

"As soon as you add the knife to the mithrium, things are going to get crazy. We'll need to—"

"Transfer it to the mold," Yinzar continues, "then pour the ice water from the silver bucket. Yes. We're ready."

Another deep breath. "We're trusting you, Sira."

"I knew you understood, Clayson."

"The way I see it, you wanna be rid of this more than any of us." I pass her the knife. When she grips it, Rugnus' shoulders tense, but his defense is unnecessary. She doesn't wanna control us.

I encourage her to come closer. Her face hardens. The freckles across the bridge of her nose and cheeks come to life in the light. She won't give the knife any more of herself. With a determined nod, she drops the relic into the mithrium.

A swell of cold wind gathers around us. The shield flickers.

"Quick," Yinzar shouts, "transfer it to the mold!"

Sira lifts the crucible and pours the liquid light into a hole in the sealed form. The crucible empties, not even a drop of liquid left inside.

Brig laughs out loud. "Opposite energy! It's working."

Sira eagerly grabs the silver bucket of ice water. That's when I realize how right I've been about her. She's glad to be rid of it, glad no one can ever use it again. Without a second of hesitation, she dowses the whole mold with the ice water, making sure some of it fills the hole in the form, that it reaches down and touches the liquid metal.

But something's wrong. The light from the metal is pulsing like a strobe light. A buzz of energy trembles through the air, shaking my bones.

This is not what happened last time.

"It's the shield!" Rugnus shouts.

Yinzar bolts toward the automated shield. "It's blocking the cooling effect!"

Jeiah grabs his arm. "You can't just take it down!"

"Everyone get close," I shout, running toward the automation machine. The second everyone is within range, I rip the tungsten cup from the machine and extend the power of my bracelet around the group.

The forge draws in every particle of energy it can find. The thick layer of ice coating the plaza cracks and fissures. A second later, the whole world transforms with silver-white light. All of us crane our necks toward the brightstorm. The uncertain flickers have ceased, and the loose rings of light tighten around the mini sun until it transforms into a moon of silver. A column of light erupts from the mold, and we all stumble away, shielding our eyes. The column shoots heavenward, uniting with the brightstorm.

Yinzar laughs gleefully. "It's beautiful!"

Something stings my face. I lift my hand to touch the spot just above my eye, and my fingers come away bloody and wet.

Another sting and a tiny cut opens on my hand. Ice, nearly invisible, whirls through the air toward the mold. A hundred million tiny attacking particles fly toward us, and my shield can only do so much.

"Behind the tree line!" Rugnus orders.

We shuffle forward, careful to keep everyone in the shield, taking shelter from the mounting storm of flying ice next to a line of trees.

The mold shatters.

Light bursts over the plaza, brighter than the summer sun. I turn away, protecting my eyes. Now that I'm not facing the light, the rush of ice particles is more visible. A storm of glimmering slivers rises from every surface around us. Even with the protection of my bracelet and the trees, a few pieces of ice cut through my clothing, lacerating my skin.

When the barrage of ice slivers stops, the whole world begins to melt. The light at my back fades into a dull silver. I whirl around, searching for the result of our recipe. The new object is trapped in a glacier five times my height. But slowly, inch-by-inch, the ice boulder melts.

Jeiah grabs my hand. "We did it."

The object we crafted hovers inside the glacier. It's heating up the ice from the inside. All at once, the outermost layer of ice breaks near the bottom, and water rushes into the plaza. We're far enough away that it doesn't knock anyone over, but the gush of water soaks my shoes.

Floating at eye level, a small crown hangs in the air.

There's movement and voices.

"What's happening?" someone yells.

A crowd gathers around us.

"It can't be." Yinzar's eyes grow twice their size.

Thiffimdal's inhabitants are free from the mithrium fallout. I can't quite catch my breath. Is it just the people in the plaza?

"Brick," Rugnus whispers. "How are these people not dead? They've been frozen for centuries."

Yinzar tilts his head to one side. "Cryogenics. If I remember right, the mithrium bomb in this city was combined with part timecraft, part ironcraft. But this? I wouldn't have guessed this was possible."

Sira breaks from our group, making for the mithrium object in the center of the plaza. Jeiah shakes her head as Sira reaches up for the crown.

Rugnus shouts, "Sira, no!"

"It's okay," I say. "No one can use it now."

I follow her to the center of the plaza to get a better look. "Go ahead. Test it."

Sira stands transfixed. "It's beautiful."

I'm euphoric. We've done it. But a ping of doubt sounds like an alarm inside my mind as she reaches for it. Her hand closes over the metal.

"It's cold. I would have thought it would still be hot. And..."

"What is it?" Yinzar asks.

"...and nothing. We did it!" Sira steps away from the crown. It remains floating. Impossible for one person to use or control ever again. "We did it. It isn't responding to me. I can't move it or use it. And does anyone else feel that?"

"I do," Jeiah says. "I thought it was just me."

"I'm happy," Sira says. "Truly happy for once. It's the crown. The silvercraft is as powerful. It must have the same radius as the shield." A giggle escapes her lips. "Clayson, we're all moving here... today."

In Geum Ide the effect of the mithrium shield was obvious—a sphere of energy encased the town in protection, all the way out to the citybarrel. Something different has happened here. An overwhelming calm fills the world. My heart bursts with peace, and joy, and healing. It can only be mithriumcraft.

Tears of joy fall from Rugnus' eye.

Jeiah blinks and kisses me unashamedly.

Astonished, my eyes stay open for a few greedy seconds watching her. I lean into the kiss—my first—reaching around to pull her closer to me. A shock pumps through my veins. She smells like burning wire and a fresh cotton t-shirt. Like electricity. As if I've caught a firefly in a bottle. Finally, she leans away, grinning.

Sira doesn't seem bothered by this at all. She hoots. "My handsome Wraithking. You did it. This is everything I wanted." She spins in a circle, her arms to the sky as if trying to accept even more peace, letting it soak into her skin like sunlight.

My body, my brain, and my lungs struggle to keep up with the fetterless pumping of my heart. No one is unhappy. No one is hurt. We gaze at the crown in unfiltered joyousness. People join us from all around cheering and crying and cheering some more. We've done it.

Far away, at the walls of the city, there's a glow of silver light, the extent of the crown's power. The whole world could come here, people could rest from fear and worry, they could play and sing and run wildly in the streets, like carefree children.

Yinzar claps me on the back. "This is what should have been done with the mithrium long ago. No one can use this for evil. The world can repair itself."

Someone budges between us and the crown.

For the moment, I don't know how to feel anything but happiness, yet something in my mind tells me I should be unhappy. Something is wrong.

"No." Sira's voice is soft, ghostly. My mind catches hold of the danger even under the powerful influence of the crown.

Vor. He shouldn't be here.

I smile at Vor. "It won't work Vor. It's out of everyone's reach."

"What's happening?" Rugnus says, unable to stop smiling.

Laughter escapes me. "You failed, Vor. Even you can't compete with the power of mithrium."

He nods slowly. "Hmm. I certainly didn't expect... but maybe there's one more little secret. A discovery, really." He reaches out to the crown and pulls it from its spot.

Once it's in his hand, his chin turns up and, for the first time, we see eye to eye. Dread fills every inch of my body.

He sighs happily. "*This* I didn't know. *This* changes everything."

"What just happened?" Andalynn says.

"I-I... no. No one can move it. I—"

Vor mocks me. "I-I... like the wrecking ball you are, I didn't even have to force you. And you somehow performed perfectly! Everyone else can leave, except you and your company. I want to deal with you more personally." He looks around at the confused faces of the citizens of Thiffimdal. "Go on, leave. Be gone!"

He's not asking. He's using the power of the mithrium crown. Exponential silvercraft. The moment he shouts his command, the surrounding crowd begins to vanish, one by one, each taking out their own budges and leaving. Controlled by an incalculable power.

The eight of us freeze, our minds captured. How can he use the crown like this? No one could move the shield.

Sira hangs her head. "No, no, this isn't right. This—"

"Quiet!" Vor's hand tightens on the crown.

Sira's throat works, but nothing comes out.

"Let her go," I demand.

Vor tamps down the royal crown of silver firmly on his own head. "See, Clayson, you're sharp. Brave even. But this is mine. Onrix is the heart of *my* dungeon."

My head is whirling. This can't be happening. Vor is Dura. He can only use the craft he gets from a willing Loamin. Vor has no dungeon. To have a dungeon, he would have to be a champion. And if he were a champion with a dungeon, he couldn't be here. He'd be stuck like all the others. This isn't real. It's some trick maybe or—

"Or what, Clayson," Vor says, reading my mind. "This is no trick. This is real. Everyone, everywhere, will obey me. No more Vor, the vacant, the servant." He laughs. "After a thousand years, millions of orders to follow, I get to force my will on everyone. Oh, I just... this feels amazing. I couldn't be happier."

"I don't—"

"Understand? I was Loamin, Clayson. I was Loamin. Don't you get it? Of course not. I didn't, not until I touched this beautiful object you made for me. The memories from my dungeon are rushing back to me so fast."

He inclines his head like he's trying to hear something. His hands roam his face like it's unfamiliar. "I was Loamin. Onrix was my greatest possession long ago. So, so long ago. I died a champion. But this body came into existence at the same time, when my consciousness was locked away in a dungeon. A thousand generations, my mind spun around inside my tomb. Protecting Onrix until someone took it out. Blackmug. Like you did with Kel, with Torlina Wolfstaff.

"It wasn't the shadowcraft that made Kel crazy. It was you. You tore down her dungeon. And you're going to help me tear down all the rest, free the champions, so they can take possession of their true bodies. Dura bodies. Become what we should have become long ago."

"That's not possible." Rugnus' words are like pebbles scraping underfoot.

My mind reels. Kel was Torlina's body? This is worse than I feared. Vor will use me to wreak havoc on this world, to destroy the dungeons. But Torlina's relief when I freed her from the dungeon... that couldn't be a trick.

The moment my dad learned I had taken the heart of Wolfstaff, he said it could mean the end of craft. Could he have known? Not only that, Vor was like Ara with craftprints, but that their spirits were trapped in dungeons? I've never liked how the Dura were treated, but Vor can't do this. He wants the end of craft. His vision for the world is not mine. How many bodies would he leave in his wake?

"I-I won't help you," I say.

"That's certainly not true. But if you insist on being so unwilling... on with the show. Clayson, grab the forgeseed, will you."

Against every instinct in my body, I obey him. It's still glowing white-hot. My shieldcraft protects me, but I know what he's planning.

He looks straight at me and commands. "Push it through someone's head. Or I can choose."

When I do nothing, my feet move on their own until I'm standing in front of Mom. Vor doesn't free her body, but I can see acceptance, kindness even, in her eyes. I scream out as my arm comes up. The forgeseed is a lump of glowing power, but my bracelet extends its protection over me—only me. I try to resist as my hand pushes the forgeseed closer to her head, but soon the skin at her temple sizzles.

She whimpers. Her eyes give me permission.

As with the snap of someone's fingers, I'm free. I come back to myself.

How? I whirl around to face Vor.

But someone else is facing him.

Ara looks right at me, the mithrium shield in her hands. She smiles, and it's the most dangerous thing I've ever seen in my life.

WAKE THE ANCIENTS

VOR AND ARA were once Loamin.

This is a truth of the universe now. An unalterable stone foundation.

Somehow their bodies existed away from their minds, minds that had been trapped in dungeons. No one knew because no Dura had ever become aware. The truth was right in front of me. Ara had felt called to the mithrium shield, and the conjurers had imprisoned her in fear.

It wasn't unfounded.

"Ara," I say.

"Clayson." She looks me right in the eye. "Give me one second."

She faces Vor.

"Illuminating, isn't it?" he says casually.

"Somewhat. But we've been awake for centuries," she hisses at him.

"Barely. I suspect you didn't know what you were?"

"No."

"Let's not pretend these infants are important to you. Join me. We can teach them a lesson. Free the rest of the champions."

The shield in Ara's hands sags a bit. Is she considering helping him?

"Ara, you're not like him," I say. "And we care about you."

She smiles kindly at me. "I *am* like him. More than you know, Clayson. I didn't see it until I touched the shield."

Vor smiles broadly. "These *Loamin* aren't worth your effort, Ara. Let's put them in their place."

Ara considers this. Her shield lowers a bit more but comes back up. "I've been hurt by them as much as you have Vor, perhaps more. But there's a difference between you and me."

Vor's eyes search our group, and something is growing inside him.

Fear.

"And what's that?"

"Do you remember what it was like to be Loamin?"

He narrows his eyes. "You know I don't."

"Neither do I. But I remember everything from the dungeon. And my guess is that you do as well. There was so much good. Loamin are strong and compassionate. They're fiercely loyal to each other. They're not our enemies."

He sighs. "You've bought into their delusions. Well, if you won't join me, I'd better be going. Work to do."

In a flash, he vanishes.

Ara's arm slackens. "Is everyone okay?"

Mom reaches up for the burn on her face. I move her hand and heal her.

"We will be," Mom says.

"How did you get here without a budge?" Rugnus asks Ara.

She gestures to the mithrium shield. "Mithrium allows me to use every type of craft. But Ergal's power—the heart of my dungeon—that's what it was made for. To protect."

Rugnus rubs his head. "This can't be happening. We made it worse."

"Where will he go?" Jeiah asks.

Ara is at a loss. "I don't know. The only place he can't go is the surface."

"Why?" Jeiah asks.

"I can feel it. And it's true for me as well. I can't go to the surface. Not in my new state, not after claiming the heart of my old dungeon. Though it *is* nice to have Ergal close to me again." She taps on the shield.

"So where then?" Jeiah asks again, her persistence shining through. "We need to follow him, stop him. With your help, we may stand a chance. Did you see how he ordered all those people to leave? A whole city?" She opens bluelink and begins reading something, her eyes hungry for information.

"Will he go after the last piece of mithrium?" Yinzar asks.

"Maybe?" Andalynn says. "But Emberfence is most likely on the surface. Or at least I hope that's where he went. And if Ara is right, he can't follow him there."

"The other Dura," I say. "Kel and Tas. We've got to get to Geum Ide."

Jeiah's hands fly outward, searching for something to steady her. "Wait. Everyone's location data… they're all budging."

"Who?" I ask.

Jeiah closes her eyes. "Everyone."

"What?" Everyone cries out at once.

Below us the plaza is empty. "He can control entire populations."

"The bombs had the power to destroy even the binary cities," Rugnus says. "Millions and millions of people, in each city. If the crown is as powerful as a bomb…"

Jeiah purses her lips into something firm and angry. "Wraithspit."

"No, no, no, no, no." Sira is pacing. "I didn't want this. I didn't want this."

"But the shield," Yinzar adds, "it can cancel out the crown. The moment Ara arrived, we were freed from Vor's control."

"What are we waiting for?" Rugnus says, Icho already in his grip.

"Wait," Jeiah says. "Please. Take Brig somewhere safe. Take him—"

"To the surface," I say, removing my bracelet and jamming it on Brig's wrist.

Brig backs away. "No way. I won't be treated like a latch—"

Rugnus disappears, reappearing only seconds later. "Safe at the cabin. Let's go."

Jeiah nods to Rugnus. "Thanks. He's not going to like that."

"It's for the best," I tell her.

I blink, and we've budged. From the top of the Bluelink building, all of Tungsten City is visible, but there are no Loamin anywhere to be seen.

"No one's left," Andalynn says.

A building—usually washed in green flames—flickers out.

"What's happening with that?" Mom points to one of the floating buildings, slowly drifting downward but close, too close, to the tree line.

Rugnus points Icho out over the city to the descending building. "Brick. We... what can we—"

The building crashes in the apex, shattering trees with a deafening sound. Fire spits into the sky, followed by smoke.

"Mechsmiths must have been working on it," Jeiah says. "Vor forced them to budge. Keep Ide, where would he be taking them?"

"Whurrimduum." Sira's hand comes to her mouth. "He'll go there next. He wants..."

Andalynn glances at me. "He's collecting everyone. Every single person under granite."

"Not if we stop him," Mom says.

Rugnus lowers Icho into the center of the group. "To Whurrimduum."

"Wait." My mind is spinning but I have to get ahead of him. "We're just chasing him. What about Geum Ide? What about the other Dura? Ara, can we get to them? Tas? Kel? Could they help us? If we have more power than Vor... He has the crown. We have the shield. But if we give craftprints to Kel and Tas..."

"Yes," Ara says. "We have to have enough to overpower him. The shield will block his influence on the people, and then we can stop him. But we need to wake up Kel and Tas."

"Trollbrick. How?"

"I remember what woke me up the first time, Clayson."

Yinzar is almost beside himself with wonder. "What was it?"

"Ergal, when it was just a ring. Exralt Blackmug, he gave it to me. I couldn't use it, but...but I woke up. Why didn't he tell me what it was? Why would he keep that a secret?"

Jeiah is nodding vigorously. "You're saying the other Dura, the one's whose dungeons have been raided, the hearts of the dungeons—you're saying they could be at least as powerful as you were? That they could use craftprints."

Ara stares at her. "Yes,"

"Tas and Kel," Mom says. "We would only need the hearts of their dungeons."

"Wolfstaff." I take the long metal staff from its place at my back. "And Tas, his must be—"

"Icho," Rugnus says. His voice is remarkably steady. "Just need to get him to touch it. It will wake him up."

"Let's get there before Vor," Ara says.

"If we can," Jeiah says. "He emptied Tungsten City in less than a minute."

"Beard and bones," Rugnus says. He budges us all once more.

It's night in Geum Ide's central square. The healed bright-storm over our heads is a purplish globe. Conjurers throng the cobblestone, strange for this time of night. Stranger still because they are all, everyone, faced the same direction.

Yinzar groans. "They're already under Vor's control. He's already here."

"No, look," I say. "They're coming out of it. The shield is working."

Ara scans the crowd. "You're both right. Vor's here, but my shield has broken his influence."

Someone yells Rugnus' name, and we all spin around to look.

Against the flow of conjurers Koglim comes striding forward wearing a huge grin. "Yes! Get melted! Bam! My guess was spot on. I found you."

"Koglim?" Rugnus says, doubt and laughter waring in his voice.

"In the flesh. Well, most of it." He lifts his shirt to reveal a divot in his stomach. "Feral wolves do not play around."

"How did you... where—"

"So, what I'm gathering," Koglim says, "especially by the determined looks in your faces—is that Vor is now—what? Super, duper, duper powerful? Pretty sure he forced every Loamin under granite here to Geum Ide. Well, not here to the settlement, but the whole citybarrel is filled with Loamin. There's got to be millions of people under his control. I mean, maybe everyone."

"And you thought to look for us here?"

"Okay, so when I was in the hospital—by the way, not cool that no one was there when I woke up, and then I couldn't find... anyway, my tattoo showed me a picture of you guys all hanging out here without me. And I thought, how am I going to get there?"

"Then Vor showed up," Rugnus says.

"Exactly. So, what have you guys been up to?" He smiles. "Something crazy, I bet."

Rugnus raises an eyebrow. "Well, Clayson's part wraith"— Koglim lifts his chin to me in acknowledgment— "uh, Dura are resurrected Loamin champions. They can use the heart of their old dungeon-like a permanent mithrium bomb." He points a thumb at my grandfather. "Yinzar's dungeon was fake, and he's not dead. Not sure what else."

"Huh," Koglim says. "No, no. That sums it up. So, do we need to go melt Vor now?"

A group of conjurers is scuffling past the fountain.

"Out of the way!" Winta's voice clears a row of conjurers from between us.

"The gang's all here." Koglim urges Winta and Hemdi into our circle. Winta looks like she hasn't slept since last Gem. And still no baby.

Andalynn leans into Rugnus and whispers something. Before Winta even sees what's happening, Rugnus uses Icho. One second Winta and Hemdi are standing next to us looking dumbfounded. The next, they're gone, along with Rugnus. They had no craft to prevent him from budging them.

Everyone's eyes go wide and shift toward Andalynn.

"What?" she says. "Winta can't help us. We did the same thing to Brig."

Sira scoffs. "You forced her to leave?"

Koglim giggles, high-pitched. "That's rich coming from you. By the way, why are you even allowed to be around us? Clayson, what's that paper thing that humans use to keep people away..."

"A restraining order?" I offer.

"That!" Koglim says, pointing to Sira. "That's what we need for you."

"Budging Winta and Hemdi was the right call," Mom says.

Rugnus reappears. "They're with Brig at the cabin. Though I think this one will permanently damage our friendship."

Ara throws up her hands. "They would have known where Kel and Tas are."

Andalynn steps before the people onto a half wall. "Everyone. Please listen to me." The conjurers turn confused eyes on her. "Vor, the former servant of the council, a Dura, has taken control of an object made from mithrium. Like the shield, but instead, it can control your minds." The murmurs rise in a wave. "We need to find Kel and Tas. Where are they?"

Someone calls out, "Saw them near the bridge."

Another few murmurs confirm this. Fingers point through town toward the main bridge that spans the gap between the two sides of Geum Ide.

Ara and Mom cut a new path in that direction, running. We rush after them.

"Can they do what Ara does now?" Koglim asks.

"No," I say, "the hearts of their dungeons haven't been combined with mithrium. But they should be able to absorb craftprints."

"You guys have been busy," Koglim approves.

We round the last corner to the bridge and run right into the two Dura. The light from Ara's mithrium shield illuminates their tall bodies.

"The second," Kel says.

"And the third and the fourth," Tas says.

"Rugnus," Ara says. "Let Tas hold Icho."

But Rugnus doesn't move. Andalynn gently takes Icho from his loose grip. "Here," she says, handing the club to Tas. "This was yours."

Ara takes the wolfstaff relic from its place at my back and passes it to Kel at the same time. The second their hands are around the objects; I notice the change. Not in the same way Vor or Ara changed with the mithrium infused objects, but a change. They become like Ara had been, tentative but aware of their surroundings.

"Where am I?" Kel says.

Tas casts his eyes toward Ara, the only one besides Kel he can look at directly. "Wh-who are we?"

"You are just waking up," Ara explains to Tas. "You were a champion. These were the hearts of your dungeons."

"You're Torlina Wolfstaff," I tell Kel. "Or you were in your last life. Now you're something different. But that's beside the point. We need your help."

"Maybe I don't want to help anymore. I've been slaving in that restaurant for hundreds of years."

In life, Wolfstaff was shrewd and calculating. In her dungeon, she ruled with cruelty. Whatever we do here tonight, I am not sure she will be our ally.

"Good bread bowl soups, though," Koglim says. Andalynn slaps his arm.

More noises rise in the night. The bridge is still ahead of us.

"We don't have time for this. Be ready to help." Ara closes whatever discussion was about to take place.

The bridge is wide enough for all of us to walk side by side. The night is slowly changing to morning. I take it as a last sign of hope before we face Vor. He must have been coming for them as well. He's standing in the center of the bridge, the loose suit coat he normally wears left behind somewhere. He glances down at the ravine, a shimmering silver crown sitting perfectly straight on his head.

"Good!" he says. "Everyone's here."

Glaris and my dad are kneeling before him. Vor rests his jagged sword on my dad's shoulder. "See how easy it is when so many willingly give up craft? False leaders for a fake world. Send Ara away, or I'll kill them both, Clayson. You know I'll do it. Just like the council. Just like Chainkeeper."

My dad twists his head around. "Don't! Clayson, don't do—"

"You think," Vor says loudly, "he will listen to you now? Should we tell him Therias? Tell him how long we've known each other? How long you've known I was like Ara. You and Glaris are such hypocrites. Hypocrites and cowards. Look what's happened to the path you chose."

Mom murmurs to me. "We knew this, Clayson. Don't let Vor in your head."

Her words are only wishes, and I know the way a wish sounds. It's the same way every time one of my dad's secrets boils to the surface and erupts over my life.

"Now that I know who I truly am," Vor says. "I will tear down every single dungeon."

"That won't end craft," Glaris says.

"But it will bring this world to its knees, where it belongs. And... here I thought I would just torture people. Now it's clear. Dura are the natural evolution of your race. We are what you should be, but only the strong become Dura. We should rule over you."

My heart pumps blood of pure metal. I shake off Mom's hands and storm onto the bridge. Vor lets me get within a few feet before he levels his sword again, shaking his head. "Ah, ah, ah."

My dad's chin drops to his chest. "This is not what was supposed to happen," he says softly. "I had no control over it. Over him. I left. This is why I left. Why we should've stayed on the surface. Everything's my fault."

That's when I see it—we're nearly the same person. Same dimples, same shame for letting others down. Allowing bad things to happen. Being out of control. Reckless. We're a reflection. His choices are all inaction. Mine are all action, but they've led to the same result.

"You knew what he was," I tell him. "You knew what he could do, and you told no one? Did nothing? Walked away? Why?"

"I thought it was for the best," my dad says.

Vor taps him on the head with the sword. "Ah, but I didn't tell you how I caused the Mithrium War in the first place. Must have forgotten. See, I used Emberfence to assassinate your parents. He thought he was under orders."

"That's not... that can't be true," my dad says.

"Secrets... am I right," Vor says. "Don't feel great, do they? Anyway, now that I have your son on my demolition team, this will go a lot quicker. See, no matter what I did, I couldn't really break things. Not like you, Clayson. I could never do enough to change things, to see the next evolution of this world. You know? Just couldn't get a good grip on things. I know why. I wasn't ready to take my place as this world's ruler. My hunch about you paid off. When I learned from Sira that you couldn't sleep, I thought maybe I could use you to get in the dreamwell. You were different. And difference has the power to transform the world. Turned out so much better than I hoped."

"You're forgetting something," I say. "Ara has the shield. So, it's a tie."

He looks past me. The others have drawn closer. "What about them?" Vor says. "Kel. Tas. Ara won't join me, but I remember being new to this world, just like you are now," his voice rises into the air, "realizing what the Loamin had done to me. What they'd turned me into."

"He's right." Kel's hand is still in Tas'. "Why would we try to stop him?"

Rugnus panics and grabs Kel's shoulder. "You can't!"

"Stop!" Sira yells so loud and long that everyone, including Vor, seems to freeze. Noticing this, she looks away, and I hadn't realized it until this moment, but her mannerisms are so much like a Dura. Her feet face away from us, her eyes are downcast. "Stop," she says like she's hushing a child.

Rugnus releases his grip, and Kel pushes through the group, dragging Tas along.

I let them walk past me. What else can I do? Force them to stop? Ara shouldn't have woken them up. It was a bad choice, but I'm the king of bad choices. I glance at my dad, whose face is contorted.

"It doesn't matter," I tell Vor. "No one in their right mind will give them craftprints if it's to help you. We all see right through you."

Vor clicks his tongue. "Sira, sweetie. Come on. You won't be safe with them. I won't let you be."

We all look at her. Her head is hanging down. She's not under his control. She lifts her chin and shakes her head, but something is left in the air. Her father's death. Her desire to just feel better. To force people to be kind. It's why she brought me to Silverlamp last year. She wanted the mithrium to make something exactly like what rests on Vor's head.

"Sira," he says. "This is what you wanted. Didn't you feel it? That peace? You helped me for so many years. Don't stop now. We are so close to realizing what you dreamed. Everyone safe, everyone happy. Don't you want that? What does it matter if I have to rule them to get it?"

"Don't," I beg her. "Please don't."

"I can't do anything else. I thought I would be safe with you." Her form melts away under a brown light. I turn around, and she's appeared at Vor's side. When she vomits, he dances out of reach with a sick look on his face.

One second.

Sira reaches forward to give her craftprint to Tas. This can't be happening.

Everyone behind me rushes onto the bridge like a wave, craft flaring in every color. Ara raises the shield. Rugnus flashes out of existence and reappears beside Vor with Icho, grabbing for the sword.

Another second.

Before Rugnus can reach him, Vor grabs Glaris and drives his sword through her down to the hilt. As he draws it out, filthy with her blood, he looks directly at me and runs her through once more. She stumbles into the railing of the bridge.

Yinzar screams.

Another second.

Tas, grimacing in displeasure, uses Sira's craftprint to control my dad. No longer under his own control, my dad places a hand on Kel. Kel's body straightens. She flexes her hands with borrowed red-lighted power. She smiles. The brightstorm continues its slow transformation into day, painting the land red as blood.

Glaris' body tumbles over the bridge, landing audibly. She's dead. She had no craft to stop her descent. Yinzar howls, charging Vor.

Ara groans, the power of the shield overcome. If it was her shield versus Vor's crown, we could overcome him—she would win—but with my father's craftprint and Sira's craftprint added to the equation, we don't stand a chance. The power of a million versus the power of a million becomes the power of a million versus the power of a million plus the craftprints Tas and Kel have taken, and she can't compete.

The bridge rumbles with destruction, the metal railings super heat. This is a copy of Sular's craft—the pin my father gave to me. The relic I gave away to Rugnus. But this craftprint was forcibly given to Kel.

Hellfire pours from the sky, brimstone, and shafts of lava—Sular's full power on display. This is what my dad is capable of. The whole world transforms into flame. A molten rock smashes down at my feet and I jump backward.

"No!" The word erupts from my lips.

Ara's face is a mask of effort, sweat, and tears, painted over a grimace of desperation. She falls back, grabs my hand, pressing something cold into my palm. "We failed. I'm sending you somewhere safe. Where Vor can't get you. Any of you."

"Stop! Let me—"

A second later, it's over.

I close my eyes in what I think will be death, but nothing happens.

Birds are chirping. Sunlight hits my eyelids. When I open them, I'm standing between the cabin and the shed. The mithrium shield, Ara's defense, hovers at eye level, but Ara is nowhere to be seen. We're above granite. Mom, Andalynn, Rugnus, Jeiah, and Koglim. No dad, no Sira, no Yinzar, no Glaris.

Glaris is dead. Murdered.

Hemdi and Brig rush over to us, but Winta isn't far behind. Though I can tell, she's worked herself into a storm of rage. It's in the tension of her muscles and a vein standing out on her temple.

I unclench my fist. The leaf Silverkeeper had left for my dad catches a ray of light. Ara. She gave this to me. Everything happened so quickly.

"We're at the cabin," Koglim says. "Melt this! What happened?"

Winta skids to a halt when she sees him. "Koglim, of course, the first thing out of your mouth would state the obvious." Winta blows out a breath. This one is long and steady. I look her over. Is she…?

"What happened to Ara?" Andalynn says.

"Didn't she say she couldn't come to the surface anymore? Neither can Vor," Rugnus points to the mithrium shield. "I guess she sent the shield with us as protection."

I try to move the shield, but it's back to being like it was in Geum Ide.

"We're stuck up here?" Rugnus says slowly.

I shrug. "I-I don't know."

"Just need a game plan." Koglim slaps his back.

"Someone, tell me what happened," Brig says.

Hemdi surveys all our faces. "I think we lost."

Winta looks up at the afternoon sun. She draws in a steadying breath. "I'm gonna have this little brick above granite?"

Andalynn grabs her hand as she leans against the woodpile. "Are you—"

"Having contractions?" She takes another deep breath through her nose and groans. "For a while now."

Andalynn moves to her first.

Jeiah takes my hand.

Mom comes to Winta's side. "One thing at a time. Come on, Winta. Let's get you comfortable. We're not leaving."

EPILOGUE

It becomes my daily ritual to feed the animals and climb the western cliff, most times before sunrise. Too early even for the dogs. There are days I start so early I find Winta, or Hemdi, or both in the machine shop with their son Echel, making every attempt to soothe him with white noise from an engine Winta rebuilt.

This day, however, everyone is on the other side of the property. Waiting for the ceremony. I can sense the soft energy of anticipation rising with the morning. I'm wearing slacks and a pressed, buttoned shirt. I shouldn't go climbing, but it will help loosen the knot of tension in my back. I can always use the quick clean to straighten up before the big event.

A single yellow light is on as I pass the shop, but it's as quiet as the mountains. The chickens and goats stir only a little as I refill their food and water. I've ended the automation of Spangler Eggs going to Tungsten City. No one's there to get them.

Finally, in the last minutes of my ritual, I take the short, well-worn path to the western cliff. Darkness shrouds the trees, but I know they've put forth leaves, and before too long, the height of summer will be here. Light will arrive earlier and earlier, making my routine seem less manic to everyone else.

Jeiah is waiting for me at the foot of the cliff. "Trying to sneak away? Predictable," she teases.

"I won't be late."

She nods, scanning the cliff. "There's a faster way to the top." She budges all the way up to the precipice and yells. "See?"

She'll stay at the top until I get there. A few days a week, she gets up early enough to wait for me at the top. Something to normalize this whole being stranded on the surface thing.

I move to the cliff. It's the same as always, but I enjoy every movement of my body, each strain on my muscles. I take the most difficult path, or rather, the one I believe to be most difficult. The stone always seems to surprise me with new places to put my hands and feet. Every time I think I know the direction I could go, every decision I could make, the stone shows me another way.

When I reach the top, Jeiah dusts off my dress shirt, shaking her head.

We sit on a long slate of stone, looking over the mountains. I watch the world prepare to unfold the day. Jeiah watches me. After a few seconds, she focuses on the forest below us.

"It's the darkest part of the morning," I say, "but in a few hours, the sun will be up."

"Things won't be all that different after the ceremony."

"I'd been doing pretty good. I wasn't thinking about my dad or Vor or the millions of people under his control."

"It's a different kind of day. Makes us all think about it. But we're doing everything we can to find a safe way back down there. Try to focus on them. It's their day, not ours."

"Ours?" Now I'm the one teasing.

She looks away. "I don't mean that. I just—"

"I know what you meant. Come on"—I pull her to her feet—"we don't wanna be late."

I turn toward the path to the cabin, but she doesn't move. She tightens her hand over mine and pulls me back in front of her. It's something she does to slow my thoughts. I'd say it's magic, but she's no silvermage. As I look into her eyes, I find the familiar blue, a blue somehow lighter in the darkness.

I try to bury everything terrible some place deep in my mind.

With a smile, she wraps both arms around me. "This is overdue."

I move my head only slightly, the air tingles, and her lips come forward. She kisses me. She kissed me once under the influence of pure joy from the mithrium crown, but this is new. Something I've wanted but didn't know how to explain to her.

It didn't need to be explained.

Every time I hold her hand, every time we sit together, it's another of her investigations. Our real first kiss is no different. I can sense her questions in the movement of her soft lips against mine. I find comfort in the depth of her feelings for me. I wanna tell her how smart she is, how encouraging and brave. I love those things about her. And the way she waits, suspending judgement, and sorting everything into truths or uncertainty. All these praises and thoughts swell inside of me, center mass, and I send them to her in the kiss.

She steps back. Taking both her hands, she turns my head in different directions as if looking for the best lighting for my features, or maybe just trying to spot something she hasn't seen yet.

"I really like you," I say.

"Hmm," she considers this, considers me. "What makes you say that?"

Of course, this is her response—further investigation—but it throws me off for a second. "I-I—"

She rubs my shoulders. "Relax, Clay. We both know how I feel about you. I think I felt this way before I even met you. What did Winta call it the other day?"

I laugh. "A celebrity crush?"

"Yes," she smiles. "A crush. I crush you."

I chuckle at this. It makes me forget everything but her. "Something like that."

We walk through the trees until we come to the clearing where the cabin stands. On the opposite side of the gravel road, there's a massive stone cottage. Green vines cover the second-story balcony, forming along the railing and around the upper windows.

Jeiah glances at the newly constructed home. "I still think you could have let Rugnus build us all a real castle. There's enough land."

"There aren't many castles in the Blue Ridge Mountains."

"Still."

We come to a small path leading into the eastern woods.

"Ready?" she asks.

I nod. The appointed spot is deep in the woods, and it takes another ten minutes to find the clearing. I don't mind. Being with Jeiah at this moment, under the cover of the trees, makes the morning more enjoyable.

We're greeted by soft blue and purple light from iridescent flowers that Andalynn and Mom planted along the path. But my eyes catch a glimmer of something orange flitting through the brush. A butterfly. And another, and another until there are dozens of butterflies dancing around us, half orange, half green. As promised, Mom has constructed a living memory garden for the ceremony, for Andalynn and Rugnus. I catch a green one and see through Andalynn's eyes, chasing a gray cat through Everbloom Garden.

I catch an orange one, and I'm Rugnus as his mother wipes away his tears. It's a party. A silver goblet that had been filled with red liquid lays spilled over a white rug.

There are dozens more. We get to see both of them in these moments as they grow into the people they are now. It's beautiful. I catch as many as I can, relishing each chance to see my friends' faces change. See them laugh, and cry, and to grow into themselves a year at a time.

The hard part is still there. In the background of every memory, the backdrop for their lives, these are the places we can no longer go. Andalynn runs through the palaces of Whurrim-duum and Rugnus trains in Tungsten City for his summation.

So much loss.

This feeling of dread and guilt stays with me until we emerge from the trees and the dazzling white gazebo is revealed. Hemdi and Winta wait to administer the ceremony. Andalynn and Rugnus test strengths using both of their arms crossed over each other. Andalynn sees me in the corner of her eye, and with a slight gesture, she beckons me to stand next to her.

I pass a semi-circle of padded stone benches, where everyone awaits the ceremony. Echel squirms in Mom's arms. Mom looks from me to Jeiah and back to me. Jeiah sits next to her brother. Brig watches the baby, making faces, eyes wide and mouth turned into a smile.

When I take my place next to Andalynn, Koglim moves next to Rugnus. Hemdi takes Winta by her hand, and they look down to the earth. A forge burns behind them. Behind that, an icy ribbon of water floats mid-air.

Closing his eyes, Hemdi takes a deep breath. "Together, place your offering in the forge."

Andalynn and Rugnus release each other's arms for only a second to place craftable metal cubes in the furnace. One is aluminum, one is tin.

Hemdi smiles and begins the ceremony. "By Ide, the love that you have crosses another threshold."

Winta smiles, adding another light to the forest. "By Ide, that love can craft something new."

Hearing his mother's voice, Echel whimpers for her.

"And in that craft," Hemdi continues, "you find a greater depth of being."

Winta's turn. "In that craft, you become together what you could not be apart—one body."

"There are those who bear witness to this."

Koglim clears his throat, wipes his eyes. "Witnessed. May Ide keep you as one."

I add my words to the ceremony. "Witnessed. May Ide keep you as one."

"This oath we make," Andalynn says.

Rugnus repeats her. "This oath we make."

"Shall not be broken."

"Shall not be broken."

A crest of brown and green light appears as a seal above them, and they kiss each other's foreheads, first Andalynn, then Rugnus. The longer kiss that follows unites them as husband and wife. Together they pour the liquid metal from the forge into a shallow mold. Winta and Hemdi take the mold and submerge it in the ribbon of water.

Rugnus and Andalynn wait until the mold is drawn out and step over to Hemdi and Winta. The mold is shattered, leaving behind a wide-rimmed bowl. Together they take the bowl representing their union. Brown and green light fills the area around them until thousands of plants and vines appear everywhere, blooming with tiny spouts of fire.

After so much loss, I bask in the beauty of this craft, and of these people I love.

Echel's whimper grows into a cry, and Mom tries to calm him, but—done with her part of the ceremony—Winta steps away, reaching out for her baby. She sits back on the bench and feeds him.

Over the next hour, the lights made from Loamin craft grow dimmer, and sunlight begins to open all the darker places in the forest. Waiting in the stone cottage, there's a taffy cake that Winta insisted on baking, and with my help, it turned out beautifully. With all their other craft, baking doesn't come naturally to Loamin—except maybe to Brig.

In the late morning, I find Rugnus standing where the camper had once stood, Stone licking his fingers waiting for him to throw a tennis ball. For fourteen years, the camper had smothered the grass, but spring has done its work, and though the cinder blocks still sit there, fresh blades of grass push through the dirt.

Rugnus looks contemplative but genuinely happy. He throws the ball and Stone goes rushing off to search for it.

"What's next?" I ask.

My question must catch him off guard because it takes him a while to respond. "We could just stay here. We already risked one trip down there. We were lucky to get away. Vor's darksmiths won't stop hunting us. We're safer under the shield."

Every time I look at Echel I think about this. There's nowhere he can go. Once he gets outside the shield, he'll suffer all the effects of the surface. And we have limited objects and a fear that if we return under granite, Vor will see us. He will come for us. And we can't use the shield as protection.

"Doesn't sound like the Rugnus I met last year."

His smile is genuine. "Maybe because I have more to lose."

"Sorry, this is not the day for—"

"It's okay."

Stone returns, dropping the ball between us. From the trees, a chickadee whistles out two clear notes over the early summer quiet, giving me a moment to determine what to say. "We need to go back down there."

"It's a wraith's cradle. We'll never fix what he's done."

"You don't mean that."

More silence, except for Stone's quiet whimpering. "No, I don't."

I grab the ball and hurl it down the gravel road.

With one last sigh, swallowed up by the day, we make for the cabin, for the friends and family waiting for us.

"Maybe it is a wraith's cradle," I say, "but that's our thing. We're not afraid to do impossible things."

If you enjoyed the world of RIMDUUM, please consider leaving a simple rating or review on Amazon or Goodreads. If, like me, you've fallen for the characters and setting of this amazing world, please share the news with your scifi/fantasy-loving friends. Word of mouth makes such a difference for creatives like me.

Pick up a signed copy of the next book over on my website. It ships directly to you! I'll stamp it with your favorite craft symbol. Don't forget to sign up for the RIMDUUM exclusive newsletter, bringing you deals, chances to read the next chapters early, and free short stories.

www.loamseedpress.com

There are so many beautiful and imaginative stories floating in the great void and you chose the world of RIMDUUM. Thank you so much! I'd love to hear from you. Feel free to contact me on social media. May all of your dreams and wishes come true. May you find something that stokes the fires of your imagination and leads you to be more and more human, and to treat other people the same. Go out there and build worlds of wonder.

Sincerely,

ABOUT THE AUTHOR

BEN GREEN has always been a storyteller. When he was a kid, he would tear apart his coloring books and assemble them into crossover stories with lots of drama and lots of glue. Then he discovered action figures and took to burning Cobra agents at the stake and writing/acting out whole episodes of Star Trek the Next Generation. As a teen, he wrote Star Wars fanfiction and began creating his own worlds on a Brother word processor with a tiny screen and floppy disks. Meaning he's also very old.

Though he grew up in Arizona and Nevada, Ben now lives in southern Minnesota where he puts his degrees in teaching, history, and technology to use as a social studies teacher for non-traditional students. He is passionate about teen issues and at-risk youth. This may be why he spends so much time with his four children, telling stories, working in the garden, and encouraging them to find something to be passionate about.

facebook.com/bengreenwrites

instagram.com/bdigitalgreen

goodreads.com/bengreenwrites

pinterest.com/bengreenwrites